TH
COULD NEVER FORGET

BY
MEREDITH WEBBER

THE NURSE WHO
STOLE HIS HEART

BY
ALISON ROBERTS

MILLS &
BOON

Wildfire Island Docs

Welcome to Paradise!

Meet the small but dedicated team of medics
who service the remote Pacific Wildfire Island.

In this idyllic setting relationships are rekindled,
passions are stirred, and bonds that will last a
lifetime are forged in the tropical heat…

But there's also a darker side to paradise—secrets,
lies and greed amidst the Lockhart family threaten
the community, and the team find themselves
fighting to save more than the lives of their patients.
They must band together to fight for the future
of the island they've all come to call home!

Read Caroline and Keanu's story in
The Man She Could Never Forget
by Meredith Webber

Read Anna and Luke's story in
The Nurse Who Stole His Heart
by Alison Roberts

And watch for more
fabulous *Wildfire Island Docs* stories
coming soon from Mills & Boon Medical Romance!

THE MAN SHE
COULD NEVER FORGET

BY
MEREDITH WEBBER

MILLS & BOON

Published in Great Britain 2016
By Mills & Boon, an imprint of HarperCollins*Publishers*
1 London Bridge Street, London, SE1 9GF

© 2016 Meredith Webber

ISBN: 978-0-263-25429-7

Our policy is to use papers that are natural, renewable and recyclable
products and made from wood grown in sustainable forests.
The logging and manufacturing processes conform to the legal
environmental regulations of the country of origin.

Printed and bound in Spain
by CPI, Barcelona

Dear Reader,

In March 2014, a group of writers from far-flung parts of the country were meeting up for their eighth or ninth writers' retreat… The first retreat originated when four of us got together for the Crocodile Creek series of books, and with other friends invited it became a yearly event—a week somewhere near a beach, for brainstorming, writing, an occasional sip of wine and, recently, great lobster for lunch at a nearby restaurant.

So there we were, Marion Lennox, Alison Roberts and myself, amongst our other friends, with a vague idea of doing something together again—a series…six books…a tropical island. We threw some ideas around, wrote notes, drew island pictures and then went home—thousands of kilometres from each other but still in touch. About halfway through that year we got serious enough to actually work out a few overall continuity ideas, and each of us decided on our characters and the bare bones of a plot for our own story.

I think it was Marion who put it all together and sent if off for editorial approval—which we got, with a few stipulations. Then began the fun of fitting the books in with already scheduled books and getting the stories written. My workload at the time was lightest, so I said I would do the first book—setting up the island itself, introducing the characters who would be in most of the books, and generally getting started.

So here, lucky reader, is the first of six books set on Wildfire Island, a small island in the M'Langi group, way out in the Pacific Ocean. Privately owned, the island is falling on hard times and in need of rescue—so rescuing it and rescues of another kind are a thread running through the books.

Enjoy!

Meredith Webber

To Linda and Alison and the writing friends
we share and love—long may Maytone survive!

Meredith Webber lives on the sunny Gold Coast in
Queensland, Australia, but takes regular trips west
into the Outback, fossicking for gold or opals. These
breaks in the beautiful and sometimes cruel red earth
country provide an escape from the writing desk and
a chance for the mind to roam free—not to mention
getting some much needed exercise. They also supply
the kernels of so many stories she finds it's hard to
stop writing!

Books by Meredith Webber

Mills & Boon Medical Romance

Visit the Author Profile page
at millsandboon.co.uk for more titles.

CHAPTER ONE

As the small plane circled above the island, the hard lumps of pain and worry that had been lodged in Caroline Lockhart's chest for the past months dissolved in the delight of seeing her home.

From the air, the island looked like a precious jewel set in an emerald-green sea. The white coral sand of the beaches at the northern end gleamed like a ribbon tying a very special parcel, the lush tropical forest providing the green wrapping paper.

Coming in from the west, they passed over the red cliffs that lit up so brilliantly at sunset that early sailors had called the island Wildfire.

As they flew closer, she could pick out the buildings.

The easiest to find was the palatial Lockhart mansion, built by her great-grandfather on a plateau on the southern tip of the island after he'd bought it from the M'Langi people who had found it too rough to settle.

Lockhart House—her home for so many years—the only real home she'd known as a child.

The house sat at the very highest point on the plateau, with views out over the sea, ocean waves breaking against the encircling reef, and beyond them the dots of other islands, big and small, settled and uninhabited, that, with Wildfire, made up the M'Langi group.

Immediately below the house and almost hidden by the thick rainforest surrounding it was the lagoon—its colour dependent on the sky above, so today it was a deep, dark blue.

Grandma's lagoon.

In truth it was a crater lake from the days of volcanic action in the area, but Grandma had loved her lagoon and had refused to call it anything else.

Below the house and lagoon was the hospital her father, Max Lockhart, had given his life to building, a memorial to his dead wife—Caroline's mother.

Around the main hospital building its cluster of staff villas crowded like chickens around a mother hen. And below that again lay the airstrip.

Farther north, where the plateau flattened as it reached the sea, sat the research station with the big laboratory building, the kitchen and recreation hut, small cabins dotted along the beach to accommodate visiting scientists.

The research station catered to any scientists interested in studying health issues unique to this group of isolated islands, and the tropical diseases prevalent here.

The most intensive research had been on the effects of M'Langi tea—made from the bark of a particular tree—and why the islanders who drank this concoction regularly seemed to be less affected by the mosquitos, which carried a unique strain of encephalitis.

As she frowned at what appeared to be changes to the research station, she wondered if anyone was still working there. Keanu's father had been the first to show interest in the tea—

Keanu.

She shook her head as if to dislodge memories of Keanu from her head and tried to think who might be there now. According to her father, a man she knew only as Luke had been working there for a short time but that had been four or five years ago.

Circling back to the southern end of the island, past the little village that had grown up after Opuru Island had been evacuated after a tsunami, she could just pick out the entrance to the gold mine that tunnelled deep beneath the plateau.

The mine had brought wealth not only to her family but to the islanders as well, but the only sign of it was a huge yellow bulldozer, though it, too, was partly hidden beneath a cluster of Norfolk pines and what looked like a tangle of vines.

Weird.

Dropping lower now, the sea was multicoloured, the coral reefs beneath its surface visible like wavy patterns on a fine silk scarf. Images of herself and Keanu snorkelling in those crystal-clear waters, marvelling at the colours of the reef and the tiny fish that lived among the coral, flashed through her mind.

An ache of longing—for her carefree past, her childhood home—filled Caroline's heart, and she had to blink tears from her eyes.

How could she have stayed away so long?

Because Keanu was no longer here?

Or because she'd been afraid he might be…

'Are you okay?' Jill asked, and Caroline turned to her friend—her best friend—who, from seven hundred miles away, had heard the unhappiness in Caroline's voice just a short week ago and had told her she should go home.

Insisted on it, in fact, although Caroline suspected

Jill had wanted to show off her new little plane, *and* her ability as a pilot.

'I'm fine, just sorry I've stayed away so long.'

'In recent times it's been because you were worried that rat Steve would take up with someone else if you disappeared on him for even a week.'

The words startled Caroline out of her sentimental mood.

'Do you really think that? Do you believe I was that much of a doormat to him?'

Jill's silence spoke volumes.

Caroline sighed.

'I suppose he proved he didn't really care about me when he dropped me like a hot cake when the story about the Wildfire gold mine being in trouble appeared in the paper.'

But it was still upsetting—wounding...

Could the man who'd wooed Caroline with flowers, and gifts and words of love, who'd wrapped her in the security of belonging, really be the rat her friends thought him?

Had *she* really been so gullible?

'Maybe he *did* meet someone else,' Caroline answered plaintively. 'Maybe he was telling the truth.'

'That man wouldn't know the truth if it bit him on the butt,' Jill retorted, then fortunately stopped talking.

Caroline wasn't sure if it was because Jill was concentrating on her landing, or if she didn't want to hurt her friend even more.

Although she'd realised later—too late—that Steve *had* been inordinately interested in the mine her family owned...

The little plane bumped onto the tarmac, then rolled along it as Jill braked steadily.

'Strip's in good condition,' she said as she wheeled the craft around and stopped beside the shed that provided welcome to visitors to Wildfire Island.

But the shed needs repainting, Caroline thought, her elation at being home turning to depression because up close it was obvious the place was run-down.

Although the strip had been resurfaced.

Could things have come good?

No, her father had confirmed the mine was in trouble when she'd spoken to him about the article in the paper. Although all his time was spent in Sydney, working as a specialist physician at two hospitals, and helping care for Christopher, her twin, severely oxygen deprived at birth and suffering crippling cerebral palsy, the state of the mine was obviously worrying him.

He had been grey with fatigue from overwork and his fine face had been lined with the signs of continual stress from the hours he put in at work and worry over Christopher's health, yet with the stubborn streak common to all Lockharts he'd refused to even listen when she'd asked if she could help financially.

'Go to the island, it's where you belong,' he'd said gently. 'And remember the best way to get over pain is hard work. The hospital can always do with another nurse, especially now clinical services to the outer islands have expanded and we've had to cut back on hospital staff. Our existing staff go above and beyond for the island and the residents but there's always room for another pair of trained hands.'

Losing himself in work was what he'd done ever since her mother had died—died in his arms and left him with a premature but healthy baby girl and a premature and disabled baby boy to look after.

'Maybe whoever owns that very smart helicopter has an equally smart plane and needed the strip improved.'

Jill's comment brought Caroline out of her brooding thoughts.

'Smart helicopter? Our helicopters have always been run-of-the-mill emergency craft and Dad said we're down to one.'

But as she turned in the direction of Jill's pointing finger, she saw her friend was right. At the far end of the strip was a light-as-air little helicopter—a brilliant dragonfly of a helicopter—painted shiny dark blue with the sun picking out flashes of gold on the side.

'Definitely not ours,' she told Jill.

'Maybe there's a mystery millionaire your shady uncle Ian has conned into investing in the place.'

'From all I hear, it would take a billionaire,' Caroline muttered gloomily.

She'd undone her seat harness while they were talking and now opened the door of the little plane.

'At least come up to the house and have a cup of tea,' she said to Jill.

Jill shook her head firmly.

'I've got my thermos of coffee and sandwiches—like a good Girl Scout, always prepared. I'll just refuel and be off. It's only a four-hour flight. Best I get home to the family.'

Caroline retrieved her luggage—one small case packed with the only lightweight, casual summer clothes she owned. Her life in Sydney had been more designer wear—Steve had always wanted her to look good.

And I went along with it?

She felt her cheeks heat with shame as yet another of Steve's dominating characteristics came to mind.

Yes, she'd gone along with it and many other 'its', often pulling double shifts on weeknights to be free to go 'somewhere special' with him over the weekend.

The fact that the 'something special' usually turned out to be yet another cocktail party with people she either didn't know or, if she had known them, didn't particularly care for only made it worse.

But she'd loved him—or loved that he loved her...

Jill efficiently pumped fuel into the plane's tank, wiped her hands on a handy rag, and turned to her friend.

'You take care, okay? And keep in touch. I want phone calls and emails, none of that social media stuff where everyone can read what you're doing. I want the "not for public consumption" stuff.'

She reached out and gathered Caroline in a warm, tight hug.

'You'll be okay,' she said, and although the words were firmly spoken, Caroline heard a hint of doubt in them.

Dear Jilly, the first friend she'd made at boarding school so many years ago, now back in the cattle country of Western Queensland where she'd grown up, married to a fellow cattleman, raising her own family and top-quality beasts.

Caroline returned the hug, watched as Jill climbed back into the plane and began to taxi up the runway. She waved to the departing plane before turning to look around her.

Yes, the shed was a little run-down and the gardens weren't looking their best, but the peace that filled her heart told her she'd done the right thing.

She was home.

Bending to lift her suitcase, she was struck that something was missing. Okay, so the place wasn't quite up to speed, but where was Harold, who usually greeted every plane?

Harold, who'd told her and Keanu all the legends of the islands and given them boiled lollies so big they'd filled their mouths.

Her and Keanu…

Keanu…

She straightened her shoulders and breathed in the scented tropical air. That had been then and this was now.

Time to put the past—all the past—behind her, take control of her life and move on, as so many of her friends had advised.

And moving on obviously meant carrying her own suitcase up the track to the big house. Not that she minded, but it was strange that no one had met the plane, if only out of curiosity.

Had no one seen it come in?

Did no one care any more?

Or was Harold gone?

How old had he been?

She didn't like the tightening in her gut at the thought that someone who had been so much part of her life might have died while she'd been away…

Impossible.

Although all adults seemed old to children, she doubted Harold had been more than forty when she'd left—

The blast of a horn sent the past skittering from her mind, and she turned to see a little motorised cart—the island's main land transport—racing towards her from the direction of the research station.

'Are you the doctor?' the man driving it yelled.

'No, but I'm a nurse. Can I help?'

The driver pulled up beside her and gestured towards his passenger.

'We phoned the hospital. Someone said the doctor would come to meet us on the way. My mate was fine at first but now he's passed out, well, you can see...'

He gestured towards the man slumped in the back of the little dark blue vehicle. He had no visible injury—until she looked down and saw his foot.

Clad only in a rubber flip-flop, the foot had a nail punched right through beneath the small toe, and apparently into a piece of wood below his inadequate footwear.

Caroline slid in beside the man and put a hand on his chest. He was breathing, and his pulse— Yes, a bit fast but obviously it had been a very painful wound.

'I think we should get him up to the hospital as quickly as possible,' she said, as a figure appeared on the track they would take.

A figure she knew, although the intervening years had stretched him from an adolescent to a man—and for all her heart was bumping erratically in her chest, she certainly didn't know the man.

Caroline slid out of the cart and took the spare seat in front while Keanu, without more than a startled glance and a puzzled frown in her direction, took over in the back, fitting an oxygen mask to the man's face and adjusting the flow on the small tank he'd carried with him.

'Give me a minute to get some painkiller into him.'

Prosaic words but the deep, rich voice reverberated through Caroline's body—a man's voice, not a boy's...

This was Keanu?

Keanu was here?

She didn't know whether to hug him or hit him, but with witnesses around she could do neither. What she really wanted was to turn around and have another look at him, but the image of that first glimpse was burned into her brain.

Keanu the man.

Now grown into his burnished, almond-coloured skin, his grey eyes—his mother's eyes—strikingly pale beneath dark brows and hair.

Straight nose, tempting mouth, sculpted shoulders, abs visible beneath a tightly fitting polo shirt.

He was stunning.

More than that, he projected a kind of sexuality that would have every female within a hundred yards going weak at the knees just looking at him.

'Come back for a break from Sydney society?'

The cold wash of words obviously directed at her fixed the trembling knee thing, while the sarcasm behind them replaced it with anger.

She turned, chin tilted, refusing to reveal the hurt his words had caused.

'I'm a nurse, and I've come back to work, but I *am* surprised to see you here after the way you cut your connection to the islands so many years ago.'

Fortunately, as Caroline had just realised their driver was listening to this icy conversation with interest, they pulled up at the front of the hospital.

The patient was awake, obviously benefiting from the oxygen and the painkilling injection.

Keanu asked the driver to lend a hand, and the two of them eased the man out of the vehicle.

'Sling your arms around our shoulders and we'll help

you in,' Keanu said, and Caroline guessed he was concentrating on the patient so he wouldn't have to look at her.

Or even acknowledge her presence?

What had happened?

What had she done?

Steely determination to not be hurt by him—or any man—ever again made her shut the door firmly on the past. Whatever had happened had been a long time ago, and she was a different person, had moved on, and was moving on again…

But walking behind Keanu, she couldn't *not* be aware of his presence. This man who'd been a boy she'd known so well was really something. Broad shoulders sloping down to narrow hips, but a firm butt and calf muscles that suggested not a workout in gym but a lot of outdoors exercise—he'd always loved running, said he felt free…

She was looking at his butt?

Best she get away, and fast.

But once they had the man on the deck in front of the hospital, Keanu turned back towards her.

'Well, if you're a nurse, don't just stand there. Come in and be useful. Hettie and Sam are on a clinic run to the outer islands and there's only an aide and myself on duty.'

He stood above her—loomed really—the disdain in his voice visible on his features.

And something broke inside her.

Was this really Keanu, her childhood friend and companion? Keanu, who had been gentle and kind, and had always taken care of her when she'd felt lost and alone?

Back then, his mother's mantra to him had always been 'Take care of Caroline', and Keanu, two years older, always had.

Which was probably why his disappearance from her

life had hurt so deeply that for a while she'd doubted she'd get over it.

Head bent to hide whatever hurt might be showing on her face, she took the steps in one stride and followed the three men into the small but well-set-up room that she knew from the hospital plans doubled as Emergency and Outpatients.

Having helped lift the patient onto an examination table, the driver muttered something about getting back to work, and hurried through the door.

Which left her and Keanu...

Keanu, who was managing to ignore her completely while her body churned with conflicting emotions.

'Nail gun?' Keanu asked the patient as he examined the foot.

The patient nodded.

'Never heard of steel-capped workboots?' Keanu continued. 'I thought they were the only legal footwear on a building job.'

'Out here?' the man scoffed. 'Who's going to check?'

'Just hold his leg up for me, grasp the calf.'

An order to the nurse, no doubt, but even as he gave it Keanu didn't glance her way.

'No "please"?' Caroline said sweetly as she lifted the man's lower leg so Keanu could see just how far through the wood the nail protruded.

She must have struck a nerve with her words, for Keanu looked up at her, his face unreadable, although she caught the confusion in his eyes.

So she wasn't the only one feeling this was beyond bizarre.

'Okay, let it down,' he said, the words another order.

Maybe she'd been wrong about the confusion.

Only then he added, 'Please,' and suddenly he was her old Keanu again, teasing her, almost smiling.

And the confusion *that* caused made her wish Jill hadn't taken off again so quickly. She had come here for peace and quiet, to heal after the humiliation of realising the man she'd thought had loved her had only been interested in her family money.

What was left of it.

'Here's a key.'

Keanu's fingers touched hers, and electricity jolted through her bones, shocking her in more ways than one. 'You'll find phials of local anaesthetic in the cupboard marked B, second shelf. Bring two—no, he's a big guy, maybe three—and you'll see syringes in there as well. Antiseptic, dressings and swabs are in the cupboard next to that one—it's not locked. Get whatever you think we'll need. I'm off to find a saw.'

The patient gave a shriek of protest but Keanu was already out of the room.

Slipping automatically into nurse mode, Caroline smiled as she unlocked the cupboard and found all she needed.

'He's not going to cut off your foot,' she reassured the man as she set up a tray on a trolley and rolled it over to the examination table. 'Hospitals have all manners of saws. We use diamond-tipped ones to cut through plaster when it has to come off, and we use adapted electric saws and drills in knee and hip replacement, though not here, of course. I'd say he's going to numb your leg from the calf down, then cut through the nail between your flip-flop and the wood. It's easier to pull a nail out of rubber and flesh than it is out of wood.'

Their patient didn't seem all that reassured, but Caroline, who'd found where the paperwork was kept, distracted him with questions about his name, age, address, any medication he was on, and, because she couldn't resist it, what he was doing on the island.

'Doing up the little places down on the flat,' was the reply, which came as Keanu returned with a small battery-powered saw and a portable X-ray machine.

'The research station,' he said, before Caroline could ask the patient what little places.

'They're doing up the research station when there's not enough money to keep the hospital running properly?'

The indignation in her voice must have been mirrored on her face, for Keanu said a curt, 'Later,' and turned his full attention to his patient.

After numbing the lower leg—Caroline being careful not to let her fingers touch Keanu's as she handed him syringes and phials—he explained to the patient what he intended doing.

'Nurse already told me that,' the man replied. 'Just get on with it.'

Asking Caroline to hold the wood steady, Keanu eased it as far as it would go from the flip-flop then bent closer to see what he was doing, so his head, the back of it, blocked Caroline's view. Not that she'd have seen much of the work, her eyes focussed on the little scar that ran along his hairline, the result of a long-ago exercise on her part to shave off all his hair with her grandfather's cut-throat razor.

Fortunately he must have been able to cut straight through the little bar of the nail, for he straightened before she could be further lost in memories.

Caroline dropped the wood into a trash bin and returned to find Keanu setting up a portable X-ray machine.

'We need to know if the nail's gone through bone,' he explained, helping her get back into nurse mode. 'And the picture should tell us if it's in a position that would have caused tendon damage.'

'Why does that make a difference?' Now he was pain-free—if only temporarily—the patient was becoming impatient.

'It makes the difference between pulling it out and cutting it out.'

'No cutting, just yank the damn thing out,' the patient said, but Keanu ignored him, going quietly on with the job of setting up the head of the unit above the man's foot.

Intrigued by the procedure—and definitely in nurse mode—Caroline had to ask.

'I thought the hospital had a designated radiography room,' she said, remembering protocols at the hospital where she'd worked that suggested wherever possible X-rays be carried out in that area, although the portables had many uses.

Keanu glanced up at her, his face once again unreadable.

'There is but I doubt you and I could lift him onto the table and with his leg already numb he's likely to fall if he tries to help us.'

Which puts me neatly back in my place, Caroline thought.

'Move back!'

Ignoring the peremptory tone, she stepped the oblig-atory two metres back from the head of the machine, watched Keanu don a lead apron—so protocols *were* ob-served here—and take shots from several angles.

That done, he wheeled the machine to the corner of

the room, hung his apron over a convenient chair and checked the results on a computer screen.

'Come and look at this. What do you think?'

Assuming he was talking to her, not the immobile patient, she moved over to stand beside him—beside Keanu, who had been the single most important person in the world for her for the first thirteen years of her life. Important because, unlike her father, or even Christopher, he'd always been there for her—her best friend and constant companion.

Until he'd disappeared.

But this Keanu...

It was beyond weird.

Spooky.

And, oh, so painful...

'Well?' he demanded, and she forgot about the way Keanu was affecting her and concentrated on the images.

'By some miracle it's slipped between two metatarsals and though it's probably hit some ligament or tendon, because the bones are intact it shouldn't impact on the movement of the foot too much.'

'And don't look at me like that,' she muttered at him, after he'd shot yet another questioning glance her way. 'I *am* a trained nurse, and have been a shift supervisor in the ER at Canterbury Hospital.'

'I don't know how you found the time,' he said as he headed back to the patient.

She was about to demand what the hell he'd meant by that when she realised this was hardly the time or place to be having an argument with this man she didn't know.

Her friend had been a boy—was that the difference?

It certainly was part of it given the way her body was reacting to the slightest accidental touch...

'Okay, so now I need you to swab all around the nail then hold his foot while I try to yank the nail out. I'd prefer not to have to cut it out.'

Caroline put on new gloves, cleaned the areas above and beneath the foot, changed gloves again and got a firm grasp of the man's foot, ready to put all her weight into the task of holding on if the nail proved resistant.

But, no, it slid out easily, and as the wound was bleeding quite freely now, it was possible the risk of infection had been limited.

'Antibiotics and tetanus injections in the locked cupboard,' Keanu told her as he examined the wound in the patient's foot. 'And bring some saline and a packet of oral antibiotics as well. Everything's labelled as we get a lot of agency nurses coming out here for short stints. I'll use the saline to flush the wound before we dress it.'

He worked with quick, neat movements, cleaning the wound, putting the dressings on—usually, in her experience, a job left to a nurse—before administering the antibiotic and a tetanus shot. He even pulled a sleeve over the foot to keep the dressings in place and keep them relatively clean.

'Now all we have to do is get you back to your accommodation,' Keanu said. 'Keep off the foot for a couple of days and find your workboots before you go back on the job. If you don't have any you can phone the mainland and have some sent out on tomorrow's plane. Nurse Lockhart and I will help you out to a cart and I'll run you back down the hill.'

'I've got workboots,' the man said gruffly. 'And I'll phone my mate to come and get me, thanks. The foreman on the job doesn't like strangers on the site.'

'Strangers on the site? What site? What's happening at the research station, Keanu?'

He touched her on the arm.

'Leave it,' he said quietly, and the touch, more than his words, stopped her questions.

Since when had her body reacted to a casual touch from Keanu's hand?

It was being back on the island…

It was seeing him again…

Remembering the hurt…

Caroline closed her eyes, willing the tumult of emotions in her body to settle. She was here to heal, to find herself again, but she was also here to work.

She cleaned up, dropping soiled swabs into a closed bin marked for that purpose and the needles into a sharps box. Their patient was now sitting on the examination table, chatting to Keanu about, she found as she edged closer, fishing.

Well, it wasn't something she wanted to discuss right now, and as she needed time to sort out her reactions to seeing Keanu again, she slipped away, heading back down the track to the airstrip to collect her suitcase.

She could walk up to the house on the path behind the hospital and so avoid seeing the source of her confusion again. And once she was up at the house—home again—she could sort things out in her head—and possibly in her body—and…

And what?

Make things right between them?

She doubted that could ever happen. He had disappeared without a word, returned her letters unopened.

But now she'd have to work with him. Was she supposed to behave as if the life they'd shared had never happened?

As if his disappearance from it hadn't hurt her so badly she'd thought she'd never recover?

Impossible.

She'd reached the airstrip and grabbed her case by the time she'd thought this far and as further consideration of the problem seemed just that—impossible—she put it from her mind and started up the track, feeling the moisture in the air, trapped by the heavy rainforest on each side, wrap around her like a security blanket.

She was home, that was the main thing.

The track from the strip to the big house led up the hill behind the hospital and staff villas.

Staff villas?

Keanu.

Forget Keanu!

For her sanity's sake, she needed to work—she'd already sat around feeling sorry for herself for far too long as a result of another desertion.

And another nurse would always come in handy on the island even if they couldn't afford to pay her. She had her own place to live and some money Steve hadn't known about tucked away in the bank.

And wasn't this what she and Keanu had always planned to do?

He would become a doctor, she a nurse, and they'd return to Wildfire to run a hospital on the island. As children, they'd shared a picture book with a doctor and a nurse that had led to this childhood dream. Had it seemed more important because they had both lost a parent who possibly could have been saved if medical aid had been closer?

Half-orphans, they'd called themselves…

But as she hadn't existed for Keanu once he and his mother had left the island permanently, seeing him here, *and* seeing him carrying out *his* part of their dream, had completely rattled her.

Trudging up the track, she shook her head in disbelief at his sudden reappearance in her life, especially now when all she wanted to do was throw herself into work as an antidote to the pain of Steve's rejection.

Could she throw herself into work with Keanu around? Even seeing him that one time had memories—images— of their shared childhood flashing through her head.

Helen, his mother, had died not long after leaving the island. Caroline's father had passed on that information many years ago, but he'd offered no explanation the year Caroline had found out she wouldn't be going to the is- land for her holidays as Helen and Keanu had left and there'd been no one to care for her.

And despite her grief at Helen's loss, she'd felt such anger against Keanu for not letting her know they were leaving, for not keeping in touch, for not telling her of his mother's death himself, that she'd shut him out of her mind, the hurt too deep to contemplate.

'I'll take that.'

Keanu's voice came from behind her, deep and husky, and sent tremors down her spine, while her fingers, ren- dered nerveless by his touch, released her hold on the case.

Why *had* he come back?

And why now?

But it was he who asked the question.

'Why did you come back?'

Blunt words but something that sounded like anger

throbbed through them—anger that fired her own in response.

'It is my home.'

'*One* of your homes,' he reminded her. 'You have another perfectly comfortable one in Sydney with your father and your brother—your twin. How *is* Christopher?'

She spun towards him, sorry she didn't still have the suitcase to swing at his legs as she turned.

'How dare you ask that question? As if you care about my brother. People who care for others keep in touch. They don't just stop all communication. They don't send back letters unopened. I was twelve, Keanu, and suddenly someone who had been there for me all my life, someone I thought was my friend, was gone.'

Keanu bowed his head in the face of her anger, unable to bear the hurt in her eyes. Oh, he'd been angry at her reappearance, but that had been shock-type anger. He'd returned to Wildfire thinking her safely tucked away in Sydney, enjoying a busy social life.

Then, seeing her appear out of nowhere, so much unresolved anger and bitterness and, yes, regret had churned inside him he'd reacted with anger. But that anger should have been directed at another Lockhart. It was regret at the way he'd treated her—his betrayal of their friendship—that had added fuel to the fire.

Guilt…

And now he knew he'd hurt her again.

He'd learned to read Caro's hurt early. He'd first read it in a three-year-old looking forward to a visit from her daddy, the visit suddenly cancelled because of one thing or another.

Usually Christopher's health, he remembered now.

Throughout their childhood, she'd suffered these disappointments, a trip back to her Sydney home put off indefinitely because Christopher had chicken pox and was infectious. Going back to Sydney at ten when her adored grandmother had died, and learning it would be to boarding school because her father worked long hours and Christopher's carers could not take care of her as well...

'I'm sorry,' he said, apologising for all the hurts she'd suffered but knowing two words would never be enough.

'I don't want your "sorry" now, Keanu. I'm here, you're here, and we'll be working together, so we'll just both have to make the best of it.'

'You're serious about working in the hospital?'

Had he sounded astounded that she glared at him then turned away and stalked off up the path?

He followed her, taking in the shape of Caroline all grown up—long legs lightly tanned, hips curving into a neat waist, and long golden hair swinging from a high ponytail—swinging defiantly, if hair could be defiant.

The realisation that he was attracted to her came slowly. Oh, he'd felt a jolt along his nerves when they'd accidentally touched, and his heart had practically somersaulted when he'd first set eyes on her, but surely that was remnants of the 'old friends' stuff.

And the attraction would have to be hidden as, apart from the fact that he was obviously at the very top of her least favourite people list, he was, as far as he knew, still married.

Not that he could blame Caro—for the least favourite people thing, not his marriage.

They'd both been sent to boarding school while still young, she to a school in Sydney, he to one in North Queensland, but the correspondence between them had been regular and intimate in the sense that they'd shared their thoughts and feelings about everything going on in their lives.

Then he and his mother had been forced to leave the island and there had been no way he could cause his mother further hurt by keeping in touch with Caroline.

She was a Lockhart after all.

A *Lockhart*!

He caught up with her.

'Look, no matter how you feel about me, there are things you should know.'

She turned her head and raised an eyebrow, so, taking that as an invitation, he ventured to speak.

'There's your uncle, Ian, for a start.'

Another quick glance.

'You must have known he came here, that your father had left him in overall charge of the mine after the hospital was finished and he, your father, that is, was doing more study and couldn't get over as often.'

She stopped suddenly, so he had to turn back, and standing this close, seeing the blue-green of her eyes, the dark eyebrows and lashes that drew attention to them, the curve of pink lips, the straight, dainty nose, his breath caught in his chest and left him wondering why no one had ever come up with an antidote for attraction.

Cold blue-green eyes—waiting, watchful…

'So?'

Demanding…

Keanu shifted uneasily. As a clan the Lockharts had always been extraordinarily close to each other and even though Ian was the noted black sheep, Caroline's father had still given him a job.

'Ian apparently had gambling debts before he came—a

gambling addiction—but unfortunately even on a South Sea island online gambling is available. From all I heard he never stopped gambling but he wasn't very good at it. Eventually he sacked Peter Blake, the mine manager your father had employed, and took whatever he could from the mine—that's why it's been struggling lately and your father's having to foot a lot of the hospital bills. Ian stopped paying the mine workers, closed down the crushers and extractors and brought it to all but a standstill.'

He paused, although he knew he had to finish.

'Then he ran away. No one knows for certain when he went but it was very recently. One day his yacht was in the harbour at the mine and the next day it was gone.'

Blue-green eyes met his—worried but also wary.

'Grandma always said he was no good,' she admitted sadly. '"In spite of the fact he's my son, he's a bad seed," she used to say, which, as a child, always puzzled me, the bad-seed bit.'

He heard sadness in Caroline's words but she seemed slightly more relaxed now, he could tell, so he took a deep breath and finished the woeful tale.

'The trouble is, Ian's damaged the Lockhart name. I don't know how people will view your return.'

'What do you mean, view my return?'

Her confusion was so obvious he wanted to give her a hug.

Bad idea.

He put out his hand and touched her arm, wanting her calm enough to understand what he was trying to tell her. Though touching her was a mistake. Not only did fire flood his being, but she pulled away so suddenly she'd have fallen if he hadn't grabbed her.

And let her go very swiftly.

'Lockharts have been part of M'Langi history since they first settled on Wildfire,' he said gently. 'Your grandfather and father helped bring prosperity and health facilities to the islands and were admired for all they did. But Ian's behaviour has really tainted the name.'

He could see her confusion turning to anger and guessed she wanted to lash out at him—well, not at him particularly…or perhaps it was at him particularly, but she definitely wanted to lash out.

She turned away instead and trudged on up the slope, spinning back when she'd covered less than three feet to reach out and say, 'I'll take my bag now, thank you.'

Cool, calm and collected again—to outward appearances.

But he knew her too well not to know how deeply she'd been affected by his words. She'd never been a snob, never seen herself as different from the other island children with whom they'd attended the little primary school on Atangi, but she'd felt pride in the achievements of her family, justifiably so. To hear what he was telling her would be shattering for her.

But all he said was, 'I'll carry the bag, Caroline, and maybe, one day soon, we can sit down and talk—maybe find our friendship again.'

In reply, she stepped closer, grabbed her bag and stormed away, marching now, striding, hurrying away from him as fast as she could.

And was it his imagination, or did he hear her mutter, 'As if!'?

CHAPTER TWO

KEANU RUSSELL WALKED swiftly back down the track. He probably wasn't needed but the hospital was so short-staffed someone had to be there. The situation at the hospital was worse than he'd imagined when, alerted by the elders on Atangi, the main island of the group, he'd come back.

He touched the tribal tattoo that encircled the muscle of his upper arm, the symbol of M'Langi—of his belonging.

'Come home, we need you.'

That had been the extent of the elders' message, and as the islanders—with help from Max Lockhart—had paid for his high school and university education, he'd known he owed it to them to come.

He'd tried to contact Max before he'd left Australia but had been unable to get on to him. Apparently, Max's son, Christopher, had had a serious lung infection and Max had been with him in the ICU.

Trying the hospital here instead, Vailea, the hospital's housekeeper, had answered the phone and told him the islands—and the hospital in particular—were in big trouble.

'That Ian Lockhart, he's no good to anyone,' Vailea

had told him. 'Max has been paying for the hospital out of his own money, because the mine is run-down and any money it does make, that rotten Ian takes.'

There was a silence as Keanu digested this, then Vailea added, 'We need you here, Keanu.'

'Why didn't *you* call me? Tell me this? Why leave it to the elders?'

There was another long pause before Vailea said, 'You've been gone too long, Keanu. I did not know how to tell you. I thought with me asking, you might not come, but with the elders—'

She broke the connection but not before he'd heard the tears in her voice, and he sat, staring at the phone in his hand, guilt flooding his entire being.

M'Langi was his home, the islanders his people, and he had stayed away because of his anger, and his mother's inner torment—caused by a Lockhart…

But if he was truly honest, he'd stayed away because he didn't want to face the memories of his happy childhood, or his betrayal of his childhood friend.

But home he was, and so aghast at the situation that memories had had no time to plague him. Although sometimes when he walked through the small hospital late at night he remembered a little boy and even smaller girl holding hands on about the same spot, talking about the future when he would be a doctor and she would be a nurse and they would come back to the island and work in the hospital her father had, even then, been planning to build.

Okay, so the ghost of Caroline did bother him—had bothered him even as he'd married someone else—but there was enough work to do to block her out most of the time.

Or had been until she'd arrived in person. Not only arrived but apparently intended to work here.

Not that she wasn't needed…

The nurse they had been expecting to come in on the next day's flight had phoned to say her mother was ill and she didn't know when she might make it. Then Maddie Haddon, one of their Fly-In-Fly-Out, or FIFO doctors, had phoned to say she wouldn't be on the flight either— some mix-up with her antenatal appointments.

Sam Taylor, the only permanent doctor, was doing a clinic flight to the other islands, with Hettie, their head nurse—another permanent. They didn't know of the latest developments but as Keanu himself had come as a FIFO and intended staying permanently whether he was paid or not, he could cover for Maddie.

And, presumably, Caroline could cover for the nurse.

Caroline.

Caro.

He had known how hurt she would have been when he'd cut her out of his life, but his anger had been stronger than his concern—his anger and his determination to do nothing more to hurt his already shattered mother.

Caroline discovered why Harold hadn't met the plane. He was in the front garden of the house, arguing volubly with his wife, Bessie. It had been Caroline's great-grandfather, autocratic old sod that he must have been, who'd insisted that all the employees working in the house and grounds take on English names.

'You come inside and help me clean,' Bessie was saying.

'No, I have to do the yard. Ian will raise hell if the yard's not done, not that I believe he's coming back.'

Watching them, Caroline felt a stirring of alarm that they had grown old, although age didn't seem to be affecting their legendary squabbles.

'Nor do I but someone is coming. Some other visitor. We saw the plane on a day when planes don't usually come, and anyway it was too small to be one of our planes.'

'Might be for the research station. Plenty of people coming and going there,' Harold offered, but Bessie was going to have the last word.

'In that case you don't need to do the yard.'

Caroline decided she couldn't stand behind an allemande vine, wild with shiny green leaves and brilliant yellow trumpet flowers, eavesdropping any longer.

'Bessie, Harold, it's me, Caroline!'

She passed the bush and came into view, expecting to be welcomed like a prodigal son—or daughter in her case—but to her utter bewilderment both of them burst into tears.

Eventually they recovered enough from their shock to rush towards her, arms held out.

'Oh, Caroline, you have come back. Now we have you *and* Keanu back where you belong, everything will be good again.'

Wrapped in a double, teary hug, Caroline couldn't answer.

Not that she would have been able to. Although she knew he was here—knew only too well—hearing Keanu's name knocked the breath out of her. But it had been the last part—about everything being good again—that had been the bigger shock.

But it also gave her resolve. If the trouble was so bad

the islanders thought she, whom they'd always considered a helpless princess, could help, things *must* be bad.

She eased out of their arms and straightened up. Of course she had to help. She didn't know how, but she certainly would do everything in her power to save the islanders' livelihood and keep much-needed medical care available to them.

Enough of the doormat.

M'Langi was her home.

'But why are you working in the house, Bessie? What happened to the young woman Dad appointed after Helen left?'

With Keanu, a voice whispered, but she had no time for whispering voices right now.

'That was Kari but from the time that Ian got here we thought it would be better if she kept her distance,' Bessie explained. 'Ian is a bad, bad man for all he's your family. In the end I said I'd do the housework. I mind Anahera's little girl too, but she's no trouble, she plays with all your toys and loves your dolls, dressing and undressing them.'

Caroline smiled, remembering her own delight in the dolls until Keanu had told her it was girl stuff and she had to learn to learn to make bows and arrows and to catch fish in her hands.

'Anahera?' she asked, as the name was vaguely familiar.

'Vailea, her mother, worked as the cook at the research station while we were caretakers there. But there's all kinds of funny stuff going on there too, so now she's housekeeper at the hospital and Anahera—she's a bit older than you and went to school on the mainland; her grandmother lived there—well, she's a nurse here so I mind her little one.'

It was hard to absorb so much information at once, so Caroline allowed herself to be led up to the house, where a very small child with dark eyes, olive skin and a tangle of golden curls was lining up dolls in a row on the cane lounge that had sat on the veranda for as long as Caroline could remember.

The cane lounge, potted palms everywhere, a few cane chairs around a table, once again with a smaller pot in the middle of it, and the swing she and Keanu had rocked in so often—*this* was coming home…

'This is Hana,' Bessie said, leading the little girl forward. 'Hana, this is Miss Caroline. She lives here.'

Caroline knelt by the beautiful child, straightening one of the dolls.

'Just Caroline will do,' she said, 'or even Caro.'

Caro.

No one but Keanu had ever called her Caro, but now wasn't the time to get sentimental over Keanu, for all he looked like a Greek god, and had sent shivers down her spine just being close to him.

She was here to…

What?

She'd come because she was unhappy, seeking sanctuary in the place she'd loved most, but now she was here?

Well, she was damned if she was going to let things deteriorate any further.

But first she had to find out exactly how things stood, and whether whoever ran the hospital would give her a job, and most importantly of all right now, she had to find the steel in her inner self to work with Keanu…

'Are you being paid, Bessie?' she asked, thinking she had to set her own house in order first.

Bessie studied her toes then shook her dark, curly hair.

'Anahera pays me for looking after Hana, but it's been a while since Harold got a wage.'

Caroline was angry. She knew their fondness for the Lockhart family and gratitude for what her father had done for the islands would have kept them doing what they could whether they were paid or not.

Knew also that the couple wouldn't be starving. Like all the islanders, and many people she knew on acreage on the mainland, they had their own plot of land around their bure—the traditional island home—and Harold would grow vegetables and raise a few pigs and chickens, but that didn't make not paying them right.

'Well, now I'm here we'll shut off most of the rooms and I'll just use my bedroom, bathroom and the kitchen. I can pay you to keep them clean and I'll vacuum through the rest of the place once a fortnight.'

Bessie began to mutter about dust, but Caroline waved away her complaint.

'Lockharts have been eating dust since the mine began,' she said, 'so a little bit on the floor of the closed rooms doesn't matter. And now,' she announced, 'I'm going down to the hospital to ask whoever runs it for a job. Even if they can't pay me, they can surely find me something to do.'

She left her case and headed back down the way she'd come. Work would give her the opportunity to find out what was going on. Even small hospitals were hotbeds of gossip.

Although…

Of course she could work with Keanu. She didn't know the man he'd become so she'd just treat him like any other colleague.

Male colleague.

Friendly, but keeping her distance…

Definitely keeping her distance, given how the accidental touches had affected her…

Lost in her muddled thoughts, she was halfway to the hospital when she remembered the only people there had been Keanu and an aide. What had he said? Hettie and Sam were on a clinic run? Caroline knew the hospital ran weekly clinics on the other inhabited islands of the group and today must have been one of those days.

That was probably the only reason Keanu had accepted her help with the injured man earlier.

She walked back up the hill, wondering why she'd thought returning to the island was such a good idea.

Wondering how things had gone so wrong, not only with the island but between herself and Keanu.

Had she judged him too harshly?

Refused to accept he might have had a good reason for stopping communication between them?

But surely they'd been close enough for him to have given her a reason—an explanation?

Hadn't they?

Totally miserable by the time she reached the house, she went through to her old bedroom and unpacked the case that either Bessie or Harold had left there.

Then, as being back in her old room brought nostalgia with it, she slowly and carefully toured the house.

Built like so many colonial houses in those days, it had a wide veranda with overhanging eaves around all four sides of it. She started there, at the front, looking down at the hospital and beyond it the airstrip, and onto the flat ground by the beach, and although she couldn't see the research station, she knew it was there, sheltered beneath huge tropical fig trees and tall coconut palms.

As she knew the village was down there, on the eastern shore, nestled up against the foothills of the plateau. The village had been built on land given by her father, after the villagers on another island had lost their homes and land in a tsunami.

Now some of the villagers worked in the mine and at the hospital, and worshipped in the little white church they'd built on a rocky promontory between the village and the mine. A chapel built to celebrate their survival.

She knew the beach was there as well, but that too was hidden, although as she turned the corner and looked across the village she saw the strip of sand and the wide lagoon enclosed by the encircling coral.

On a clear day, from here and the back veranda, she'd have been able to see most of the islands that made up the M'Langi group, but today there was a sea haze.

The western veranda formed the division between the main house and the smaller copy of it, an annexe where Helen and Keanu had lived.

No way was she going there now, although their home had been as open to her as hers had been to Keanu.

This time she entered the house through the back door, through the kitchen with its different pantries opening off it and the huge wooden table where she and Keanu had eaten breakfast and lunch.

The pantries had provided great places for hide and seek, although Grandma's cook had forever been shooing them out, afraid they'd break the precious china and crystal stored in them.

Caroline opened the door of one—empty shelves where the crystal had once reflected rainbows in the light.

The sight sent her hurrying to the dining room, on the eastern side of the main hall. Looking up, she saw with relief that the chandelier still hung above the polished dining table.

Grandma had loved that table *and* the grandeur of the chandelier. She had insisted Caroline, Keanu and Helen join her there for dinner every evening, the magic crystals of the chandelier making patterns on the table's highly polished surface.

Helen would report on anything that needed doing around the house, and talk to Grandma about meals and what needed to be ordered from the mainland to come over on the next flight.

Grandma would quiz Keanu and Caroline about their day at school—what they'd learned and had they done their homework before going out to play.

Ian might have sold her grandmother's precious crystal to cover his gambling debts but at least he'd left the chandelier.

He must have been desperate indeed to have packed the delicate objects before sending them out on the boat that made a weekly visit to the harbour at Atangi.

Before or after he'd started skimming money from the mine?

Taking away the livelihood of the workers?

Shame that she could be related to the man brought heat to her cheeks, but what was done was done.

Unless?

Could she do something to help set things to rights?

Refusing to be waylaid, she continued with her exploration. Next to the dining room was the big entertaining room Grandma had always called the Drawing Room—words Caroline still saw in her mind with capital letters. Here, at least, things remained the same. The furniture, the beautiful old Persian carpets—Ian couldn't have known they were valuable.

But the elegant, glass-fronted cabinets were empty. Grandma's precious collection of china—old pieces handed down to her by *her* mother and grandmother—was gone.

That was when tears started in Caroline's eyes. Ian had not only stolen physical things, he'd stolen her memories, memories of sitting on the floor in front of the cabinet while Grandma handed her one piece at a time, telling her its history, promising they would be hers one day.

That she'd lost them didn't matter, but the treachery of Ian selling things he knew had been precious to his mother turned her tears to anger.

Taking a deep breath, she moved on into Grandma's sitting room.

The little desk she'd used each day to write to friends was there, and Caroline could feel the spirit of her grandmother, the woman who, with Helen, had brought her up until Grandma's death when Caroline was ten.

Opening off the wide passage on the other side were large, airy bedrooms, all with wide French doors and folding shutters that led onto the veranda. The filmy lace curtains still graced the insides of the windows, although they were beginning to look drab.

Grandma's was the first room, the huge four-poster bed draped with a pale net, the faint scent of her presence lingering in the air. There'd always been flowers in Grandma's room, as there had been on the dining-room table and the cabinets in the drawing room...

Leaving her exploration, she hurried out into the garden, minding the thorns on the bougainvillea as she pulled off a couple of flower stems, then some frangipani, a few yellow allemande flowers, some glossy leaves, and white daisies.

Back inside she found vases Ian must have considered too old and cracked to fetch a decent price. She filled them with water and carried them, one by one, into the three rooms where flowers had always stood.

Soon she'd do more—head into the rainforest for leaves and berries and eventually have floral tributes to Grandma that would rival the ones she used to make.

But there was still half a house to explore.

Her father's room was next, unchanged although the small bed beside her father's big one reminded Caroline of the rare times Christopher had come to the island. The visits hadn't lasted long, but she and Keanu had always shared their adventures with him. They would put him in his wheelchair and show him all their favourite places, probably risking his life when they wheeled him down the steep track to Sunset Beach.

The next room must have been Ian's, then three smaller, though still by modern-day standards large, rooms—hers in the middle.

But as she poked her head into Ian's room it was obvious he hadn't been living there as the furniture was covered in dust sheets that seemed to have been there for ever.

'He lived in the guesthouse.'

Bessie had come in and now stood beside Caroline, looking into the empty, rather ghostly room.

The guesthouse was off the back veranda opposite Helen and Keanu's suite of rooms, but detached and given privacy by a screen of trees and shrubs.

'I don't think I'll bother looking there,' she said to

Bessie. 'It was about the only place on the island Keanu and I weren't allowed to play so there'd be no memories.'

She was back on the front veranda when she heard the *whump-whump-whump* of a helicopter.

Now she could go down to the hospital and ask for a job.

Right now before she'd let her doubts about working with Keanu solidify in her head.

Or perhaps tomorrow when she'd worked on a strategy to handle working with him…

He had to go up to the house and make peace with Caro, Keanu decided, not skulk around down here at the hospital.

Sam and Hettie would employ her, that much was certain, so he would be working with her. But doctor-nurse relationships needed trust on both sides and although all his instincts told him to run for his life, he knew he wouldn't.

Couldn't.

M'Langi was more important than these new and distinctly uncomfortable reactions to Caro. Finding out what had been happening and trying to put things right—that was what the elders expected of him.

So he was here, and she was here, and…

He sighed, then began to wonder just why she was here. He'd never totally lost touch with what Caro was up to, being in contact with her father all through his student years, asking, oh, so casually, how she was doing.

And friends from the islands, staying at the Lockharts' Sydney house on a visit or while studying, would pass on information. So now he thought about it, he'd known she'd studied nursing, because he'd smiled at the time to think both of them were fulfilling at least the beginning of that childhood promise.

But he'd never expected her to return to Wildfire to actually finish the job, especially as he'd known a little of the life she'd been leading. Known from the Sydney papers he would buy up in Cairns, for the sole purpose, he realised, of torturing himself.

He might pretend he'd bought them for the business section, which was always more comprehensive than the one in the local paper, but, if so, why did he turn to the social pages first, hoping for a glimpse of Caro—a grown-up, beautiful Caro—usually on the arm of a too-smooth-looking bloke called Steve, to whom she was, apparently, 'almost' engaged.

What the hell did 'almost' mean?

It couldn't have been jealousy that had made him feel so bad—after all, he'd been the one who'd not almost but definitely married someone else. Someone he'd thought he'd loved because she'd brought him out of the lingering misery of his mother's death, his loneliness and his homesickness for the island.

So kind of, in a way, he'd betrayed Caro not once— in disappearing from her life—but twice, although that wasn't really true as trysts made between twelve- and fourteen-year-olds didn't really count.

Did they?

It was all this confusion—the unresolved issues inside him—that was making him angry, and somehow the anger had made her its target.

Which was probably unfair.

No, it was definitely unfair.

Especially as she was obviously unhappy. He'd put that

down to her seeing him again, which would be natural after the way he'd behaved towards her.

So maybe he should stay well out of her way.

Except he'd always hated it when Caro was unhappy. And if he'd caused or even contributed to that unhappiness, which he must have, cutting her off the way he had so long ago, then shouldn't he do something about it?

At least see if they could regain a little of their old friendship.

Friendship?

When one glimpse of the grown-up Caro had sent his pulses racing, his entire body stirring in a most unfriend-like manner?

Not good for a man who was probably still married...

On top of which, he was torn between two edicts of his mother. The childhood one, always spoken when the two of them as children had left the house, plainly spoken and always understood: take care of Caroline.

Then, as his mother had been dying from pancreatic cancer that had appeared from nowhere and killed her within six weeks, while he, a doctor could do nothing to save her. *Then* she had *cursed* the Lockharts...

Well, Ian Lockhart anyway.

Anyway, wasn't he beyond superstitions like curses?

He shook his head to clear the memories and useless speculation, checked the few patients they had in the hospital, then let out a huge sigh of relief when he heard the helicopter returning.

He almost let himself hope it was bringing in a difficult case, something to distract him from the endlessly circling thoughts in his head.

Hettie and Sam had left the hospital's makeshift ambulance down near the helicopter pad so Keanu walked down to the airstrip, not really wishing for a patient but ready to help unpack anything they might have brought back. And it would be best to break the news about the FIFO nurse and Maddie not coming now, rather than leaving it until the morning.

Would he tell them about Caroline's arrival?

He'd have to at least mention it.

Sam would be only too delighted to have an available nurse.

And he would be doomed to work with the woman he didn't really know but had been instantly attracted to in a way he'd never felt before.

It was because of the old friendship. The attraction thing. It had to be, but with any luck, after the way he'd treated her, she'd want to have as little to do with him as possible.

He was almost at the helicopter now, and could see Sam and Jack Richards, the pilot, lifting out a stretcher.

Good! That means work to do, Keanu thought, then realised how unkind it was to be wishing someone ill. But it was only when he saw the patient that he felt a flush of shame at his thoughts. It was old Alkiri, from the island of Atangi, the elder who had been one of his and Caro's favourite people and true mentor when they had been young.

He moved closer and greeted the elder in his native language, touching the old man's shoulder in a gesture of respect.

Even through the oxygen mask, Keanu could see the blue tinge on their patient's lips and he wondered just how old Alkiri might be.

'He had a fall, perhaps a TIA as apparently he'd been falling quite a lot recently.'

TIA—transient ischemic attack—often a precursor to a full-blown stroke. Had Alkiri been putting these falls down to old age? He was a private man, unlikely to seek help unless he really needed it. Yet, as Caroline's grandfather's boatman, he had not only lived here at Wildfire but had taken two small children under his wing. It was he who had taken them and the village children to and from the school on Atangi, teaching them things about the islands, and life itself, that to Keanu were as important as the learning he'd had at school.

He should tell Caro Alkiri was—

He stopped the thought before it went any further. It had been automatic for he knew she'd loved the old man as much as he had—and probably still would...

But he was no longer the boy who'd run through the house, calling for his friend to pass on a bit of news.

And she was no longer the girl he'd always wanted to find so he could tell—

They strapped the stretcher into the converted jeep, especially modified for just that reason, then Jack and Hettie rode back to the hospital, Sam walking with Keanu to check on any news and pass on information from the clinics on the other islands.

The scent of a nearby frangipani hung in the air, but today such a reminder that he was home didn't soothe Keanu as it had on other days, on other such walks with Sam, or Hettie or whoever had done the clinic run.

He gave Sam the news that neither Maddie nor the FIFO nurse would be arriving the next day, assured Sam he was happy to work full time, then hesitated.

'More?' Sam asked quietly.

'There *is* a nurse,' Keanu answered, and something in his voice must have alerted Sam.

'She's a problem? Drinker? Chain smoker who'll insist on cigarette breaks? Axe murderer?'

'She's a Lockhart,' Keanu answered, and watched as Sam smiled and shook his head.

'That doesn't make her a bad nurse, Keanu. I assume she's Max's daughter, the girl you grew up with. And don't look at me like that—nothing stays secret on this island for long.'

Sam stopped walking and turned towards Keanu, his usually smiling face set in a frown.

'Are you saying you can't work with her?'

'Of course not,' Keanu responded, possibly too quickly. 'But the Lockhart name isn't held in much regard here at the moment. I was wondering about the patients.'

'Of course you were.'

Sam smiled again.

'Considering all the good Max Lockhart and his parents and grandparents before him have done for the islands, I doubt the one bad apple will have totally ruined the name. I do hope not, because we need her. But speaking of Ian, Hettie and I discovered he'd stopped in at Raiki after he left here and took not only the locked box of drugs we kept in the clinic there, but also the clinic nurse.'

'Why on earth?' Keanu had trouble taking in this information. 'Drugs, maybe—he's on a boat, could have injuries and presumably anything he doesn't use he'll sell—but the nurse? I assume she went willingly.'

'Apparently so, but it leaves Raiki without a nurse. The drugs we can replace, but she was one of the first nurses trained when Max set up the programme to help any islanders wanting to do nursing. Most of them lived in his house in Sydney while they were at university, but she was one of the few who came back here to work.'

'But the others will be helping people even if it's not here,' Keanu pointed out, mainly to cover the stab of guilt he'd felt at Sam's statement. It had reminded him that he, too, hadn't come back—well, not until he had been reminded of his duty...

'So, when do I get to meet her?' Sam asked.

'I imagine she'll come down in the morning. She did help out soon after she arrived earlier today when we had a bloke come up from the research station with a nail from a nail gun in his foot. It wasn't much of a test of nursing but she seemed to know what she was doing.'

Sam smiled again before walking on.

'Poor girl!' he said. 'Already damned with faint praise.'

Poor girl indeed, Keanu muttered to himself. If she was still a girl everything would be okay.

Or would it?

She'd been nothing more than a girl when he'd hurt her and for all he'd told himself she wouldn't miss his letters, and would probably be relieved not to have to write back, given all the friends she would have made at school, he'd never quite believed it.

'I could take you up to the house and introduce you this evening if you like,' he offered.

Sam studied him for a minute.

'Let's just wait for her to come to us,' he suggested, then he grinned. 'And let's hope she's early as apparently she'll have to start work straight away.'

CHAPTER THREE

A BEAUTIFUL YOUNG woman with long, lustrous, dark hair piled up beneath a dodgy-looking nurse's cap, and wearing what was apparently a uniform of green tunic and green three-quarter-length pants greeted Caroline with a smile and, 'Can I help you?'

'I'm looking for Sam,' Caroline explained.

'Rather you than me,' the woman replied. 'He's in the little room he calls his office, probably setting fire to the paperwork. Straight along the passage and on the left.'

Caroline turned to follow the directions.

'I'm Anahera, by the way, but everyone calls me Ana,' the dark-haired woman added.

Caroline turned back.

'Oh, I've met your daughter. She's adorable. I'm Caroline Lockhart.'

Caroline held out her hand but couldn't miss the hesitation or the look of wariness in Anahera's eyes before she took the proffered palm and shook it.

But 'Oh!' was all she said, turning back into the small ward behind her where Caroline could see four occupied beds.

Farther down the passage she found the room, knocked briefly then answered a peremptory 'Come in.'

'Caroline Lockhart, I presume?'

The good-looking man behind the desk looked up briefly from the paperwork he was shoving from one pile to another, then frowned down at it.

'Never become an administrator,' he muttered, pushing the lot back together into an untidy heap.

'Don't like paperwork?' Caroline asked, but she was smiling as she said it. There was something immensely likeable about this man.

'Who does? The problem is I'm already short on staff and I've still got to waste time doing blasted paperwork.'

'Can't you get the dog to eat it? Isn't that the classic homework excuse?' Caroline suggested, seeing the warm brown eyes of the Labrador lying on Sam's feet under the table.

Sam flashed her a grin.

'I did try that but the wretch keeps spitting it out. Hospital dogs are too well fed. But let me introduce you. This lazy, too-well-fed beast is Bugsy, Maddie Haddon's dog. Maddie is one of our FIFO doctors but rather than fly Bugsy back and forth she leaves him here. Unfortunately she can't make today's plane and as he usually knows when she's due in, he's decided I'm the best substitute for his owner.'

Sam paused and studied Caroline for a moment.

'I'm also a nurse short, and Keanu told me you were here. Want a job?'

'As long as it doesn't involve sorting that mess you've made of those papers you're shuffling. I can certainly help in other ways.'

Humour lit his eyes.

'Nice back massage? Rub my feet?'

'In your dreams!' Caroline retorted, deciding she quite liked this rather strange man.

'But I could fill in for your missing nurse,' Caroline added, refusing to be beguiled by gleaming eyes. 'I'm a nurse and you're apparently one nurse short.'

'Keanu said you're a socialite.'

One more black mark against the man who'd hurt her so badly.

'Well, you may not have noticed but there's not that much social life around here, and a socialite without a social set is superfluous to requirements, while a nurse might just fill in for the one who isn't coming, if you're willing to give me a chance.'

Now she had his attention.

'Touchy, are you?' He looked her up and down. 'I suppose you have the right bits of paper—degree, references.'

'Right here,' she said, pulling the paperwork she'd grabbed and stuffed in her back pocket before leaving the house.

Caroline began to relax.

Well, not *relax* relax—that would never happen with Keanu somewhere near—but some of the tension she'd been feeling drained slowly out of her.

'It seems you've been away from the island for a long time,' Sam said, riffling through the papers but, she suspected, speed-reading every word. 'Why have you come back?'

'I don't think that's relevant but I did hear the island was in trouble.'

'And you thought coming here to nurse would cure things?'

Caroline shook her head.

'Boy, are you a grump! I didn't even know there'd be a nursing position available, although I had intended working here for nothing if necessary, but this place was my home—*is* my home—and I'll be damned if I'm going to sit back and let it fall apart without at least trying to find out what's been happening and what can be done to save it. My dad would be here as well, only he— Well, there's a family problem.'

Sam raised his head and looked at her.

'He's a great man, your father. He does the best he can. Lobbying for government support, fundraising. Ever since the mine stopped paying its promised share for the hospital, I think he's put his entire salary into it. I just do what I can.'

'So, do I get a job?'

Sam studied her a little longer.

'The nurse who was coming was a FIFO—Fly-In-Fly-Out—the term more commonly used in mining communities. It means you're on duty for two weeks then off for one, and you can take the flight to the mainland for that week off if you wish.'

'Which leaves you with only one nurse—Anahera—for a week?'

'Not really. The FIFOs overlap and we have another permanent. You haven't met Hettie yet—Henrietta de Lacey—only don't dare ever call her Henrietta, she'll lop off your head with the nearest implement. She's our head nurse and is permanent staff and she's the one you should be speaking to about this job, but she's doing another clinic run. It's not usual to do two in one week, but there's a lot to sort out. The clinic on Raiki is short of drugs, not to mention a nurse, so Hettie's gone out there to replace the drugs then scour the islands to see if she can get one of the nurses from another island to cover Raiki for a while. How are you in a helicopter?'

Caroline was wondering what had happened to both the drugs and the nurse from Raiki when she realised she'd been asked a question. She grinned at him.

'Do you mean can I fly one or do I throw up in one?'

'Definitely the latter. Pilots we have.'

'I'll be fine, but do nurses always do the clinics or do the doctors go out to the other islands as well?'

'Doctors too,' came the swift reply, although Caroline had already forgotten what she'd asked as she'd sensed a presence in the room behind her, and every nerve in her body told her it was Keanu.

'Sorry to butt in, boss.'

His deep voice reverberated around the room.

'But Alkiri, the old man you brought in from Atangi, is having difficulty breathing—I think his end is very near. Okay with you if I sit with him?'

Sam nodded, then turned to Caroline.

'If you want to start work now, go sit with Keanu. Just see Alkiri is propped up in a comfortable position and moisten his lips for him if he needs it. Turn his head a little—'

'So saliva can drain out,' Caroline finished for him. 'I *have* done this before, you know.'

Sam nodded again, then added softly, although they were already alone in the room, 'I'd like you there for Keanu. He's known the old man all his life. He's the elder who asked Keanu to come back to the islands. It will be hard for him.'

Caroline nodded.

'Alkiri would have known he was dying,' she murmured, remembering the uncanny sense the islanders seemed to have about death. 'Maybe he wanted Keanu by his side.'

She left the room to be with Alkiri and Keanu, though she doubted *he'd* take comfort from her presence.

Sitting on the opposite side of the bed from her childhood friend, she took the old man's dry hand, feeling bones as fragile as a bird's beneath the papery skin.

'It's Caroline,' she said very quietly. 'Do you remember teaching me to weave fish traps?'

To talk or not to talk to the dying was a much-argued topic, but Caroline thought Alkiri deserved to know she remembered, and perhaps to let his mind drift back to happy times he'd had with the two children.

'Then you'd take us out in your old boat to show us where to put them up against the reef.' Keanu took up the story equally quietly, but looking at him, Caroline wondered if the sadness in his eyes was not all caused by the elder's approaching death.

Caroline swabbed the saliva from the old man's mouth, while Keanu started a story about Alkiri's frustration at not being able to teach Caro to split a coconut properly.

'I still can't,' Caroline admitted, 'although they're everywhere in the city shops now and people are going crazy for coconut water.'

'I've been looking into that and have talked to the elders,' Keanu said quietly. 'Wondering if the craze for it might provide a viable source of income for the islanders. After all, it's not just the water but every bit of a coconut is used in one way or another. I've got an accountant who's done a lot of set-up work on new businesses looking at the figures.'

Her thoughts hadn't quite got that far but the splitting of coconuts had started her thinking that way.

She risked a glance towards him. Surely they were not still going to be able to read each other's thoughts, especially now, when her thoughts, since meeting him again, had been almost wholly taken up with how magnificent he looked.

Keanu was as fine a specimen of manhood as she'd ever seen, and although just looking at him generated unwelcome reactions in her body, she couldn't resist a sneaked glance now and then as she tried to analyse her reactions.

She turned her attention back to Alkiri, speaking quietly again, more memories tumbling into her head. Keanu offered some of his own, adding to hers—shared lives.

At some stage she heard a plane come in—bringing stores but not the staff that had been expected, Caroline guessed. Then some time later it took off again. They talked on...

There were long silences between Alkiri's rattly breaths, some so long she feared their old friend had already died. Until suddenly he roused, opened his eyes and looked from one to the other, smiling.

'With both of you here, I am at peace. Please keep me here when I am gone. Wildfire was always my true home,' he whispered in a thin papery voice, and then the breathing did stop.

For ever.

Caroline couldn't bring herself to pull the sheet up over the old man's face. Very gently, she closed his eyes, and straightened the sheet across his body.

'*Can* we bury him here or would his family want him back on Atangi?' she asked, finally meeting Keanu's eyes across the bed.

Keanu shrugged, and, sensing the grief he was trying

hard to hide she went to him, unable not to offer comfort to her old friend, and put her arm around his wide shoulders.

'Come on, let's have a cup of tea while we think about the arrangements.'

He walked with her, but blindly, although the fact that he was not aware of her didn't bother Caroline one bit. She was far too busy battling all the reactions just touching Keanu's body had caused in hers—hoping the deep breaths she was taking to suppress the weird emotions were going unnoticed by her companion.

But her heart raced, her head spun, and every nerve in her body tingled with excitement.

Ridiculous, she told herself. This was 'old friend' reaction and not sexual at all, although it *did* feel…

Sexual?

Vailea was in the kitchen. She took one look at Keanu's stricken face and pulled out a chair for him.

'I heard you were back,' she said, her voice cold enough to douse the fires just touching Keanu had set alight. 'Come to bring more trouble to us?'

'No, of course not. I've come to work.' Caroline tried to sound reassuring, but Vailea's words and attitude had stung.

What on earth had been going on? Was it more than Ian's poor management? Selling off the family heirlooms wouldn't have affected anyone outside the family, so what else had happened or was happening? What had Bessie said about the new housekeeper? Something about Ian…

'I've come to make Keanu a cup of tea,' she said as Vailea's eyes continued to study her, a malevolence Caroline couldn't understand clear within them.

'I'll take care of him,' the older woman snapped, and

Caroline, only too pleased to escape the extremely un-comfortable atmosphere, left the kitchen.

'Boy, this is going to be fun,' she muttered to herself as she made her way out of the hospital.

Keanu could deal with Alkiri on his own—do whatever needed to be done. She was damned if she was going to stay around and be insulted. Once Hettie, the head nurse, returned later today and gave Caroline her roster, she could work out how best to avoid Vailea altogether.

Vailea *and* Keanu.

Although there was something about Vailea's reaction to her that seemed more personal than a general hatred of all Lockharts...

Keanu walked up to the house at six. He'd spent two hours talking to the elders on Atangi, making arrangements for Alkiri's funeral. The elders had agreed he could be buried on Wildfire and they would send over people to help with the practicalities and some cooks to prepare the food.

'Is there somewhere we can all gather?' the man he'd been speaking to had asked. 'I think the little church and its hall would be too small.'

Keanu thought of the big longhouse that had once been the centre of the research station and assured the elder that somewhere could be found. There was always the Lockhart house if nothing else worked out.

They settled on a service at ten in two days' time.

Now, given that they might need the house, he had to make peace with Caro, although he doubted he could ever explain his angry reaction to her arrival—far too complicated and quite unwarranted, really.

Caroline was sitting on the veranda, watching the sun

sink into the sea, dropping below the western cliffs lit up with the brilliant fiery red that gave the island its name.

He took the steps three at a time in long, deliberate strides, then slumped down on the top one, not looking at her but out at the dying colours of the sunset.

'Why *did* you come back?' he asked, almost gently, although being this close to her had started all the physical reactions again, and the confusion of that made him feel...

Angry?

Not really, more unsettled...

'Why did you?' she countered.

'I was asked,' he said, trying desperately to pretend that this was just a conversation between two old friends. Which, of course, it was—wasn't it?

'The island was in trouble, the community was in trouble. It's my home and I love it. Of course, I had to come back.'

'And yet you ask me why I came? To tell you the truth, I didn't know things were this bad until I got here. I just wanted—needed—to come home.'

'And now you're here?

She turned towards him, her eyes alight with determination.

'I have to find out what's been happening. How everything's gone so terribly wrong. Do you honestly believe the island means less to me than it does to you? That this isn't my community as well?'

Her gaze drifted back to the sunset, so he guessed there was a bit more to the answer than that. But whatever it was it had caused a break in her voice and he wanted more than anything in the world—more even than saving the livelihood and well-being of the islanders—to comfort her, to take her in his arms, hold her close, smell the Caro scent of her, and never let her go.

Like she'd want *that*!

He also wanted to ask her about Christopher. She hadn't answered earlier. But he knew it was too painful a subject to bring up when they were so estranged, so he stuck to practicalities.

'So, what do you think you can do?' he asked instead, his voice rougher than it should be as it scraped past the emotion in his throat.

'Find out what's been going on, for a start,' she said. 'All the predictions from the geologists showed the mine had many years to run. I don't doubt Ian's been embezzling the money it's been earning but it can't *just* be that.'

Keanu hid a smile. That sounded so like the young Caroline—his Caro—on the trail of some possible crime—suspected cruelty to some chickens being only one of her campaigns.

Memories were dangerous things…

Better to stick with the present and practicalities, discuss what facts he *did* know, although they were few enough.

'Did you know Ian leased out the research station?' he asked.

'He's leased the research station? Why on earth would he do that?'

'Money, why else! It had been run-down for a while. Fewer and fewer people using it. Then he somehow found this wealthy Middle Eastern guy who wants to set up an exclusive resort. The local residents are a bit uneasy about it, but heaven knows we need all the income and employment we can get.'

'Well, it explains the guy with the nail in his foot. Does my dad know?'

'I assumed he did but the negotiations certainly went through Ian, and no one here seems to know anything about it.'

'Dad would never have trusted Ian to negotiate, and he'd never have made a decision without consulting the elders. He sent Ian here mainly to keep him out of trouble. It's the way Dad feels about family. He thinks even the black sheep deserves a chance to redeem himself, but from all I'm hearing about our particular black sheep, it's impossible.'

She sighed then added, 'The guy with the nail in his foot—he's working there? Work's going on now?'

Keanu nodded. 'And has been for some time.'

'I want to have a look.'

'You can't. The whole place is fenced and gated. That patient yesterday wouldn't even let us drive him back down there. He had his mate come back to the hospital, remember?'

'But this is our home! We can go wherever we like.'

Keanu hid a smile. This was Caro at her most imperious. And hearing her, hearing the old Caro sent a piercing pain through his chest.

'You want to argue with the guards? They'll never accept your authority. Besides, legally, I would think now this man has leased it, it's his land for as long as the lease states.'

'But Dad doesn't know anything—if he did he'd have told me. Come on, Keanu, you must know something.'

'All I know is that some rich man is turning it into a resort. A chap called Luke Wilson was doing some research here a few years ago and apparently this rich bloke knew Luke from somewhere. That was enough for Ian to make contact with him and that's what happened.'

Keanu paused, trying to think—to get it right.

'I wouldn't be surprised if he's already achieved his aim for the resort—there's been a hell of a lot of activity going on around the place. Container loads of stuff taken off huge ships and ferried ashore on barges, imported workers everywhere.'

'But the research station? That was my great-grandfather's legacy to the whole of M'Langi, designed to provide facilities and housing to anyone who wanted to investigate or study ways to improve the health of the islanders through science. Your father was one of the first to work there. I know my grandfather and Ian resented putting money into it, but I'm sure it was legally tied up so the mine had to keep supporting it.'

'And if the mine couldn't?' Keanu asked. 'Isn't it better to lease it to someone with money than let the idea die completely?'

Caroline stared at him, trying to work out what might be going on behind this conversation.

As far as she was concerned, there was a lot of very strange stuff lingering in the deep recesses of her mind and fluttering along the nerves in her body, yet Keanu was sitting there, about as sensitive as a boulder.

Whatever. She was finding out things she needed to know so she had to set aside all the physical manifestations of the boulder's presence and seek more information.

'You mean this mystery millionaire is going to keep the research station going? So why build luxury accommodation?'

Keanu shrugged.

'Who knows, but that's what's happening because Sam's been carrying on with some of Luke's research into why the islanders don't suffer from encephalitis to the extent their counterparts in other island groups do and he's been wanting to use the laboratories there. Apparently, they've said he can as soon as the renovations are completed.'

'Weirder and weirder,' Caroline muttered, but the worst of the weirdness was what was going on in her body. She'd been, what, thirteen when she'd last seen Keanu? And with her isolated life on the island then boarding school, had probably been a late developer. And although his disappearance from her life had devastated her—even broken her heart—it had been a child's heart that had been broken, a child's love betrayed.

What she was feeling now had nothing childish about it, and if she was going to be working with him, seeing him every day, she'd better get over whatever it was PDQ.

Practicalities—they would be the best antidote to this Keanu business.

'Let's go and see,' she suggested. 'I'll grab some bottled water and a torch, and we'll go take a look.'

'We can't,' Keanu answered flatly, killing the small spark of excitement taking some action had lit.

'And why not?' she demanded, the young Caroline again.

'I've already told you, it's fenced off. Visitors to the resort won't be bumped along a rocky track—they'll travel down there by helicopter.'

'They can't have fenced the whole place. Not the beach and the reef and that rockfall around the corner of Sunset Beach.'

'So?'

'We'll just have to find our way either around or over this fence and see what's happening for ourselves. We'll go down to the beach for a start, and walk to the rock-fall then figure it out from there. We've swum around it in the past, but it might be low tide. We should at least go and have a look.'

She was twelve again and grinned at him.

'Come on, Keanu, it will be an adventure, just like old times!'

Keanu studied the beautiful, *smiling* woman in front of him and knew that while her features might have changed as she'd matured, her determination obviously had not.

He heard his mother's voice, back when they'd been young, saying look after Caroline—words to a child that were now coming back to haunt him. He'd *have* to go along on this ridiculous escapade because there was no way he could let her go alone. The very thought of her prowling around down there made his blood run cold, not to mention what might happen if she tried to climb the rockfall on her own.

Apart from which, he had to admit, he *would* like to know what was going on at the northern end of the island, and he could check out if they'd rebuilt the longhouse and if it would be suitable for Alkiri's funeral feast—should they get permission to use it.

'Are you going like that?' he asked, looking at the short shift dress she wore.

'Of course,' she replied. 'It's faded so much it almost looks like camouflage, although I didn't choose it for that—just pulled it out of the cupboard. I'll slip on some soft dive boots in case we have to swim.'

He hoped like hell they wouldn't have to swim, because the thought of seeing that shift wet and clinging to her body was already causing a definite stirring in his lower abdomen.

The thought of helping her down the cliff path, taking her elbow on a tricky bit, touching her at all, had been bad enough, but the wet shift image was torturous.

Yet he'd seen Caroline naked often enough, when they'd shucked off their clothes to swim in the lagoon by the house—but that had been boy-girl stuff, kid stuff—and she hadn't had breasts then...

Dear heaven, was he losing his mind?

He knew his mother had had good reason for leaving the island—Ian Lockhart had made sure of that—but he wondered if she'd also been thinking of what might happen as he and Caroline went through puberty? Feeling as she did about Ian, his having a relationship with Ian's niece might have been too much...

Caroline was back, soft dive boots—more like ballet slippers—on her feet and a small backpack on her back. She passed a second one to him.

'A camera with a long-distance lens,' she announced. 'Apparently, Ian didn't know of Dad's interest in photography or he'd have found them and sold them off as he seems to have done with everything else of value in the house.'

Keanu thought of the beautiful pieces of porcelain Caro's grandmother had collected—and Caro had loved—and knew without asking that they'd be gone.

Well, he hadn't been able to save her treasures, but he sure as hell was going to do everything he could to keep her safe in her mad quest to save the island. At least in *that* quest they'd be partners once again.

He slung the backpack over his shoulder and reached out to take her arm.

'Let's go,' he said. She moved away from his outstretched hand, but undeterred he added, 'It *will* be like old times!'

Except all his senses were on full alert, his body buzzing just being near her, so who the hell knew what would happen if she actually swam!

CHAPTER FOUR

THEY WALKED SWIFTLY to the clifftop, muscle memory in
their feet remembering the path possibly better than their
brains did. Above them, in the thick rainforest, birds were
settling down for the night, rustling among the leaves.
Then down the rocky track with its views out over the
reef to the ocean beyond. The path they took was now
overgrown in places as if it had been rarely used since
two adventurous children had left the island.

'How long have you been here?'

Caroline, following him with one hand on his backpack, asked the question.

'Three weeks.'

The answer came easily. Three weeks of shock as
he'd tried to accept the island as it was now and work
out what had happened.

'Have you seen the Blakes?'

Keanu shook his head.

'They were long gone when I got here. The old man,
your grandfather, appointed Peter not long before he died
and your father was happy to leave him in charge of the
mine when you were born and he had to take Christopher to the mainland for constant medical supervision.'

'Dad liked the fact that Peter was an engineer as well as having practical knowledge as a miner, and he was as honest as they come.'

'Probably too honest for Ian,' Keanu said. 'He decided he could do the job better and sacked Peter. Then, with Peter gone, Ian announced he'd take over the running of the mine as well as everything else on the island.'

'No wonder it's run-down,' Caro said tartly. 'Ian couldn't manage his way out of an open door.'

'Harsh!' Keanu said, turning to take Caro's hand and help her over a particularly tricky bit of the path.

'Well, you know he couldn't. The only things he was ever interested in were money and women and gambling, although I imagine the order changed according to the situation.'

And even in the dim light of early evening reflected off the sea she saw the pain on Keanu's face, the stricken look in his eyes. She remembered something strange that Bessie had said about it being better if Kari kept her distance from Ian, and started to connect the dots...

'Oh, Keanu, not your mother?' She reached for his shoulders and pulled him close, wrapping her arms awkwardly around his body. 'Is that why you left? Why didn't she tell my father? Or the elders? Or the police? Do something to get him stopped?'

Keanu eased out of her grasp and looked down at her, his face now wiped as blank as she'd ever seen it.

'He didn't assault her, if that's what you're thinking,' he said. 'What he did was worse.'

Bitterness as harsh and hurtful as Caroline had ever heard leached from every word so each one was a separate prick of pain—into her skin, through her flesh and into her heart.

But worse than rape?

What could she say?

Much as she longed to know more, she knew by the cold finality in Keanu's voice that the conversation was finished.

He had turned and was moving on and although she longed to ask him if that's why he'd never contacted her, she knew she wouldn't—couldn't. In fact, she knew the answer.

Somehow or other, a Lockhart had hurt his mother— an unforgiveable sin.

They stumbled their way down to the beach then, staying in the shadows of the fringing coconut palms, made their way to the rockfall.

The tide was in, the small ripples of water inside the reef splashing up against the rocks.

'So we swim,' she said brightly, wishing they could get back to the not easy, but easier atmosphere they'd shared as they'd started down the cliff. 'But I doubt Dad's camera's waterproof so what if I go around first then climb up on the lower rocks on the other side and you pass it to me, then you swim around?'

'Haven't changed much, have you? Bossy as ever!' Keanu muttered, and Caroline hid a smile—the old Keanu was back with her again, if only temporarily.

It was far worse than he'd expected, Keanu realised as Caro, the thin wet shift clinging to every curve of her body, appeared on the other side of the rockfall, reaching up and out for the rucksack.

He'd taken off his shirt but his shorts would be wet

as he clambered ashore, so his reaction would be obvious, though it was darker now and maybe she wouldn't notice…

Well, he could hardly leave her alone on the other side of the rockfall—not with his mother's order, the 'take care of Caroline' one, still echoing in his ears.

He swam, emerging from the lagoon and flapping at his shorts to conceal the evidence of his reaction.

'We'd better move into the shadows of the palm trees,' he said, deciding it was time to take charge. 'And walk quietly. You don't know who might be around.'

'What, like fierce Alsatian guard dogs that will rip us to pieces without a second thought?' Caroline muttered. 'I wonder if I can still shin up a coconut palm.'

Keanu smiled at the image, although he was thinking more of the darkness the shadows would provide. At least in the shadows beneath the palms he wouldn't be able to see the way her full breasts were outlined by the wet shift, or the way it was indented into her navel, and raised slightly over the mound of her sex.

He had to stop thinking about wet shifts and sex and concentrate or they'd be caught for sure.

As they approached the first of the bures that had once housed visiting scientists they heard voices, but not close.

'That sounds like people over beyond the kitchen where the little staff bar used to be,' he murmured to Caroline.

The helicopter pilots, back when there had been three or four and so they'd had more time off than other staff, had always frequented it, not by creeping down the cliff and swimming around the rockfall but by walking down the track from the airfield—the track now fenced off, guarded and gated.

A lone light shone in the first of the bures, but even from outside Keanu could see the place had had a lot of money spent on it. Stone walls where mud had been, a marble deck with a deep spa bath shaded by thick vegetation.

'This isn't accommodation for visiting scientists,' Caro whispered to him. 'It's luxury accommodation for the very wealthy who want absolute privacy and can afford it. See how each bure has been separated from the next by a thick planting of shrubs, most of them scented, like that huge ginger plant over there.'

'But what of the laboratories and the communal kitchens and dining rooms?' he argued. 'Surely people paying the kind of money they'd pay to stay here aren't all going to eat together?

'Let's see.'

Keanu took her hand, ignoring the shock of excitement such an impersonal touch had caused. He led the way towards the kitchen area, although always off the path that, even in the dark, looked freshly raked and would show their footprints.

What had been the kitchen and adjoining open eating area seemed shrouded in scaffolding, until they crept closer and realised the old longhouse had been included in the renovations. It was now a longer, wider building, still open at the sides to catch the breezes, exactly like the meeting halls on the other islands, where feasts were held and elders met to make rules or administer judgment. Only better—fancier…

The kitchens must be behind it, but so was the bar because the noise was louder now.

'We can't go farther,' Keanu said firmly. 'We'd be caught for sure. We'll have to rely on Sam to report on the laboratories when he's able to go back to work in them. And there's no way we can take photographs, the flash would alert someone for sure.'

He half expected Caro to argue—she'd always been the one more willing to take risks—but to his surprise she turned back into the bushes.

'Come on, we'll go back the way we came before someone finds us.'

Caroline smiled to herself, realising Keanu was now as intent on this expedition as she had been.

But holding Keanu's hand was distracting, and he was pulling her along, far too close to his body, which was beyond distracting. She began to tremble and suspected it wasn't nerves or cold, although he stopped in a partic-ular dense patch of shadow and pulled her into his arms.

'You're cold,' he whispered, folding her against his body, the action making her tremble even more. His bare skin was warm against hers, his body hard where hers was soft. And her reaction to it was so startling she prob-ably would have done something stupid like kiss him if he hadn't been rubbing his hands up and down her arms, obviously trying to warm her, although the trembles had nothing to do with the cool night air.

A boulder—it confirmed her suspicions. No matter what weird reactions she was having to this reunion—to his closeness, his body—he was feeling nothing for the woman trembling in his arms.

A rustle in the bushes broke them apart, and although it was only an inquisitive lyrebird, it was enough to re-mind them of where they were and the inherent danger of being caught there.

But red flags of warning of another kind waved in

Caroline's head as they crept back to the beach. Her reaction to Keanu holding her had to be a rebound thing. Devastated by Steve's rejection and reunited with her childhood friend, she'd really only wanted comfort.

Right.

So why was her body throbbing with what felt very like desire, not to mention an even deeper regret that the kiss hadn't happened?

Ridiculous! A relationship between them just couldn't happen. Not only had her uncle Ian done all he could to blacken the Lockhart name among the islands' population but he'd—what?—assaulted Keanu's mother?

Although he'd said worse than assault...

Little wonder Keanu had broken off all contact with her—and probably distrusted anyone who bore the Lockhart name.

At which stage she fell over, making enough noise as she landed in a baby palm tree to awaken the ghosts of the dead.

'What is wrong with you?' Keanu growled, hauling her to her feet. 'You're blundering along as if you've got your eyes shut.'

She could hardly tell him the line her thoughts had been following so she got back onto the edge of the path and resumed walking quietly along it.

'Tomorrow night we could walk along the fence,' Keanu said, breaking a silence that had stretched a little tautly between them.

'I might be on duty. I haven't met Hettie yet, let alone get a roster from her.'

'Come to think of it, you probably will be on duty,' Keanu told her. 'Anahera does extra day shifts so she can be at home with Hana in the evenings. Besides which we probably wouldn't see much—the plantings are too thick.'

'On duty all night?' Caroline ignored his fence conversation because she was interested in the set-up at the short-staffed hospital, although she'd get back to him ordering her around some other time. They'd been a pair, a partnership, in all the right and wrong things they'd done, and now here he was, giving orders...

'No, three to midnight. We have a couple of local nurses' aides who share the night shifts between them.'

'And who supports them?'

Keanu sighed.

'It's a small hospital, Caro, and either Sam or whatever doctor is here is always on call. Hettie, too, for that matter. The staff quarters are just at the back of the hospital and it takes exactly two minutes to get from one of our apartments to the wards.'

'You've timed it?'

They'd reached the beach and paused beneath the palm trees, talking quietly while they checked that no one else was taking a midnight stroll.

'I've done it,' Keanu told her. 'More than once. The aides are good, but they know what they can handle and what they can't. The system could be a lot better but it works.'

It didn't seem right to Caroline that Hettie was the nurse always on call, but until she knew more about the hospital, there was nothing she could do.

She was concentrating on hospital staffing issues because Keanu's use of her childhood name—his casual use of 'Caro'—had started up the disturbances the warming hug had caused.

'It seems quiet, let's go,' she said, and led the way across the sand to the shadow of the rockfall.

To Keanu's relief the tide had gone out far enough for them to wade around the rocks. Given the effect that holding her had had on his body, he didn't think he could handle seeing the wet shift again.

He had no idea why Caro had returned to the island, certain her coming to help because she'd heard it was in trouble wasn't the whole story.

What had happened to that sleazy-looking guy called Steve who was always with her in the society pictures?

Had he dumped her?

Keanu shook his head, angry with himself for even thinking about Caroline's private life, but angrier for feeling sorry for her. It was bad enough he'd become involved in tonight's escapade, but to have held Caro in his arms, felt her body pressed to his...

He must have been moonstruck!

They were scaling the rocky cliff path now and he paused to look around for a moon but failed to find one.

'Are you grunting?' Caro asked. 'I know it's steep but I thought you'd be fitter than that.'

'I was *not* grunting,' he told her, voice as cold as he could make it.

'Wild pigs, then,' Carol said cheerfully, although he knew she didn't for a minute believe it.

Though would she have believed he'd been grunting at his own stupid thoughts?

'Bright lights ahead,' the woman he shouldn't have held in his arms said cheerfully, and he locked away the past and moved himself swiftly into the present.

Bright lights indeed.

'The helicopter must have brought in a patient from an

outer island,' he said, lengthening his stride so he passed Caro as he hurried towards the scene of the action.

Hettie had one end of the stretcher they were unloading, Jack, the pilot, holding the other end. He could see Manu, their one remaining hospital orderly, running towards the airstrip, Sam not far behind him.

'Tropical ulcer gone bad,' Hettie said as Manu took over her end of the stretcher and Sam and Keanu arrived. 'I'm actually dubious about it. I think it might be worse than that.'

'A Buruli ulcer?' Sam queried, and Hettie shrugged. 'We'll need to test it.'

She spoke quietly but Keanu knew they were all feeling tension from the words she'd spoken. Tropical ulcers were common enough and in many cases very difficult to treat, but the Buruli was a whole other species, and could lead to bone involvement and permanent disability.

'Is it common here?'

He'd forgotten about Caro but she was right behind him, so close that when he swung around to answer her his arm brushed against her breast.

And restarted all the thoughts he was sure he'd locked away.

'Not as common as in some islands in the west Pacific,' he told her, then he caught up with Hettie, who was following the stretcher up the slight incline to the hospital.

'I've got a new recruit for you here,' he said. 'Sam's probably told you Maddie and the FIFO nurse weren't coming in today, but Caroline dropped from the skies yesterday and she tells us she's a nurse.'

He ignored the glower Caro shot at him as she stepped past him to introduce herself to Hettie.

'Caroline Lockhart,' she said, holding out her hand, while Keanu watched the meeting with some trepidation.

'Of the hilltop mansion Lockharts?' Hettie demanded, ignoring the proffered hand.

'Yes, and proud of it,' Caro said quietly but firmly. 'And I'd rather be judged by my work than the house I live in.'

Hettie pushed errant bits of hair off her forehead and sighed.

'Fair call,' she said softly, and this time, to Keanu's relief, *she* held out *her* hand. 'It's just been too long a day trying to work out how to replace a resident clinic nurse on Raiki Island.'

'What happened to her?' Caroline asked, and Keanu knew the answer was going to hurt her.

'Apparently she went off with your uncle Ian—she and all the drugs.'

'She what?' Caroline swung towards Keanu. 'Does my father know all that's been going on? Know his brother's stooped so low as to rob an island of their drugs, not to mention their nurse?'

'It was only discovered yesterday.' Hettie answered for him, and her voice was gentle. 'And as Ian's gone off in his yacht to who knows where, there's very little your father or anyone else can do about it.'

Keanu read the pain on Caro's face as she realised exactly why the Lockhart name was mud. The harm Ian had done reached out across all island life and all the islanders.

Following the little procession up to the hospital, Keanu felt deeply sorry for her, sorry for the pain the slights against her family must be causing her.

But the Caro he'd known would have pushed away any offer of comfort and tossed her head to deny any pain.

He glanced towards her and saw her chin rise.

This Caro wasn't so different. She'd take them all on and prove all Lockharts weren't tarred with the same brush.

And seeing that chin tilt—reading it—his heart cramped just a little at the sight of it. The woman she'd become wasn't so different from his Caro after all.

'A Buruli ulcer?'

Caroline had caught up with him so the question came from his right shoulder.

He glanced towards her and even in the poor light on the track he could see the remnants of her hurt.

He wanted to put his arm around her shoulders and pull her close. Comfort her as he had when she'd been a child, hurt or lonely or bewildered by her motherless, and usually fatherless, situation.

But with all the new disturbances she'd caused in his body, giving her a comforting hug was no longer an option.

Professional colleagues, that's all they were.

'It's not that common but it's a nasty thing if left untended, as this one may have been. Often it starts as a small nodule, hardly bigger than a mosquito bite, so the patient just ignores it, but the infection can lead to a bigger ulcer forming, destroying skin and tissue. If it's left too long there can be bone involvement, even loss of a limb.'

'Sounds like a similar infection to leprosy.' She was frowning now, no doubt thinking back to her years of study.

'Spot on,' he told her. 'The bacterium causing it is related to both the leprosy and tuberculosis bacteria.'

'Can you test for it here or do you have to send swabs to the mainland? Wouldn't that take days?'

Hettie answered for him.

'We're fortunate in that Sam is an avid bacteriologist in whatever spare time he has. Although the research station's closed at the moment, he still loves poking around in the little lab we have at the hospital and breeding who knows what in Petri dishes. If anyone can test it, he can.'

Caroline realised she'd have to rethink the laid-back, handsome doctor who ran the hospital. He obviously had hidden depths because even the simplest of biological tests was painstaking work.

They'd reached the hospital and, unsure of her part in whatever lay ahead, she followed the troop inside.

The patient was young, maybe just reaching teenage years, from French Island, so called, Caroline knew, because a French square-rigged sailing vessel had once foundered there, the sailors staying on, intermarrying with the locals, until rescued many years later.

Caroline concentrated on the now instead of on the past. The boy, Raoul—French names still being common—had been lifted onto an examination table, and Sam, assisted by one of the nurses' aides who had been waiting at the hospital, was carefully removing the light dressing Hettie had used to cover the wound.

Caroline swallowed a gasp. This was no small nodule like a mosquito bite but a full-blown leg ulcer, the edges a mess of tattered skin and deeper down, tender, infected flesh.

'I'm going to take a swab,' Sam was saying to the patient, 'but even before I test it, I'm going to start you on antibiotics.'

'It generally responds well to a combination of rifampicin and streptomycin,' Keanu explained quietly. 'If that doesn't work, there are other combinations of drugs we can use, usually with the rifampicin. The other combinations haven't been fully tested but the options are there.'

Tension she hadn't been aware she was feeling eased a little, but she hated the thought of the possibility of this young lad losing a leg.

'Okay, everyone out except Mina,' Sam said, using a shooing motion with his hand. 'She and I can handle it from here. Keanu, you might introduce our newest staff member to Jack. And Hettie, if you're not too tired, I've left Caroline's details on your desk, but you might want a chat with her yourself.'

Great, Caroline thought. A perfect end to a perfect day—an interview with a woman who obviously hated her entire family.

But Keanu had taken her elbow, and all thoughts but her reactions to his closeness fled from her mind.

'Come out and meet Jack Richards,' he said. 'There's a staffroom through here—we can have a coffee or a cold drink.'

A bit social for an introduction, Caroline thought, but apparently the pilot called Jack usually made for this staffroom when he returned from a flight. And, yes, he was sitting there, legs outstretched on a tilting lounge chair, draining the last dregs from a can of cola.

With his head tilted back, she could see a jutting jaw, and the breadth of his shoulders suggested muscle rather than fat. Here, in the light, she saw he was tall, but solid rather than rangy. His dark hair was cropped close to his scalp as if he ran an electric razor over it every now and then by way of hairdressing.

He had a strong face, a slightly skewed nose that suggested football in his youth, and smooth olive skin. But by far his most arresting feature was a pair of dark blue eyes, which, Caroline guessed, missed very little.

He set the empty can down on a small side table.

'God, I needed that,' he said. 'The day was a disaster from beginning to end. First the consequences of the disappearance of the drugs and the nurse from Raiki. You can imagine how angry the residents were. Then we headed over to Atangi because there are two nurses there and Hettie hoped one of them would cover Raiki until we got someone.'

'Did you get someone?' Caroline asked, intrigued by this idea of a helicopter flitting between the islands as casually as a city commute.

'Yes, I think so. Hett's still negotiating. Anyway, who do we find but a mum who'd mistaken clinic days and brought in a toddler for vaccination? A toddler who hated needles. Poor kid, who doesn't? He screamed like a banshee as Hettie gave him his triple antigen. Of course, the father came in and got stuck into Hettie and the scene developed into something like an old-time TV comedy, only it wasn't really funny because the poor kid was genuinely terrified.'

'Then French and the ulcer,' Keanu said, turning from the urn where he'd been making a coffee—holding out the cup to Caroline, who shook her head.

'Yeah, we had a call from the nurse there, whipped over and collected the lad, then to top it all off we were caught in a very nasty crosswind on the flight home. I know we have to expect that at this time of the year—it's the start of cyclone season—but heaven help us if there's an emergency call tonight.'

'You're the only pilot?' Caroline asked, sitting down on the couch across from Jack.

'Sorry, I'm supposed to make the introductions,' Keanu said. 'Jack, this is Caroline, new nurse. Caroline, this is Jack Richards and, yes, at the moment he's our only pilot. Although there's relief on the way Friday when the second flight for the week comes in. That's right, isn't it, Jack? A FIFO coming in to give you a break?'

'Yeah, young Matt Rogers is due to come in on Friday's flight.'

'You don't like him?' Caroline asked, unable to not hear the distaste in Jack's voice.

'Only because he's younger, and fitter and better looking than our Jack here,' Keanu teased, 'and they both share a very keen interest in the beautiful Anahera.'

'Who at least ignores us both equally,' Jack said with such gloom Caroline had to smile.

'I can't blame any man being attracted to her—she *is* beautiful,' Caroline said, now wondering if the nurse was ignoring these two suitors because she had her eye on someone else.

Someone like Keanu?

And if Vailea's daughter fancied Keanu and Vailea was thinking him a good match, maybe that's why she'd shown such animosity to Caroline. Everyone on the island would know the two of them had grown up together...

She must have sighed, for Keanu said, 'Come on, you're tired. I'll walk you up to the house.'

Jack straightened up in his chair.

'*The* house?' he said. 'Like the Lockhart mansion? Since when did our nurses get lucky enough to stay there while important blokes like me sleep in little better than prefabricated huts?'

'Since their surname is Lockhart,' Keanu said, enough ice in his voice to stop further speculation. 'And *all* the hospital buildings are prefabricated, as you well know. It makes it much easier to pack them into shipping containers and land them here, then it only needs a small team of men to put them together.'

He turned to Caroline.

'Prefab or not, the staff villas are really lovely so just ignore him.'

Jack was ignoring them both. He was still staring at Caroline.

'You're a Lockhart?' he said with such disbelief Caroline had to smile.

'Did you think we all had two heads?' she asked, but Jack continued to stare at her.

Maybe she *had* grown a second head.

But two heads would give her two brains and she only needed one—even a part of one—to know she didn't want Keanu walking her home. Her feelings towards him were in such turmoil she doubted she'd ever sort them out.

For years she'd hated him for his desertion. Hadn't he realised he'd been her only true friend? Even after they'd both gone to boarding school, he'd still been the person to whom she'd poured out her heart in letter after letter.

Her homesickness, the strange emptiness that came from being motherless, the pain of her time spent with Christopher, who couldn't respond to her words of love— writing to Keanu had been a way of getting it out of her system.

So he knew everything there was to know about her life, from her envy when other girls' parents came to special occasions to the realisation that, for her father,

Christopher and the hospital on Wildfire were more important than she was.

She'd told Keanu things she'd never told anyone, before or since, then suddenly, he'd been gone.

Nothing.

Until now, and although the confusion of seeing him again had at first been confined to her head, since he'd held her—if only to warm her—it was in her heart as well.

Damn the man.

'I don't need you to walk me home,' she said when they'd left the staffroom. 'I *do* know the way.'

'And *I* know there are a lot of unhappy Lockhart employees—or ex-employees—on the island at the moment, and while I don't think for a minute they'd take out their frustration on you, I'd rather be sure than sorry.'

So he was walking her home to protect her. Looking after Caroline as his mother had always told him to when they'd been children.

She felt stupidly disappointed at this realisation then told herself she was just being ridiculous.

As if that kind of a hug meant anything. And anyway she didn't want Keanu hugging her.

That just added to her torment.

'What employees and ex-employees are upset?' she asked to take her mind off things she couldn't handle right now.

'Just about all of them,' Keanu replied. 'But mostly the miners, and although some of them are from other islands, a lot of them live in the village. They've had their hours cut and the ones who've been sacked haven't been paid back wages, let alone their superannuation.'

'But if Ian's gone, who's here to pay them or to cut hours? Who's running the mine?'

'Who knows? Ian's disappearance, as you may have gathered, is fairly recent. He was here last week, then suddenly he was either holed up in the house or gone.'

'Gone how?' Caroline asked as they reached the front steps of the house, where Bessie had left a welcoming light burning.

'Presumably on his yacht. It was a tidy size. One day it was in the mine harbour and the next it was gone.'

'But the mine's still operating?'

Keanu nodded.

'Then we should go down and check it out.'

'Go down to the mine?' Keanu demanded.

Caroline grinned at him.

'Not right now, you goose, but tomorrow or whenever we can get some time off together. That's if you want to come with me.'

'Well, I damn well wouldn't let you go alone, although why you want to go—'

'Because I need to know—*we* need to know. Without the mine there's no way we can keep the hospital going, not to mention the fact that the entire population, not just those here on Wildfire, will lose their medical facilities as well as their incomes.'

She was so excited her eyes gleamed in the moonlight, and it was all Keanu could to not take her in his arms again, only this time for a different reason.

But if holding her once had been a mistake, twice would be fatal.

And he was still married—or probably still married, even if he hadn't seen his wife for five years.

Did that matter?

Of course it did.

He could hardly start something that she might think would lead to marriage if he couldn't marry her.

So forget a hug.

'We can't run the mine,' he said, far too bluntly because now a different confusion was nagging at him.

She shook her head in irritation.

'Then we'll just have to think of something.'

He had to agree, if only silently. The continued survival of the hospital—in fact, of all the health care in the islands—depended on support from the mine.

'I imagine once we know what's happening we can find someone who can,' he said, reluctantly drawn in and now thinking aloud. 'Some of the local men have worked there since it opened, or if they're not still there we could find them. We want men who trained under Peter Blake or maybe beg Peter to come back.'

'And pay him how?' Caroline demanded.

Keanu held up his hands in surrender.

'Hey, you're the one who wanted to think of something. I'm just throwing out ideas here. You can take them or leave them.'

He saw the shadow cross her face and knew he'd somehow said the wrong thing.

'Is that how you felt about me back then? That you could take me or leave me? Yes, Ian obviously hurt your mother, but what did *I* do to *you* to make you cut me out of your life?'

She was angry—beautiful with anger—but he stood his ground, then he leaned forward and touched her very gently on the cheek.

'You were never right out of my life, Caro,' he said quietly, his hand sliding down to rest on her shoulder.

Momentarily. He turned and walked swiftly back down the track, not wanting her to see the pain her words had caused written clearly on his face.

But she was right. He *had* come back to see what he could do to save the hospital, and saving the mine should have been the obvious starting place.

But joining forces in this crusade would mean seeing more of her, working with her outside hospital hours, feeling her body beside his, aware all the time of the effect she had on him, aware of her in a way he'd never been before, or imagined he ever would.

Physically aware of the one woman in the world who was beyond his grasp—the woman whose trust he'd betrayed when she'd been nothing more than a girl…

Caroline watched him stride down the path, long legs moving smoothly and deliberately over the rough track, stance upright, broad shoulders square…

Was it just the length of time since they'd seen each other that was making things so awkward between them, or was Keanu still brooding over whatever had happened to make him stop writing to her? Even stop reading her letters…

'Bother the man,' she muttered to herself, climbing the steps and wandering through the house towards her bedroom.

Her bedroom. Still decorated with the posters of the idols of her teenage self.

Of course, with Ian gone, she could have the pick of any of the six bedrooms in the house, but her room felt like home, even if home was an empty and lonely place without Keanu in it. Helen *and* Keanu. Their rooms had been in the western annexe, but the whole house had been her and Keanu's playground—the whole island, in fact.

Stupid tears pricked behind her eyelids as memories of their youth together—their friendship and closeness—threatened to overwhelm her.

Pulling herself together, she ripped the posters off the walls. One day soon—when she'd done the things she *really* needed to do, like visit the mine, she'd find some paint and redo the room, maybe redecorate the whole house, removing all traces of the past.

Except in your head, a traitorous voice reminded her.

But she'd had enough of traitorous voices—hadn't one lived with her through most of her relationship with Steve?

She'd learned to ignore it and could do so again.

Although, with Steve, maybe she'd have been better off listening to it. Listening to the whisper that had questioned his protestations of love, listened to the niggling murmur that had questioned broken dates with facile excuses, listened to her friends…

Had she been so desperate for love, for someone to love her, that she'd ignored all the signs and warnings?

'Oh, for heaven's sake, get with it, girl!' she said out loud, hoping to jolt herself from the past to the present.

There was certainly enough to be done in the present to blot out any voices in her head.

Work was the answer. Nursing at the hospital, and during her time off finding out exactly what had been happening on the island.

CHAPTER FIVE

THE PREVIOUS EVENING Hettie had disappeared by the time Caroline had finished talking to Jack, so she wasn't sure if she was employed or not. Deciding she had to find out, she walked down to the hospital at seven-thirty the next morning.

It was already hot and the humidity was rising. Jack's mention of cyclones had reminded her that this wasn't the best time of the year to return to the island—although she'd spent many long summer holidays here and survived whatever the weather had thrown at her.

Hettie was in a side ward with the patient she'd brought in the previous evening, and it was, Caroline decided, almost inevitable that Keanu would be with her as she examined the wound.

'Will you have to cut away the ulcerated tissue?' she asked, walking to the other side of the bed and peering at the ulcer herself.

Hettie looked up, beautiful green eyes focussing on Caroline.

Focussing so intently Caroline found herself offering a shrug that wasn't exactly an apology for speaking but very nearly.

'I came down to see if you had work for me to do—a

slot in the roster perhaps, or some use you could put me to?'

Hettie was still eyeing her warily, or maybe that was just her everyday look. She was neat—a slim figure, jeans and a white shirt, long dark hair controlled in a perfect roll at the back of her head—and attractive in a way that made Caroline think she'd be beautiful if she smiled.

'What do you know about Buruli ulcers?' Hettie asked, and, breathing silent thanks for the instinct that had made her look them up on the internet, Caroline rattled off what she'd learned.

Then, aware that the internet wasn't always right, she added, 'But that's just what Mr Google told me. I haven't had any experience of them.'

To her surprise, Hettie smiled and Caroline saw that she *was* beautiful—that quiet, unexpected kind of beauty that was rare enough to sometimes go unnoticed.

'You'll do,' Hettie said. 'Welcome aboard. It's hard to work to rosters here, but there's always work. Maddie, one of our FIFO doctors, usually does the checks on the miners but she didn't come in and the checks are due— or slightly overdue. You'd know the mine, wouldn't you? Perhaps you and Keanu could do that today?'

Excitement fizzed in Caroline's head—the perfect excuse to go down to the mine.

'What kind of checks do we do?' she asked Hettie, ignoring Keanu, who was arguing that she was too new in the job to be going down to the mine.

'Just general health. They tend to ignore cuts and scratches, although they know they can become infected or even ulcerated. And we've got a couple of workers— you'll see their notes on the cards—who we suspect have chest problems and aren't really suited to working underground. But you know men, they're a stubborn lot and will argue until they're blue in the face that they haven't any problems with their lungs.'

'Stubborn patients I do understand,' Carolyn said, smiling inwardly as she wondered if seemingly prim and proper Hettie had experienced many run-ins with stubborn men in her own life. She certainly seemed to have some strong opinions when it came to men in general.

'As a matter of course,' Hettie continued, 'we check the lung capacity of all the men and keep notes, and those two aren't so bad we can order them out of the mine. Yet. The hospital is, in part, funded by the Australian government, and the health checks at the mine are a Workplace Health and Safety requirement.'

'More paperwork for Sam,' Caroline said, and Hettie smiled again.

'He does hate it,' she agreed before turning to Keanu. 'You're not tied up, so you can take Caroline down there. You can show her where all the paperwork is kept, and the drugs cabinet we have down there.'

'If Ian didn't pinch it when he left,' Keanu muttered, but Caroline couldn't help feeling how lucky they were, to both have this excuse to visit the mine.

And although more time with Keanu was hardly ideal, this was work, and all she had to do was concentrate on that.

If she was gathering whatever impressions she could of what was happening at the mine she'd hardly be aware Keanu was there.

Hardly.

Stick to business!

'So, who do you think will be in charge of the mine

now Ian's gone?' she asked Keanu as they took the path around the house that led to the steps down to the mine.

He stopped, turning around to take her hand to help her over a rough part of the track where the stone steps had broken away.

'Ian's never really been hands-on, leaving the shift bosses to run the teams. Reuben Alaki is one of the best,' he said, speaking so calmly she knew he couldn't possibly be feeling all the physical reactions to the touch that were surging through her.

'I remember Reuben,' she managed to say, hoping she sounded as calm as he had, although she was certain there'd been a quiver in her voice. 'His wife died and he had to bring his little boy to work and your mother looked after him. We treated him like a pet dog or cat and he followed us everywhere.'

Fortunately for her sanity the rough bit of track was behind them, and Keanu had released her hand.

'That's him, although that little boy is grown up and is over in Australia, getting paid obscene amounts of money to play football.'

Then of course Keanu smiled, which had much the same result on her nerve endings as his touch had.

'Good for him,' Caroline said cheerily. 'Maybe you should have gone that way instead of becoming a doctor.'

Then you wouldn't be here holding my hand and smiling at me and totally confusing me!

Lost in her own thoughts, she didn't realise Keanu had stopped. He turned back to face her, his face taut with emotion.

'We had an agreement,' he reminded her, and now a sudden sadness—nostalgia for their carefree past, their happy childhood—swept over her.

'What happened to us, Keanu?' she whispered, forgetting the present, remembering only the past.

'Ian happened,' he said bluntly, and continued down the path.

Guilt kept him moving, because he *could* have kept in touch with Caroline, but in his anger—an impotent rage at his mother's pain—he had himself cursed all Lockharts.

Of course it had had nothing to do with Caroline, but at the time fury had made him blind and deaf, then, with his mother's death, it had been all he could do just to keep going. Getting back in touch with Caroline had been the last thing on his mind.

'All the files are in the site office,' he said, all business now as they reached the bottom of the steps.

He pointed to the rusty-looking shed sheltering under the overhang of the cave that led into the mine.

'That's Reuben there now. Let's go and see him.'

He knew Caroline was close behind him, aware of her in every fibre of his body, yet his mind was crowded with practical matters and he needed to concentrate on them—on the now, not the past...

The rumbling noise from deep inside the tunnel told him the mine was still being worked, but who was paying the men? And the crushing plant and extraction machine were standing idle, so they could hardly be taking home their wages in gold.

'Who's paying the men?' Caroline asked, as if she'd been following his train of thought as well as his footsteps.

'Reuben will tell us.'

Reuben stepped out of the shed to shake Keanu's hand, then turned to Caroline.

'New nurse?' he asked.

'But old friend, I hope, Reuben. It's Caroline Lockhart.'

Reuben beamed with delight and held out his arms to give Caroline a hug.

'You've grown up!' Reuben said, looking fondly at her. 'Grown up and beautiful!'

And from the look on Caroline's face, it was the first friendly greeting she'd received since her return.

'And your father? How is he?' Reuben asked.

'Working too hard. I hardly see him.'

'Working and caring for that poor brother of yours, too, I suppose. Same as always,' Reuben said. 'Me, I did that when my wife died but later I realised pain didn't go away with work. I have a new wife now and new family, and my big boy, he's rich and famous in Australia—sends money home to his old man even.'

'That's great, Reuben,' Caroline said, and Keanu knew she meant it. Her affinity for the islanders had always been as strong as his, and they had known that and loved her for it.

'So, what's happening here, Reuben?' he asked to get his mind back on track.

'Well…'

Reuben paused, scratched his head, shuffled his feet, and finally waved them both inside.

'The men working the bulldozer and crusher and extraction plant hadn't been paid for more than a month so they walked off the job maybe a month ago.'

He paused, looking out towards the harbour where

machinery and sheds were rapidly disappearing under rampant rainforest regrowth.

'The miners are in the same boat, but they believe they'll eventually be paid. I think their team bosses sent a letter to your dad some weeks ago and they're waiting to hear back, hoping he'll come. They're happy to keep working until they hear because most of them—well, they, we—don't need the money for food or fancy clothes. It just puts the kids through school and university and pays for taking their wives on holidays.'

The words came out fluently enough but Keanu thought he could hear a lingering 'but' behind them.

'But?' Caroline said, and he had to smile that they could still be so much on the same wavelength.

'The miners—they mine. It was the crusher team that did the safety stuff. Your uncle's been putting off staff for months, and he started with the general labourers, saying the bulldozer boys and crusher and extraction operators could do the safety work when the crusher wasn't operating, but now they've gone.'

'Then the miners shouldn't be working,' Keanu said. 'You've got to pull them out of there.'

Reuben shook his head.

'They've got a plan. They're going to stockpile enough rock then come out and work the crusher themselves for a month and that way they can keep the mine going. The miners, they're all from these islands, they know the hospital needs the mine and they need the hospital and the clinics on the islands. Because they're younger, a lot of them have young families—kids. Kids have accidents—need a nurse or a doctor...'

Keanu sighed.

He understood that part of the situation—but nevertheless the mine would have to shut! Safety had to come first and their small hospital just wasn't equipped should a major catastrophe like a mine collapse happen.

Caroline's heart had shuddered at the thought of the miners working in tunnels that might not have been shored up properly, or in water that hadn't been pumped out of the tunnels, but the best way to find out was to talk to them.

'Well, if there are people working here, shouldn't we start the checks?' She turned to Keanu, and read the concern she was feeling mirrored in his eyes. 'How do you usually handle it?'

But it was Reuben who answered her.

'I'll ring through to the team and they send one man out at a time—we do it in alphabetical order so it's easier for you with the files. I'm a bit worried about Kalifa Lui—his cough seems much worse.'

'Should we see him first?' Caroline asked, but Keanu shook his head.

'He'll realise we've picked him out and probably cough his lungs up on his way out of the mine so his chest's clear when he gets here. Better to keep to the order.'

Reuben had placed a well-labelled accident book in front of Caroline and a box of files on the table where Keanu sat.

Index card files?

Caroline looked around the office—no computer.

Ian's cost-cutting?

She didn't say anything, not wanting to confirm any more Lockhart inadequacies or bring up Ian's name unnecessarily.

Keanu was already flipping through the files, and

Reuben was on the phone, organising the check-ups, so Caroline opened the book.

But she was easily distracted.

Looking at Keanu, engrossed in his work, making notes on a piece of paper, leafing back through the files to check on things, she sensed the power of this man—as a man—to attract any woman he wanted. It wasn't simply good looks and a stunning physique, but there was a suggestion of a strong sexuality—maybe more than a suggestion—woven about him like a spider's web.

And she was caught in it.

The memories of their childhood together were strong and bitter-sweet given how it had ended, but this was something different.

'Aaron Anapou, ma'am.'

Jerked out of her thoughts by the deep voice, she looked up to see a dust-smeared giant standing in front of her.

'Ah! Hi! Actually, Keanu's doing the checks. I'm Caroline—I'm the nurse.'

She stood up and held out her hand, which he took gingerly.

'You should have gloves on, ma'am,' he said quietly.

'But then I might miss a little gold dust sticking to my fingers.'

Aware that she'd already held up things for too long, she waved him along the table towards Keanu, who already had the first card in front of him.

Reuben had helpfully laid out the medical implements between the two of them—a stethoscope, ear thermometer and covers, and a lung capacity machine. So what did she do? Act as welcoming committee? Wait for orders?

Behind her desk Reuben had also opened the doors on what looked like a well-stocked medical cabinet.

Maybe she did the dressings.

But, in the meantime, there was the accident book to go through. She looked at the recent pages, then flipped back, interested to see if there were always so few accidents recorded.

It wasn't hard to work out when the crushing and extracting operations had closed down as most of the reported accidents had been caused by some chance contact with some piece of the machinery.

In the background she heard Keanu chiding men for working in flip-flops instead of their steel-capped boots, listened to explanations of water not being pumped out, and her heart ached for the days when the mine had been a well-run and productive place.

'If you're done, you can give me a hand.' Had Keanu guessed she'd been dreaming?

The next miner hadn't tried to hide the fact he'd been working in flip-flops—they were bright green and still on his feet. The skin between his big toe and the second one, where the strap of the sandal rubbed, was raw and inflamed, and a visible cut on his left arm was also infected.

Caroline worked with Keanu now; he cleaned and treated wounds, handing out antibiotics, while she did the lung capacity tests and temperatures.

'I'm surprised there are any antibiotics to give out,' she said when there was a gap between the miners.

'I keep the keys of the chest and no one but me can ever open it,' Reuben said firmly. 'I suppose it was too big for Mr Lockhart to take away and he couldn't break the bolt, although I think he tried.'

Caroline sighed.

Her uncle had left a poisonous legacy behind him on what had once been an island paradise.

And, given her name, she was part of the poison.

'We definitely have to close the mine.' Keanu's voice interrupted her dream of happier times, and she realised the parade of miners—a short parade—from the mine to the table had ceased. 'It would be irresponsible not to do it.'

'And *that* will damage the Lockhart name even more,' Caroline muttered as shame for the trouble her uncle had caused made her cringe.

He touched her quickly on the shoulder. 'We'll talk about it later,' he said, pulling the accident book from in front of her and checking the few notes she'd made.

'Given the state of the mine, there've been remarkably few accidents,' he said. 'Unless, of course...' he looked at Reuben '...you haven't been recording them.'

Reuben's indignant 'Of course I have,' was sincere enough to be believed, especially when he added, 'But remember, not all the men are working. Only this one team at the moment.'

'But even if there haven't been many accidents, that doesn't mean there won't be more in future,' Caroline said, seeing the sense in Keanu's determination that the mine should close.

So what could she do?

Find out whatever she could?

'Reuben, would you mind if I looked at the accounts and wages books?'

He looked taken aback—upset even.

'I'm not checking up on you, but it would help if I could work out how much the miners are owed. I know

Dad would want them all paid. Do you have the wages records on computer?'

'It's all in books, but I keep a copy on my laptop,' Reuben told her, disappearing into the back of the office and returning with the little laptop, handing it over to her with a degree of reluctance.

'We *do* have to close it down,' she admitted to Keanu as they climbed back up the steep steps to the top of the plateau. She was clutching the laptop to her chest.

'You're right,' he said, 'but do you think the men will stop working just because we say so? I'll phone your father—he's the one to do it, and if he can't come over, he can send someone from the Mines Department, someone who might carry some weight with the miners. They could come on Friday's flight.'

Keanu got no answer to his common-sense suggestion. *She's plotting something*, he realised as they climbed back up the steep steps to the top of the plateau.

He knew Caroline in this mood and more often than not whatever she was up to would be either rash or downright dangerous.

But he had worries enough of his own. The elders had placed their faith in him to save the livelihood of the island and the continuation of medical facilities.

'Do we have to go straight back to the hospital or can we sit down with a coffee and work out what to do? I can try to get in touch with Dad,' Caroline said as she led the way towards the house, as if assuming he would agree.

Keanu followed, but hesitated on the bottom step of the big house, his mind arguing with itself.

Of course he could go in—it was just a house, the place where he'd spent so much of his childhood.

Yet his feet were glued to the step.

Caro turned back.

'You're not coming? Do you think we should go back? Bessie would get us some lunch and we could have a talk.'

Then, as if they'd never been apart, she guessed what he was thinking, headed back down to where he stood, took his hand and gently eased him down onto the step, sitting close beside him, her arm around his shoulders.

'Tell me,' she said, and although she spoke softly, it was an order, and suddenly he needed to tell, as if talking about that day would help banish the memories.

He looked out over the island, down towards the sea surrounding it, green-blue and beautiful.

Peaceful…

'I came home on an earlier flight. One kid had measles just before the holidays so they closed a week early. I didn't tell Mum, wanting to surprise her.'

And hadn't he surprised her! The memory of that ugly, desperate scene lived on in his nightmares. He concentrated on the view to block it out of his mind even now…

'I walked up from the plane and into the house. I knew Mum would be in there—dusting or cleaning—she loved the house so much.'

Had Caro heard the break in his voice that her arm tightened around his shoulders?

'They were in the living room, on the floor, on one of your grandma's rugs, like animals.'

He turned to Caroline, needing to see her face, needing to see understanding there.

'I thought he was raping her. I dragged him off, yelling at him, trying to punch him, and…'

'Go on.'

The words were little more than a gentle whisper but now he'd gone this far he knew he had to finish.

'He laughed!' The words exploded out of him, his voice rising at remembered—and still lingering—anger. 'He stood there, pulling up his shorts, buttoning his shirt, and laughed at me. "Do you think she didn't want it?" he said. "Wasn't begging for it? Go on, Helen, tell him how desperate you were to keep what was nothing more than an occasional kindness shag going."'

'Oh, Keanu! I can only imagine how you felt and your poor mother—'

'I lost it, Caro! I went at him, fists flying, while Mum was covering herself and gathering clothes and telling me to stop, not that I did much good. At fifteen I was a fair size, but nothing like Ian's weight. He eventually pushed me to the ground and told me to get out, both of us to get out. He'd ask the plane to wait so we could pack then be out of there.'

'But it was your home, Keanu. It always had been. Grandma had promised that before I was even born!' Caro hauled him to his feet and hugged him properly. 'Anyway, after I arrived Helen was employed by Dad, not Ian.'

Keanu put his hands on her shoulders and eased her far enough apart to look into her face.

'Ian's words destroyed Mum. She refused to talk about it except to say she'd always known she wasn't the only one. I realised then it had been going on for some time. But to humiliate her like that, in front of me—it was more than she could take! When we got back to the house in Cairns she phoned your father to say she wouldn't be there to look after you during the holidays and that she'd retired. No other explanation no matter how often he phoned, even when he visited. With the admiration she had for your father, there was no way she could have told him about it. She just shut herself away from life, then only a few years later she was gone.'

Caro drew him close again, wrapping her arms around him, holding him tightly.

'Oh, Keanu,' she whispered, the words soft and warm against his neck. 'At least now I understand why you deserted me. How could you have had anything to do with any Lockhart after Ian's behaviour to your mother?'

Was it the release of telling her the story, of her finally knowing why he'd cut her off that made his arms move to enfold her?

He didn't know—he only knew that he held her, clung to her, breathing in the very essence that was Caroline—his Caro. And like a sigh—a breath of wind—something shifted between them…an awareness, tension—

Attraction?

You're married.

Probably.

He didn't actually leap away from her embrace, but the space between them grew.

They were friends, but whatever this new emotion was, it hadn't felt like friendship.

Had Caro felt it?

Were warning bells clanging in her head?

For once he had not the slightest idea of what she was thinking, but deep inside he knew that, whatever lay ahead, he couldn't do anything to hurt her, not again, which meant not getting too involved until he knew he was free.

Something had obviously happened between her and

Steve because she was back on the island and he could
see she was hurting.

Abandoned again by someone she loved?

Wouldn't he have to do that if his divorce didn't go
through?

Get out of here and sort it out!

'You have lunch here,' he said, aiming for sounding
calm and composed—sensible—although his whole body
churned with emotion. 'I'll go back to the hospital and
talk to Sam. He'll know the best way to close down the
mine.'

Caroline nodded. 'Yes, good idea.'

Perhaps she hadn't felt what he'd felt when they'd
hugged, because she'd never sounded more together—
practical, professional—putting the past firmly behind
her.

But then, she'd always been a superb actress, having
grown adept at hiding her feelings.

Though usually not from him…

CHAPTER SIX

HAD THEY BEEN going to kiss?

Surely not!

But Caroline was very relieved he'd pulled away, and hopefully without seeing her suddenly breathless state.

And if he hadn't?

Would that surge of attraction have led to a kiss—right there on the front steps of the house?

Her heart ached for him after hearing the story of his return from school, his mother's humiliation, and imagining the pain the pair must have suffered, leaving the place that had been their only true home.

Her first reaction had been numbness. After Bessie's chance remark about no woman being safe around Ian, she'd imagined rape, but humiliating Helen as he had done had been emotionally so damaging. How impotent Keanu must have felt in the face of Ian's callousness.

Of course she'd had to hug him!

But hugging Keanu had never felt like that before!

Hugging Keanu had never produced that kind of mayhem in her body. Not even Steve, who'd never failed to boast about what a great lover he was, had ever managed to evoke something like that.

Or was that unfair to Steve?

He hadn't really boasted of his prowess, it was just the impression she'd got from his confidence, and the fact that other women had envied her the man who had wooed her with flowers, and gifts and promises of undying love.

Actually, now the hurt was gone and she could look back rationally, it had been the undying love thing that had got her in the end; the fact that this person had come into her life, vowing to be there for ever—to never let her down or abandon her. That last had been the clincher.

How stupid had *she* been?

A practised lover, he'd sniffed out the silly issues she had with abandonment—with the loss of so many people in her life and the distraction of others—and had worked on it!

Jilly had been right, she was well out of that relationship, and as the days had turned into months Caroline had realised that as well, glad the man she'd thought she loved had turned out to have not only feet of clay but whole legs of it!

And Keanu?

She closed her eyes and breathed deeply then decided she wouldn't think about that right now. She had more important things to consider, the first being to find some way to pay the miners what they were owed.

She didn't think it would go all the way to restoring the Lockhart name but those people had worked for her family—they deserved to be paid.

And they would be.

She'd phone Dad, talk to him about the mine closure and the problems Ian had left behind him on the island— the damage he had done to the Lockhart name.

Although could she add that much more worry to his already over-burdened shoulders?

An image of her twin rose up in front of her—Christopher's crippled, twisted body, his lovely blue eyes gazing blankly towards her as she talked to him, the pigeon chest battling for every breath…

No, she couldn't pull Dad away from Christopher, especially right now when he had been hospitalised again…

So it was up to her.

Or was she fooling herself?

'Nurse Hettie phoned to say she expected you back at the hospital.' Bessie appeared at the front door. 'I told her you're having a late lunch and will be down soon.'

Bother!

'Thanks, Bessie, I'll go right now.'

'You'll do no such thing. You come into the kitchen and have lunch.'

'But Reuben gave Keanu and I fruit salad and cold juice. I don't need lunch.'

'You do need lunch!'

Realising it was futile to argue, she went into the kitchen to eat the gargantuan sandwich Bessie had prepared for her.

Footsteps on the veranda sent Bessie scurrying from the kitchen, and Caroline carefully wrapped the remainder of the sandwich and popped it into the fridge.

The deep voice she heard was definitely Keanu's.

Her heart made a squiggly feeling in her chest as she hurried to the front veranda.

'There was no need for you to come up, I just had to wash and put on a clean top—it was dusty down there.'

Keanu nodded, just that, a nod, the story he'd shared with her like a glass wall between them.

Or had it been the hug?

Whatever, he'd turned away and started back towards

the hospital, pausing only to explain, 'Hettie's done two trips the last two days so she's taking a break, but the patient with the Buruli ulcer needs the skin around it debrided and the wound cleaned, and Anahera has her hands full with the other patients.'

Other patients?

Caroline realised with a start how little she knew about the hospital and what was going on there. She was a nurse, and the patients should be her first concern, not worrying how to pay the money owed to the miners.

She followed Keanu down the path, ignoring the hitch in her breathing at the breadth of his shoulders and the way his hair curled against the nape of his neck, catching up with him to ask, 'Do we use the treatment room where I first saw him or the operating theatre?

'He doesn't need a full anaesthetic, just locals around the wound, but the theatre is more sterile so we'll do it there.'

Caught up in what lay ahead, Caroline set aside the disturbances Keanu's presence was causing and concentrated on the case.

'Are we using the theatre because the ulcer bacteria are easily transmitted?'

Keanu shook his head.

'We've no idea how it's transmitted, although the World Health Organization has teams of people in various places working on it. Using the theatre is a safeguard, nothing more.'

'And debriding tissue?'

He turned to look at her as they reached the hospital.

'Are you asking questions to prove your worth as a nurse or because you're genuinely interested?'

The deliberate dig took her breath away but before she

could get into a fierce, and probably very loud, argument with him, he added, 'I'm sorry, that was unfair. I'm so damned mixed up right now.'

He sighed, dark eyes troubled, then touched her lightly on the shoulder.

'The thing about Buruli is that it produces a toxin called mycolactone that destroys tissue. We have the patient on antibiotics but they are taking time to work, so we're going to clean it up in the hope that we'll kill off any myolactone spores.'

Caroline's mind switched immediately to nurse mode. They'd need local anaesthesia, scalpels, dressings, dishes to take the affected skin to be disposed of in the incinerator.

And she had no idea where that was or, in fact, where any of the other things were kept. Instead of prowling around in the dark with Keanu last night, she should have been checking out the hospital.

She must have sighed, for Keanu said, 'It's okay, Mina will have everything set out for us.'

He *was* still reading her mind!

And, given some of the thoughts flashing through it, that could prove very dangerous—*and* downright embarrassing.

The ulcer was inflamed and looked incredibly painful, but the young man was stoic about it.

Keanu injected local anaesthetic into the tissue around the wound, then checked the equipment while he waited for it to take effect.

'I want to keep as much of the skin intact as I can,' Keanu said, speaking directly to her for the first time. 'I'll trim the edges and try to clean beneath it. I'll need you to swab and use tweezers to clear the damaged bits as I cut.'

Caroline picked up a pair of forceps. The wound was long but reasonably narrow, and she could see what Keanu hoped to do. If he could clean out the wound he might be able to stretch the healthy skin enough to stitch it together.

'If you stitch it up, would you leave a small drain in place?'

He glanced up from his delicate task of scraping and cutting and nodded. Seeing his eyes above the mask he was wearing made her heart jittery again.

This was ridiculous. She was a professional and any interaction between them, at least at the hospital, had to be just that—professional!

She selected another pair of forceps and lifted the skin towards which he was working.

He continued to cut, dropping some bits in one dish and some in a separate one.

Intrigued, she had to ask.

'Why the two dishes?'

He glanced up at her with smiling eyes and any last remnants of hope about professionalism flew out the window—well, there was no window, but they disappeared. That smile re-awoke all the manifestations of attraction that she'd felt earlier, teasing along her nerves and activating all her senses.

'I think I mentioned Sam's a keen bacteriologist,' Keanu was explaining while she told herself she was being ridiculous. 'He's never made Buruli a particular study but he'll be interested to look at it under a microscope. The more people around the world peering at it the better chance we have of developing a defence against it. It's not so bad here in the West Pacific but in some African and Asian nations when it's not treated early it attacks the bone and causes deformities or even loss of limbs.'

'I don't want to lose my leg,' their patient said firmly, and Keanu assured him that no such thing would happen.

'We've got you onto the drugs early enough and once we clean it up you should be fine.'

Keanu was being professional—purely professional.

Until he looked up, caught her eye, and winked.

'I think that's it,' he said, much to her relief. It had been an 'I'm finished' wink, nothing more.

Yet her reaction suggested that keeping things purely professional between herself and Keanu would prove impossible—from her side at least.

No way! She was stronger than that. And she had plenty to occupy her mind. The sooner she could get the back payments for the miners sorted out, and get the mine closed until it could be made safe, the better it would be for the hospital, and if she concentrated on that—

'Okay, I'll get Mina to do the dressing. I think we deserve a coffee.'

She glanced at the clock—they'd been standing over their patient for more than two hours and probably did deserve a coffee.

Well, she could do coffee…

Except he was smiling.

Possibly not.

'What I need more than coffee is a tour of the hospital so I know where everything is and what patient is where. I'll do the dressing then maybe Mina can show me around.'

Keanu could hardly argue, although he could alter the plan slightly.

'Let's stick with Mina doing the dressing and I'll show you around instead.'

Caroline's reaction wasn't what you'd call ecstatic.

More resigned, if anything, but after being distracted by the telling of his mother's distress and their departure from the island earlier, he was hoping to have a chat about the situation at the mine—to find out what she was thinking.

Because she *was* thinking of something she could do to help matters. He'd known her too long and too well not to have picked that up.

But he could hardly ask about it while touring the little hospital and introducing patients, so he'd have to find another time.

'There are four wards, if you can call small two-bed spaces *wards*. Three on this side, with sliding doors that can close each of them off, although most of the time we leave it open for the breezes.'

He led her into the first of these, which, at the moment, had two patients, young men from another island who had taken the tide too lightly and had been injured when the boat they'd been in had overturned on the reef. 'As you can see,' Keanu pointed out, 'one has a broken arm, the other an injured ankle, and both have quite bad coral grazes—'

'Which can easily become infected if not treated promptly and continually.'

Keanu nodded. Anyone who grew up in the islands knew about infections from coral so he wasn't going to give her any brownie points for that. But walking with her, talking with her—even professionally—was so distracting to his body he couldn't help but resent her presence.

If she wasn't here—

No, he was glad she was here.

She belonged here, just as he did. He just had to get over this physical attraction thing.

Be professional.

'The patient in the third bed, in what's technically another ward, you might recognise—Brenko, Bessie and Harold's grandson. The flying surgeon took out his spleen last week after he'd had an accident on his quad bike. More muscle than sense, haven't you?'

The young man grinned, and the patients, who had been quiet as Keanu had brought the stranger into the room, all began to talk at once.

Was she really Caroline Lockhart? How could any Lockhart show her face here? What was going to happen with the mine?

The questions, and the animosity behind some of them, must have hurt Caroline deeply because he heard her sigh with relief when he stopped the talk.

'Caroline is here as a nurse, so if you don't want her jabbing you with unnecessary needles, you'd better start treating her with respect. She's spent more time in these islands than some of you have been alive and is not to blame for anything her uncle did.'

The anger that underlined Keanu's words quietened the young men, then Brenko said, 'I'm glad you're back, Caroline. I still have the ukulele you gave me when I was little.'

Caroline smiled at the memory, but Keanu guessed that one happy memory wouldn't make up for the animosity that had been thick in the air around her.

He led her through the next small room, this one closed off with the shutters. An elderly woman patient was sleeping soundly, although the young men's voices could be heard quite clearly.

'Unstable diabetic,' Keanu murmured.

'It's the curse of all the Pacific islands,' Caroline replied quietly, and he nodded, then, feeling the hurt he knew she would be nursing, he put his arm around her shoulders and gave her a quick squeeze.

She shot away as if he'd burned her, then must have realised her reaction had been a little extreme and moved close again.

But not close enough for hugs or squeezes, however sympathetic.

In the fourth room, a young woman was sitting up in bed, nursing her baby, Anahera standing by in case either of them needed a bit of help.

'We don't have a maternity ward because we transfer all pregnant women to the mainland at thirty-four to thirty-six weeks, depending on the advice of our flying obstetrician, but this little fellow arrived early,' Keanu explained, smiling at the sight of the mother and child.

'By rights he shouldn't be here. His mum was to be going out on today's flight,' he continued. 'But Hettie and the local midwife who delivered him suspect his dates were wrong. As you can see, he's a good size and he's feeding lustily.'

He turned to smile at Caroline.

'In all truth, we love having him here—we've all gone a bit soft. Because the women and their babies usually fly in and go straight to their homes, we don't get to see the babies except on clinic runs. Consequently, we're happy to keep these two here just in case anything goes wrong. We've got them isolated in this room to keep them clear of any infection.'

'Because you don't know how Buruli ulcers are transmitted?'

'Exactly.'

'The lad with the ulcer will be transferred to the ICU across the passage, beyond the theatre, once Mina has finished dressing the wound. It's next to the recovery room and ICU is probably a grand name for it but it's got a ventilator and monitoring equipment in it. The lad doesn't need it but it does keep him isolated.'

Caroline nodded her understanding.

'We're not finished, are we?' she asked. 'Don't you have linen cupboards and drug cabinets and instruments and sterilisers and a million other things that a hospital, even a small one, needs? Where's your radiography department, for a start?'

'Through here,' he said, moving into a separate wing. 'The theatre you've already seen and all the sterilising stuff is in an annexe off that. Cupboards for sterile clothing, etcetera are also in the annexe, and there's a shower and locker room next to that and beyond the theatre is Radiography.'

'It's well planned,' Caro commented.

'We've your father to thank for that,' he said. 'And him to thank for us having the best and latest in radiography machines. Money from the mine put in the basics— X-ray and ultrasound—and the Australian government donated a mammography machine, but he won a grant from one of the big casinos to put in a CT machine. He really does everything he can for the island and the hospital.'

'The hospital and Christopher,' Caro pointed out, and Keanu heard the catch in her voice. Did she think her father cared more for the hospital and his son than he did for his daughter?

Keanu remembered that as a child Caro had felt guilty

about her mother's death, and Christopher's cerebral palsy, blaming herself for both problems, but there was no way Max would feel that.

'That was bitchy!' she said suddenly. 'Both the hospital and Christopher need him far more than I do. And Dad has so much on his shoulders, the least I can do is understand that and do whatever I might be able to do to lift some of the burden.'

Keanu wanted to argue that she had every right to feel left out, but he wondered if Max's avoidance of the island whenever possible was entirely to do with work and his disabled son, or was it that he was still haunted by his young wife's death?

Would too many heartbreaking memories lay siege to him whenever he was here?

Caro was wandering around the equipment, checking it all.

'So, what do you think?' he asked, dragging his mind from the Lockhart family tragedies to the present.

'It's great equipment for a small hospital but, given the isolation, I'd say it's all necessary. And I can see why Dad's been working his butt off, not only for money to keep the place afloat but doing all the lobbying with business and government.'

The way she spoke told Keanu she saw little of her adored father, but as he watched she shrugged off whatever she was thinking and tugged at one of the curtains that screened off various sections of the room.

She poked her head out from behind the curtain and grinned cheekily, doing terrible things to Keanu's heart, lungs, not to mention his determination to keep things professional between them.

'We didn't think of all of this when we decided to become the doctor and the nurse on Wildfire, did we?'

'Didn't know "all this" existed,' Keanu reminded her, hoping he sounded more in control than he felt.

Trying to get her and the past out of his mind, he remembered the look on her face as they'd come back from the mine and his wanting to find out what she was up to.

'The laundry cupboards and other stuff are closer to the kitchen and even if you don't want a coffee, I do.'

She followed him obediently, said hello to the cook when he introduced them, then politely but adamantly refused to answer any questions.

'To tell you the truth, Keanu, I have no idea what I can do to sort out all that's happened at the mine, but I know I have to do something. The hospital needs a functioning mine, and the islands need the hospital, so we can't just let it all fizzle out. Besides, it was a Lockhart who caused all the problems, so it's up to me to at least try to do something to sort it out.'

But what?

The question bugged him, to the extent that he found himself, much later, when all was well in the hospital and Sam and Hettie both on call, walking up the hill, skirting the lagoon, to the house where he'd grown up.

They'd grown up.

He climbed the steps but once again hesitated on the veranda, reluctant to go in.

'Caro?'

His call was tentative—pathetic, really.

'If you want to see me you'll have to come in,' she yelled from somewhere inside, and he guessed from the direction of her voice that she'd be sitting at the big table in the dining room, pen and paper at hand, trawling through the information on the laptop.

Of course he could go in. It had been his home as much as hers, and although as a Lockhart she probably had more rights, his mother had run the place for years.

Until…

Then Caro was there, so much sympathy in her eyes he thought his heart might crack.

She put both arms around him and drew him close.

'I know it must be dreadful, having to walk through here again, but I'm in the dining room, and you have to do it some time. Standing out here isn't going to banish the memory, now, is it?'

Her hair touched his shoulder, soft as silk, and the woman smell of her filled his head with fantasy.

So much so, his arms returned her hug until it became more than a hug and they were kissing—gentle, exploratory kisses that nonetheless sent fire throughout his body and a throbbing need deep inside it.

Eventually—fortunately—she eased away.

'Well, that was weird,' she said lightly, before leading him firmly into the house.

But it was more than weird, it was dangerous. The attraction he was feeling was obviously mutual, but there were so many ifs and buts about it…

She'd led him into the dining room, and Keanu looked at the bits of paper scattered across the shining surface.

'What on earth are you doing?' he demanded.

'I'm trying to work out exactly how much the workers are owed, and once I know that I'd like to know how much it costs to run the mine on a weekly or monthly basis.'

'And then you'll know how much you need to win on Lotto to fix everything up,' Keanu finished for her.

She glared at him.

'You may mock, but while it might be hard to find money for projects like this, it would be impossible if we don't know what we need. If I can work out a kind of ballpark figure, we can take it from there—get some investors, speak to banks, big businesses, whatever. It might be beyond us whatever we do, but at least we'd know we tried.'

Keanu understood what she was saying and a tiny spark of light flickered in his brain. The seed of an idea he couldn't yet grasp.

Kind of hard to grasp at glimmers of ideas in his head when most of it was occupied with telling his body that a sympathy kiss from Caroline meant nothing, and the fact that his body was attracted to hers was probably nothing more than their closeness in their childhood, and he was still married...

Probably.

Was she feeling the awkwardness too, that she suddenly bundled up all her bits of paper into a very rough pile and said, 'The moon's up, let's go for a walk. I haven't been down to the lagoon since I got back—there always seems to be something else to do.'

She made it sound like a peaceful stroll down to one of their favourite childhood places, but his body screamed at him to resist at all costs. The moon was not just up, it was full. The lagoon would be bathed in its soft glow, as would the woman with whom he was strolling.

But when had he ever been able to say no to Caro?

Once outside, in the light of the said moon, Caroline realised what a stupid idea it had been. Bad enough that she'd already been kissing Keanu, kissing him and wanting to keep kissing him. It was more than weird, it was scary.

But wonderful.

That thought filled her with a kind of awe…

And how was she going to cope with Keanu *and* moonlight, twin attractions, twin magic?

But she could hardly back off now, so she strode down the slightly overgrown path they'd used as children towards the end of the lagoon just above the small waterfall, where a large, flat rock only inches above the level of the water gave a wonderful view, not only of the entire lake but of the village beneath the plateau.

Keanu caught up with her as she reached the thicker rainforest that protected the waterhole, reaching out a hand to steady her as the track was rough. Roots and vines conspired to catch at their feet and they brushed against each other often.

Definitely not one of her better ideas.

The touch of his hand had been enough, but skin on skin contact, no matter how accidental, had made goosebumps rise on her arms and neck as her nerve endings battled with the notion that this was Keanu—just a friend!

They reached the lagoon, and trod carefully around its rocky edge towards the small opening through which the water tumbled its way down a rocky path to the flat land below.

And there was their rock. Caroline hurried on, anxious to be there as if sitting in such a familiar place would protect her from all the unfamiliar reactions she was getting from being around her old friend.

But once he'd joined her she realised the rock had shrunk.

Ridiculous, they had grown, so now they sat, close

together, feet flat, knees raised, hands looped around their legs.

Very close together!

And in spite of the moonlight, the lagoon looked dark and mysterious, the surface silvered, but with a sense of hidden depths lurking beneath that shining skin.

Hidden depths...

The man beside her would have those too, not deliberately hidden but ideas, emotions, even ethics and beliefs that developed with maturity so for all she thought she knew him, she really didn't.

'I have got one idea to get the money,' she said tentatively, as the side of her body closest to Keanu heated towards fever level. 'Do you remember Dad explaining to us—well, to me, I suppose, but I'm sure you were there—that my mother's parents had left their house in Sydney jointly to Christopher and me? They'd also left most of their money, which was apparently considerable, in trust for Christopher and the interest on that pays for his full-time carers and the housekeeper and upkeep on the house.'

She leant forward so a curtain of hair saved her from looking at Keanu's face. Studying it in the moonlight that picked out the strong bones of his cheeks and jaw, the straight line of his nose was just too distracting.

'I vaguely remember, but is this story going somewhere?' Keanu replied, moving slightly and tucking her protective curtain back behind her ears, presumably so he could see her face, for he'd turned to study her at the same time.

She felt the brush of his fingers as he moved her hair, could feel his eyes on her skin—soft eyes, gentle, understanding, like a caress...

'Well, it might be—it *could* be a solution,' she said, her voice wavering as her body reacted to his gaze, *and* realised just how stupid this was all going to sound. 'I thought if I could borrow enough money by mortgaging my half of the house, we might just be able to get the mine working again and eventually there'd be money over and above what it pays to the hospital for me to repay the loan.'

He hesitated for a moment, then slipped his arm around her shoulders, as if preparing her for a hug when he disappointed her with his reply.

'Caro…' His voice was deep and husky and his arm tightened around her shoulders. 'I know you said it was your first idea, but if you don't mind my saying so, it isn't the best idea you've ever had. What if we can't get the mine going again, and the bank forecloses and Christopher loses his home?'

'But surely they'd…' Caroline protested, so flustered by Keanu's touch she'd forgotten what she'd meant to say.

'Only take half a house?' Keanu finished for her, showing just how ridiculous the idea had been.

Had she looked so disappointed that Keanu used the arm around her shoulders to pull her closer? A comforting hug, nothing more, but given where her comforting hug to him had led earlier, she really should pull away.

Except it *was* comforting.

Too comforting…

For Keanu too, as he suddenly let his arm slip and got back to practicalities?

'Now, as you were right about knowing a ballpark figure for the amount of money we need,' he said, 'let's go back to your notes and see what we can come up with.'

He stood up, reaching down to help her to her feet,

then keeping her hand in his, not exactly imprisoned because she knew she could pull hers out but firmly, as if he wanted it there.

Here she went again, feeling things between her and Keanu when in reality it was nothing more than their old friendship.

Back in the house, she made tea, and put out biscuits Bessie had cooked that day, carrying them through to the dining room where Keanu was already going through her figures.

Or would have been if he hadn't been holding the old notebook she'd pulled out of her room to use the blank pages in it, running his fingers over the hearts and flowers she'd drawn on the cover—the hearts with the arrow running through them, linking her initials to his.

She snatched it out of his fingers.

'It's the first thing I could find to write on,' she muttered. 'But to get back to the mine, the closest I've got to a total is the wages owed and the full wages for running the mine—from figures back when Peter was here. I just need weekly or monthly running costs from Reuben and we'll have some idea of what's needed.

'We can get them later,' Keanu assured her, taking the book from her but flipping back to the cover of the book and smiling at her. The teasing warmth of that smile sent ripples of what felt very like desire downwards through her body.

'I was ten, just look at the figures!' she snapped, but he kept smiling.

Damn the man. It was just so much easier being near him when he wasn't smiling.

But they stood up together, the air between them dense with tension.

In the end it was he who broke the spell, stepping back, so they stood, a foot apart, still looking into each other's eyes.

Then Keanu smiled, and she regretted the foot of space between them, because right then there'd be nothing she'd have liked more than to be locked in his arms.

Locked in his arms?

As in romance?

'You loved me when you were ten,' he reminded her, before turning and walking quietly out of the room, down the hall, across the veranda and down the steps.

Gone…

CHAPTER SEVEN

As he'd mentioned, Keanu was off duty, and Anahera and an aide Caroline didn't know were working in the hospital when Caroline arrived the next morning.

'Sam's in his office,' Anahera told her. 'And Hettie says she's taking a day off, which she should, but I bet she's doing paperwork in her little villa—she finds it hard to stop, although she does love exploring the island, swimming in the lagoon and climbing around the waterfall. She has a true passion for this place.'

'And you?' Caroline asked, glad to have an opportunity to chat with Anahera even if they were only counting drugs in the dangerous drugs cabinet.

Anahera didn't answer for a moment, then, to Caroline's surprise, she said, 'Well, me, I'm just glad you've turned up. The island is my home and I'm happy here with Hana, but since Keanu's arrival, Mum's been trying to push us both together.'

'Not interested?' Caroline said as casually as she could.

'Once bitten, twice shy,' Anahera answered obliquely. 'Not that being interested in Keanu would do me any good. Even Mum's realised how he is around you.'

Caroline felt heat in her cheeks.

'It's just because we've always known each other,' she said, then realised how lame she'd sounded.

The drugs all counted and checked off on the list taped on the cabinet door, the pair of them walked through the hospital.

'Do you want to change the dressings on the coral cuts while I do some bloods?'

It was good to be doing routine nursing work and now they'd accepted her, the lads with the coral cuts were fun. She took off the old dressings, cleaned the wounds, which were looking good, applied antibiotic ointment and covered them again.

By the next day, she guessed, they'd be able to go home.

She and Anahera had a coffee in the kitchen with a slice of extremely good hummingbird cake, and were just finishing it when Keanu appeared.

'Can you come down to the airstrip?' he asked, by-passing any politeness. 'There's an emergency call-out to Atangi. Hettie's done two flights the last two days so Sam suggested you come along to see what we do.'

You'll be okay, just don't touch him more than neces-sary, the sane voice in her head said firmly, but the pro-fessional part of her mind was focussed firmly on what lay ahead.

'What kind of an emergency?' she asked.

Keanu was hurrying beside her now, long strides eat-ing up the ground.

'Pregnant woman, thirty weeks, having severe cramps.'

He paused—both feet and words—and turned to look at Caroline.

'We'll see how she is when we get there, maybe just bring her back here. Atangi's a good clinic for you to see first, as it has a fairly well-equipped and stocked operating theatre. Before the hospital was built, the flying doctors used it for their emergency visits.'

'Thirty weeks, so we'll take a humidicrib and resus gear?'

'Already in the chopper.'

They'd reached the airstrip, where Sam was talking to Jack.

'You're okay to do this?' Sam asked, looking at Caroline.

'Very okay,' Caroline assured him, not adding that she was actually excited at the thought of going to Atangi after so long a time. You could hardly tell your boss you were excited that someone was ill.

The flight was short, but so beautiful it brought tears to Caroline's eyes. The translucent green water over the reefs, the deeper blue of the sea between the islands, then there was the harbour at Atangi.

'Did you remember Alkiri telling us about the harbour being blasted through the coral by the Americans during the Second World War?' Keanu asked as they dropped down to land on a marked circle next to a building Caroline recognised as the clinic.

As children, she and Keanu had been brought here for their immunisations, and occasionally treated by the resident nurse for minor injuries.

'It seems funny, being back,' she said as she followed Keanu out of the helicopter, feeling a now-familiar tension as his hand held her arm to steady her.

Keanu leaned back in to pull out a backpack, and Caroline knew it would contain all the emergency equipment they might need.

'The clinic is actually well stocked and we probably

won't need anything apart from the mobile ultrasound unit that's in here, but it's just as easy to take the lot.'

He spoke to Jack, who'd shut down the engine and disembarked, carrying the portable humidicrib and another bag of equipment.

'You'll stand by?'

Jack shifted uneasily from one foot to the other.

'Actually, I'd like to take a look at the engine. It was missing a bit on the way over, which sounds as if a little moisture has got into the Avgas. Last night was cooler than we've had and the supply tank I used to refuel was close to empty so there could have been some condensation in it.'

'Which means?' Caroline asked, pleased she hadn't heard the missing beat of the engine.

'I'll drain the tank—get an empty drum from the store to put it into—and refill the chopper tank here. We keep a small tanker of Avgas here because we often need to refuel, and it's useful if we're doing search-and-rescue work, which is co-ordinated from here.'

'How long?' Keanu asked.

'Three hours tops,' Jack replied cheerfully.

Three hours! They wouldn't be rushing the pregnant woman back to Wildfire.

Keanu introduced the local nurse, Nori, the name reminding Caroline they'd been at school together. They hugged and exchanged greetings, although Keanu broke up the very brief reunion with a reminder that they had a patient.

Their patient was standing in a corner of an examination room, bent over and clinging to the table. A large woman, it was hard to tell she was actually pregnant.

'Baby's coming,' she said as they came in. 'Soon.'

'Are you able to get up on the table so I can examine you?' Keanu asked in his deep, caring voice.

'No way! I'm not getting up there. The baby's coming now.'

Nori was plugging in the crib to warm the mattress in it, and fitting an oxygen tube to the inlet, so Caroline grabbed a small stool that seemed to have no apparent purpose and pulled it over so Keanu could squat on it while he felt the woman's stomach for the strength of the contractions.

Nori had laid out clean towels, gloves and various instruments on a trolley beside the table. Caroline put on gloves, took a towel, just in case the baby did come unexpectedly, and checked that suction tubes and scissors were among the instruments.

If the baby popped out limp, they would have to resuscitate it, but at least they had the humidicrib to keep it pink and warm on the way back to Wildfire.

Keanu was talking quietly to the woman in their own language, and Caroline knew enough of it to know it was mainly reassurance, although he slipped in a question from time to time. Apparently this was her sixth child, so she probably knew more about childbirth than either she or Keanu.

She was thinking this when the woman gave a loud cry and squatted lower, Caroline getting her hands down quickly enough as a watery mix of fluid rushed out.

The baby followed, straight into Caroline's waiting hands—sure and steady hands, although inside she was a mix of trepidation and elation.

The little one cried out, protesting her abrupt entry into the world but with her little fat hands clutching the umbilical cord as if she was ready to take on whatever it had to offer her.

Certainly not a thirty-week baby, more like thirty-six, perhaps even full term.

Keanu reached out a hand to help Caroline and her precious bundle up from the floor, then took the child and passed her to her mother.

The look of love and joy on the woman's face as the baby nuzzled at her breast brought tears to Caroline's eyes.

Keanu was clamping the cord, ready to cut it, but the woman took the scissors out of his hand.

'I do this for my babies,' she told him, cutting cleanly between the clamps.

She passed the baby back to Caroline, who put her down gently on the table on a warm sheet Nori had taken from the crib. Carefully, she wiped the tiny baby clean, suctioned her nostrils and mouth, Keanu taking over for the Apgar score, then Nori produced another warm sheet and Caroline swaddled the little girl, whose rosebud lips were pursing and opening like a goldfish's, instinct telling her she should be attached to her mother's breast.

Yet Caroline's arms felt reluctant as she passed the baby back, which was ridiculous.

As if arms even knew what reluctance was…

Nori led the woman to a comfortable armchair and said she'd take care of things from now.

Caroline made to argue but Keanu shook his head, just slightly, and led her out of the clinic.

'The islanders have their own rituals for disposing of the placenta,' he explained as they stood in the sun, feeling it warm on their skin after the cool of the air-conditioning inside. 'Before the hospital the islanders had their own midwife—sometimes two—who cared for all the pregnant women. When you and Christopher were born, your father called for one of these women but it was beyond her ability to save either Christopher from injury, or your mother. Your father then decided that all women should have their babies on the mainland and when young women went to the mainland for training as nurses, the midwives stopped passing on their skills.'

'But now?' Caroline asked. 'Seems to me someone having their sixth baby wouldn't have got the dates wrong—and then there's the baby who was in hospital when I arrived.'

'Exactly,' Keanu replied with a grin that made her stupid heart race. 'Now they have the hospital and helicopter as back-up, I think they've decided with a little cheating they can have an island birth. In fact, one of the local nurses is over in Sydney, doing some advanced midwifery training. It might not be traditional midwifery but at least, when she returns, the island women will have the option of staying here.'

'Which is wonderful,' Caroline declared, smiling herself at the remembered feel of the little baby dropping into her hands. 'So now?' she added, feeling that standing in the sun smiling inanely was probably making her look like an idiot. 'Can we go for a walk? It is so long since I was on Atangi, I need to get the feel and smell of the place back into my blood.'

Keanu swallowed a huge sigh.

He could hardly say no. The baby was fine and whatever was going on inside the clinic was islander business—and women's business at that.

The problem was that the look on Caro's face as she'd

stared in wonder at the baby she'd caught had stirred all kinds of uncomfortable thoughts in his mind, and unease in his body.

He'd felt tension from Caro's closeness the whole time they had been in the room and although he was professional enough to not let it affect him, now he wasn't fully focussed on something else, the awareness had grown.

It was because of the notebook, and something to do with sitting on the rock and feeling her hurt when he'd pointed out the flaws in her idea—feeling her disappointment, although she was smart enough to know it would never have worked. Up until then, he'd been able to explain away his physical reactions to her by the fact she was an attractive woman—nothing more than normal physical reactions.

But this was Caro…

'I *can* go for a walk by myself,' she said, obviously sensing his hesitation.

Get over it, he told himself.

'No, it'll be an hour before Jack finishes his refuelling,' he said to her. 'Why don't you wander down to the harbour while I go and see a couple of the elders about Alkiri's funeral?'

She hesitated, and he wondered if she was feeling the same awkwardness that was humming through his nerves.

'Come with me or I'll come with you,' she said quietly. 'Let's be friends again.'

He heard the plea in her voice and a faint tremor in the words caused a pain in his chest.

'Can we just be friends?' he asked.

Fire sparked in her eyes.

'Oh, for heaven's sake, Keanu, I don't know that any

more than you do. But there's stuff that needs to be done, things we can do to help the situation here, so surely we can get over all that's happened between us in the past and this inconvenient attraction business that's happening now and work together to make things better.'

She paused, then added in a quieter voice, 'Our friendship was special to me and, I think, to you. Maybe the reward for our efforts would be finding that again.'

He put his arm around her shoulders and drew her close although every functioning brain cell was yelling at him to keep his distance.

The lovely eyes he knew so well looked into his—wary and questioning.

'Our friendship was the most important thing in my life, Caro,' he admitted. 'That will never change.'

She half smiled and shifted so her body wasn't touching his—apart from his arm, which still rested on her shoulders.

'Thanks,' she said, and moved away completely, then in a tone that told him any emotional talk between them was done she added, 'Let's go and see the school first.'

But that was a mistake.

The first thing they noticed—everyone noticed—in the schoolyard was the huge old curtain fig tree, so called because air roots grew down from the branches, forming a thick curtain around the trunk.

And behind that curtain, like hundreds of children who'd attended the school over the years, they'd once shared a very chaste kiss. Her grandma had died and Caroline had known they'd both be off to mainland schools the following year, and for some reason—playing hide and seek most probably—they'd both ended up beneath the fig.

Not that an innocent kiss between a ten-year-old girl and a twelve-year-old boy meant much, but the memory sent a tingle up her spine.

'All the kids are in school,' Keanu murmured. 'Should we?'

Of course they shouldn't but she was ducking between the trailing roots right behind him, letting him take her in his arms, turn her towards him, and lift her head to his, to relive that first kiss.

In actual fact, it was nothing like that first kiss, more like a first kiss between two people attracted to each other and early on in the courtship.

Tentative, exploring, tasting and then tempting, Keanu felt heat rise in his body, and strained to keep things— well, not exactly casual, more noncommittal, if such a thing was possible.

When Caro began kissing him back as if her life depended on the joining of their lips, the contact of their tongues...

Or was it he who'd intensified things—he couldn't think straight, could barely think at all, except that there was no way he should be kissing Caro like this when his life was such a mess.

It was a silly, sentimental thing to do, but there was nothing silly or sentimental about the way their lips met, the teasing invasion of Keanu's tongue, her own tangling with it, the heat in his body as her hands pushed up his shirt to touch his skin, no doubt matched by the heat in hers as his hand slid down her neck towards her breast.

A hundred questions jumbled in her head. Was this just attraction? Or perhaps leftover love from their youth? And hadn't attraction led her into trouble with Steve? No, she could answer that one honestly—it had been his attention to her that had made her lose her head with Steve.

But this kiss—this kiss was different. This kiss was amazing—

So why was she so bamboozled?

'Damn it all!'

The explosive words broke the spell.

'I thought we were trying to be friends,' he muttered, taking her hand and almost dragging her out from under the tree. 'Do you realise I could have made love to you right there under the tree with half of Atangi walking by? Why on earth would you kiss me back like that?'

'Oh, so it's all my fault?' Caroline retorted. 'Anyway, we're both adults and if we feel like it, why shouldn't we kiss?'

She could feel the heat in her cheeks, the disappointment and relief battling for supremacy in her body.

Not that he'd know it because she was stalking away from him, throwing back over her shoulder, 'Anyway, it was your fault—you started it!'

But hearing the words they'd flung at each other so often in childhood fights, she felt a deep sorrow for all they'd lost...

Or had they?

What about the friendship they'd decided to rediscover?

'Nice walk?' Nori asked brightly when they returned to the clinic, any further exploration totally forgotten.

'It had its moments,' Caroline replied, then proceeded to ask Nori about her family, marital status and children, a conversation that lasted until Jack returned to tell them they could head back to Wildfire.

* * *

Not interested in the brilliance Nori's three-year-olds were already showing, Keanu had moved into the theatre to check their patient. She was dozing in the big chair, the baby sleeping against her breast.

The sight brought unexpected emotion welling up inside him, bringing a thickness to his throat.

Time he was out of there…

'Coming back with us?' Keanu said to Caro, who was still deep in a conversation about Nori's children.

Which made him wonder as she said, 'Yes, sir!' and followed him out of the clinic, why she'd never married the Steve guy and had children of her own.

Apart from their medical ambitions, if he remembered rightly they had been going to get married and have ten children.

Ten?

'Did you know Nori has six children—three sets of twins?'

Keanu shook his head. She'd been talking to Nori— talking about children—so it was a fairly innocuous thing for Caro to have said. But coming right on top of the thick throat and his memory of the past, it shook him. There were far too many things going on his head that he didn't want her picking up on, although he wouldn't have minded having a few clues about her thoughts.

Fortunately, by the time they arrived back on Wildfire he had an excuse to escape. He had to concentrate on the arrangements for Alkiri's funeral and the first thing on the list was to try entry to the research station via the gate, and get permission from whoever was in charge.

Should he ask Caroline to accompany him?

She'd been anxious to know what was happening at the station but walking with her through the scented tropical dusk with her was too much to contemplate.

He went in to see Sam, inevitably battling paperwork in his office, to check he wasn't needed at the hospital.

'You're free to go, mate,' Sam told him, 'and I've already got their okay. In fact, the bloke who's the foreman down there actually contacted me to see if I'd like to come down and see the laboratories, and I asked him about the longhouse. But if you want to check it out, just explain who you are to the gate people. Sounded to me that, now they've finished, they're happy to have people see what they've achieved.'

Sam's eyes slid away from his, and Keanu turned to see Caroline standing there.

'You want to go with Keanu and see the renovations down the road?'

'We're allowed in?' She sounded so delighted Keanu could hardly say he didn't want her with him.

'As of today,' Sam was assuring her.

At least she wouldn't be wearing a wet shift, Keanu told himself, but somehow that wasn't comforting at all. She'd been in the same mid-calf pants and uniform shirt when they'd kissed under the tree…

The foreman's name was Bill and he was at the gate talking to the guard there when Keanu and Caroline arrived.

'Sorry about the fence, but the boss wanted the place secure—or as secure as anything can be with so much beach frontage. It was mainly to keep out adventurous kids during the building process, and the fences and guard will remain because the laboratories will have some evil chemicals in them. Not that they won't be locked as well, and I imagine there'd be more kids coming by boat than down from the hospital, but what he says goes.'

'Who is he?' Caroline asked, so excited to be 'invited' to the station that she was barely registering Keanu by her side.

Well, almost barely.

'Some fellow from the Middle East apparently. I get my orders from his—what do they call him?—Australasian manager. He's from the Middle East as well, but speaks English the same way the Queen does.'

Caroline smiled. Children from all over the world were educated in top English public schools so undoubtedly all of them spoke 'like the Queen does'.

Keanu was talking to Bill, so Caroline dawdled behind them, trying to identify all the different scents. She saw the jasmine creeping up the fence—soon it would be smothered—and the broad leaves of the ginger plant, their drooping white bulb-like flowers giving out what was probably her favourite perfume. Or did she prefer the frangipani that was dominant now—?

'You with us?' Keanu asked, and she realised how far she'd fallen back. He and Bill were at the door of the newly renovated and freshly painted laboratory block.

She caught up as Bill unlocked the door, and she gasped at the difference. Admittedly, it had been thirteen years since she'd been in the lab—back when she'd had her last holiday here with Keanu and Helen.

After they left it had never been the same and she'd used the excuse of spending more time with Christopher to avoid island holidays.

'It's been completely redone,' Keanu was saying. 'No

wonder Sam's so excited about it. But do you know if there are people booking to come here to use it?'

Bill shook his head.

'Not my department, but we have been hurrying to finish everything and be out of the way because the boss—the big boss—is planning some kind of exclusive, very clever scientists' get-together some time soon.'

They went to check the longhouse next, and once again Caroline could only gape in amazement. Rebuilt in the style of the island meeting places, thatched roof—probably with something underneath the palm thatching to stop it leaking—and open on all sides, it was finished with the best of materials, with cedar benches polished to a glowing shine, weavings hanging from the rafters, mats and cushions strewn around the floor. It was an island longhouse for today and for the future.

'It's totally awesome,' she said, shaking her head because it was hard to take it all in.

'And we can use it for Alkiri's funeral feast?' Keanu asked, as if he already knew this had been agreed.

'Sure thing,' Bill said. 'It will be a good test of the fire pits.'

'It's even got fire pits?'

She sounded so incredulous both men smiled, but she followed them beyond the building where, sure enough, a deep pit had been dug with a more shallow one beside it, big stones, firewood and white sand stored neatly in the bottom of open wooden cupboard-like structures beside it.

'We've had some of the local community here, doing the mats and cushions, and they told us about the fire pits. A big one for the fire that heats the stones, then a shallower one for the stones to go into when they're hot, baskets for the food and bags and sand to cover it all up. Have we got it right?'

He was obviously anxious, but Keanu clapped him on the back and said, 'Fantastic, mate, it's just fantastic.'

Caroline had opened one of the top cupboards and found the baskets for the food stacked inside it. The next one held the sacks that would wet and placed across the food before the lot was covered with sand to keep the heat in and help the meal steam-cook.

The thought that she'd actually be here and celebrating with a *hangi* made her turn to Keanu in delight.

'Won't it be great? It's so long since we've been to a *hangi*!'

'Great if we don't have to cook it,' Keanu reminded her, but Bill assured them both that local staff had already been employed for the station and they were bringing in more people for the celebration of Alkiri's life the following day.

'Apparently people will come from all the islands, and as we're leaving soon, it will be kind of a reward for our workers to be here for the party.'

Bill hesitated then added, 'Although that sounds a bit rough, partying when someone's dead.'

'Not here,' Keanu assured him. 'Here we celebrate a life that enriched all who knew him—or her if it's a woman's funeral.'

Bill seemed content, but Caroline considered what he'd said.

Had *she* enriched anyone's life?

She rather doubted it.

Christopher's maybe.

He'd certainly enriched hers, getting through each day of pain and illness with a smile always ready on his face for her or their father. During the 'Steve years' as she was starting to think of them, she'd seen less of her brother and really regretted it. Love, or what she'd thought was love, had made her selfish.

They were walking back up to the hospital while these thoughts coursed through her head.

'You okay?' Keanu asked, and she realised she'd dropped behind again, drifting through the past.

Which, considering the confusion she was feeling in *his* presence, might have been a safer place.

'Fine,' she lied, and hurried to catch up with him.

CHAPTER EIGHT

IT WAS A day without end, or so it seemed to Caroline when they returned to the hospital.

'Would you mind keeping an eye on things while Keanu, Hettie and I have some dinner?' Sam greeted her. 'Hettie's cooking because Vailea's already preparing for the funeral feast and there's stuff the three of us have to go over, including juggling the roster for the funeral tomorrow.'

'No worries,' Caroline assured him, 'though you'd better tell me what to do in an emergency. Do I go to the back door and yell?'

'Oh, you don't know the system? Of course not, you've barely arrived and we haven't stopped working you. See the panel by the door? It was an ingenious idea worked out by your father. You hit the blue button for me—it rings in my room—the green for Hettie—and the red that will clang all through the villas for all hands on deck.'

'No fire alarm?' Caroline teased, and Sam pointed to the regulation fire alarm box set beside the panel.

'Open that one and press the button and they'll hear you over on Atangi! And the village will have men here almost as fast as the staff can get here. The hospital's very important to all the islanders—and they've your father to thank for that.'

Caroline thought the conversation was over, until Sam added, almost under his breath, 'Although we'd prefer to be thanking him in person.'

'My father loves the island. All M'Langi. I can hear it in his voice when he talks about it, asks questions. But my mother's death, and Christopher... It seems he blamed himself, and now he says both the hospital and Christopher need him more on the mainland. Over there he can keep a watch on Christopher's care and also make money and lobby for money to keep this place going.'

Sam sighed and departed, but the conversation had brought Caroline's mind back to the problems at the mine. Of course mortgaging half a house had been a stupid idea, but Keanu hadn't come up with anything better.

Keanu...

The kiss...

Setting the past and the future firmly out of her mind, she went into the big ward, where she discovered that the boys with the coral cuts had been released. The woman with unstable diabetes was sleeping once again, as was their patient with the Biruli ulcer. The woman with the baby had also gone, so all she had to do was hang around in case she was needed.

And use the time to try to sort out the mess inside her head.

Start with the mine—there had to be *some* way...

But how could she think when she was hungry? She headed for the kitchen, where she found several salads made up in the main refrigerator.

'Staff salads,' the note attached to the shelf said, so

she took one, went back into the desk in the ward to keep an eye on her patients and ate it there.

Thinking, almost subconsciously, of the grandparents she'd barely known.

How terrible for them to have lost their daughter—their only child—so far away from home. Max had flown his wife's body back to Sydney to be buried there, and had taken first his babies, and later his toddlers—well, Christopher had never actually toddled—to visit their grandparents.

But both of them had been dead before Caroline was six so it was difficult for her to summon up more than an image of a defeated-looking old man and woman.

Defeated by grief, she'd realised, much later.

'Are you okay? You must be tired. I can take over here if you like.'

Keanu's arrival interrupted her unhappy thoughts.

'No way. I have a feeling if I handed over, or even had you standing by, it would reinforce everyone's opinion of the worthlessness of all Lockharts.'

Keanu smiled, something she wished he wouldn't do, at least when she was around.

'Hettie will be over soon and she'll stay until Mina comes on, but I can at least hang around and keep you company. I'm being Maddie this week and she was on call so I might as well be here.'

He pulled a chair over from beside the wall and sat beside her at the small desk, far too close.

Caroline managed to manoeuvre her chair a little farther away from him but he was still too close. She could feel the force-field of him, as if the very air around him had taken on his essence. It was because of the kiss—

she knew that. It had done something to her nerves and spun threads of confusion through her head.

'I talked to your father,' he said, startling her out of thoughts of kisses and physical closeness. 'He can't get over at the moment but has asked me to make sure the mine is closed, at least temporarily until he gets a chance to look at things and maybe get it going again.'

'*You* talked to Dad?'

'I thought it might be easier, the mine closure, coming from me and not a Lockhart. I know how distressed you are about the damage Ian's done to the family name.'

Caroline turned so she could study him.

'And you think you telling them will make a difference? It's still the Lockhart mine, and with everyone connected to it now losing their incomes, of course the blame will come back on the Lockharts.'

She was so upset she had to stand up—to move—pacing up and down the silent ward while her mind churned.

It was the right thing to do—she knew that. It was far too dangerous for the miners to keep working without the tunnel being shored up.

'I'll do it,' she said, suddenly weary of the whole mess, and when Keanu started to argue she even found a tired smile.

'Best all the blame lands on us,' she told him. 'We don't want everyone hating you as well.'

Keanu shot up from his chair and took her hands.

'No one will ever blame you, Caroline,' he said, and the feel of her hands in his—the security of her slim fingers being held by his strong ones—fired all her senses once again.

She eased away from him.

'I have patients to check, and it's probably best if you go, because it's too easy to be distracted when you're around.'

'Really?'

He smiled as if she'd given him a very special gift, then leaned forward to peck her cheek before leaving the room.

Keanu went back to his quarters but was too restless to settle down. His phone call to Max, the closing of the mine and his still-vague idea of how to save it, his increasing attraction to Caroline—all were drawing him further and further into the web that was the Lockharts.

He couldn't help but think of his mother, so humiliated by Ian.

Probably already ill, she'd never really overcome their banishment from the island. It was as if Ian's words had left an enduring scar in her mind, and poison in her body. In his mother's mind, the happy Lockhart days had gone, and the stories of the Lockharts taking her in after her own family had disowned her and her husband had died had been long forgotten.

Almost without orders from his brain, his feet took him back out of the villa that was currently his home and up the hill to the grassy slope behind the big house to where his father was buried among dead Lockharts and other islanders who'd lived and worked on Wildfire.

To the grassy slope where Alkiri would be laid to rest tomorrow…

Keanu sat down by his father's grave, idly pulling a few weeds that had recently appeared, trying desperately, as he often did, to remember his father.

But memories of a two-year-old were dim and not particularly reliable so all he had were the stories his mother had told over the years.

His father, bright star of the school on Atangi, had been sent to the mainland for his high-school education, all the costs met by the Lockhart family. From boarding school he'd gone on to university, studying science, and returning, with the woman he'd met and fallen in love with, to Wildfire to work at the research station and begin the first investigation into the properties of M'Langi tea.

His mother's tales had told of their early adventures, the two of them roaming the mountains on the uninhabited islands, in search of the special tree from whose bark and leaves the tea was made.

He'd been two years old when his father, working with a local friend, had been killed by a rockfall on an outer island.

Two years old when his mother and he had moved into the comfortable, self-contained annexe off the big Lockhart house. It was only after Caroline and Christopher were born, and their mother died, that old Mrs Lockhart had offered his mother a job—helping with the baby and generally running the house.

'I thought I might find you here.'

Caroline's voice startled him out of his reverie.

'What are you doing? What about your patients?'

'Hettie sent me home. Sam's just checked our patients and decided Mina can manage them.'

She sank down beside him on the grass.

'When I came back to work at the hospital,' he told her, 'I brought my mother's ashes here and scattered them in the grass.'

'So she and your father could be together.'

Caroline spoke quietly, a statement, not a question.

She rested her hand gently on his shoulder, and his skin burned beneath the touch, his body warring with his mind, wanting her so badly, yet here, beside his mother—

He *had* to tell Caro.

Now, before anything went any further...

But she was so damned insecure, wouldn't his marriage—for all it was over now—seem like a further betrayal?

Hurt her as much as his deserting her had?

She slid her hand down his arm to grasp his fingers.

'Come on,' she said, 'let's visit my mother now.'

They'd done this so often as children, coming to the little cemetery, sitting among the graves, talking to her mother and his father, telling them what they'd been doing, laughing, and sometimes crying.

They reached Charlotte Lockhart's memorial—a simple stone with her name and the words 'wife and mother'—Max having given the initial of her name to both her children.

'Hold me,' Caroline whispered, and Keanu put his arms around her and drew her close, feeling her softness, her breasts against his chest, long silky hair tickling his neck, covering his hands that now held her to him.

She raised her head, and he caught the glisten of tears in her eyes.

Her eyes were shadowed with memories, and not happy ones. This was Caro, so he kissed them, first one and then the other, his lips sliding to her temple, teeth nibbling at her ear lobe, kisses along her jaw, although her mouth—that wide, sensual mouth—had always been his destination.

Or so it seemed as he tasted her, his tongue sliding around her lips, delving, probing.

Had her mouth opened to him?

Were her lips responding?

For a moment it seemed as if she might have been a statue, then, with a groan that started somewhere down near her toes, she kissed him back, her mouth moving on his, her hands exploring his shoulders, arms, neck, gripping at his hair, his head, holding his mouth to hers as if her life depended on it.

They were in a graveyard.

His parents were here…

Somehow his lips had slipped lower, kissing her neck, while she pressed hers against his head and murmured his name. His hand had slid beneath her shirt, found a breast, a full breast that felt heavy in his hand. His thumb strayed across the nipple, already peaked by the heat of the kiss.

She'd dragged his head back to kiss his lips, so he gave in and let her, matched the heat of her kisses, and the little moan she gave as his fingers teased the taut nipple was like honey in his mouth.

Had his legs given way that he was on his knees, still holding Caroline, their bodies pressed together? Moonlight cast shadows from the trees around the graveyard, picked out writing on the stone beside which they knelt.

Charlotte Lockhart.

Wife and mother…

Wife!

'This is crazy,' he whispered as he eased himself away from Caroline, his body throbbing with need, hers hot within his hands, which had settled on her shoulders. 'I'm sorry, there's something I should have said—told you—have to tell you.'

Blue-green eyes—dazed with desire?—stared at him and she shook her head, as if trying to take in his stumbling words.

She released the grip she'd had on his shirt, raised her hands to lift his off her shoulders, then bowed her head so the hair on the top of her head brushed against his chest.

He saw her shoulders move as she took a deep breath, then she lifted her head and looked at him, into his eyes, hers questioning now but so beautiful.

Too beautiful to hurt?

Perhaps he could contact his lawyer first, before he told her, find out the situation…

Coward!

He took her hands in his and eased her back down onto the ground.

'So tell,' she said quietly.

But words wouldn't come. *I'm married* seemed too blunt, far too hurtful.

'It's about attraction,' he finally began. 'About attraction and love and how there can be one without the other but how do you know at the beginning?'

'Are you talking about our attraction?' she asked, her head turned not to him but towards the distant sea, so all he could see was her profile—no emotion…

'Not really but in a way, yes, and I should have told you earlier. I should have told you when it happened—but we'd been apart so long and I really didn't know how to. And I certainly should have told you before I kissed you.'

Now she turned to him.

'It's something bad, isn't it? You're already married, or engaged? I should have guessed. Why wouldn't you be?'

She went to rise, but he caught her hand and kept her on the grass beside him.

'Married but separated for five years,' he finally admitted. 'It was attraction, nothing more, but we didn't discover that until after we were married. We weren't exactly virgins, but Mum's greatest pain, later when she did eventually talk about Ian, was that she'd lost her moral compass—the ethical code by which she'd always lived. And that was in my mind—some half-formed ethical code that said if we were having sex we should get married. We'd met at uni, as physio and medical students—our paths crossed often—and the attraction was definitely there. Marriage seemed a great idea, but something didn't gel. We didn't fight, we didn't hurt each other, we just kind of drifted in different directions and in the end sat down and talked about it and agreed it had been a mistake.'

He ran out of words and leaned back on his elbows, looking up at the silvery moon above them.

'Where is she?' Caro asked.

He shrugged.

'She went to Melbourne. We didn't keep in touch, nor did we get around to divorcing. I don't know why— perhaps because it seemed like admitting what a huge mistake we'd made. Anyway, a couple of months ago she contacted me, told me she wanted a divorce and sent the papers. She'd met someone else, sounded so happy I was pleased for her, so I signed the papers. They'll go before a judge some time soon, then a month and a day later I won't be married any more.'

Caroline had sat, stunned into silence, as Keanu told his tale. Somehow, in all her thoughts of Keanu over the years, the fact that he might marry had never occurred to her.

Not that it should matter, but obviously it did, because her heart was hurting, and her throat was tight, and what she really wanted to do was hit out at him.

But why shouldn't he have married?

Wouldn't she have married Steve if he hadn't dumped her when the mine had gone bad?

'Did you think of me at all?'

She wasn't sure where the question had come from, but heard it make its way out of her dry mouth.

'Only every minute of the ceremony, which is when I realised how wrong it all was. But I put that aside, and gave the marriage all I had, Caro. Moral compass stuff again. We were friends as well as lovers and I didn't want to hurt her.'

Now Caroline was sorry she'd asked the question, sorry about so much, but the pain in her heart remained and she knew she had to get away—think about this, work out why now, when it was all over, it was hurting her.

Why his being married was so ridiculously hurtful, especially as he wasn't really married at all…

And shouldn't he have told her all this before they'd kissed—the first time, not the last time?

Even if he wasn't *married* married, shouldn't it have been mentioned in passing?

She touched his shoulder as she stood up, then made her way up to the house, her mind so full of conjecture it felt too heavy for her neck.

Vaguely recalling, through a foggy haze of lust and shock, that Keanu had mentioned something about her being on duty at six, Caroline got herself out of bed, dressed, ate a lamington Bessie had apparently baked the previous day, drank a glass of milk and headed down to the hospital.

This time of the year, it was light by five in the morning, but half an hour later than that the morning still had a pearly glow and the sound of the birds waking up, the calm sea beyond the rainforest, and a sense of the world coming alive with a fresh new morning filled her with unexpected happiness.

True, there were problems but right now nothing, but nothing, seemed insurmountable.

Inevitably, Hettie was already there, in spite of Caroline being twenty minutes early.

'Anahera's off duty today and will be helping her mother with preparations for Alkiri's funeral. In fact, the fire's already been started in the fire pit.'

Fire? Fire pit?

The words seemed hard to understand in a hospital, until Carolyn remembered where she was and what was happening today—a funeral and funeral feast.

'Keanu's also gone down to the research station to help set everything up,' Hettie added. 'I'll take a look at the young lad with the ulcer before I hand over. I don't think the medication is working. I'll talk to Sam about changing the combination, but watch him carefully and if there's any sign of fever get Sam or Keanu here immediately.'

The diabetic patient was up and dressed.

'Doesn't want to miss the funeral feast,' Hettie said dryly. 'I'll sign her out later.'

She turned to Caroline.

'Okay, so you'll only have one patient, but that's largely because everyone knows we're short-staffed and puts off coming to see us, either here or at the island clinics. But our one patient needs all the care we can give him, never forget that, and if you don't get one or two coming up from the feast with burnt toes or cut fingers I'd be very surprised. Apparently, the festivities kick off at ten—well, the funeral part, anyway.'

She paused, then added, 'I understand Alkiri was a friend of yours and you'd really like to be there, but the foreman wants to show Sam and me the laboratories—showing off, I suppose—and Keanu's doing the oration so he has to be there. Our second aide will be here with you. Her shift doesn't begin until eight, but if there's any problem at all, phone me or Sam—our cell numbers are by the phone in the main office.'

Caroline took it all in, and much as her heart longed to be there to say goodbye to Alkiri, she knew being left here was a sign of her acceptance. Lockhart or not, Hettie was trusting her.

What Caroline hadn't realised was that the statement—'Anahera is helping her mother with the celebration feast'—meant Vailea was not in the kitchen. Apparently, nurses here made and served breakfast to their patients when called upon to do so.

Vailea—bless her heart, or perhaps her organisational skills—had a list of all meals up on a corkboard near the door. Not only were the meal menus there, but they had the requisite 'GF' for gluten free, and a little heart beside ones suggested for heart patients.

Back to her patients—checking their notes: no dietary restrictions for either of them.

According to—

'How are you doing?'

Keanu was there, right behind her.

'I thought you were busy with the *hangi*,' she said,

needing to say something as an almost overwhelming rush of what could only be lust weakened her knees.

She was *still* feeling that lust thing?

He was married!

And he hadn't told her.

Anyway, might he not be right about the dangers of attraction, which was just a weaker word for lust?

And shouldn't she show *some* reaction to this information?

But what?

'Too many cooks,' he said lightly, and she had to grapple her way back through her thoughts to where the conversation had started. 'I'm not needed until a lot later. I'm doing the oration.'

The lightness vanished from his voice with the last sentence, and yet again Caroline's first instinct was to hug him.

But hugs led to—

Well, trouble.

Change the subject.

'You've been down to check? They've got the fire going?'

He nodded, so close now she could see the smooth golden skin of his face—the strong chin he must have shaved extra-carefully this morning.

And being that close, *he* must be able to see she was having difficulty breathing.

She ducked behind a table, and he stood opposite her. 'And?'

'The women are hanging flower leis and putting huge baskets of leaves all around the place. It's really beautiful, Caro.'

'Sounds lovely but I've got to get breakfasts,' she managed, although her mind was on the kiss they'd shared the previous evening, not bacon and eggs.

'I know,' he said, his voice husky, his eyes unreadable. 'I really wanted to tell you I went down to see Reuben this morning just to confirm the order to close the mine.'

The broad shoulders that had felt so solid beneath her hands lifted in a shrug.

'I said it was a health and safety issue and, as a doctor overseeing that, I had the authority to issue the shutdown notice.'

Caroline sighed.

'That was silly. You've put yourself into the firing line of the workers' anger now. They already hate the Lockhart name, so what harm could a little more hate do? And as it's Ian's fault that the mine's in the state it's in, it's a Lockhart issue anyway.'

Keanu's sigh was almost as deep as her own.

'We'll just have to wait and see,' he said quietly. 'Reuben's going to get someone in from Atangi to fence the site and he was going to tell the small crew still working as soon as I was out of sight.'

'So they wouldn't rend you limb from limb?' Caroline queried, although she couldn't find even the slightest of smiles to go with the suggestion.

'Probably,' Keanu agreed. 'But it's done now, so that's one less thing for you to worry about. Let's get started on these breakfasts.'

He'd done it so she could stop worrying about it?

'Weren't you talking about making breakfasts?'

One word, and a practical one at that, yet tingles still ran down her spine.

'Of course. I've only got two and shortly I'll be down to one patient, but would you mind asking them what they fancy for breakfast? Vailea's left a list—there's scrambled, boiled or fried eggs, bacon, baked beans, toast and jam, and I think there's cereal.'

'I might have to have the lot to wake me up,' he said before turning and walking out of the kitchen.

To wake him up?

It hadn't been *that* late when they'd parted.

So, had he, like she, lain awake long into the night, rethinking the kiss?

Or had he been thinking about his marriage?

About his wife?

Though perhaps he'd been worried about the mine closure and his decision to be the one to tell Reuben? Kept awake by things that had nothing at all to do with the heated, almost desperate kiss and the discussion that had followed it.

CHAPTER NINE

FINDING THE RATHER large kitchen altogether too small to share with Caro, Keanu delivered the breakfast orders and departed, excusing himself by explaining he wanted to change the dressings on the Buruli ulcer, which was causing both him and Sam a lot of concern.

It wasn't responding to the medication, the young lad was in severe pain and the flesh was continuing to deteriorate, as was the lad's general condition.

'Are you sure nothing got into it before you came in here?' he asked as he deadened the area around the wound to clean it yet again.

'Could have.' A shrug strengthened the typical boy reply.

'Like what?' Keanu asked, but all he got that time was a shake of his head.

He put the new dressing on the wound, wrote up stronger painkillers and was departing when the young aide, having just started on duty, brought in the breakfast tray.

Time he was gone, yet his feet led him to the kitchen.

'Hettie tells me she'll be here just before ten so you can come down to the longhouse.'

All he got for a reply was a frown, although eventually she must have summoned up enough courage to speak.

'I—um—I'm not sure, Keanu. I really don't like funerals—even the island celebratory ones. I hate that people say all the nice things about someone after they're dead and can't hear them. Why don't people tell them that stuff before they die?'

Keanu moved across the kitchen towards her and put his arms around her.

'You did tell him, Caroline, when we sat with him before he died. He knew how much he meant to you and if you don't want to come down, of course you shouldn't. I guess Hettie just assumed you would want to.'

He felt her body rest against his and tension drain from it. He longed to kiss her, but now he knew where kisses led…

He shouldn't have come close enough to touch her, let alone give her a hug, at least until they'd had time to talk about last night's revelations. About how she felt, about whether it mattered at the moment that he was still married…

So he let his lips brush the soft, golden hair on the top of her head and eased away from her.

'I'll bring you some food later,' he said, and got out of the place before the regret that he *hadn't* kissed her overcame his common sense.

The longhouse was busier than he'd expected, and he could pick out people from every inhabited island in the group. The harbour down at the mine would be crowded with boats and the old truck would have been ferrying locals from there to the research station all morning.

Someone had put a row of chairs at one end of the building, and he and the elders took their places there. The crowd grew quiet when he spoke, talking with love of the man he'd known—the young, strong man who'd been a master boatman, often called upon to rescue people who had foolishly put out to sea when the weather was bad.

He reminded his people of some of the history of M'Langi that Alkiri had passed on to him, true tales and folklore, fascinating stories for two story-hungry youngsters.

And finally he asked for others to speak, and speak they did. A flood of reminiscences followed, first the elders, then ordinary people whose lives Alkiri had touched.

Swallowing a lump of emotion as he listened, he was almost glad Caro wasn't here. Always a softie, she'd have been in floods of tears by now.

Caro…

A disturbance of some kind at the back of the long-house brought him out of his reverie—useless reverie, in fact.

There were raised voices, angry voices, then one of the men departed, maybe told to leave by someone senior to them.

But the bits and pieces of talk he'd heard suggested the man was going to the hospital. He could see Hettie and Sam sitting with the works foreman, Hettie having obviously returned when Caroline had explained she wasn't coming down.

Caroline!

The man was a miner…

With a very hasty excuse to the nearest elder he departed, following the man up the hill, hurrying to catch up, to get in front of him.

He recognised him.

Definitely one of the miners he'd seen the other day.

He called to him but in spite of the early hour the man had probably been drinking and nothing could make him deviate from his determined path.

Keanu was close on the miner's heels when he reached the gate near the airstrip and there Keanu diverted from the miner's path, taking the back way, which he knew was shorter, running now, his heart thudding in his chest, reaching the hospital and racing in, calling for Caro.

He must have looked and sounded like a madman because she reached out her hand and rested it on his arm.

'Calm down, Keanu, tell me what's up.'

'Go back to the house—no, he'll go there next. Go out the back. My villa is the lowest one. Go inside and lock the door.'

He could hear the man by now, ranting about the closure, and knew how close he must be.

'Go now,' he said to her, but she stood her ground, wanting an explanation.

The phone broke their stalemate and she answered it, turning back to him to say, 'That was Hettie to tell you Sam and some of the young men are on their way. On their way where? What's happening?'

But it was too late for explanations. The angry man was already on the hospital steps, his voice crying out for a Lockhart and, woman or not, any Lockhart would do.

'I can't have them coming in here—there are patients, well, one patient. I'll go out and see him.'

Keanu grabbed her shoulders as she started to move past him, pulling her back, thrusting her towards the kitchen.

'At least go in there and lock the door. *I'll* talk to him!'

He turned away, sure the man wouldn't hurt a woman,

yet only half sure. Who knew what a man made brave by cava might do?

'She's not here,' he said, meeting the man on the veranda. 'And she's not up at the house so don't bother looking there. Anyway, I'm the one who closed the mine, and it was for the safety of all the miners. It's a temporary measure until we find some money to give everyone their back-pay and start things up again.'

'That's what you say, Keanu, but for all your closeness you're not a Lockhart and we all know what *they* can do.'

The man pushed forward, but Keanu blocked the doorway.

'This is a hospital, not a boxing ring,' he reminded them. 'Let's talk about this in the garden.'

No one moved—well, the man threw a punch, which missed Keanu's jaw by a whisker but still served to fire his anger.

He hit back, knocking the culprit down the steps.

It had been stupid. He knew that immediately, because now he'd made the man look foolish, and that had angered him even more. He righted himself and pressed forward again and this time the punch that was thrown connected, knocking Keanu sideways against the doorjamb. He'd barely straightened when he felt a shove from behind, and Caroline stood there, hands on her hips and fury in her eyes.

'That's enough!' she said. 'Keanu's right, this is a hospital. And you are right as well—it *was* a Lockhart who brought the troubles on you. But he was one bad apple. Do you think I'm not as upset as you all are?'

The answer was another roar of anger. Keanu spun Caroline behind him.

'Go and protect the patients—lock the ward doors if you can, or put furniture against them.'

Would she do it?

No time to find out but somehow he had to protect her.

'Caroline's right about the one bad apple,' he said to the man who still loomed on the steps. 'But he's gone now and I know the Lockharts are doing all they can to fix things, Caroline in particular.'

'The mine's closed—what can *she* do?'

'Find the money to get the mine started again, to pay the wages you're all owed. But in the meantime, think of the other things the Lockhart family has done for you— and will continue to do in the future. You've got kids. If you chase them off, and the hospital closes, where do you go when one of your kids is stung by a stonefish? And what job will you have if you don't allow us time to get the mine operating again?'

It had certainly quietened him down.

'Now move away, we don't want trouble here.'

The new voice made them turn. Sam was there and with him a group of elders and young men, very strong young men.

'Shame on you,' the senior of the elders said. 'You do something like this on a day when one of our most re-vered friends is being laid to rest. And now the feast is ready—let us celebrate his life.'

The fight seemed to ooze out of the man, although Keanu wondered if he might return.

Or worse, raid the house while Caroline slept in-side it…

CHAPTER TEN

Sam returned to the celebration. As guest of the resort foreman he had to stay for the feast, but Hettie insisted on remaining at the hospital.

'You go down,' she said to Caroline, who shook her head.

'Go down there where people hate the very mention of my name? I know that lout was drunk, but he was probably expressing the sentiments of most of the community. I doubt if anything will ever restore our name, given the amount of damage Ian's done—and I only know little scraps of it.'

'Something will work out,' Hettie said, but with so little conviction Caroline knew she was only being kind.

She probably didn't think much of the Lockhart family herself.

And who could blame her?

'Then I'll just head up to the house,' she said to Hettie, thinking she'd phone her father just to talk to him, to ask about Christopher, then...

Get back to the books.

'You will not go up to the house,' Hettie said firmly. 'Not until Keanu, or Jack or Sam are here to go with you, and then only to get whatever you need, then you can come back down here and stay in one of the empty nurses' villas.'

It bothered Caroline that even Hettie was being protective. Surely there wasn't that much risk.

Well, she could forget the phone call, but she had to do something.

And surely all this fuss was overdone...

Hettie had disappeared so Caroline slipped out of the hospital, taking the back path up to the house in case the angry man was still lurking around. It took her only minutes to collect what she wanted, then she headed back down the track, not to one of the nurses' villas but to Keanu's place.

Somehow she knew she'd be safe in Keanu's place.

The door was unlocked and as she entered and looked around, she had to smile. Helen had insisted they both keep their rooms neat and tidy and it was obvious the rule had stuck with Keanu for longer than it had stuck with her.

The little place was neat and functional. The design offered a largish room with a sitting space, a dining space and beyond that the kitchen. Off that, to the right, was the bedroom, complete with double bed—did married couples often choose to work here?

She smiled to herself at the naivety of the thought. Of course there were likely to be relationships among staff working in such an isolated place. Wasn't Jack hoping to win over the beautiful Anahera?

But going into Keanu's bedroom and what was presumably a bathroom off it was a step too far, so she dumped the little notebook and laptop on the dining table.

And sat down to do some work.

She still didn't have the running costs of the mine but

Reuben would know, or once she found Peter she could get a rough figure from him. Where they'd get the money she didn't have a clue, but somehow she had to do this. She made up neat lists. The back pay she could put a figure against but superannuation had a question mark, as had running costs. And she'd have to work out how much pay was owed to Bessie and Harold.

On top of that, if she was going to continue to live at the house, she should check what food was there. The next flight was Friday—she should order supplies…

As she paused, considering what to do next, she heard the music from the longhouse. It flowed through her blood and sent her fingers tapping until she stood up and began to move. She would never have the lithe grace of the islanders but she couldn't help swaying her hips to the rhythm of the music.

Keanu had teased her…

Had she summoned him up by thought wave that he appeared in the doorway? She stopped her movement immediately before he teased her again.

'Don't tell me you've actually done what you were told,' he said, then he looked at the book and laptop on the table. 'Well, not entirely, you obviously went up to the house to get those and I'll bet no one went with you.'

'Everyone's back at the party—I was quite safe,' she retorted, then sniffed the air and looked at the basket he carried in one hand.

'You've brought food? Oh, Keanu, thank you. It is so long since I tasted *hangi* meat and vegetables.'

She pushed the laptop to one end of the small table and hurried into the kitchen area, finding plates on her second foray into the cupboards and cutlery in the top drawer she expected it to be in.

Keanu had taken a cloth off the top of the delicacies in the basket and the aromas made Caroline's mouth water.

He divided the food onto the two plates, stopping when she protested it was too much. But the delicious, tender pork, the taro and potatoes disappeared from her plate in no time, conversation forgotten as the food took them back to happier times when they'd often attended island feasts.

'Were you dancing as I came in?' Keanu asked when she'd pushed her plate away unfinished, and he'd slowed down his eating enough to talk.

'Maybe moving just a little,' she admitted. 'As you've told me so many times, girls with European blood can't dance.'

He smiled, remembering, as she had been, and sadness for those lost days filled her soul.

Keanu read the sadness in her eyes and knew what she was thinking.

'Our childhood was truly blessed,' he said quietly.

He set down his knife and fork and pushed his plate away, but as Caroline stood up to take it, he reached out and took her hand, closing his fingers around hers.

Just that touch sent messages he didn't want to acknowledge streaming through his body, but he needed to say what he had to say.

'I want you to stay here tonight, Caro. The rabble-rousers—if it turns out to be more than one—will probably be too drunk to do anything other than sleep but in case they want more trouble, they certainly won't go door to door in the hospital quarters in search of you.'

She eased her hand out of his and stepped back.

'No way. They could attack the house,' she reminded

him. 'Not find me there, and become angry, burn the place. I can't stay here, Keanu. I'll get Bessie and Harold to stay there with me if you really believe there's any danger.'

She hesitated, and he sensed she wanted to say more.

But she returned to gathering up the dishes, taking them to the kitchen, putting leftover food into the refrigerator—busywork while she avoided him in case he asked what was going on.

'Aren't you in charge over at the hospital?' she asked when she'd finished cleaning. 'If you don't mind, I'll stay here until the party is over, then track down Bessie and Harold to ask them about tonight.'

Bessie and Harold, both well into their sixties, would be fine protection. He supposed if she was insistent about staying in the house, he'd have to stay there too, which, in fact, would be preferable to both of them staying here, her in the bed—he'd insist on that—and him on the couch, aware in every fibre of his being that she was there, so close.

And how could he return to that bed when she'd departed?

Wouldn't he always feel her presence there? Smell the Caro scent of her on the sheets and pillowslip?

'I'll be over at the hospital,' he said, knowing he had to get away from her before he was completely tied in knots. 'Hettie's very worried about the ulcer—worrying if we've misdiagnosed it as it seems to be getting worse, not better. You call when you're going up to the house and I'll walk you up.'

For a moment he thought she'd argue, but instead she flipped him a snappy salute, said, 'Yes, sir!' and opened her notebook again.

* * *

She wasn't going to stop Keanu sleeping in the house—
Caroline was only too aware of his stubbornness—but
it would be better than having him sleeping in the big
house somewhere far from her, rather than right next
door, through partition walls that wouldn't hold back
the essence of him that seemed to fill her whenever he
was near.

Every time she closed her eyes she felt the kiss they'd
shared in the graveyard—felt the longing in her body for
them to have taken it further.

But wasn't it too soon?

Of course it was.

And he was married.

Her senseless mental meandering led nowhere so she
sighed, gathered up the books and was halfway up the
hill before she remembered she was supposed to summon Keanu to guard her on her walk.

But Bessie and Harold were there, arguing on the track
not far from her, so she was safe.

'We are staying at your place tonight and don't you
argue, missy.'

She'd caught up with Bessie and Harold, and on this
subject they were obviously united for Bessie spoke and
Harold nodded his head very firmly.

Harold and Bessie she could handle in the house.

But Keanu?

He came at nine.

Bessie had made a salad to go with leftover pork from
the feast, and she, Harold and Caroline had eaten it at the
kitchen table, Bessie refusing to eat in the dining room.

'Makes me too sad to see that lovely chandelier and
think of your grandma polishing each crystal,' she said,

by way of explanation. And in truth Caroline felt much the same way—plus she still had papers spread across the table, and although it looked like a mess, she knew where to put her hand on every record there.

She was sitting on the swing seat on the front veranda, watching the last flights of the seabirds—dark whirling shadows against the early evening sky, returning to their roosts on the island.

They were a fairly good reflection of her thoughts at the moment—dark and whirling.

The cause of her distraction appeared on the track below the house, striding resolutely up from the hospital accommodation, clad now in linen shorts and a dark green T-shirt—a man at home in his environment.

And wasn't she at home in hers?

Of course she was and the shiver of whatever it was that had coursed through her body was probably only relief at seeing him.

Except that she hadn't been frightened by the loud voice and accusations earlier and she was reasonably sure that man and all the others would have drunk themselves stupid and collapsed into bed by now.

'Evening,' he said, touching a forefinger to an imaginary hat.

'And good evening to you,' Caroline replied. She could do this—she really could. All she had to do was completely divorce herself from all the manifestations of attraction that the wretched man was causing in her body.

But when he sat down beside her on the swing, took her hand and began to push the swing gently back and forth with his foot, she lost what little resolve she'd managed to gather, rested her head on his shoulder and swung with him, just as they had so many times in the past.

The moon rose majestically from the water, the birds had quietened and a peace she hadn't felt for a long time spread through her veins.

So even when Keanu turned to press a light kiss on her shoulder she barely reacted.

That was if you could define a small electric shock as barely...

'Nice here, isn't it?' he said, and although she'd swear neither of them had moved, their bodies were now touching from shoulder to hip and their clasped hands were in Keanu's lap.

Worse was the cloud that had wrapped around them, some unseen yet almost tangible blanket of desire.

Or maybe he couldn't feel it.

Maybe it was just her.

Being silly.

Imagining things.

'Not going away, is it, this attraction?' he said quietly, and she knew it wasn't imagination.

'Not really,' she answered, although the truth would have been *not at all*.

He turned away from a fascination with the moon to look directly at her.

'So, how do we tell?'

'If it's love?' she asked, guessing his earlier experience of attraction had made it hard to use the word. 'I wonder...'

Although maybe she *knew*.

Didn't her heart beating faster when she caught a

glimpse of him, or heard his voice or even thought of him suggest it had to be love?

Was lying sleepless in her bed, her body wired, wanting…?

Him!

Was that love?

Or was it old friendship mixed up with attraction?

For a long time he didn't speak, and she wondered if he'd been giving it the same thought she had but had come to a different conclusion.

'So much has happened between us,' he said quietly. 'I let you down once before, Caroline, and please believe me when I say that it hurt me too. Then marrying. Not telling you. I let you down again. But now—now I'd cut off my hand if it would help you to forgive me.'

Her heart was juddering in her chest, the beat every which way, while some kind of madness filled her mind—a madness begging her to take him to her bed, to rip off all his clothes and dispense with the agony that was attraction.

With Harold and Bessie here?

So lighten up!

'And what would I do with a bloody hand?' she teased, and though he laughed, she hadn't quite achieved her aim for he'd let go of her hand and wrapped his arm around her shoulders, drawing her closer, close enough to look into her eyes and probably see through them to the muddle in her head.

The kiss, when it inevitably came, was like nothing she'd experienced before. A barely there brush of lips on lips, then butterfly kisses across her cheeks, her eyelids and her temple.

With maddening deliberation, his mouth eventually returned to hers, but only to tease again, his teeth nibbling softly at her lips, tongue darting in to touch her tongue, withdrawing, darting, departing so her lips were hot then cool, and the pressure building within her was volcanic—a volcano about to blow.

He must have kicked with his foot, for the swing began to move again, and the movement lulled her senses, so when his tongue invaded her mouth and his hand brushed against her breast, she sighed and leaned into him, welcoming him, kissing him back, the intensity of the kiss growing until it blotted out her mind.

It was such a cliché, sitting on a porch swing, kissing like this.

Keanu was desperately trying to keep a grasp on reality, to keep his mind from going blank and letting his body take over all his actions.

They'd stop soon—well, they could hardly make love out here, especially not when there might be murderous miners wandering around.

But right now kissing Caroline was filling his soul with delight. His body wasn't quite so delighted, wanting more than fervid kisses.

Did he love her?

Her tongue was tangling with his, and he felt almost painfully aroused, but he couldn't break the kiss, couldn't pull his lips from hers, his arms from around her body.

She was his.

That was what the kiss was saying.

His kiss, and her response, making a statement.

About the future?

Or about attraction?

'Go to bed,' he whispered, his lips close to her ear. 'Maddie is back tomorrow, and a FIFO nurse is joining her, so we'll both have time off. We'll talk.'

'About?' she murmured back.

'About us, and our future, and attraction and love and all kinds of things.'

She smiled and kissed him gently on the lips, her eyes bright with unshed tears.

Tears of happiness this time, the brilliance of her smile told him that.

He stood up and pulled her upright, then turned her and nudged her towards the front door.

'I'll sleep on the couch out here. Reuben's got some sensible young men staked out around the veranda, and Harold's in a swag in the kitchen.'

He knew she was going to protest, so he kissed her again—swift and hard—then pulled back.

'Go,' he said.

CHAPTER ELEVEN

KEANU WAS DOWN at the hospital early—just the thought of Caroline asleep inside the house had been enough to keep him sleepless. Deciding to use the time productively, he stopped in at the office, realising it had been a couple of days since he'd dealt with his emails. He logged on to the computer and drummed his fingers as he waited for the screen to load.

And suddenly, there it was. An email from his solicitor in Cairns. So it was official—just like that, and without a word exchanged between him and his ex, his marriage was dissolved. He was a free man, although in truth he'd never been free. Not from the only person who'd ever held his heart. Just what did this mean for him and Caroline? In so many ways this wasn't the right time, but if not now, then when? If she could forgive him, then maybe, just maybe, she could love him.

But Keanu was roused from his musings by the sudden appearance of Sam in the office.

'Keanu, I'm glad you're here. I've just been looking at that ulcer again. The more I see it, the more convinced I am that we're dealing with something different here. I'd value a second opinion.'

Forcing his thoughts back to his work, Keanu nodded briskly. 'Of course. I agree that there's more to this than meets the eye. Has our patient said anything else about it to you?'

Sam shook his head as he pushed open the door to the ward, Keanu following right behind. They made their way to Raoul's bedside, where Keanu leant over to examine the uncovered wound.

'It's not looking good,' Keanu agreed, frowning in concentration.

'Not only that, but according to the limited testing I've been able to do, and our patient's response to the medication—or total lack of response—it just has to be something else, but I've no idea what eats away at the flesh so badly and just continues to degrade the wound.'

'Hydrofluoric acid.'

Keanu wasn't sure where the answer had come from, though apparently it had surfaced from some deep recess in his mind.

Which must have been working, for all he felt like a very confused zombie what with all that was happening in his personal life right now…

Sam turned to face him, grabbed his arm and steered him back out through the door.

'What did you say?'

'Hydrofluoric acid,' Keanu repeated, but with more certainty this time. 'Dreadful stuff. It just eats away at the skin and flesh and if you happen to drink it you're done for.'

'Well, I'm glad you kept that little bit of information to yourself until we were away from the patient. I don't think I've ever heard of it—though I probably did as a student—but I've never come across it as an acid burn. Except…' He paused in thought. 'Now I look at the wound as an acid burn it's starting to make sense. But this—what did you call it?'

'Hydrofluoric acid. It's the only acid that eats through glass so has to be kept in plastic containers. Years ago a very small concentration of it was used in a product for taking rust marks out of clothing but I think that's been banned now.'

'So why on earth would anyone have any of it on the fairly isolated islands of M'Langi? If it's as dangerous as you say, you can't just order a gallon or two off the internet.'

'I doubt a plane would carry it. But someone's brought it back here in hand luggage or by boat. Apparently there *are* places you can buy it. I imagine it has commercial uses of some kind or it wouldn't still be manufactured.'

Sam frowned at him.

'But why?'

Keanu heard the plane coming in, hopefully bringing relief staff, but Sam showed no desire to go rushing off to meet it.

'Keanu?'

Neither would he until he got an answer.

'It dissolves glass,' he repeated. 'And glass is made of sand, which is very degraded quartz, and gold comes in quartz veins. You pop a piece of gold-bearing quartz into a jar of hydrofluoric and, *voilà*, in a couple of days you have wee nuggets of gold.'

Sam was staring at him in disbelief.

'You're saying men steal gold-bearing quartz from the mine?'

He hadn't really been saying that—hadn't wanted to mention the matter at all—but they had a patient…

'Not all of them, and I'd say theft was rare back when

the place was properly managed, but those who haven't been paid for a while probably feel they deserve it. Some of them might pinch it anyway—no one's perfect.'

He certainly had Sam's attention now.

'So, it's possible our patient had been fooling around with probably his father's acid and splashed some on his skin. Wouldn't he know?'

Keanu shook his head.

'Maybe not straight away, and when it started to hurt—from all accounts it's extremely painful—he didn't want to tell anyone about it because I'm sure he'd been forbidden to go near it, let alone open the lid of the container. Sniffing the fumes in close quarters can do horrible things to your lungs. No, he was hardly likely to tell his family what he'd done.'

'Treatment?'

Again Keanu could only shake his head.

'I was a child when I heard about it and even if the treatment was discussed it would have gone over my head. Best you get onto the internet or call the poisons centre back in Oz.'

Sam sighed, but before he could say anything a gorgeous and very pregnant young woman with short auburn curls, startling green eyes and a smile that lit up the air around her swept into the hospital.

'Maddie!' he and Sam cried in unison, holding out their arms and somehow gathering her in a three-way hug.

Which was when Caroline walked in.

Now was not the time to fill Caro in on his divorce; instead, Keanu made the introductions.

'Maddie, this is Caroline Lockhart. She filled in for us this week when the FIFO nurse didn't come.'

'And has been doing a great job,' Sam added.

He'd interrupted Keanu's, 'Caroline, this is Maddie Haddon, one of our favourite FIFO doctors.'

'Your only FIFO doctor now you've decided you'll be permanent, Keanu,' Maddie corrected as she held out her hand towards Caroline.

The introduction was interrupted as Bugsy, obviously hearing his mistress's voice, came hurtling towards her.

Maddie crouched awkwardly to hug her ecstatic dog.

'So much for my walking him twice a day,' Sam complained, 'but now you're here, Maddie, do you know anything about hydrofluoric acid?'

Maddie looked a little startled but she accepted Sam's hand to help her upright again, and shrugged her shoulders.

'That's the stuff that melts glass so has to be kept in plastic containers,' she offered.

'I think we've already established that. Come through to the office and you can tell me all your news—check-up okay?—while I look up how to treat a hydrofluoric burn.'

They disappeared along the corridor, and Caroline followed Keanu into the young lad's room. He could feel her closeness—aware of her in a way he'd never been before.

'You think it's an acid burn?' she asked him, all business.

Keanu wasn't sure what to feel. Last night they'd sat together and talked of love and attraction, and his body clamoured to greet her with a kiss—at least a kiss...

But work was work.

Caroline was by the patient's bed, leaning forward to examine the wound, so Keanu joined her, pushing the swirl of emotions inside him out of his mind with the practicalities of work.

He bent over Raoul and spoke quietly to him.

'Did you spill something on your leg?'

The slightest of head movements, but definitely a very subdued yes.

'Can you tell me what it was?'

Another shake of the head, this one just as definitely negative.

'You're not going to get into trouble,' Keanu said gently, 'at least not from us, but we do need to know so we can treat it before it gets any worse.'

How he was enduring the pain now, Keanu didn't know, having heard horror stories of hydrofluoric burns.

'Calcium glucanate gel,' Sam announced, coming in to join them by the bed. 'We don't have it but I can make it up. In the meantime, Caroline, would you take a blood sample so can we check if it's affected his electrolytes and, Keanu, can you flush the wound again to remove the cream we've been using?'

He turned to Raoul.

'If you'd told us—' he began, but Keanu held up his hand.

'We've had that conversation and he's very sorry.'

Sam nodded and disappeared again, no doubt to mix the solution he needed.

Caroline tightened a ligature around Raoul's upper arm then tapped a vein inside his elbow. She was so aware of Keanu's presence she could feel her skin growing hot and tight.

While Keanu was doing nothing more than flush a wound?

Concentrating, remembering all her training, she slid the needle into the vein, released the ligature and drew out blood for testing, telling herself all the time that a strange conversation during one night on a swing didn't mean anything.

Or did it?

He said they'd talk.

She asked Raoul to hold the cotton-wool ball to the tiny wound while she set aside the phial and found some tape.

Professional, she could do it, for all her nerves were skittering with the…promise, maybe, that had been last night.

Pleased to escape Keanu's presence, she took the blood through to Sam.

'And?' Maddie prompted.

Caroline wondered if she looked as puzzled as she felt. 'And what?'

Maddie smiled at her.

'Just because I've been off the island doesn't mean I haven't been keeping up with the gossip. And that tells me that you and Keanu have renewed your old childhood friendship, though possibly the word *friendship* isn't quite enough to describe your relationship.'

'For heaven's sake, we've barely spent ten hours alone with each other and the gossip mill has us…'

She didn't have the words she needed.

'Practically married?' Maddie kindly put in.

Caroline sighed. Well, Keanu was married, just to somebody else, so no matter what island gossip suggested a real marriage between herself and Keanu wasn't even an outside possibility for the near future.

'Things haven't got quite that far,' she muttered, unwilling to share more with a virtual stranger.

'Well, there's still time,' Maddie said. 'Now, didn't Sam say you could take a break? Go home.'

Home.

The island *was* home to her and she'd been so happy here since her return. Disturbed by the problems, of course, and confused by her attraction to Keanu, but none of that had spoiled the feeling that she was back where she belonged.

Home.

Keanu.

What was *he* thinking?

Caroline sighed and headed up to the house, using the track past the lagoon, thinking a swim might clear her head.

But up at the house the bookwork beckoned. She hadn't got the maintenance and other day-to-day working figures of the mine from Reuben. Hoping he'd still be in the office there, organising the fencing off of the mine, she headed down the steep steps once again.

Keeping busy to keep her mind off Keanu.

But he was already there, sitting with Reuben in the shed.

Why wouldn't he be?

No reason, but something about the way the pair of them looked at her made her feel uneasy.

Keanu was the first to speak.

'We're just sorting out something here, Caro,' he said, and for some reason his voice sounded tight.

As if they'd been discussing her?

Of course they wouldn't have been…

'I'll see you later at the house,' he added, and knowing a dismissal when she heard it, she turned and headed back up the steps.

But halfway up she saw the faint marking of an old track, grassy now, and grown over with enthusiastic tropical vines and plants.

Had she been thinking of the grotto that she noticed it?

She certainly hadn't the last time she'd climbed the steps.

But her feet were already on the barely there track, picking their way through the tangled regrowth, quickening her pace where the track was clear but taking her time to find a way around where thorn bushes formed a barrier.

Hot and sticky, not to mention covered in burrs, she finally reached the pool where the water cascading down from the lagoon came to rest before trickling on past the village to the sea.

She breathed in the humid air, catching scents she couldn't quite identify, resting for a moment before turning towards the waterfall.

'You're being silly,' she told herself, speaking the words aloud in the hope they might stop this trek back into the past.

Didn't work, and she kept going, arriving eventually at the hidden space behind the waterfall, the water making music all around her, the thick fern growth giving the space a special magic.

He'd married someone else.

She told herself this was okay, only to be expected—of course he would have married, and it was only the small child she'd once been that was bleating *But he's mine* deep inside her head.

She sat on a rock, her clothes damp from spray, and tried to make sense of her life as it was—not as she'd once imagined it would be.

'Caro, are you in there?'

Keanu's voice.

How had he guessed?

And of course it wasn't anything to do with linked thoughts.

'Caro,' he called again, and this time she knew she'd have to answer.

'I'm in the grotto,' she called, and within minutes he was there beside her, sitting on what had always been 'his' rock.

'How did you know?' she asked.

'It was obvious that someone had been along the old track and as you were the only one stupid enough to be coming down here on your own, I just followed your trail.'

'Stupid enough?' she demanded, angry but not sure whether it was because her thinking time had been interrupted or because his presence always caused her tension.

'There could have been a landslip or a bit of the track washed away.'

'Well, there wasn't, and I'm quite safe, so you can go off and do whatever you were planning to do with Reuben.'

'Which was to come and see you,' Keanu told her, not as excited now as he'd been earlier, not quite as sure she was going to like the idea. And he'd already decided that now was not the time to mention his divorce. Other matters were more urgent after all.

'I was talking to Reuben about the mine. I talked to the elders about it yesterday, and spoke to your father this morning. Something you'd said about finding someone to invest in it—once we knew how much we needed—

sparked a kind of shadow of an idea in my head, and it wasn't until yesterday at the funeral that I worked out what it was.'

He paused, waiting for a comment, perhaps a little excitement, or even a cool 'And?'

But there was no response so, feeling even more uncertain, he ploughed on.

'Reuben isn't the only islander with a son making good money on the mainland, so it seemed to me that the islanders themselves might like to invest in the mine, form a company of some sort, a co-op perhaps—and take it over.'

'Take it over?'

Caro's voice was scratchy.

'Completely?'

'That's why I had to talk to Max. I knew he'd know which way to go, the company or whatever, and of course he'd have to agree to the idea.'

'And he did? He's happy for the islanders to take over the mine?'

Keanu was worried now. He'd really expected excitement that he'd sorted out the problem, perhaps a little hesitation as Caro considered it. But not this flat, unemotional questioning.

Unable to work it out, he went with answering.

'Yes, of course. He was annoyed he hadn't thought of it himself. Of course, it can't happen overnight, but within maybe six months we could have the mine up and running again and money going into the hospital—that would still be part of the arrangement—with the shareholders benefiting as well.'

'And you never thought to talk to me about this?'

Not flat and unemotional now—no, now she was upset, although he couldn't fathom why.

'There's been no time,' he said, hoping to sooth whatever was bothering her. 'As you can imagine there's still so much to do. It's mainly been just contacting people.'

It was hard to see her expression in the gloom, but he saw the way she stood up, and knew from the way she held her body that she'd be glaring down at him.

'Contacting everyone but me!' she said. 'Do I not count? Wasn't I part of this save-the-mine project from the beginning? Wasn't I the one who got the books and put the figures together? Then suddenly it's all "Don't worry your little head about it, the men will fix it" and you don't even mention it to me?'

He stood too, and put a hand on her shoulder—a hand that was quickly shrugged off.

'Caro—' he began.

But she was already walking away, pausing only to say, 'You could have mentioned it as we sat on the swing, as we talked about love and what love was. I thought it was sharing, doing things together—not everything, that would be silly—but this was a joint project at the beginning, then suddenly it was all yours. I don't know how to feel, Keanu. I don't even know why I feel the way I do, when obviously it's the ideal solution for the mine, but right now I just have to get away by myself and try to work out what I really want from love.'

And with that she disappeared from the grotto, not going back along the track but climbing the rocks at the side of the waterfall.

She was as sure-footed as a cat, so he didn't worry about her going that way, and he knew it would be pointless trying to argue with her in the mood she was in, so he sat on his rock in the place where they'd practised getting married, and wondered just how things had gone so wrong.

She climbed the rocks to the top, skipped over the flat rocks where she'd sat with Keanu—had it been only a few days ago?

Keanu.

He'd sorted out the problem at the mine—or would eventually—and he'd spoken to her father.

But not to her.

Did he really know her so little he'd thought she wouldn't want to know?

After all the work she'd done on the figures, of course he had to know. Had to realise the responsibility—family responsibility—she felt towards it.

And didn't he even consider just how hard this might be—hearing that a chunk of her life, her heritage, had been taken from her without any discussion?

It wasn't that she wanted the blasted mine. As long as it continued to support the hospital, she couldn't have cared less what happened to it.

Somewhere deep inside she knew she was being silly, that it was just a mine. And she knew full well that without it the hospital couldn't keep going.

She made her way along the track to the house, still feeling wounded no matter how she tried to rationalise it.

Had Keanu talked to her about his idea, made her part of it right from the start, she knew she'd probably feel differently about it.

Probably even be as excited as he was about it.

She'd reached the hospital and was about to climb the

hill to the house when Sam caught up with her, his face
so serious she knew something was wrong.

Very wrong!

'You father phoned,' he said gently. 'Christopher has
taken a turn for the worse. He'd like you home.'

Panic flooded her body. She'd always known this day
would come. Known, too, that it was getting closer.

But now…

'He's sending a plane for you. You've got two hours.
You father will send a car to meet the plane at Sydney
airport.'

Caroline supposed she'd heard the words, but her total
focus was on her brother, willing him to stay alive until
she got there.

She'd been selfish, thinking only of her own unhappiness when she'd fled to the island, and now—

Shutting off *that* thought, she hurried up to the house.

Keanu left the grotto. He'd told Reuben he'd go over to
Atangi to talk to the elders again—tell them he'd spoken
to Max. Reuben was phoning them and they'd be waiting
for him, no doubt filled with excitement and ideas about
how they'd manage the mine.

He went down to the village where he kept a boat he'd
bought from one of the locals almost as soon as he'd arrived back on Wildfire, half thinking he should have
let Caro know where he was going, but he was already
running late.

Plus, he needed to consider her reaction before he
talked to her again. Out on the water he could think
straight. Right now he felt there was a lot of thinking
that needed straightening. Not only was the issue of the
mine hanging between them but the knowledge that he

had to tell Caroline that he was free, that his divorce was final worried at him too. Just how would she react to that news? Given the sour response to his plans for the mines and his ill thought-out decision to get the ball rolling without first consulting her, he imagined that trusting him with her heart was furthest from her mind right now...

He headed towards Atangi, easing the boat over the shallow part of the reef.

The little engine pushed them through the water and the tension he'd been feeling eased.

So *was* it love he felt for her?

Adult love?

Enough to build a future on? Now that he finally had a future?

It was hard to tell because he'd always loved her and even when he'd cut her out of his life rarely a day had gone by without something reminding him of her.

And now she was here, back on Wildfire where it had all begun, and he couldn't begin to work out...

What couldn't he work out?

Whether or not he loved her?

No, that part was settled, but there were so many different kinds of love.

No, he was playing with words.

He loved Caroline, and he was pretty sure that Caroline loved him. And if that was the case they could sort out the rest.

Hadn't they talked of love on the swing?

But had he *told* Caro that he loved her?

Had he actually said the words?

He tried to think but his mind went blank with shock

at his own stupidity. That he, who knew Caro probably better than anyone else did, hadn't told her how he felt.

Her whole life had been filled with the uncertainty of love. Not that she spoke of it, or wallowed in self-pity. No, his Caro just got on with things. Like being left with her grandma for a start, then boarding school, and all the times her father hadn't come. Even Christopher kept his best smiles for his father.

So of course she'd be uncertain about his love, then taking the decisions about the mine away from her— that was how she'd have seen it—would have been the last straw.

He had to see her, tell her he loved her, that more importantly he was now free to love her. He'd start with that *then* sort out the mine business. He'd see the elders, go back to Wildfire.

Full of resolve, Keanu pulled into the harbour at Atangi, thinking not of the meeting but of the night ahead.

If only Keanu was here, Caroline thought as she flew over the Pacific. With him beside her she could face anything.

Was that what love was about?

Having someone to lean on, someone there to help you through the rough times as well as celebrate the good ones? She'd been stupid, reacting as she had to Keanu's suggestion about the mine co-op. She wasn't even sure why she'd reacted as she had.

And blaming Keanu...

Though if he really loved her, the way she now realised she loved him, wouldn't she be the first person to discuss it with?

Even before he knew it might actually work?

Of course not, that was a petty and stupid way to think.

She'd been unfair, but the calm way he'd announced *he'd* sorted out the mine problem, leaving her out completely, had temporarily blocked all rational thought and she'd struck out at him.

And now, heading further and further away from him, she couldn't tell him—couldn't say she was sorry and agree it was an ideal answer to the problem, even if she felt that a little bit of herself had been cut off.

In her head, the mine had been as much a part of Wildfire as the house she knew was home.

But stuff had gone from it and the house had still been home.

She'd phone Keanu as soon as she was in the car on the way to the hospital and tell him she was sorry.

Tell him she loved him.

Tell him she needed him?

Was it too soon for that?

CHAPTER TWELVE

RETURNING TO WILDFIRE, and heading straight to the house to tell Caro he loved her—this mission becoming more urgent by the moment—Keanu was disconcerted to hear she'd gone.

Because she was upset with him?

But Bessie was still explaining and he forced himself to listen.

Christopher... Sydney...charter flight...

He thanked Bessie and headed for his villa. Thankfully, he could get the regular flight out of here the next day. He sat at his computer, booking a flight from Cairns to Sydney, and arranging a hire car to be waiting at the airport.

Praying all the while—for Christopher, for Caro and for himself a little—hoping he hadn't left all he wanted to say until it was too late.

Mrs Phipps, the housekeeper, older now and somehow smaller, opened the front door of the Lockharts' Sydney house and squinted uncertainly up at him.

'Do I know you?'

'It's Keanu, Mrs Phipps. I used to come here sometimes during the holidays to play with Caroline and talk to Christopher.'

'Keanu?'

Her voice was slightly disbelieving.

'But you're much bigger now. You've grown. Of course you've grown! But welcome. You've come to be with Caroline, I suppose. They're up at the hospital—she and Dr Lockhart. Christopher's very poorly again.'

He didn't need to ask what hospital. There was an excellent private hospital just a few blocks away and the professional staff there all knew and loved Christopher, treating him with special care.

'Thank you, Mrs Phipps,' he said and turned away.

'But don't you want to leave your bag? You'll stay here surely?'

He looked down at the bag he was carrying, having decided a taxi was easier than a hire car in a city he didn't know well.

Would he stay here?

Would he be wanted?

He wished he were as certain as Mrs Phipps seemed to be.

'Best not,' he said, 'but thanks.'

And with that he headed down the ramp, out onto the street and up the road to where the hospital was built to look out over a part of Sydney's magnificent harbour.

With the money the twins' maternal grandparents had left in trust for Christopher, he would always have twenty-four-hour care, private hospitals and the best of doctors and specialists. So this hospital was a special place, and he would be getting the best possible treatment here.

But Keanu's heart quaked at the thought of Caro losing her brother. They might not have been physically close but there'd always been a special bond between them. Even as a child, if she woke with a nightmare in the night his mother would be sure to get a call the next morning to say Christopher wasn't well.

Poor Caro.

Would she let him comfort her? Take whatever support he could offer her?

Or had he hurt her too badly for that?

Once at the hospital, he asked a friendly receptionist if he could leave his bag behind her counter, then enquired about Christopher's whereabouts.

'He's in Room 22 on the second floor, but I think it might be family only. Dr Lockhart and his sister are in with him right now. He's very frail.'

The woman blinked back tears, and Keanu realised just how special Christopher was to all those who'd come in contact with him.

He tapped gently on the closed door of Room 22 then eased it open. Max was asleep in a big chair by the bed, while Caroline was sitting close to the bed, Christopher's hand clasped in hers, her head bent over it, possibly dozing as well.

He opened the door wider, and a slight squeak made her turn.

'Keanu?'

She mouthed his name, set Christopher's hand down on the bed and got up stiffly from the chair, easing out the door and closing it behind her.

'What are you doing here?' she demanded, but fairly weakly as her exhaustion clearly showed in the shadows under her eyes and the taut lines drawn in her skin.

'I hadn't said I loved you, really loved you—the now

you not the past or anything else, just you,' he replied, and realised how lame it sounded when he saw the puzzled look on her face.

'I just wanted you to know. I know I don't deserve your love after the way I treated you, but somehow it seemed important to tell you anyway. We talked all around it at times, but on my way to Atangi it came to me that I'd never said the words. Not properly...

'There, I have more I need to talk to you about, much more, but that's the crux of it,' he added a little later, when the only reaction from the woman he loved had been a bewildered stare.

'Now, how bad is Christopher? You look exhausted and I've never seen your father look so grey. Why don't you take him home for a proper sleep and I'll sit with Christopher? I'll call you the moment there's any change and don't bother about that stuff I said, just go home and rest for a while.'

'You'll sit with him?'

Teardrops sparkled on her eyelashes, and it was all he could do not to kiss them away.

'Of course I will. Don't you remember when he had measles at the island that time and I'd had them so I was okay and I sat with him every day? We like each other.'

Caro reached up and kissed his cheek.

'I'll get Dad,' she said, nothing more, but somehow Keanu felt it was enough.

For now...

Max and Caro left, Max shaking Keanu's hand in welcome, and thanks and goodbye.

'We won't be long,' he promised, 'but don't hesitate to call if there's any change.'

'I won't,' Keanu promised, then he watched them

walk away, Caro turning at the door to give him a puzzled look.

Keanu took his place in the chair Caro had been using and took Christopher's hand in his, holding what was little more than a bag of frail bones and skin very gently.

He massaged the skin, just rubbing it, and, remembering himself and Caro sitting with Alkiri, he began to talk, quietly but clearly.

'It's Keanu, mate. I've sent the others home to sleep. You're causing them a bit of worry at the moment. Anyway, I'm glad I've got this chance to sit with you because there's a lot I have to tell you. I love her, you see, your sister, though I'm not sure how she feels about me. For a while there, back on Wildfire, I thought she might love me back, but I've made a bit of a mess of things so it's hard to tell.'

He paused, then continued, this time gently rubbing Christopher's withered arm, spreading cream on it he'd found on the table by the bed.

'If she does love me, mate, I want to let you know that I'll never let her down. I did before because I didn't want to hurt my mum, and then again, recently, when I told her I'd married someone else. But you have to believe me, that part of my life is over, it's really over now that my divorce has finally come through. And I swear to you, Christopher, that I will never do anything to hurt her again. She's so special, your sister, that she deserves the very best, and although I know I'm not that, I'd do my darnedest to become it just for her.'

Was it his imagination or had Christopher's eyes fluttered open, just momentarily?

Keanu kept talking, moving to the other side of the bed to put cream on the hand and arm over there. He talked of the island, of how well the hospital was doing and how much his family had done for the people of M'Langi.

He talked about the day outside, cool but cloudless so the sun sent sparkly diamonds of light dancing across the waters of the harbour.

'I guess you've seen it like this before if they always put you in this room, but it's magic to me. I'd like to buy her a diamond, but then I think of her eyes and wonder about sapphires. I don't suppose you have any idea of her stone preferences? Not that she's likely to want anything from me. I kind of did something that upset her.'

And this time the eyelids definitely fluttered, and Keanu could have sworn he'd felt a tiny bit of pressure from the claw-like hand clasped in his.

'But I guess if she doesn't love me, there's not much I can do.'

Definite pressure this time. Keanu looked up at the nurse who'd remained in the room to do the regular obs and update Christopher's chart.

'Did he move his fingers?' the young man asked. 'I'm sure he did, and his eyelids fluttered as well.'

'I'd better get the family back,' the nurse said.

'They won't have had much sleep.'

The nurse was obviously torn.

'I'll give them another ten minutes and phone the house. The housekeeper will know whether to wake them.'

'Maybe suggest she wake Caroline. I'm sure Dr Lockhart has been more sleep deprived than she has.'

The nurse did his checks, agreed that all the signs were that Christopher might be improving, then left the room.

'Of course you're improving,' Keanu said. 'I'll want

you around for the wedding, you know. That's if she'll have me.'

He took a deep breath and put all thoughts of love and weddings out of his mind.

'Do you remember,' he said, letting go of his hand and moving down to massage Christopher's toes now, 'how we took you swimming in the lagoon that time you were visiting? Mum put you in a life jacket and we all lay on our backs in the water and looked up at the sky through the canopy of the rainforest.'

Christopher's eyes, so like Caroline's, opened slightly and Keanu could swear he was actually looking at him.

Christopher's smile might be but a shadow, but Keanu's answer was a broad grin.

'And what about when we took you down to Sunset Beach in your wheelchair but the path was too steep and we tipped you out, and when we got you back in, we had to spend ages wiping red sand off you so your nurse and Mum wouldn't know?'

Open eyes *and* a smile!

Keanu's hand surged with joy.

'Oh, Christopher, we had such fun!'

'Didn't we?' a quiet voice said, and Keanu looked up to see Caro on the other side of the bed.

'Where did you come from? I thought the nurse was going to let you sleep for ten minutes before she rang the house.'

Caroline came into the room and sat down in the chair she'd been in earlier. She took Christopher's other hand in hers, leaned forward to kiss his cheek, then finally looked at Keanu.

'I never left,' she said. 'I went as far as the lift with Dad then thought of something.'

She hesitated, heart pounding, knowing what she wanted so much to say, but still held back by uncertainties she couldn't name.

'Thought of something?' Keanu prompted.

She nodded, saw Christopher's eyes open, looking at her, urging her on, it seemed.

'I hadn't told you I loved you either. I'd wanted to but I hadn't. I was upset about the mine business—stupid really when it's a good idea—then Dad phoned to say he'd sent the plane to bring me home and all I could think about was Christopher. Then, when I came back just now, I heard you talking to him—I stood and eavesdropped and put my finger to my lips so the nurse wouldn't betray me and now I want to tell Christopher something too.'

She lifted his hand and pressed her lips to it.

'I love this man Keanu, Christopher, and I do hope you approve because without him I don't think I could go on. He is part of me, part of my heart and soul, and always has been, and now that I understand why he broke away, well, I love him even more, because that was done from love—love for his mother.'

She reached across the bed and took Keanu's hand in hers.

'And in case Christopher didn't tell you, I like sapphires.'

Max, alerted by the nurse, came in to a surprising tableau. His son, who'd been lingering close to death for days, was not quite alert, but definitely had his eyes open and a lopsided smile on his face, while his daughter shone with luminous radiance, sitting with her hand linked in Keanu's across the bottom of the bed.

And Keanu's face wasn't exactly doleful either.

'You two got something to tell me?' he asked.

'I'd like to marry your daughter,' Keanu said.

'But not right away, Dad,' Caroline assured him. 'There's a lot of stuff to sort out at the island and when we're married there, I want it to be the perfect, happy, heavenly place it used to be.'

'I presume you'll let me know a date,' Max said, smiling at the pair. 'Now, I'm sure you've got plenty to say to each other so leave me with my son, and go make your plans.'

* * * * *

Don't miss the next story in the fabulous
Wildfire Island Docs *series:*
The Nurse Who Stole His Heart
by Alison Roberts.
Available now

THE NURSE WHO
STOLE HIS HEART

BY
ALISON ROBERTS

Published in Great Britain 2016
By Mills & Boon, an imprint of HarperCollins*Publishers*
1 London Bridge Street, London, SE1 9GF

© 2016 Alison Roberts

ISBN: 978-0-263-25429-7

Our policy is to use papers that are natural, renewable and recyclable
products and made from wood grown in sustainable forests.
The logging and manufacturing processes conform to the legal
environmental regulations of the country of origin.

Printed and bound in Spain
by CPI, Barcelona

Dear Reader,

If you were asked to think of the most romantic setting ever, where would it be? A candlelit dinner? A walk in a forest with dappled sunlight filtering through the canopy? In front of a crackling fire on a winter's night? Or maybe a beach on a tropical island—at sunset?

Those all work for me, that's for sure, but there's obviously something about the tropical island beach that puts it closer to the top of the list for many people—which probably explains why travel agents use those stunning images of couples on beaches to advertise islands.

I've been lucky enough to visit Hawaii, Fiji and Samoa. I'm also lucky enough to have writer friends who love island settings for romantic stories as much as I do, so when the opportunity came up to work together we were all excited.

Wildfire Island is the star of our fictitious archipelago of M'Langi. It has a beach that is so famous for its amazing sunsets it gave the island its name. It also has a hospital, and a team of people who all have their own stories.

This is Luke and Anahera's story. They've both kept huge secrets from each other and have to deal with the repercussions of having them revealed. What are those secrets and how do they do that?

Read on and find out…

With love,

Alison xxx

For Meredith and Linda with very much love xxx

Alison Roberts is a New Zealander, currently lucky enough to live near a beautiful beach in Auckland. She is also lucky enough to write for both the Mills & Boon Romance and Medical Romance lines. A primary school teacher in a former life, she is also a qualified paramedic. She loves to travel and dance, drink champagne, and spend time with her daughter and her friends.

Books by Alison Roberts

Mills & Boon Medical Romance

The Honourable Maverick
Sydney Harbour Hospital: Zoe's Baby
Falling for Her Impossible Boss
The Legendary Playboy Surgeon
St Piran's: The Wedding
Maybe This Christmas…?
NYC Angels: An Explosive Reunion
Always the Hero
From Venice with Love
200 Harley Street: The Proud Italian
A Little Christmas Magic
Always the Midwife
Daredevil, Doctor…Husband?

Visit the Author Profile page at
millsandboon.co.uk for more titles.

CHAPTER ONE

STEPPING OFF A plane could be more than stepping onto unfamiliar ground.

Sometimes it was like stepping back in time.

The heat of the early evening was the first thing that Luke Wilson noticed. The kind of heat laced with moisture that felt like the anteroom of a sauna. Why on earth had he chosen to fly in a suit?

Because that was what internationally renowned specialists in tropical diseases wore when they were invited to be a keynote speaker at an exclusive conference?

The smell was the second thing that hit Luke as he walked from the plane towards the golf cart that was clearly waiting to transport him to his accommodation at Wildfire Island's newest facility—a state-of-the-art conference centre.

He'd already shed his jacket on the small private plane that he'd boarded in Auckland, New Zealand—the last leg of a very long journey from London. Now he loosened his tie and rolled up his shirtsleeves as he breathed in the scent of fragrant blossoms like frangipani and jasmine being carried on a gentle, tropical breeze.

And it was the smell that did it.

It smelled like…

Oh, man…it smelled like Ana.

The emotional reaction slammed into him with far more force than he had anticipated. A mix of guilt. And loss. And a longing that was still powerful enough—even after so many years—to make him wonder if his knees were in danger of buckling.

He shouldn't have come back here.

'Let me take that for you, Dr Wilson.' The smiling young island lad held out a hand to take his small suitcase. 'Hop on board and I'll take you to your bure. You've got just enough time to freshen up before the cocktail party.'

Cocktail party? For a moment, Luke hesitated—his brain fuzzy from a mixture of displacement and the opposing time zone. Oh, yes…this was the 'meet and greet' session before this exclusive conference started tomorrow. A chance to reconnect with his esteemed colleagues from all over the globe who shared his passion—the ambition to make a real difference in the world. Harry would be there, too, of course. More formally known as Sheikh Rahman al-Taraq, Harry was a patient turned friend who was bringing that ambition close enough to touch…

Luke's suitcase was strapped onto the back of the cart and the young man was giving him a curious look, clearly aware of his hesitation.

'You ready, Dr Wilson?'

Luke gave a single, curt nod, defying jet lag as he focussed on what lay ahead for the next couple of days. The nod dispelled any ghosts as well. Anahera didn't live here now. She'd moved to Brisbane almost as soon as he'd left Wildfire Island nearly five years ago. The weird sensation—a curious mix of opposite ends of the spectrum between dread and hope—was nothing more than a waste of mental energy.

'I'm ready.' He climbed onto the cart, smiling at his chauffeur.

'I just don't get it.' Sam Taylor, one of the permanent doctors at Wildfire Island's small hospital, shook his head as he stirred his coffee. 'All the comings and goings and the research centre being fenced off for so long. Now we have private jets coming in and it seems that we have a boutique international conference venue on Wildfire Island. Why here?'

Anahera Kopu shrugged. 'It's a gorgeous place. Different. Exotic enough to attract people who might need an inspiring break as a background to sharing knowledge and doing the kind of networking that's important in the scientific world.'

'I get that. But I still don't understand why someone would choose a place as exotic as the M'Langi Islands. How did they even know about us? And can you imagine how much it has cost? Who's behind it and why has it been such a secret?'

Anahera shook her head. 'I have no idea. But it's not the only secret on this island, is it?'

Oh, help…what an idiotic thing for her—of all people—to say. She had been keeping something huge a secret from all the people who meant the most to her—her mother and her colleagues and friends who were her wider family.

Sam grinned. 'Do tell, Ana…you must know a few more than me. You grew up here and I'm just a newbie.'

Anahera kept her tone light enough to make the conversation impersonal. She'd had plenty of practice at steering conversations in a safe direction.

'No, you're not. You've been here for years now.' She turned on the hot tap and reached for some dishwashing liquid. 'You arrived just after I went off to Brisbane to do my postgrad training, didn't you?'

'Mmm…when the research station was just that. A research station. Now we find out it's been added to and turned into some exclusive resort that's going to be used for medical think tanks and—not only that—there's a rumour that apparently there's been some amazing breakthrough that's going to be announced. Something that could change our lives. Don't you think someone might have told us about that? What do you think it is?'

'No idea. Unless they've come up with a new vaccine, maybe?'

'Doubt it. That takes years and years and more money than anyone would want to throw at an isolated group of Pacific islands. I reckon it's got something to do with that M'Langi tea they make and how it seems to protect some islanders from encephalitis. Did you know that research started on that decades ago?'

Oh, yes…Anahera had known about that. Not that she was about to share any details. She didn't want to think about it, let alone tell someone else. Unbidden, a memory surfaced of sitting in a swinging chair as a tropical twilight morphed into night. Of arms—heavy but so welcome—resting on her body as she lay back against the chest of the man who was telling about his curiosity regarding the tea. She shook the memory off with a head shake that was visible but fortunately appropriate to a dismissive comment.

'I think they'd decided that the only benefit of the tea was some sort of natural insect repellent so that mosquito bites were less likely and therefore people were less likely to contract encephalitis from them. It's hardly going to change our lives.'

Sam sat down at the table. 'I guess not. What we really need is for the aerial spraying to happen to control the mosquito problem. I wonder if anyone's managed to get in touch with Ian Lockhart yet. He's the person who should be organising it.'

Anahera shrugged. 'Not that I know of. He seems to have fallen off the face of the earth. I wouldn't be surprised to hear he's in Vegas, gambling away any recent profits from the mine.'

'If it doesn't happen soon, we could be in for a few nasty cases this year. We don't want another Hami, do we?'

'Heavens, no.' Anahera could feel her face scrunching into lines of distress. She would be in tears in no time if they started talking about the little boy they had lost to encephalitis a couple of years ago. It had been the most heart-wrenching case of her nursing career so far. Almost unbearable, because the little boy had been the same age as her own daughter.

'Maybe we'll find out at this cocktail party. You all set, Ana? Got a pretty dress?'

'I'm not going.'

'But you're invited. We all are.'

'Doesn't mean I have to go. I want to spend some time with Hana. I haven't seen her all day.' Anahera dried the mug and put it back in the cupboard.

'Bring her, too.'

She laughed. 'Take a three-year-old to a cocktail party? I don't think so... Besides, I said I might stay on till ten p.m. if Hettie decides she wants to go before taking over the night shift.'

Anahera could feel a faint flush of warmth in her cheeks as the quirk of Sam's eyebrow made her realise that she had just pulled the rug out from beneath her excuse of wanting to spend more time with her daughter.

'I just don't feel like being social, okay? I had enough of that kind of thing in Brisbane. Not my scene.'

'There'll be interesting people to talk to who'll only be here for a couple of days. Experts on things like dengue fever and encephalitis. I'm looking forward to hearing what the latest research is all about and any improvements to treatment, never mind what the secret announcement is.'

'And I'll look forward to you telling me all about it tomorrow.' Anahera's tone was firm. Clipped, even. She didn't want to hear people talking about research into tropical diseases. It was too much of a reminder of conversations long past. Like the ones about the M'Langi tea. And the dreams of someone who had planned to change the world for the better. She'd bought into those dreams a hundred per cent, hadn't she? Because she'd been going to be by his side while he made them happen. Even now, that sense of loss could tighten her throat and generate that unpleasant prickle behind her eyes.

'There's going to be a *hangi*. You love *hangis*.'

'I know. Mum's in charge of it, which is why she's left us to sort the patients' meals tonight.' A quick glance at her watch and Anahera had the perfect excuse to leave. 'I'd better go and get on with the observations and medications round so I can feed everyone before they want to go to sleep.'

Sam shook his head, clearly giving up. 'I'll help with the obs and do the meds. We've only got a few inpatients so it won't take long. Then I'll have a shower and get spruced up while you're playing chef.'

The shower was exactly what he'd needed to clear the jet lag and sensation of displacement but, if anything, it only added to Luke's amazement.

Like the rest of this luxurious bure tucked into the tropical jungle edging the beach, this bathroom could have been plucked from a five-star resort. The walls were an almost flat jigsaw of boulder-sized stones and the floor a mosaic of grey pebbles inset with white ones that made a tribal design of a large fish. The soap was faintly scented with something that smelled like the island— jasmine, maybe—and the towels were fluffy and soft.

Wrapping one of those towels around his waist, Luke stepped back into the round sleeping area where the mosquito nets, still tied back over the huge bed, rippled gently in the sea breeze coming through the louvered windows. He could hear voices outside. People greeting each other as they made their way from the other bures to the meeting hall where the cocktail party would probably be under way already.

None of these dwellings had been here the last time. There'd been a rustic cabin or two that had been used by visiting marine scientists but they'd been closer to the laboratories and had clearly been demolished to make way for the new meeting hall. Luke had never needed to use one anyway. He'd come here to work at the hospital as part of his specialist training in tropical diseases so he'd stayed in one of the cabins set up for the FIFO— Fly-In-Fly-Out—staff that provided medical cover and a helicopter service for the whole group of islands and managed to keep a surprisingly excellent, if small, hospital running.

Even the local people who helped staff the hospital had been excellently trained. Like the nurses.

Like Ana…

Luke pulled on a short-sleeved, open-necked shirt and a pair of light chinos. He combed his hair but decided not to bother eliminating his five o'clock shadow. This evening, in particular, was a gathering of people who knew each other well and they'd been invited to relax here. For the next couple of days the intention was for them to enjoy a tropical break while they shared new ideas and then brainstormed the best way to use this facility in the future.

Outside, the sun was already low and the heavy fragrance of the lush ginger plants screening his bure from the next one made Luke draw in a deep breath. He'd only taken a couple of steps before he turned back, however. How ironic would it be to come here and end up as a patient? Digging into his bag, he found the tropical-strength insect repellent he'd brought and gave himself a quick spritz. He slipped the slim aerosol can into his shirt pocket to take with him in case one of his colleagues had not been so well prepared.

Like the accommodation bures, the meeting hall had been designed to blend with island style. It had a thatched roof and was open on all sides with polished wooden benches and woven mats on the floor. A table had been set up as a bar, and a man peeled away from the group gathered in front of it.

'Luke. It's so good to see you.'

'Harry.' Luke took the outstretched hand but the greeting turned into more of a hug than a handshake. They were far more than colleagues, thanks to what they'd gone through together years ago. 'I can't believe what you've achieved here.'

'It was your idea.'

'Hardly. I suggested using the laboratories as a base to attract new research. I didn't expect you to run with it to the extent of creating the world's most desirable conference venue.' Luke shook his head. 'You don't do things by halves, do you, Harry?'

'I needed a new direction. Or maybe a distraction.'

Luke's gaze dropped to his friend's hand. 'How is it?'

'Oh, you know… I won't be stepping back into an operating theatre any time soon.' Harry turned away with a smile. 'Let me get you a nice cold beer. Unless you'd prefer something else? A cocktail, perhaps?'

'A beer would be great. But don't worry. I'll get it myself. And I need to say hello to people.' Luke followed Harry towards the bar but got sidetracked on the way when he noticed an acquaintance. 'Charles…it's been far too long. How are things going in Washington, DC?'

'It was snowing when I left.' Charles—an American expert on dengue fever—grinned broadly as he gestured towards their stunning view of the beaches and sea beyond the jungle. 'Have to say, this is a bit of a treat.'

'It's a great place. If you walk past the rock fall at the end of the beach in front of the bures you'll get to Sunset Beach. On an evening like this the cliffs light up like they're on fire. That's how this island got its name.'

'Is that so? You've obviously done your homework.'

'Not exactly. I've been here before. When I was starting my specialty training in tropical diseases I came out to do a stint at the hospital here.'

A short stay that had only been intended to enhance his training but which had ended up changing his life.

Haunting him…

He'd known he would encounter ghosts here but they were so much more powerful than he had anticipated. He should have made it impossible for Harry to persuade him to return but how could he have missed this inaugural event when he'd been present at the moment the dream had started? When he'd been the one to suggest the setting?

'I heard about the hospital.' A tall, blonde woman with a Scandinavian accent had joined them. 'Is it usual for such an isolated group of islands to have such a well-equipped medical centre?'

'Not at all. It's thanks to the Lockhart family that it came about. They discovered the gold and started the mine and the research station.'

'And the mine did well enough to pay for setting up the hospital?'

'Not exactly.'

Another ghost appeared because it was impossible not to remember when he'd first heard this story himself. He'd been walking hand in hand with Anahera, on their way to the best seat in the house for the dramatic show that nature put on every evening at Sunset Beach. He could actually hear the sad notes in her voice as she'd filled him in on a bit of island history.

'It was a family tragedy that made it happen. A premature birth of twins that led to the death of their mother and one of the twins being severely disabled. Their father—Max Lockhart—devoted his life to making sure such a thing would never happen again. He studied medicine himself, lobbied the Australian government for funding and encouraged local people to get trained. I believe he even paid for some of that training out of his own pocket.'

'Amazing...' Charles murmured. 'And now he's set up this conference centre? He's a man with vision, that's for sure.'

'Someone else had this vision.' Luke looked up to smile in Harry's direction. He was outside now, with a group of islanders, and they were taking the top layer off a cooking pit. Steam billowed out and a delicious smell wafted in through the open walls of the meeting house. 'Have you met Sheikh Rahman al-Taraq?'

'I heard a lot about him when I made enquiries after getting the invitation for this meeting. A surgeon, yes? Isn't he funding some extensive research into vaccines for encephalitis? How come a surgeon got so interested in a tropical disease?'

'You'll have to ask him about that.'

'I'll do that. Maybe over dinner. Whatever it is they're dishing up out there smells fantastic. I'm starving...'

'I don't like fish pie.'

'There'll be some ice cream later, Raoul. As long as you eat your veggies.' Anahera tried to sound firm but she was smiling as she delivered her last dinner tray. 'You won't be eating hospital food for much longer anyway. Didn't I hear Dr Sam say you might be able to go home tomorrow?'

'He's going to see how well I go on the crutches. And talk to my mum about getting to clinics to get my bandages changed.'

'Yes...you've got to keep that leg clean. You don't want to have to have any more operations.'

'I'm going to have a big hole in my leg where the ulcer was, aren't I?'

'Not a hole, exactly, but it will be a big scar and a dent where there isn't so much muscle. And you're going to have to work on building up your other leg muscles with the exercises we've taught you. You've been in bed for a long time.'

'Ana...'

She turned swiftly at the urgent tone of the call to see Sam in the doorway of the two-bed ward.

'Sam...I thought you were at the cocktail party.'

'I was on my way. Got a call. You *have* to come with me.'

Anahera tucked back a stray tress of long dark hair that was escaping the knot on the back of her head. She glanced down at her uniform of the green tunic and three-quarter-length pants that were looking a bit worse for a long day's wear and she shook her head, but Sam was already turning. His voice got fainter as he headed towards their small theatre suite.

'*Now*, Ana. It's an emergency.'

Any thoughts of how she must look vanished as Anahera ran after Sam. He was lifting the heavy life pack in one hand and reaching for an oxygen cylinder with the other.

'What's happened?'

'Could be a heart attack. One of the visiting doctors. Ten out of ten chest pain and nausea. Grab the resus kit and let's go.'

Manu, the hospital porter, had a golf cart already running outside the door.

'Maybe I should stay,' Anahera said. 'We can't leave the hospital unattended.'

'I'll stay,' Manu told them. 'And Hettie's on her way.'

'I need you,' Sam said as he stowed the gear on the back of the vehicle. 'You're the one with the intensive care training. If we have to intubate and ventilate, I want you helping.'

Ana climbed onto the cart. Sam was right. This was exactly the sort of scenario she had covered with her extensive postgraduate training. She could deal with something like this without a doctor around, if necessary, and the opportunity to keep her skills fresh didn't happen that often.

They bounced down the track as Sam opened the throttle. It wasn't that far to the new development but it was far enough to have Anahera running through all the possibilities in her head. Would they find their patient in a cardiac arrest? At least there were plenty of doctors there who could provide good-quality CPR but they would need the defibrillator to have any hope of starting a heart again.

It was almost an anticlimax to rush in and find nothing dramatic happening. A group of people were standing quietly beside a table covered with abandoned plates of food. A middle-aged man was sitting on the floor, propped up by a large cushion. Another man was crouched beside him with a hand on his wrist, taking his pulse. The woman standing beside them, directing a breeze from a fan to the patient's face, was Anahera's mother, Vailea Kopu, who was the first to spot their arrival.

'They're here,' she said. 'You're going to be fine, Dr Ainsley.'

'I'm fine already,' the man grumbled. 'I keep telling

you, it's only indigestion. I ate your wonderful food too fast, that's all.'

Sam crouched beside the man. 'Let's check you out to make sure. I'm Sam Taylor, one of the resident doctors here.'

'This is Charles Ainsley.' The man monitoring the condition of their patient turned to look at Sam. 'He's sixty-three and has a bit of a cardiac history…'

Anahera wasn't hearing any of their patient's history. Her hands were shaking as she opened the pockets of the life pack and pulled out the leads they would need to do a twelve-lead ECG and check whether the heart's blood supply was compromised.

She couldn't look up but she didn't need to.

She would have known that voice anywhere…

How on earth had the possibility of Luke Wilson attending this elite conference not occurred to her?

But it had, hadn't it? She'd been avoiding any mention of the upcoming event because that thought had been haunting her. Not attending the cocktail party because she didn't want to hear people talking about research into tropical diseases had been a blanket denial. There was only one person she would really dread listening to. Or meeting. The visiting medical specialists would only be here for a couple of days, she had told herself. It would be easy to stay out of the way.

Much easier not to even know whether Luke was present.

She'd been right to dread this. Even the sound of his voice was overwhelming enough to have her whole body trembling. What would happen if she looked up and made eye contact?

He was still talking to Sam. '…Stable angina but he's due for a coronary angiogram next month.'

'Let's get an ECG,' Sam said. 'Have you had any aspirin today, Charles? Used your GTN spray?'

'I took an extra aspirin for the flight. Forgot my spray.'

'No problem.' Having unbuttoned the shirt, Sam reached for the leads that Anahera had attached sticky dots to. 'Grab the GTN, Ana. And let's get some oxygen on, too.'

Ana…

Her name seemed to hang in the air. Had Luke heard? Or had he recognised her already and was trying to ignore her presence?

Dammit…her hand was still shaking as she pulled the lid from the small spray pump canister.

'Open your mouth for me,' she directed. 'And lift your tongue…'

'I can do that.' A hand closed over hers to remove the canister and there was no help for it—she *had* to look up.

And Luke was looking right back at her.

For a heartbeat nothing else existed as those hazel-green eyes captured her own with even more effect than the touch of his hand had—and that had been disturbing enough.

Her body froze, and she couldn't breathe. Her mind froze as it was flooded with emotions that she'd thought she would never experience again. The love she had felt for this man. The unbearable pain of his betrayal.

And then something else made those memories evaporate as instantly as they'd appeared.

Fear…

This wasn't supposed to be happening. It was dangerous. She had to protect more than her own heart and that meant she had to find the strength to deal with this and make sure nothing was allowed to change.

Determination gave her focus and an unexpected but very welcome sense of calm. It was Anahera who broke the eye contact and found that both her voice and her hands had stopped shaking.

'Fine. I'll put the oxygen on.'

The moment had mercifully been brief enough for no one else to have noticed. Or maybe it hadn't. Sam looked up after sticking the final electrode into place.

'This is Anahera,' he told Luke. 'Our specialty nurse.'

'Yes.' Luke pressed the button on the canister to direct a second spray under their patient's tongue. 'We've met before.'

'Of course…' Vailea was still standing beside them, providing a cool breeze from the palm-frond fan. 'I knew I'd seen you before. You came here to work in the hospital a few years ago.'

'I did.'

'You had to rush away, though… Your wife was ill?'

Oh…God… There it was again. The pain…

'Yes.' The monosyllable was curt. Grudging. Maybe Luke didn't want to remember the way they'd parted any more than she did.

The only blessing right now was that there were only two people in this room who knew what had happened during the few weeks that Luke had been here and only one who knew what the aftermath had been.

Anahera just had to make sure that it stayed that way.

Ana…

Hearing that name had been a bombshell Luke hadn't been expecting.

Oh, he'd seen the green uniform that looked a bit like a set of scrubs from the corner of his eye and had realised the attending doctor had brought an assistant to help carry all the medical gear, but he'd been so focussed on relaying all the information he'd gathered about Charles that he hadn't looked properly.

And then he'd heard her name. Had seen the way her hand had been shaking as she'd struggled to get the cap off the GTN spray pump. It had been an unconscious reaction to take the canister from her hand. Ana had been struggling and he could help. The consequence of touching her hadn't entered his thoughts at all so no wonder it had been another bombshell.

But both of those shocks—hearing her name and touching her skin—were nothing compared to looking into her eyes for the first time in nearly five years.

How could that be so powerful?

They were just a pair of brown eyes and he must have met hundreds of people with that eye colour over those years. How could a single glance into this particular pair make him feel like the ground beneath him had just opened into a yawning chasm?

It was like the difference between putting a plug into an electrical socket and somehow sticking your finger in to access the current directly.

And Ana had felt it, too. He'd seen the shock in her eyes but then he'd seen something he'd never expected to see. Something that squeezed the air out of his chest to leave a vacuum that felt physically painful.

He'd seen *fear*, he was sure of it.

'It's gone.' The voice of their patient sounded absurdly cheerful. 'The pain's completely gone.'

No. Luke rocked back on his heels, his gaze seeking Ana's again.

Charles might well be feeling fine but Luke had the horrible feeling that, for himself, the pain had only just begun.

CHAPTER TWO

ANAHERA WASN'T LOOKING back at Luke and it felt like deliberate avoidance.

She had the nasal cannula hanging from her hands, one end attached to the oxygen cylinder, the other end ready to loop around their patient's ears, and she was looking at Sam.

'Keep really still for a tick, mate. I'm going to get a twelve-lead ECG printed out and then we'll see what's what.'

There were a few seconds' silence as the life pack captured a snapshot of the electrical activity of the heart and then printed out the graph. Luke looked around, as if he needed to remind himself of why he'd come here when he'd known about the risk. Okay, he'd thought that the worst he would face would be the memories but there'd always been the possibility that Ana might have come home again, hadn't there? He'd pushed it aside. He was only going to be on the island for a couple of days, in the company of his professional colleagues and a good friend. He wouldn't be facing anything he couldn't handle.

But here he was. Facing something he had no idea how to handle.

Anahera was *afraid* of him?

He'd hurt her *that* badly?

An unpleasant crawling sensation began to fill that space in his chest. He felt like a jerk. A complete bastard.

His gaze had tracked the other conference attendees standing in a sombre group waiting to hear the verdict on Charles Ainsley's chest pain but he ended up looking at Anahera again. This time her head was bent close to Sam's as they both studied the ECG. He could hear her voice.

'There's no sign of any ST segment elevation. I can't see any depression that might show myocardial ischaemia either, can you?'

She was speaking softly, her tone measured. He hadn't even remembered hearing her speak like this, maybe because the memory of the last time he had spoken to her had been so very different.

She'd been so angry that he'd finally tracked her down and called her while she'd been on shift at that hospital in Brisbane.

'What's the problem, Luke? Is London a bit boring? You feel like cheating on your wife again?'

She hadn't been about to let him say any of the things he'd wanted to say.

'I don't want to hear it. I never want to hear from you again. Ever...'

The anger had been contagious in the end. She'd hated him. How could love turn to hate as decisively as if a coin had been flipped?

It couldn't. That had been the conclusion Luke had come to. It couldn't happen if the love had been real. Yes, you could throw the coin in the air but there was magic in real love and the coin would always land the right side up.

He could never hate Anahera. Not in a million years.

He would have given her the chance to explain. He would have listened.

And forgiven her anything.

Even now, he could forgive the way she was deliberately avoiding his gaze. How could he not when he'd seen that fear in her eyes?

'It's looking good, isn't it?' Charles was smiling. 'I told you it was only indigestion.'

'It's more likely it was angina, given how quickly it's gone with the GTN.'

'In any case, I'm fine.' Charles began to peel off the electrodes. 'I'm sorry to have given everyone a fright. It's my fault for forgetting my spray.'

'Keep this one,' Sam said. 'I'd still like to run some more tests. I've got a bench top assay for cardiac biomarkers. If I take a blood sample, I can pop into the laboratory here and have a result in no time.'

'Have a drink instead,' Charles said. 'And some of the amazing food.' He waved at his colleagues. 'Please carry on with your dinners,' he directed. 'Another life saved, here.'

A relieved buzz of conversation broke out and there were smiles all round. Anahera was still looking serious, however, as she coiled wires to tuck them into a pocket of the life-pack case.

He had to say something.

'It's good to see you, Ana. I…I wasn't expecting to.'

'No.' The wires had tangled a little and she shook them. 'I wasn't expecting to see you either.' Her soft huff of breath was an embryonic laugh. 'Silly, I guess. This is your field.' The wires were being coiled more tightly than necessary. 'It's a long way to come, though, and I wouldn't have thought you'd…'

What? She wouldn't have thought he'd want to come anywhere near this place again? The brief glance in his direction as her sentence trailed off made him feel like he was a stranger to her. Not someone to be afraid of now but someone to be ignored?

'I thought you were living in Brisbane.' Luke could have kicked himself the moment the words came out. It made it sound like the only reason he'd come back here was because he'd thought she was safely a very long way away.

But that was the truth, wasn't it?

'Sorry to disappoint you.' The pockets on the life pack were snapped shut, and Anahera got to her feet. 'I moved back home a couple of years ago.'

'I'm not disappointed.' He attempted a smile. 'And it *is* good to see you again.'

A lot of time had passed. Surely they could find a way to connect on some level? He wanted that, he realised. More than was probably good for him.

He wanted to see her eyes the way he remembered them, not full of fear that he might hurt her again. Or so distant he wasn't even being acknowledged for who he was. Or who he had been.

What he really wanted was to see Anahera smile, but it wasn't going to happen, was it?

And then it struck him. She wouldn't be afraid of him if she knew the truth. She wouldn't feel that avoiding him was the best way to cope either.

Something else crept into the odd mix of his feelings.

A glimmer of hope, perhaps?

Maybe this was an opportunity for both of them to lay some ghosts to rest. So that they could both move on with their lives without being haunted by what had happened between them.

* * *

'You stay.' Anahera zipped up the resus kit after Sam had taken the blood sample Charles had finally agreed was a good idea. 'You were coming here anyway. I can take all the gear back to the hospital.'

'Are you sure?' Sam was watching their patient rejoin the gathering. 'I would quite like to keep an eye on him for a while. It's only going to take a few minutes to run the assay.'

'I'd like to see the laboratory again.' Much to Anahera's discomfort, Luke hadn't followed Charles to the other side of the meeting hall. 'It sounds like you've got more gear in there than there was when I was last here.'

'I'll bet. You should come and see the hospital, too. You wouldn't have had the CT scanner when you were here. Or the ventilator we've got for intensive care either.'

'You've got a CT scanner? Wow...'

'And Anahera, here, is a qualified intensive care nurse. She could pretty much do my job, to tell the truth. She did paramedic training in Brisbane, too. She's the best at intubating if you've got a difficult airway.' Sam laughed. 'But you probably know that. You guys must have kept in touch since you were here?'

'No.' Luke and Anahera spoke at the same time but their tones were very different. Luke's held regret. Anahera's was firm enough to sound like a reprimand. No wonder Sam gave her such a surprised glance.

She shrugged, her smile wry as she tried to excuse her tone. 'You know how many FIFOs we get. If we kept in touch with them all we'd never have time to do our jobs.'

Slipping the straps of the resus kit over her shoulders, Anahera bent to pick up the life pack in one hand and the oxygen cylinder in the other. She managed a brief glance at Luke. Another smile even, albeit a tight one. 'Enjoy your visit,' she said. 'I hope the conference is worthwhile.'

'Let me carry some of that for you.'

She avoided his gaze. 'I'm fine.'

Surely Luke could see that she needed to get away from him? Someone certainly could. Anahera could feel her mother's curious gaze all the way from where she was serving food again.

Had she been wrong in assuming that only she and Luke knew what had happened when he'd been on the island that first time? How close they had become?

If Vailea was busy putting two and two together, it could make things a whole heap more difficult.

'No, you're not.' Sam took the heavy life pack from her hand. 'Don't be such a heroine, Ana. You make us look bad.'

Sure enough, another man was coming towards them, clearly intent on helping.

Anahera smiled at Sam. 'Go on, then. Just to make you feel better.'

It would make her feel better, too, to have company as she walked away from Luke. She straightened her back. She had friends here. She used her now free hand to wave at her mother, who smiled back. She had family here, too. Luke was the outsider. If he presented a threat, she had plenty of people on her side.

And maybe he would retire gracefully. Sam had paused as Luke introduced him to the man who'd joined them.

'This is Harry. Sheikh Rahman al-Taraq. He's the person who's responsible for all of this. The man who's making it his mission to find a way to beat encephalitis, amongst other tropical nasties.'

A sheikh? Anahera blinked. This was all getting a little surreal.

Sam shook the sheikh's hand. 'I can't wait to talk to you,' he said. 'I've got a few minutes to spend in the laboratory and then I'll be back.'

'Mind if I come with you? I'd like to see how the labs are shaping up. We've put quite a lot of new equipment in there. Luke, you should come, too.'

'Oh?'

'I might have another job for you—after you've given your keynote address tomorrow. We've got a bit of research to set up, here. A clinical trial, I'm hoping.'

'I'm only here for a couple of days, Harry.' Luke's laugh sounded a bit forced. Nervous even?

If that was the case, he wasn't the only one feeling like that. Anahera started walking towards the golf cart again. This was getting rapidly worse. She needed a safe place to try and get her head around it all. She couldn't wait to get back to the hospital.

No…maybe she'd ask Hettie to stay on to start her night shift early. The safe place Anahera really needed was at home.

With her daughter.

Bessie, the housekeeper at the Lockhart mansion who looked after Hana when Anahera was at work, had been happy to babysit tonight.

'She's been no trouble,' she said. 'Went to bed and off to sleep like an angel.'

'That's where you need to go, too, Bessie. You look

tired. Thank you so much for your help. I don't know what we'd do without you.'

The hug from the older woman was soft and squashy and full of love, and it took Anahera straight back to the kind of simplicity her childhood had been full of.

It made her want to cry.

'I am tired,' Bessie admitted. 'But I'm also very happy. Miss Caroline and Keanu are coming back very soon so I want the house to look perfect. We might have a wedding to get ready for.'

Anahera smiled. Keanu was another permanent doctor on Wildfire Island and, along with Sam, was a very good friend. Caroline was a Lockhart—the twin who had come into the world unscathed. 'It is very happy news. But don't go overdoing things.'

'Tell your mother that, too. She's working too hard. She has her job at the hospital and now she's taking on more work at that resort place.' Bessie shook her head as she gathered up her basket and cardigan. 'So much is happening on the island at the moment. I can't keep up…'

'I know. I feel like that, too.' Especially right now. 'But they're good things, Bessie. The mine closing has been a disaster for everybody, and Caroline's going to try and fix things. And the conference centre is going to create more jobs and bring in some money. I heard that there's going to be some new research projects happening, too. It's all good.'

But Bessie was frowning. 'You don't look so happy about it, Ana.'

Anahera summoned a genuine smile and words of reassurance as she waved Bessie off. She was going to have to be careful what showed on her face for the next few days. At least it would be a while before her mother came home. She had time to get things sorted in her head.

And her heart.

It was easy to do that. All she needed to do was tiptoe into the room where Hana lay sleeping in her small bed inside the mosquito netting that was printed with pretty pink butterflies. The nightlight was also a butterfly with glowing wings—because Hana had had a passion for butterflies ever since she'd been a baby—and it gave enough light to see her daughter's face clearly as Anahera pulled the netting back. She stroked the tangle of golden curls back from the little face and bent to press a gentle kiss to the soft olive skin of Hana's cheek.

Hana stirred. She didn't wake but she smiled in her sleep and her lips moved in a contented whisper.

'Mumma…'

'I'm here, darling. Sleep tight. Love you to the moon and back.'

She stole another kiss and then let the netting fall back to protect the precious little body, but for a long moment she didn't move. This was what she'd needed more than anything. To feel this love.

To remind herself that everything had been worth it and that she had no regrets.

There were things that she needed to do, like finding something for dinner, having a shower and finding a clean uniform for work tomorrow, but they could all wait until her mother was home. A quiet moment to herself seemed more important and Anahera chose to curl up on the old cane chair in the corner of the veranda that was bathed in moonlight and the scent of the nearby frangipani bushes.

Maybe it was the moonlight that was her undoing. Or

the sweet scent of the tropical flowers. It was probably inevitable that she had to revisit her past, given the shock of seeing Luke, and maybe it was a necessary step in order to get past it and move forward again. Or at least get herself together enough to make sure her mother didn't guess the truth.

She couldn't know, could she? If she'd had even the tiniest suspicion she would never have made that casual remark that had sliced open old wounds for her own daughter.

'You had to rush away, though... Your wife was ill...'

It had been such a secret thing—their love affair.

How naïve had she been to think that had been because it had been so precious to them both? A private joy that might change when others knew about it?

But it had seemed like a natural progression, too, because of how it had started—as an almost telepathic conversation of glances and accidental touch as an undercurrent to the open conversations of two people getting to know each other. It had been Anahera who'd made the first move. Offering to show Luke the drama of Sunset Beach had been an invitation to let whatever had been happening between them grow and, for her, that first kiss had only confirmed that her heart had already been stolen.

And it would have changed things if others had known. Her mother would have been afraid that she would lose her. That Anahera would follow Luke back to London and forget her island heritage. Her work family would have worried about how they would replace her and she herself would have had to face the possibility of giving up so much for a new life, and she hadn't been ready for that. She had wanted to stay in the safe bubble of no one else knowing for as long as possible. To revel in the bright colours and extraordinary happiness of being so completely in love.

How ironic was it that she'd ended up having to flee and start a new life anyway? Alone. Or so she'd thought until the disruption and heartache had settled enough for her to realise what was happening to her body.

And Luke? Well, he'd had his own reasons for wanting to keep their love affair a secret and it hadn't had anything to do with how precious it was, had it?

Tapping into that old anger wasn't going to help, though. She'd made a conscious decision to let it go the moment she'd first held Hana in her arms. To feel thankful that it had happened even. Oh, it had resurfaced sometimes in those first months of trying to raise her daughter alone, when the fatigue and financial pressures and homesickness had got on top of her, but coming back to Wildfire Island had fixed that. She'd been back for more than two years now and she had all the support she needed. A job that she loved and the joy of watching her daughter grow up in the same place she had. A place filled with such extraordinary beauty and countless butterflies.

Her life was exactly the way she wanted it to be.

The last thing she'd expected—or wanted—was to be reminded that something was missing. The kind of something she'd found with Luke Wilson. The one thing she had known she would never find again, especially coming back to the isolation of her childhood home, but the sacrifice had been worth it.

For Hana.

Anahera was so happy here so there was a new anger to be found that her happiness had been ambushed like this. The sooner she could get Luke and all the associated baggage out of her head, the better.

She closed her eyes on a sigh, unable to ignore it any longer—the thing she knew wasn't going to be fixed when Luke left the island in a few days. Something that had always been there but which had suddenly become a whole lot bigger. Which might, in fact, get even worse when Luke had gone again.

The guilt that Luke had no idea he was Hana's father…

Something unexpected was happening for Luke, quite apart from seeing Anahera Kopu again.

A unique alchemy of personalities that was creating an energy that Luke had been unsuccessfully trying to resist ever since the 'meet and greet' cocktail party.

He recognised it as the kind of connection he'd found with Harry over the weeks he'd treated him in London. It was more than the beginnings of a significant friendship—it was a meeting of like minds that was inspirational enough to have the possibility of achieving something amazing.

Sam Taylor might appear to be extraordinarily laid back but there was a passion for what he did running quite close to the surface and his charm was a force to be reckoned with. Add that to the more brooding intelligence and determination of Harry, along with the kind of resources he had to make things happen, and Luke was finding himself to be the meat in an increasingly interesting sandwich.

Which was why—despite thinking it wasn't the best idea—he found himself visiting Wildfire Island's hospital during a break on the second day of the conference, when the other attendees had been taken out to one of the outer islands to go snorkelling and visit a turtle colony.

He didn't want it to seem like he was forcing his company on Anahera. If there was any chance of being able to talk and possibly resolve their unfinished business, it wasn't going to happen in front of other people. It wasn't going to happen as the result of a planned meeting either, but the hope of finding her by chance was fading after Luke's long walk along the beaches and through the village yesterday evening.

And this was a professional visit to the hospital. He and Sam had a lot to talk about.

The only space for that discussion appeared to be the room that staff gathered in to take a break. There was a kitchenette for preparing hot drinks or food and a small fridge that Sam opened to reveal an impressive stock of cold drinks. The couch looked as though it was a comfortable space to nap on a night shift, and Luke could see a neatly folded blanket and a couple of pillows tucked neatly behind it. A couple of reclining lounge chairs and a table filled the rest of the available space and one of the lounge chairs had an occupant.

'G'day, mate.'

'Jack—this is Luke Wilson. The encephalitis expert I was telling you all about. Luke—this is Jack Richards, our number-one helicopter pilot.'

Jack got to his feet and extended his hand. 'It's a privilege to meet you, Luke. You've certainly fired Sam up. Haven't seen him this excited in years.'

Luke shook his hand. 'It's an exciting development, that's for sure.'

'What would you like, Luke?' Sam still had the fridge door open. 'Something cold or a coffee or tea?'

'I'd love a cup of tea,' Luke admitted. 'Haven't had one since I left London and it's starting to feel a long time ago.'

'Might have one myself.' Sam grinned. 'Get in touch with my English roots.'

'Where are you from?'

'Up north. Did my training in Birmingham.'

'What brought you here?'

Sam shrugged. 'I love my sailing. Brought my yacht here to do a FIFO stint a few years back and I liked it so much I never left.'

There was more to the story than that, Luke thought, but he wasn't about to talk about it. He turned back to Jack, keen to ask what kind of challenges his job presented, but his gaze slid past the helicopter pilot as someone else entered the staffroom.

'Sam?' Anahera was holding a clipboard. 'Can I get you to sign off on the antibiotics for Kalifa Lui?' She stopped abruptly in the doorway as she spotted Luke. He could see her neck muscles moving as she swallowed and then she cleared her throat as she broke the eye contact almost instantly. 'I think he's going to need some more Ventolin, too. The wheezing hasn't improved much since he came in.'

'Sure.' Sam paused in his task of making tea to take a pen from his shirt pocket and scribble on the clipboard. 'Have you persuaded him to stay overnight?'

'I'm working on it. I don't think he understands how serious a chest infection can be on top of his chronic lung disease, though. He wants to get back to work.'

'What work?' Jack asked. 'He's a miner and the mine's been closed. It's not safe any more.'

'They're not allowed down the mine but a lot of the

men are working to try and improve the safety so they can open it again. They're desperate to get their livelihoods back.'

'I'll come and talk to him soon,' Sam said. 'And if I can't convince him, I'll get his wife, Nani, in here. She'll sort him out.'

'Okay...' Anahera turned to leave, and Luke stared at her. Was she not even going to acknowledge him?

'Stay for a few minutes,' Sam said. 'There's something Luke and I are going to discuss and it involves you.'

'I...I need to get back to Kalifa.'

'He's had his first dose of antibiotics, hasn't he?'

'Yes.'

'And his first nebuliser is still going?'

'Yes.'

'And one of the aides is in the ward with him who can come and find us if there's any deterioration in his condition?'

Anahera just nodded this time. Still without looking at Luke, she came and sat down on one of the kitchen chairs around the table.

Sam put down two mugs of tea and gestured to Luke to take another seat. Jack watched them.

'Maybe I'll leave you to it. Go and polish the red bird or something.'

'You're welcome to stay,' Sam said. 'In fact, you'll probably be involved as much as Ana. Have a seat.'

Jack looked intrigued. Anahera was looking wary.

'What's going on?' she asked.

'You both know the really exciting news.'

'You talked about it enough yesterday.' Jack grinned. 'We have a vaccination available for M'Langi encephalitis that's been approved for clinical trials.'

'That's right.'

Jack's grin faded as he looked at Luke. 'From what Sam was saying, it was one hell of an opening address that your friend made.' He turned to Anahera. 'You had a day off yesterday so you weren't here to hear that story, were you? About the sheikh and his investment?'

'Ah…no. I did briefly see the sheikh at the conference centre and I also heard about the new vaccination. The whole island's talking about it.' She smiled at Luke. 'It's amazing news.'

'It's thanks to Luke that it's happened,' Sam said. 'There's already the vaccination for Japanese encephalitis but there were plenty of other varieties to choose to work on next. It was Luke's connection to these islands that made M'Langi the lucky one.'

'I've never forgotten my time here,' Luke said quietly. 'I think about it every day.'

A flush of colour darkened Anahera's olive skin. The hidden message had been received loud and clear. It hadn't been just the island that he'd thought about every day, had it? He'd been thinking about *her*…

'But the thanks should go to Harry,' he continued. 'He's the one who's put an extraordinary amount of time and money into getting this vaccination developed.'

'Which he couldn't have done if you hadn't saved his life.' Sam turned his gaze to Anahera. 'You should have heard him talking,' he told her. 'There wasn't a dry eye in the house by the time he'd finished telling us how close to death he was when he got encephalitis. How Luke was there with him twenty-four seven in the ICU, fighting for his life as if it was his own. That it was that kind of devotion that made Harry determined to give something back to thank him and to try and stop other people having to go through what he went through.'

The praise had been embarrassing yesterday. He'd only been doing his job after all, but watching Anahera's reaction to the story made it feel very different. There was something in her eyes that was making him feel proud instead of embarrassed. There was respect there. And something warmer—as if she was feeling proud of him, too?

'I always knew you'd go on to do great things,' she said softly. 'It's a great story.'

'Sounds like you have, too. Paramedic and ICU qualifications? An expert in difficult airway management? How long did you stay in Brisbane?'

'About two years.' Anahera's glance flicked away the moment Brisbane was mentioned, and Luke could almost feel a change in temperature around him as any perceived warmth got sucked out.

She really didn't want to talk to him about Brisbane, did she?

Why? Had the opportunity for postgraduate training been compelling for more than professional reasons? Because it had meant a fresh start—away from the place she had met him?

No. He was reading too much into it. She hadn't cared that much or she wouldn't have dismissed him with such devastating effect after all the effort he'd made to track her down. She'd moved on with her life, that was all. And what she'd done with it was none of his business.

Fine. He could move on, too. He could start with this conversation.

'Harry has plans for some research projects that can only happen here,' he said. 'One of them involves travel to some of the outer islands, which is where you come in, Jack. He's only just heard about this M'Langi tea and he thinks it could be important.'

'Why?' Anahera was frowning. 'It only has insect repellent qualities, doesn't it?'

'Exactly,' Sam said with satisfaction. 'Controlling the mosquito population by reducing habitats that support breeding and personal protection by clothing and repellents are the mainstay of prevention of mosquito-borne disease. Repellents are only ever applied externally. It could be a real breakthrough to discover something effective that can be taken systemically. Did you know that there were an estimated seventy-seven thousand deaths worldwide in 2013 from encephalitis?'

'You've got some data on which islands have the lowest incidence of encephalitis, haven't you?' Luke asked. 'That's where we'll need to go to collect samples and find out exactly how they brew that tea.'

Sam nodded. 'From memory, I'm pretty sure it's French Island, and that's where the particular hibiscus bushes that they make the tea from grow, but I'll check.'

'French Island?'

'Apparently there was a shipwreck there long ago. A French square-rigged sailing vessel. The crew survived and so we have a fair bit of French blood mingling with the islanders'. We still get some French sailors turning up, intrigued by the historic link.'

Curiously, Anahera didn't seem to want to be hearing any of this. She got to her feet.

'I really need to get back to my patients. I can't see how any of this involves me.'

'You're due to do the clinic on French Island in the next couple of days, aren't you?'

'Oh...you want me to collect some tea-leaves? Talk to the locals?'

'No. I want you to take Luke with you.'

That shocked her enough to freeze her movements, except for the direction of her gaze, which flew to Luke in alarm. 'But the conference finishes today, doesn't it? Don't you have to get back to London?'

There was that fear again. It was just a bit over the top, wasn't it? He'd been keeping his distance and it had to be obvious he wasn't going to force his company—or anything else—on her.

'Harry's persuaded me to stay on for a bit. To set up the research projects and get the protocols in place for a clinical trial of the vaccination.'

Anahera turned to Sam. 'Maybe you should do the clinic instead of me, then. I don't have anything to do with research and you love it.'

She was trying to avoid him again. Luke could feel himself frowning and barely registered Sam's smile as he spoke.

'Don't worry, we'll sort out the logistics. Why don't I give you a tour of the hospital while we talk? You'll be wanting to get back for the last session of the conference.'

Jack got to his feet as well. 'Time I did some work, too. Nice to meet you, Luke. I look forward to transporting you around the islands very soon.'

Anahera was leading the way as they all left the staff-room. The layout of the hospital still felt familiar to Luke. The U-shaped building with small wards on one side, Outpatients, kitchens and the staffroom in the middle and the ED, ICU and Radiography—that now, apparently, had gone high-tech with CT and ultrasound equipment available—on the other side. The wide covered walkway linking the wings surrounded a lush tropical garden that boasted a pretty pond in its centre.

The walkway was as spacious as he remembered and the overhead fans kept everything deliciously cool as they added to a sea breeze coming in from the garden.

There was more than a breeze coming in from the garden at the moment, though. An older woman who was carrying a small child could be seen ahead of them.

And, again, Anahera froze.

'*Bessie*…what are you doing here? What's happened?'

Luke could see that the child—a tiny girl—had been crying. Her hand was wrapped in what looked like a bloodstained tea towel.

'It's nothing to worry about,' the woman said. 'Just a little cut but it took a while to stop the bleeding and Hana got upset. I said we'd come and find Dr Sam and Mummy.'

Mummy? One of the other nurses here, perhaps? Luke, like everyone else, had stopped walking. Now the island woman stopped, too, as the child in her arms wriggled free. As soon as the girl's feet touched the floor, she was running. The tea towel unwound itself and fell to the floor as she threw her arms up in the air.

'Mumma…' The word was a sob.

Anahera was crouching, arms out, ready to catch the little girl. She scooped her up and held her close, pressing her cheek to a fluffy cloud of pale curls as she murmured reassurance.

And then she looked up and her gaze met Luke's.

He knew he must look like an idiot, with his jaw still hanging open, but this was the biggest shock yet since he'd set foot on Wildfire Island again.

There could be no mistaking the relationship between these two with the way this child had her arms wound so tightly around Anahera's neck and the palpable comfort she was clearly receiving from having found the person she needed most.

Anahera was a *mother*?

He had to swallow his shock. At least no one else seemed to have noticed. Jack was behind him and Sam was focussed on the child.

'Have you got a sore finger, sweetheart? Can you show Dr Sam?'

'It's all right, darling,' Anahera said. 'It's not going to hurt. We just want to see.'

A tiny hand appeared from behind her mother's neck and then a forefinger uncurled itself. The cut was quite deep but small.

'She found a piece of broken glass,' Bessie said unhappily. 'She was helping me clean out a cupboard.'

'You know what?' Sam asked cheerfully.

The small head moved slowly from side to side.

'I think I've got a plaster that's just the right size for a finger like that. And it's got a picture on it. Do you know what that picture might be?'

Big dark eyes widened. 'A flutterby?'

Sam grinned. 'Sorry, not a butterfly this time, button. Would a princess do instead? A Cinderella plaster?'

The smile was tentative.

'Didn't Cinderella have butterflies on her dress?' Anahera said. 'I'm sure she did. We've got the book at home, haven't we, Hana?'

Hana. So this exquisite child had a name that sounded like an echo of her mother's shortened name. She had her mother's gorgeous dark eyes, too, but her skin was much lighter and her hair very different from Anahera's midnight black.

'She's beautiful,' Luke heard himself saying aloud. 'How old is she?'

The moment the words left his mouth he realised, with what felt like a body blow, that it was possible he was looking at his own daughter here.

For a long moment there was a silence so complete it felt like everyone else here knew the significance of what the answer to his query could be. In the end, it was Hana who spoke.

'I'm *free*,' she told him.

'Three,' Anahera corrected her. 'Three and a *half*, even.'

The mental calculations were so easy to make, it took only a few seconds. Add on nine months for a pregnancy. Count up the years and months since he and Anahera had had that last, incredible night on Sunset Beach.

The difference was six months. There was no way that Hana was his child.

It should have been a huge relief.

So why was he left feeling so crushed?

Maybe because it was the final proof that Anahera hadn't cared enough. She'd moved on so fast she'd found someone else and become pregnant in the short space of a few months. For all Luke knew, Hana's father was also here on Wildfire Island. He might come through the same door any moment now.

Luke swallowed hard as he checked his watch. 'I might head back, Sam,' he said. 'We'll have plenty of time for this tour in the next few days, and, as you reminded me, I don't want to miss the last session of the conference.'

He didn't look back as he fired his parting words. 'It's what I actually came here for, after all.'

CHAPTER THREE

'WHAT'S UP, ANA?'

'Nothing.' Anahera didn't look up from her task of packing the large plastic bin that was on the bench, surrounded by a wide array of supplies.

'You don't seem yourself, that's all.' Sam was leaning against the doorframe of this storage room in the hospital's theatre annexe, having delivered the chilli bin with the lunch that Vailea had packed for the team doing the clinic run to French Island today.

Anahera turned away from him to stare at a shelf. 'Don't tell me we're out of urine dipsticks… I know we've got people who aren't managing their type two diabetes very well on French Island.'

Sam took a step into the room, reached past her shoulder and picked up the jar that had been right in front of her.

'Thanks.' Anahera cringed inwardly. 'Guess I was having a "man" look.'

'If you're worried about blood-glucose levels, a blood test is far more sensitive.'

'I know that.' The words came out as an unintentional snap and she hurriedly modified her tone. 'If the level's high enough to show up in urine then we'll know treatment is urgent. I've found that the occasional patient is more likely to agree to give a sample of urine than get stuck with a needle, even if it is just in a finger. I've already packed the BGL kit. I need the dipsticks for the antenatal checks, too.'

'Okay...'

She could feel Sam watching her. Maybe she hadn't undone the damage that that uncharacteristic snap had done.

'Sorry,' she muttered. 'I didn't sleep that well last night and I guess I'm a bit put out, having to take someone else with us today. It'll put us under pressure to get through the clinic cases so I have time to take him into the village to talk to people and get samples of the leaves or bark or whatever it is they use off the hibiscus plants.'

'Hmm...' Sam still hadn't left the room. 'Why is it that I get the impression you don't like Luke? I'm going to be working with the guy and he seems great. Is there something about him I should know?'

'No.'

'But you've met him before. You know him better than I do.'

Anahera almost laughed at the understatement. She could only hope that her smile wasn't wry.

'He's an awesome doctor. Hard-working and very, very smart. And he cares a lot about his patients.' She was keeping her hands busy, packing syringes and swabs into the plastic bin. Then she reached for the pregnancy test kits and had to close her eyes for a heartbeat. Sam was a good friend. Maybe he deserved to know that Luke wasn't completely honest. That he couldn't be trusted.

'I know...you should have heard that sheikh guy talking about him. Harry made him sound like God's gift to medicine.'

'Mmm…' It really was time to change the subject. 'Has Jack called to say the chopper's ready yet? We should get going soon. And if Luke's not here on time, we'll have to go without him.

'I'll find out.'

It was a relief to be left alone to finish her packing. Anahera really needed a few minutes to herself. A few deep breaths should do it, along with bringing her focus back to the task at hand so that she didn't find herself staring at something on a shelf that she couldn't see.

But the deep breathing didn't do what it was supposed to do. It didn't even melt the edges off that hard knot that seemed to be lodged in her belly.

Guilt, that was what it was.

She'd told Sam she hadn't slept that well last night but the truth was she'd tossed and turned so much that she'd barely slept at all.

It didn't matter how many times she went over and over that incident at the hospital when Hana had been brought in because she couldn't change the impressions she'd been left with. If anything, they only became crisper.

For a start, there'd been that unexpected and shocking reaction to seeing them together. A flash of imagining what it could have been like if they had become a family. A slicing pain of loss so deep that it was fortunate it had vanished as instantly as it had attacked.

Luke's face had been as easy to read as a large-print book. She'd seen the shock of discovering that she was a mother. Had seen the moment when it had occurred to him that *he* could possibly be Hana's father. And then she'd seen something that was shocking to *her. Disappointment?*

Did he want a child?

Even if he didn't, he had the right to know he had one, didn't he?

Oh, God…the guilt stone was getting steadily bigger and it had sharp edges that were giving her shafts of pain like colic.

Maybe reasoning would soften the edges, seeing that deep breathing hadn't done the trick.

She was deceiving him for everybody's sake.

His, Hana's, her mother's and her own.

She'd been over this ground so many times it was a familiar route. It was ironic how that casual conversation Luke had had with Sam yesterday was always her starting point.

Because one of those French sailors, intrigued by the history of the island, had been her father.

He'd come here, fallen in love with both the islands and her mother, and they had married and built a house on Atangi—the main island of this group. Her father, Stefan, had planned to create a premium tourist destination where people could come and sail and dive. It would bring money in to the islands and allow him to do what he loved most for the rest of his life.

He'd missed his homeland, though, and he'd taken Vailea and baby Anahera back to France for an extended visit to meet his family. They'd lived on the outskirts of Paris for three months.

'It was *so* cold,' her mother always said. 'And I couldn't speak the language. Even with you and Stefan there, it was the loneliest time. I wanted to be with him but part of me was slowly dying.'

They'd come back to the islands but things had changed. The islands were a place for a holiday for Stefan now and they couldn't be real life. Heartbroken, her parents had finally agreed they had to live apart. Vailea would visit Paris once a year in summer and Stefan would come to Atangi during the French winters. He'd never made it, even once, however, because he'd died after a diving mishap that had given him a fatal dose of the bends.

The first-hand knowledge of the heartbreak that trying to live in different worlds could produce was a sound starting point, wasn't it? Anahera had lived in Brisbane where the climate was far more like her homeland than London could ever be, but she'd ended up miserable and homesick. When she thought of London, it was always grey and people had to wear thick clothing and carry umbrellas all the time. Had she really thought—in those heady weeks of being so utterly in love—that she could have gone to live in London with Luke?

It could never have worked.

Hana would have to go there, though, if he knew he was her father. He would, quite rightfully, expect to be able to spend extended time with his daughter and, with his career, it wasn't likely that he could take time off to visit a remote part of the Pacific at regular intervals.

It was too easy to imagine the worst-case scenario. Arguments about schooling that might lead to a battle not to have Hana sent to an English boarding school. A taste of a different life that might lead to her teenage daughter deciding she would rather live full time with her father in a place that offered so much more in terms of social life and excitement.

Maybe it was the fear of loss that was the real driving force in this deception.

And, if she was completely honest, Anahera didn't want to share her precious daughter with the man who had broken her heart. He didn't deserve to have the unconditional love that this amazing little girl with the biggest heart in the world gave so freely.

Did that make her a bad person?

If it did, Anahera had decided long ago that she would live with the guilt of being one.

How much easier had that burden been to carry when Luke had been just a memory? Having him here in person was so much worse.

Unbearable even.

And now she had to spend a whole day in his company?

She had to press a hand to her belly as another knife-like cramp took hold.

'Ana?' Sam's voice floated through the doorway. 'Jack's all set and Luke's already at the helipad.' He came through the door just as Anahera straightened her back and summoned all her willpower to ignore the pain. 'Let me carry that bin for you.'

Getting a bird's-eye view of the islands from the cockpit of a helicopter was so much more spectacular than the limited scope of a small plane's window.

Luke was sitting in the front beside Jack and he had a grin on his face. 'Look at that…the sea's so clear you can just about see the coral in the reef. And the fish…'

'Gorgeous, isn't it? I never get sick of my office.' Jack's voice came through the headphones Luke was wearing. 'That's Atangi, there. The biggest island by land mass and the one that's been settled the longest. That's where the main schools are. It's where you grew up, isn't it, Ana?'

'Yes.' Anahera was sitting in the cabin of the helicopter, behind Luke so he couldn't see her. 'Until Mum started working at the hospital. We moved to the village on Wildfire after that and I took the boat to school.'

Luke hadn't known that. What had they talked about all those years ago? Maybe he'd done too much talking and not enough listening but it was too late to start now. Anahera had barely glanced at him when she'd arrived at the helipad and he hadn't been able to think of anything to say after a simple 'Good morning' because there'd been too many questions zipping through his head, starting with who looked after her daughter when she was at work and what did her husband do? And then he'd taken notice of her hands as she'd helped Jack load supplies into the chopper and he'd seen the absence of a wedding ring and that only led to more questions that he'd probably never get the chance to ask because it seemed like Anahera didn't even want to talk to him.

He shouldn't have let Harry and Sam talk him into extending his visit but that had been before he'd known about Anahera's daughter. When he'd still had that vague hope that maybe he and Anahera could clear the air between them. That he would be able to finally explain…

The chance of that happening had evaporated in the shock of finding out how conclusively Anahera had already moved on with her life. Why would he want to make things harder for himself by reopening old scars?

But what if she wasn't married? If whoever she had moved on with was no longer in her life?

No. He didn't want to go there. Didn't even want to think about it.

'What's that island?' he asked to distract himself. 'That round one, off to the left there. I never visited the other islands when I was here last time. I had no idea there were so many.'

'There are a lot. Most of them are uninhabited, though. That round one is Opuru. It got evacuated after a tsunami a decade or two ago and that's when the village on Wildfire got built. Before that, it was only the Lockharts and their house staff that lived here. The mine workers would all commute, mostly from Atangi.'

'Where's French Island?'

'A bit farther out. Not as big as Atangi and not as mountainous as Wildfire. It's got a lovely reef, though, and there's still the wreck of the ship it was named for. Divers love it. With the sea so clear, there's a point on one of the hills where you can see the bones of the whole ship. It's pretty spectacular.'

'I'd love to see that.'

'I could show you,' Jack said. 'We might have time, depending on how many people turn up for the clinic, of course. I stay close, in case Ana needs a hand.'

'I'd like to help with the clinic, too. If that's okay, Ana.'

'It won't be necessary.' Anahera's voice was cool. 'A lot of the people on this island don't speak much English so I'd have to translate everything and that would just slow us down. Jack and I do this on a regular basis and we've never had a problem we couldn't deal with. But thanks for the offer.'

Luke lapsed into silence as the helicopter dipped lower, heading for the landing point on French Island. The warning was clear and it was timely. If it felt like this to get a professional offer rejected, he would be wise not to make himself vulnerable on a personal level.

He wasn't wanted. Maybe he never really had been.

The patients waiting for the clinic to open were already sheltering from the sun under the spreading branches of an enormous fig tree.

Anahera could see a couple of pregnant women, mothers holding small children and a few elderly people who had family members there to support them. As she greeted everybody on the way in to open up the clinic building, she was already making a mental note of everything she would need to do. Rough bandages on limbs meant a wound that would need cleaning and dressing, possibly suturing. Her diabetic patients needed testing to make sure their blood-sugar levels were under control, either by medication or the lifestyle changes she was trying to encourage. The people with hypertension needed their blood pressure checked and, if the levels weren't improving, she'd need to talk to them about how compliant they were being with taking their tablets.

Antenatal checks for the pregnant women were important, too, and sometimes it took a lot of persuasion to get the mothers-to-be to leave their families in order to go to the mainland to give birth. Lani was worrying her at the moment.

'Your baby is still upside-down,' Anahera told Lani when it was her turn for a consultation. 'I'd like you see the obstetrician when she comes to Wildfire next week. Can you come across on the boat? Like you did for the ultrasound?'

Lani's gaze shifted to the silent, elderly woman who was sitting on a chair beside the window, and she lowered her voice. 'There's no one else to care for my mother during the day. My father is out fishing and my husband works on Atangi. It's difficult…especially since my brother and his family went to live in Australia.'

'I know.' Lani's mother had had a stroke a year ago and had been left with a disability that needed constant care. She had lost the use of one arm, her speech was unintelligible to anyone other than Lani and she had difficulty swallowing.

'Leave it with me, Lani. I'll arrange something. Maybe we can get someone to come here to help. Or we can arrange for your mother to come with you, like she has today.'

What would happen if the flying obstetrician deemed the birth high risk and advised Lani to go to Australia for the last weeks of her pregnancy was another problem. Anahera would need to bring it up with Sam and the other staff at their next clinical meeting. They might have to admit Lani's mother to the hospital to care for her until Lani was home again.

The morning flew by as Anahera treated her patients. Whenever she went outside to call the next person in, it was impossible not to look around to see how Luke was passing the time.

She'd been very unwelcoming, telling him his help wasn't necessary. She could imagine the look that Sam would give her if he found out. Or what he would say.

You had a doctor there and you made him just sit and wait for you? That's crazy, Ana. We need all the help we can get here. You know that.

She did know that. So the new guilt, added to what was already there, was taking the shine off a day that she normally loved. But she remembered how well they had worked together all those years ago. How they'd felt like the perfect partnership right from the first case they'd shared, and she didn't want to feel that professional rapport again. Things were hard enough as they were.

And Luke didn't seem to be feeling bad about being left out. When she went outside with Lani and looked at the long bench under the fig tree, he was no longer sitting there. In fact, half of the waiting patients weren't there any more either. A burst of laughter and a child's gleeful shriek revealed what was going on. A game of barefoot football. Village children had gathered and it seemed like the captains of the two teams were Jack and Luke.

For a moment Anahera watched the game, a smile spreading over her face, and, for the first time today, the knot in her stomach eased a little.

Luke looked so happy. He didn't need to speak an island dialect to connect to these children and they were loving this game. Could they tell that the way he was trying to block their access to the improvised goal was all for show and he was actually making it easier for them? The triumphant shouting when Luke was dramatically waving his fists in the air to indicate frustrated defeat suggested that they didn't and the joyful laughter meant that it didn't matter even if they did know.

And then a small boy tripped as he was running and fell hard, raising a cloud of dust from the bare patch of ground. Luke was there before the dust even began to settle, scooping the child up and settling him on one hip as he checked for any injury.

Anahera could see the concern on his face. The gentle way he was examining small limbs. And then he tickled the little boy and they both burst into laughter.

The stone in Anahera's belly seemed to turn into jelly.

She had forgotten how great Luke had been with children. That instant rapport that paved the way for making it easy for him to care for them. That patience and kindness that always won over even the most frightened children in the end.

It had been one of the first things she had loved about him.

She had thought about what a wonderful father he would make one day and how his children would adore him.

It wasn't the heat or dust that was making her throat close up.

It felt more like overwhelming sadness.

Luke set the child down on his feet and he ran off to join his friends. Luke was still grinning and he wiped dusty hands on his already smeared white shirt and then he looked around and caught sight of Anahera and the grin faded. He looked wary rather than happy now.

As if his change in mood was contagious, the game broke up. Anahera had to blink back tears. The happiness had been snuffed out and it felt like it was her fault.

'Alika? Can you come inside now, please? It's your turn…'

Finally, the clinic was over.

Luke watched as Anahera locked the door of the simple hut. Jack picked up the supply bin, which was almost empty, in one hand. He had the chilli bin that had held the sandwiches and cold drinks they'd had for lunch in the other.

'I'm going to drop these back to the chopper and then have a swim,' he said. 'Luke's already had a dip but I'm still filthy from that game of footy. Take your time in the village, Ana, but it'd be nice to get back to Wildfire before dark.'

'I thought you were going to come with us. Didn't you want to show Luke the shipwreck?'

'You know where it is.' Jack began to walk away. 'Have fun.'

Luke eyed Anahera. She met his gaze but neither of them smiled.

'Let's go, then,' he said. 'I've got all the snap-lock bags I need for samples and a notebook for recording information about the tea brewing.'

'Okay.' Anahera's nod was brisk. 'It's not too far to the village but we'd need to take a slightly longer route if you want to see the shipwreck.'

Did he want more time with Anahera?

This was an unexpected opportunity as he'd also thought that Jack would be joining them for the visit to the village. And it could well be the only chance he was going to get to have a private conversation with her.

'Yes.' His hesitation had been brief. 'I would like that. Very much.'

Their path took them uphill along a forest track, and Luke wasn't bothered by the silence between them because it added to the magic of the rainforest. It had been so long since he'd walked a track like this and he'd forgotten how intricately intertwined the plant life was. Spaces between the tall, smooth trunks of the trees that stretched to form the canopy were crowded with tree ferns and palms and ginger plants. There were dense tangles of vines that were a startling contrast to spectacular bursts of colour from orchids. Overhead branches had epiphytes and aerial moss competing for room. The raucous screech of parrots and a hum of insects were the only sounds other than twigs breaking beneath their feet.

They emerged from the forest into an area that had been cleared enough for grass to grow. There were some goats farther up the hill but Anahera led him towards a rocky patch that looked disconcertingly close to where the ground fell away steeply.

'Don't go too close to the edge,' she said. 'And test the rocks before you stand or sit on any of them. Sometimes one goes rolling off. The big ones are safe.' She scrambled carefully over some small rocks to climb onto the biggest one that jutted out towards the sea. Luke followed and found there was plenty of room for two people and the surface was quite flat. It provided a viewing platform with a stunning panorama of the ocean a long way below. The water was an astonishing shade of turquoise and so clear the ghostly outline of the ancient shipwreck was instantly recognisable.

'Wow…' Luke shaded his eyes from a sun that was getting lower in the sky and stared down. 'That's amazing…'

'Mmm. I love it here.' To Luke's consternation, Anahera walked calmly to the edge of the rock and folded herself gracefully to sit down with her legs dangling in space.

He followed a little more cautiously.

And there they were. Totally alone with the most stunning view imaginable spread out in front of them, with countless islands in every direction and the curve of reefs sheltering some of them and the changes in sea colour from pale turquoise to the almost navy blue of the deepest ocean. The intense heat of the day had faded and a gentle breeze was playing with the long strands of Anahera's ponytail. As if to make the moment perfect, a gorgeous gold-and-black butterfly came within touching distance as it flew past.

Luke was unlikely to get a better opening to a conversation.

'How cool is that?' He smiled. 'A flutterby.'

A huff of laughter escaped Anahera and it was the first time Luke had seen a genuine smile on her face in his presence. The kind that made the corners of her eyes crinkle and her whole face light up.

'You're not three, Luke. I don't think you get to call them a flutterby.'

'But why not?' It was so good to see her smile. It felt like that impenetrable barrier had just become transparent. 'It's such a brilliant word. It's exactly what they do, isn't it? Look…'

Sure enough, the stunning insect was fluttering, rising and then swooping as if it needed to explore its surroundings thoroughly.

'It's a beauty,' Anahera murmured. 'Hana would love it. She's had this thing for butterflies since she was tiny. I had her outside having a kick in the sun when she was only a few weeks old and she saw her first butterfly. That was when she smiled for the first time and it was the biggest grin.' Remembering it was making Anahera smile again and her expression was so tender it made Luke's heart ache.

'She's a very beautiful little girl. You must be very proud of her.'

'I am.'

'And her dad? He must be over the moon to have a daughter like Hana.'

There was a moment's silence that felt heavy. Awkward.

'He's not in the picture,' Anahera said.

Oh… Luke's heart missed a beat. 'Did…you meet him in Australia? At the hospital?' Had he been another doctor, like himself, perhaps? Or maybe a paramedic when Anahera was doing that part of her postgraduate training?

She seemed to be still watching the path the butterfly had taken, even though it had disappeared. 'He was a doctor.' She took a long inward breath that came out as a sigh. 'I had Hana in Brisbane and…and there was never any chance of a relationship with her father so… so I came home. To my family. My mother raised me by herself. History repeats itself sometimes, doesn't it?'

It didn't have to. The flash of bitterness that Anahera had chosen a path that didn't include him was ugly enough for Luke to squash it instantly, before its poison could tarnish this moment. He cleared his throat and searched for a way to change the conversation's trajectory.

'She looks very happy. When she doesn't have a sore finger.'

'She is. She loves the islands.' Anahera's tone lightened. 'There are more butterflies here.'

It was a neat, verbal circle that indicated that that topic of conversation was over. The silence was longer this time but it didn't feel so awkward. If anything, Luke was feeling more hopeful. Knowing that Anahera wasn't in a committed relationship with Hana's father made it more acceptable, somehow, to revisit the past.

'I'd forgotten,' Luke said quietly, 'how beautiful so many things are here. Like the ocean and the forest and the wildlife. The only thing I never forgot…was you.'

He could feel the way Anahera froze beside him. Could feel the transparency of that barrier fading so that it was becoming solid again. And then she moved, pulling her legs up over the edge of the rock and getting to her feet in one fluid movement.

Her voice was like ice. 'Did you tell your wife, Luke? About cheating on her?'

'No.' His response was so quiet he didn't think she'd heard.

'Maybe you should.'

'I can't do that.' Luke got to his feet slowly. His muscles felt heavy. Stiff. 'My wife died, Ana. Years ago. A few weeks after I left Wildfire.'

She was shocked. Her face turned back towards him. Her mouth opened and then closed, as if there'd been no words available. The breeze was still playing with the long strands of her ponytail and a few hairs caught on her lips but she didn't brush them away, she just kept staring at Luke.

'She was sick.' The words sounded wooden. The movement of her hand as she finally scraped the hair free of her lips was impatient. 'I knew that was why you had to rush back.'

'Not exactly. She woke up.'

The stare was back again, this time accompanied by a grimace of incomprehension. Disbelief, perhaps.

Luke's mouth felt dry. This wasn't exactly the scene he'd imagined when he'd hoped for the chance to tell Anahera the truth. Sitting on Sunset Beach, holding hands might have been nearer the mark. Standing on a windswept rock with a dangerous cliff and the skeleton of a long-ago wrecked ship far below made it all far too dramatic.

'She'd been in a coma for three years,' he said. 'It was the first time I'd been away from her and she'd opened her eyes and asked where I was. Yes, I had to rush back.'

Again, Anahera had no words.

'And, yes,' Luke continued quietly. 'I was married when I was with you but it didn't feel like cheating. My marriage was over the day of the accident that put Jane into that coma, although it took a very long time for me to accept that.'

'Was…was she still awake when you got back to London?'

'No. She never opened her eyes again. I sat with her every day and held her hand but she just slipped away, bit by bit. And then it was finally over. After the funeral, I tried to call you. Someone at the hospital told me you'd gone to Brisbane so I kept trying. I wanted you to know…but…'

He didn't need to finish his sentence. He could see that Anahera remembered that conversation as well as he did. And now she knew she'd accused him and judged him guilty without knowing all the facts. She looked… appalled. Her gaze slid away from his and, after a long silence, she cleared her throat.

'We should get to the village,' she said. 'If we don't go now, we won't have enough time before Jack wants to leave.'

They walked in silence again, but Luke was okay with that. Anahera needed time to process what he'd told her. Maybe it would make a difference or maybe it wouldn't, but that was okay, too. He'd been able to tell her the truth and that was enough to bring a sense of peace.

It was Anahera who broke the silence, when they'd left the forest track and were walking under an avenue of coconut palms near the beach.

'How did it happen?' she asked. 'The accident, I mean?'

'Jane was a competitive swimmer. She used to train at a local pool early every morning as soon as it opened. Sometimes the only other person there was the guy who ran the aquatic centre. On that morning, he'd been doing something in the office and when he came out he saw her floating face down in the pool. They think she must have slipped on the tiles and hit her head. He got her out and started CPR but…it was too late. She'd been without oxygen for too long.'

'That must have been devastating. I'm…I'm so sorry, Luke.'

Was she sorry for what he'd been through or did the apology include the way she'd treated him?

The look in her eyes suggested it was both. Maybe she wanted to say something more but their arrival at the village had been spotted and a bunch of children were running towards them.

'Football, mister! Come with us…' The small boy who'd taken the tumble in the game they'd had earlier took hold of Luke's hand and tugged on it. Small, grinning faces surrounded them.

Anahera shook her head and spoke to the children in their own language. The persuasive sounds turned to disappointed ones but the small boy still kept hold of his hand as they walked between the first bures of the village.

'Marama, the woman we're coming to see, lives here.'

Anahera pointed out one of the simple dwellings. 'She's going to show you how she makes the tea and take us to where the bushes grow.'

Except Marama wasn't at home. Anahera asked the children but they shrugged and shook their heads so they wandered farther into the village. Luke recognised a young pregnant woman he'd seen attending the clinic today. She had one arm around the older woman who'd been with her, supporting her shuffling gait, and she had a basket in her other hand, filled with what looked like taro roots.

'Marama's in Tane's house,' she told Anahera in response to her query. 'He's her son and he's very sick.'

Even if they hadn't been looking for Marama they would have had to go and see what was wrong.

And something was very wrong.

Tane—a young man in his early twenties—was in the grip of a seizure as Anahera and Luke entered the bure. Several people were crouched around him, trying to hold his limbs still. A woman was trying to put a stick between his teeth.

Anahera touched the woman's wrist and spoke quietly but urgently. The woman took the stick away and one by one the others let go of the man's body. Someone shifted a cooking pot farther away and another ran outside.

'I've told him to go and get Jack,' Anahera told Luke. 'We need the resus kit. And a stretcher.'

'Can you find out what's going on? Do you know this man? Is he epileptic?'

'Not that I know of. He's running a high temperature. I can feel the heat from here.' She began asking questions of the people around her and then she translated the answers.

'His wife, Kura, says that Tane was complaining of a bad headache yesterday and he was shivering. Marama gave him herbal tea but it didn't help. He was very sleepy this morning, which was why they didn't bring him up to the clinic. This is the first seizure he's had.'

'No history of any recent head injury?'

'No.'

'I can't tell if there's any rash.' Luke leaned closer to peer at Tane's bare chest but the dark skin was gleaming with sweat.

'The light's not good enough. Here…I've got a penlight torch.'

'Great. I'd like to check his pupils as soon as I can. Might give us a clue to his intracranial pressures.'

The jerking of the man's limbs was lessening. His eyelids flickered and he began groaning and then his eyes opened and he started shouting—a look of absolute terror on his face. Luke wasn't going to get a chance to check pupil sizes and reaction to light any time soon.

Anahera spoke to him, her tone reassuring and her touch intended to calm, but Luke could see that they needed help. Drugs that would take control of whatever abnormal things were going on in Tane's brain.

He'd seen many patients like this but having to deal with what was clearly very serious in a remote island village was alarming. Anahera was taking it in stride, however. At her direction, the young woman who was probably Tane's wife had produced a bowl of water and a cloth and was sponging him to try and bring his temperature down. Thankfully, the dreadful shouting and distressed movements stopped as Tane seemed to be overtaken by exhaustion. His head fell back on the woven bedding and his eyes drifted closed. That was when Anahera looked up and caught Luke's gaze.

'Are you thinking what I'm thinking?'

'Encephalitis?' Luke nodded grimly. 'Can you find out if he's had a mosquito bite recently?'

Anahera's face fell as she listened to the people around her. 'There's been a lot more mosquitoes around recently,' she relayed to Luke. 'Lots of people have been bitten. We need to get Tane to hospital as soon as possible, don't we?'

Like the cavalry arriving, Jack came running, the resus kit looped over his shoulder and an oxygen cylinder in his hand. Behind him, two of the villagers were carrying a stretcher.

'You'd better take over,' Anahera told Luke. 'You're the expert. Tell me what you need me to do.'

'Let's get fluids up and get some diazepam on board. We'll have to wait till we get back to Wildfire to do the necessary tests, like a lumbar puncture. When we see how well he's maintaining his airway after sedation, we'll know whether we need to intubate.'

Luke crouched beside Anahera as she opened the kit and pulled out the IV kit and drug roll. He took the gloves she handed him and pulled them on. Her movements were swift and competent. She put a tourniquet on Tane's upper arm and swabbed his elbow with an alcohol wipe. Luke had only just finished snapping the latex gloves into place when she peeled open a cannula package and held it out for him.

He hadn't worked in partnership with Anahera like this since he'd left Wildfire Island.

And it felt good.

Better than good.

It felt…right…

As if something that had been broken had been un-expectedly fixed.

CHAPTER FOUR

THE FLIGHT BACK to Wildfire Island was a race against time.

There was so much to do and everything was so urgent that there was no space in Anahera's head to even recall, let alone think about, the bombshell that Luke had dropped in telling her about his wife.

When they got their desperately ill patient to the hospital the pace picked up even more but at least there were extra hands to help and the facilities available were enough to surprise Luke.

'You've got a bench top scanning electron microscope?'

'Down in the research centre laboratory.' Sam nodded. 'I'm no microbiologist, though. It's more a hobby for me—a programme of self-tuition. I use all the other gear more—to do all the standard blood tests like a full blood count, glucose and electrolytes and things like toxicology screens.'

'I've done more than enough with an electron microscope to recognise a flavivirus in a CSF sample. Thanks, Ana...' Luke picked up the syringe of local anaesthetic from the trolley prepared for the next diagnostic procedure needed.

Anahera stayed to help keep Tane in position for the lumbar puncture, lying on his side with his chin tucked down and his knees bent up. She made sure that there was no disruption to his IV fluids or oxygen supply and then listened to the conversation between Sam and Luke.

'We'll start him on acyclovir until we can rule out herpes simplex.'

'And antibiotics? What about meningitis or a brain abscess?'

'We'll do a CT next. Can't believe you've got CT capability now. It's a huge advantage. I wouldn't want to be waiting for a plane to get here from Australia.'

'Must still seem limited to what you have on hand in London.'

'It's enough. It's not as if we've got anything more than supportive treatment for any forms of encephalitis other than herpes simplex.' Luke glanced up as he waited for the drops of clear cerebrospinal fluid to drip into the test tube. 'You happy with ICU protocols for managing a case like this, Ana?'

Her nod was confident. 'I'll get the head of the bed elevated thirty degrees and keep the room quiet and not brightly lit. Daily fluids need to be dropped to three quarters of routine maintenance. I'll keep a close eye on any signs of increasing intracranial pressure with vital sign monitoring and if we need to intubate, I can monitor the ventilation. I'll stay in tonight—I just need to give my mother a call and let her know I won't be home.'

Luke turned to Sam. 'You've got other nurses available, haven't you?'

'No one has Ana's ICU experience. And no one has your expertise in managing an encephalitis case.' Sam pressed on the puncture site as Luke removed the needle from Tane's back. 'I hope you're not planning on leaving any time soon?'

One corner of Luke's mouth curled up. 'I think I'll be here for a bit longer. Unfinished business…'

Anahera focussed on keeping Tane's oxygen mask in place as they rolled him onto his back but her heart skipped a beat. Was she included in what Luke had meant by that cryptic comment?

But Sam was nodding. 'Yeah… Jack said you hadn't even got near one of the hibiscus bushes to collect your bark samples. I guess we'll have to get you out to French Island again.' He clicked the side rails of the bed into place. 'Do you want to take the CSF and blood samples down to the lab? I'll have the CT scan done by the time you're back.'

Anahera watched Luke leave. Sam was happy enough with his interpretation of Luke's 'unfinished business' but she was quite sure that the research into M'Langi tea was only part of it.

The bigger part was the unfinished business of a relationship that had gone so very wrong.

And it seemed that the blame for that could be laid squarely at her own feet. Not only was she guilty in having made a judgement without knowing the facts, she had just made things a whole lot worse by lying to Luke.

She hadn't really lied, had she?

It was the early hours of the morning now and Anahera was sitting beside Tane's bed, listening to the soft beep of the cardiac monitor and watching the rise and fall of her patient's chest.

Sam and Luke were in the staffroom, hopefully catching a little sleep on the comfortable reclining chairs. Hettie was here to help with the nursing but there were other patients that needed care, and Tane couldn't be left alone, so Anahera's offer to stay on had been appreciated.

She had seen respect in Luke's expression when she'd offered to take on the intensive nursing. Admiration, even.

He wouldn't look at her like that if he knew...

Lying by omission was still lying, wasn't it? It was the trick to lying convincingly, wasn't it, to make sure that there was an element of truth in the lie. Of course Luke had believed her. It was true that Hana's father was a doctor. That she'd been born in Brisbane. And that there'd never been any chance of a relationship with her father.

Except there had been, hadn't there?

She'd been there when Vailea had come in with the shocking message that his wife was asking for him back in London, and her reaction had been instant and damning.

She'd turned her back on Luke and walked away, without giving him any chance to say anything.

And she'd done it again when he'd tracked her down and phoned her in Brisbane. When she'd known she was pregnant and it could have made all the difference in the world if she'd given him the chance to tell her the truth.

Instead, she'd gone through her pregnancy and the birth of her baby alone. All those struggles of coping with a new baby by herself. Of not knowing whether she'd been doing the right thing and the fear that something was really wrong when there hadn't seemed to be any way to comfort her infant. Those awful moments of misery when she'd simply been too tired to cope and had had to keep going without anyone there to encourage or reassure her.

Surely that had been punishment enough for her mistake?

No. Thanks to her deception today, there would be more punishment to come if she did tell Luke the truth.

He had been honest with her and he deserved the same respect in return, but the implications of reciprocating were so huge she couldn't begin to get her head around them.

Her life—and those of the people she loved more than life itself—would change for ever.

It would also destroy any trust that Luke had in her.

And that mattered more than she wanted to admit.

As if her patient was aware of the tension building inside Anahera, a grimace appeared on his face and then the muscles of his body seemed to shrink and stiffen. Within the few seconds of registering what was happening, Tane was once again in the throes of a seizure. Anahera hit the alarm button on the wall, which she knew would sound in the staffroom, and then did her best to stop IV lines tangling or pulling free from the forceful jerking of Tane's arms.

It was Luke who came into the room.

'How long has he been seizing again?'

'About a minute.'

'Have you given another dose of diazepam?'

'No.' Was Luke disappointed with her performance already? 'I've been trying to secure the IV lines. I didn't have enough hands…'

'Of course you didn't.' The flash of Luke's smile wiped out any impression that he had been criticising her. He reached for a drug ampoule and syringe. 'We'll add in some phenobarbitone.'

Anahera turned her head to glance at the monitor as an alarm sounded. 'His oxygen saturation is dropping.'

Luke nodded, glancing up as he injected the drug. 'We need to get effective control of his airway and then I can juggle meds to see if we can stop the intracranial pressure rising any further.'

'Do you want me to set up for an RSI?'

Luke nodded again. 'Do you think we can manage that on our own? Sam and Hettie are a bit tied up with a baby that's come in with bronchiolitis and is in quite severe respiratory distress.'

Anahera caught Luke's gaze again and held it for a moment. Ideally, a rapid sequence intubation procedure needed a team of three people, an assistant to the person in charge of the airway and someone to manage the drugs. A clear memory surfaced of how well she and Luke had worked together in the past. Could they still do that?

It felt like nothing had changed.

'No problem,' she said. 'I'll set up.'

She worked swiftly, moving a suction unit, having checked that it worked, and then exchanging Tane's oxygen mask for nasal prongs that would keep oxygen running while they worked on securing his airway. Then she unrolled a pack on the top of a trolley, revealing the range of endotracheal tubes, stylets, airways and the laryngoscope and blades that would be needed.

The new medications had controlled Tane's seizure so they had a window of time that would make intubation easier. Luke already had the extra drugs lined up.

'You good to go?'

'When you are.'

'Got a cric kit there?'

The need to create a surgical airway by a cricothyrotomy was an emergency backup in case the intubation attempt was unsuccessful and they had a still paralyzed patient who had no way of breathing for himself. Anahera nodded but then caught Luke's gaze.

'You won't need it.'

Luke maintained the eye contact long enough for Anahera to get the message that he had just as much confidence in her own skills and, despite how critical the next few minutes were going to be, she felt herself relax.

It was still there—that professional connection that had made them such an amazing team.

Luke's focus was completely on the task ahead the instant he looked away. 'Let's pre-oxygenate.'

The procedure went like clockwork. During the three minutes of pre-oxygenation the equipment, drug dosages and monitoring were all checked. Sedation and then the paralysing drugs were administered. Luke obtained visualisation of the vocal cords easily and the tube to secure Tane's airway was slipped into position. Luke's focus was still a hundred per cent on their patient at this point, as he confirmed the correct positioning of the tube by listening to Tane's chest. Anahera's tasks of securing the tube and attaching it to the ventilator were automatic enough for her to find her focus shifting somewhat.

To the doctor rather than the patient.

This wasn't the first time they'd worked together. It wasn't the first time they'd been alone, doing something that had the potential to go wrong with disastrous consequences for the patient either, but it *felt* like the first time.

Anahera's instincts had told her that their professional

rapport was still there but she'd forgotten how it actually felt to work with someone where there was such a smooth professional connection it was like one person having an extra pair of hands. She'd never experienced it with anyone else, including all the intensive care specialists she'd worked with in that huge Brisbane hospital. Was it just Luke? Did he achieve that kind of rapport with whoever was assisting him?

Maybe not. He looked away from the ventilator settings and caught her gaze.

'I always knew you were good,' he said quietly. 'But you've even better now. That was a real pleasure.'

The praise sparked a glow of warmth and then Anahera remembered that this was Luke praising her and something weird happened inside her chest—as if a plug had been jarred loose and a leak had sprung from what had been a tight seal. A leak that rapidly turned into a small torrent of…feelings.

The feelings she had once had for Luke that made his praise so much more than professional approval or respect.

Was it even possible to stop loving someone you had once felt so strongly about?

Apparently not. Not in her case, at least…

She had to tear her gaze away from Luke's. Had to move. If she could walk she would feel the ground beneath her feet and it would dispel the alarming sensation that the foundations of the life she had built for herself were not in the process of crumbling. Unfortunately, it seemed that her brain and her body weren't quite in sync and she almost stumbled. Luke's hand caught her arm and steadied her.

'Whoa… You okay, Ana?'

The touch of his hand would have been quite enough to make things worse but it came with the sound of her name and a tone of genuine concern that made her want to cry.

She pulled in a ragged breath but no words emerged.

'You're exhausted,' Luke said quietly. 'Things are under control here now. I'm going to review meds and sedation and then I'll see if Hettie's free to come and cover for you. You need some rest.'

It wasn't rest that Anahera needed as much as some space. Distance from Luke so that she could get that emotional plug securely back where it belonged. She closed her eyes and drew on a strength she hadn't known she possessed.

'I'm fine,' she said. 'I just need a bit of fresh air. I'll stay until the day shift gets here. I… I'll go and sit in the garden for a minute.'

She had always loved it that the three wings of Wildfire Island's hospital were U-shaped and surrounded a lush patch of tropical garden that had a pond and more than one space to sit comfortably and enjoy the serenity and delicious scents of the flowering plants like frangipani and jasmine. At night it took on a life of its own, with pale blooms shining like stars amongst dark green foliage and the chorus of the tiny frogs that called the pond home. The relaxing sound of the trickle of the water feeding the pond was a bonus that wasn't heard in the daytime, thanks to the bustle of people and birdlife.

It was deliciously cool, too. Anahera sat close to the pond and breathed in the last of the night air. The light was also beginning to change and a new day was about to begin. A new day in the life she had chosen for herself and her precious child. And with every breath she reminded herself that this was home and they were safe. Nothing had to change unless she wanted it to.

The frogs falling silent warned her that she wasn't alone any more, even before she heard the rustle of leaves as shrubs were brushed and the sound of approaching feet on the path. It had to be Luke—unless he'd told someone else to come and find her.

She kept her eyes closed as she registered the sounds and even a change in the air as someone sat down on the bench beside her, but she knew she had been right. She had no need to open her eyes to confirm who it was. How weird was that—to recognise someone so easily without seeing them or hearing their voice? Even more astonishing was to feel as though she was more present herself because of having him in the same space. More…alive…

'You okay?'

The query was soft and that concern that had almost been her undoing was still there. Anahera knew she had to open her eyes. If she didn't, he would touch her again to see if she was all right and she couldn't afford to let that happen.

But when she opened her eyes, it was to find Luke looking directly into them with an expression that told her she was the only thing in the world that mattered to him at this moment.

The way he'd looked at Tane when his patient's life had been his only focus.

The way he'd looked at her once, so long ago, just before he'd kissed her for the very first time.

Any intention to reassure him about her well-being died on her lips. Anahera could only stare back at him. At his eyes and then at his lips as the memory of that first kiss ambushed her head and then took her heart captive.

Maybe those memories were written on her face somehow. Or maybe it was some kind of telepathy.

Whatever it was, the hands of some invisible clock were whirring backwards, faster and faster, taking them both back in time.

It wasn't dawn any more. It was sunset. They weren't sitting on a wooden bench in a well-kept tropical garden. They were standing on a beach with soft sand beneath their bare feet.

And Luke had touched her face—just like this—his fingertips tracing the line of her cheek and jaw as if they were the most beautiful sculpture on earth. With just a single fingertip he brushed her lower lip so gently it felt like the whisper of a butterfly's wing and that was when Anahera knew how lost she was.

Lost in time.

Lost in love.

This kiss was as inevitable as the rising of the sun behind the mountains of this island but Anahera didn't see that first real glow of its appearance because she had closed her eyes again the moment Luke's lips touched her own and then she was aware of nothing but the pleasure of his touch.

A feeling of coming home after the longest journey would have been more than enough to deal with, but that wasn't enough for her body. Or her heart.

Pleasure escalated into desire.

She wanted more.

She *needed* more.

The force of that desire was so shocking she had to pull back and break the contact.

Instinct was telling her to run. To get away before she lost that unexpected strength she'd been able to tap into when she'd realised her feelings for Luke hadn't changed. But the commands her brain was issuing were being totally ignored by her body. She couldn't move. She couldn't even take a breath.

Anahera was trapped by Luke's hands that were still gently cradling her head. By the way he was still looking at her. By the way his breath was released in a poignant sigh.

'Oh, Ana... Nothing's changed, has it?'

CHAPTER FIVE

LUKE REALISED HE couldn't have been more wrong the moment the words left his lips.

Everything had changed.

The way Anahera had responded to his kiss told him something she had been keeping so well hidden, maybe she hadn't even realised it herself.

It was still there—that astonishing connection he'd never known could even exist between two people.

A connection that had brought them together in the first place, professionally and then personally, to explode into an emotional force that made the word *love* seem too small to encompass.

Or maybe she still didn't realise it. Or didn't want to admit it.

She shook her head just enough to dislodge the touch of his hands and she looked as though she wanted to turn and run but she was frozen—her huge, dark eyes filled with something that made his heart want to break.

Fear?

Yes…the flash of what looked like enormous relief a moment later confirmed that awful impression. Someone was calling her name.

Rescue was at hand.

'Ana? You out there? Have you seen Luke?'

He could help her, too. Give her a few moments of peace to realise that she was, in fact, safe. That he would never do anything to hurt her.

Not again…

'I'm here, Sam.' Standing up and moving onto the path that led to the pond made him visible. 'I was just catching a breath of fresh air. What's up?'

Turning his head, he could see that Anahera was going to accept the gift of privacy, but the way she had buried her face in her hands was just as heartbreaking as the fear he had seen in her eyes.

This was no fairy-tale reunion, then, with the glow of a happy-ever-after lighting the way forward.

But it *was* something that needed resolution. If things were left like this it was clearly going to haunt them both, probably for the rest of their lives. And Luke already knew the damaging effects that could have because he'd been living with it for nearly five years.

People used the term 'the love of my life' all the time but it was only in recent years that Luke had come to understand what it really meant. Yes, there were many, many people in the world that you could be compatible with. Could love, in fact, and go on to have a very happy life in their company, but, for some people, there was one who stood on a different level and if you were lucky enough to connect with them, nothing would ever be the same.

For Luke, that person was Anahera. Every time he thought of her—and barely a day went past in his life when something, however tiny, didn't remind him—the thought was accompanied by a sense of loss. Of losing something that he knew he would never find again be-cause…well, because Anahera was the love of his life.

And maybe…just maybe—despite the devastating evidence to the contrary that she'd had a child with an-other man—Anahera's life had been affected as well. She wasn't with the father of her child any more, was she?

It took a moment to tune in to what Sam was saying.

'…so I thought if you took the morning meeting and briefed the day staff, you could get some sleep. I'll give you a pager and we can send a driver if there's any de-terioration in Tane's condition. Or we can find a bed in the hospital for you to crash on.'

'That would be better. The next twenty-four hours are going to be critical. Maybe longer. How did you go with getting the chest X-ray?'

'That's what I wanted to show you. You were right about those crackles in both lung fields. There's bilateral pulmonary oedema.'

Luke nodded grimly as he followed Sam down the corridor. 'I suspect his pulmonary status is going to get worse. If it develops into ARDS, we're looking at a week or more of intensive care before we can expect any im-provement.'

'Should we consider evacuating him?'

'There's no point. All that can be done is supportive measures and we can do that here. This way, he'll at least have his family nearby.'

'We? Are you saying you'll stay that long?'

'I'll contact my department later today. As far as I know, I don't have anything in my diary that couldn't be handled by my senior staff and…and I could do with a bit more time. We need to set up that research project and I haven't collected those tea-leaves yet.'

He had another reason to want more time and that it was personal rather than professional failed to make it any less important. That kiss had changed something huge. An unspoken rule that Luke had been living by for far too long had just been exposed as being unfounded in truth. Work wasn't more important than anything else life had to offer and it wasn't the only route to happiness or fulfilment. It may have been a successful strategy to bury himself in his profession to the extent that he could ignore every other aspect of his life but he couldn't do that any longer.

Not after *that* kiss.

He knew it might be one of the hardest things he'd ever had to do, but somehow he had to find a way to talk about this with Anahera. Really talk, openly and honestly. And the hardest thing about that was likely to be getting Anahera to agree to have that talk.

In the meantime, burying anything personal by focussing totally on the welfare of someone who desperately needed his professional expertise was not only vital but a retreat into a comfort zone he really needed right now.

The sun was almost halfway visible above the mountains by the time Anahera removed the shelter of her hands and exposed her face to the world again.

Good grief…how long had she been sitting there like a stunned rabbit, unable to break the spell of that kiss or to move herself from being trapped beneath the weight of that onslaught of long-buried feelings?

Not to mention the shock of what had seemed so blindingly obvious in the silent communication of that kiss. Even if Luke hadn't said that nothing had changed, she would have known that he still wanted her. Still loved her?

No. She tried to shake that thought away. She had been the one who'd been head over heels in love and dreaming of a future. If what was between them had been strong enough for Luke to have intended keeping her in his life, surely he would have told her about the little complication that his *wife* represented?

The flash of anger was almost a welcome addition to the kaleidoscope of emotions because it was so very familiar. Anahera had relied on it as a way through the heartbreak of what had been an ultimate betrayal.

It didn't feel quite the same now, though. It had lost its power because she knew the truth.

What could she hang on to now as a framework to make such big decisions about the future?

'*Ana*…they said I might find you out here.' Her mother's face creased with concern. 'You look… You haven't been crying, have you?'

'Oh, Mum.' It was such a comfort to have her mother sit on the bench beside her and to be folded into the arms that had always made anything so much easier to bear. 'It's been quite a night.'

'So I heard. Tane's very sick, isn't he?'

'I'm afraid so.'

'His family are on the way to sit with him. I'm going to make sure we've got enough food for everybody.' Vailea sighed. 'I wish there was more I could do to help. At least we're lucky enough to have a world expert in treating encephalitis here.'

'Luke won't be here for long, Mum. He'll have to get back to his work in London.'

'Hettie tells me he's put off going back so he can look after Tane. And it's even more important that the research gets going so that we don't have more cases like this in the future. He's a wonderful man, isn't he?'

'Mmm.' The sound was choked. The emotional cauldron Anahera was immersed in had just been stirred again. She felt ridiculously proud of Luke for putting his own life on hold to help Tane. There was a wash of relief that he wouldn't be walking out of her life in the immediate future but there were also newly sharpened edges to the guilt and a deepened dread of the consequences if she told him the truth.

It was all too much. She wanted to bury her face against her mother's neck and stop trying to hold back her tears. She wanted to tell her everything and ask for advice but she already knew what her mother would say. Vailea had been horrified that Hana's father had apparently walked out of their lives and had never wanted contact with his child. She couldn't understand how any parent could do that. How disappointed would she be with her own daughter if she found out that it was Anahera who had forced that lack of contact?

So she choked back the tears and pulled herself out of the embrace that had the potential to weaken her resolve and turn their lives upside down before she was ready to do that herself. At least she had a small reprieve of time to choose when—or if—she was ready.

'How's Hana? Did she miss me last night?'

'Of course. But she's learned to take times like this in her stride.' Vailea smiled. 'She's such a happy little soul. I took her up to Bessie at the house, and she danced up the path, flapping her arms. Said she was being a flutterby today.'

Anahera's smile wobbled and she couldn't stop a tear escaping. And then another one.

'Tch…' Vailea smoothed the tears away with her thumb. 'You're just too tired, darling. Hana's fine. Bessie loves her as much as we do. She's safe and happy and she'll be even happier when she sees her mumma later. What you need is some sleep. And some food. When did you last have something to eat?'

'I…I guess it was the sandwiches you made for us to take to French Island for the clinic run yesterday.'

Vailea's huff of sound was appalled. 'Come with me. I'm going to whip up some scrambled eggs for you. You can't sleep properly on such an empty stomach. And then you can go home.'

'I need to talk to Sam and see what the roster is like. We're going to need extra staff for the next few days. Tane will have to have someone with him at all times and I'm the only nurse with intensive care training.'

'You can talk to him while you're having your breakfast. I'll make sure those doctors come and eat as well.'

Breakfast with Luke? Knowing that every time she looked at his face she would be remembering that kiss? Falling back into the whirlpool of the feelings that had surfaced? She couldn't do it. Not yet. The thought of having to try was disturbing enough to push Anahera to her feet.

'I'll tell Sam you're making breakfast but I'll find something at home. Or I'll pick a mango or pawpaw on the way. I'm so tired I think I'd be sick if I tried to eat something hot.'

Vailea simply nodded and smiled. 'I'll have something ready for you when you get back.'

Their paths diverged as they entered the covered walkway between the hospital rooms and the garden.

'Sleep well, my love,' Vailea said by way of farewell. 'Love you…'

'Love you, too.'

Anahera needed to turn right to go in search of Sam, who would either be with Tane or in the staffroom, but, for a long moment, she watched the tall figure and straight back of her mother as she headed towards the kitchens.

She had always had something ready for her. Food, shelter, acceptance, love…

Anahera barely remembered her father, even though there were plenty of photographs and she'd been told so often that her daddy loved her.

Exhaustion took on a peaceful edge suddenly and the whirlpool stopped spinning.

She didn't need anger any more. She could use logic as a framework, along with the evidence that her own history provided. Parents that belonged in different worlds couldn't forge a family no matter how much they might want to. She could use her head instead of her heart.

How selfish would it be to put her own needs or desires ahead of those of her child? Or her mother, for that matter, when Vailea was still devoting her life to her daughter and her granddaughter?

So she still loved Luke. And maybe he still wanted her. But the love story, if that was what it was, had been doomed before it had even begun. The best thing for everybody would be to close the book and walk away.

And maybe that was the answer. If she could persuade herself that those things were all that needed to be said, they might be able to part on good terms—with a clean slate to begin the rest of their lives. Okay, so her slate wouldn't be completely clean, but in a way, she would be telling him *why* she couldn't tell him the truth and that could—hopefully—make that lump of guilt a bit easier to live with.

She just needed to find an opportunity to talk to him.

Luke had known that finding an opportunity to even suggest a private talk to Anahera would be difficult, but he hadn't bargained on it being impossible.

In the few hours she had gone home to sleep, members of Tane's family and community began to arrive and fill spaces in and around the hospital and any free moments for any member of staff were taken up with making sure these people were kept informed and offered all the support they needed.

Given the available space and the need for such intensive monitoring, only one person at a time, other than his wife, Kura, could be allowed to sit with Tane, and these people were all frightened. They were listening to every beep of the monitors and watching everything that was done, desperately waiting for any sign that would give them hope.

The atmosphere was sombre. Knowing that Tane's eight-month-old son was among the family members being cared for outside the intensive care unit added to the tension. When Anahera arrived back at the hospital in the early afternoon, Luke was with Tane, adjusting the parameters of the ventilator again. Kura was on a chair pressed against the head of the bed, her hand touching Tane's cheek, and his mother, Marama, was standing behind Kura, her hands resting on the young mother's shoulders. They watched Hettie slip out of the room to allow Anahera to take her place, and Luke could feel the intensity of the way they waited for Luke to greet her.

Even a meaningful glance between the doctor and nurse, who understood far more than the family could, had the potential to be easily misinterpreted, which might add to the suffering of the people who loved this young man in their care. But Luke already knew that and he was an expert in shutting anything remotely personal out of the professional sphere. That only hours ago kissing this woman had shaken his world so hard it was still rattling was irrelevant. His greeting was no different than it would have been if Sam had come into the room and eye contact no more than polite.

Thankfully, Anahera was clearly in exactly the same space. She moved close enough to brush his shoulder but her gaze was on the ventilator settings and her swift glance showed that she recognised the significance of every change he'd just made.

The glance hadn't gone unnoticed.

'What's wrong?' Kura whispered. 'Is he getting worse?'

'His breathing is getting harder for him.' Anahera slipped past Luke to touch Kura's hand. 'We can help by changing the settings on the machine, like how much oxygen we give him and what the pressure needs to be to get it right into his lungs.'

Both women looked bewildered, and Anahera switched languages. After answering many questions, the women nodded and turned their attention back to Tane. Anahera stepped back.

'It was harder than I thought it would be to explain positive end expiratory pressure and how it helps to increase it.' A line appeared between her eyes as she scanned Luke's face. 'Have you had any sleep?'

'Not yet.' That Anahera clearly cared how he was did something weird to Luke's heart, as if it was filling up with a physiologically impossible amount of blood that was warmer than it should be as it got pumped to every cell in his body.

'Where's Sam?'

'Doing a round of the other inpatients. I don't think he's slept yet either.'

She was still holding his gaze. This might seem like no more than a professional exchange to anyone around them but it *was* more. So much more. They were more than simply a team working as a single unit towards the same goal. The bond was laced with concern. A tenderness that offered hope for the future?

'I'll hold the fort in here. Just bring me up to speed.'

'I've charted all the drugs here.' Luke picked up the chart on the end of Tane's bed. 'The lorazepam and morphine seem to be enough to be keeping him comfortable and maintaining ventilator synchrony. His temperature is stable but I'd like to see it come down further.'

'I'll give him a sponge bath. That's something that Kura will be able to help with. I'll show them how to massage his hands and feet, too.'

Luke nodded. The more they could involve Tane's family in his care, the better. It was no surprise that Anahera would already be planning how to do that. How to care for every member of his family as well as her patient. Everything she did was tinged with the extraordinary amount of love she had to offer.

Was her concern for him purely because he was in her orbit right now? That curious warmth in his body had faded enough that he knew he would probably dismiss it later as a combination of tiredness and imagination.

'I want to get another chest X-ray in a few hours. We'll

need to put in a gastric tube for enteral feeding but that can wait a little while, too.'

It was Anahera's turn to nod. 'Until you're rested.' She was already turning back to her patient. 'I'll call you if anything changes.'

Luke almost smiled as he left the room. He'd been dismissed but he was happy enough to go. He'd be no use to anyone unless he got some sleep. Maybe he had imagined the secret level he and Anahera had been communicating on for a few seconds there but he had absolutely no doubt that she could—and would—provide the best care that Tane needed.

Tragically, even the best care wasn't going to be enough for this young islander. Tane's condition deteriorated slowly over the next twenty-four hours and, early the next afternoon, his heart gave up the struggle and stopped. The desperate attempts of the medical team were unsuccessful in getting it started again and the ventilator was finally switched off when his family could return to surround his bed. Even his small baby was silent in his mother's arms as the final impression of life faded.

The whole hospital fell silent as the news spread and people gathered to comfort each other. And then the tears began. Luke was close to tears himself as people came up to him to thank him for everything he'd done. The generosity of their gratitude in the face of his failure was overwhelming, and the grief was contagious.

He had failed. And it hurt.

'Get some rest, mate…' Sam's grip on his shoulder was tight. 'We'll take care of everything here.'

Anahera was right behind Sam. She had Tane's baby in her arms and the pain of failure got a whole lot sharper. They'd not only lost a young man in the prime of his life;

a wife had lost her husband and a baby had lost his father. Pain morphed into anger. Not at himself, because he knew he'd done everything any doctor could have done—this anger was at the unfairness of life and the suffering dealt out to people who had done nothing to deserve it.

'The family want to take Tane home,' Anahera said. 'I'll help get him ready. We'll need the death certificate filled in…' She hesitated and bit her lip, her gaze barely touching Luke's.

'I'll do that,' Sam said quietly. 'We just need you to sign it.'

Luke's nod was grim. 'Just show me where the forms are. I'll do it.' He had been the physician in charge of the case and this was his responsibility. 'And then I'll get out of everybody's way. There's nothing more for me to do here.' He shook his head. He couldn't keep a lid on his anger any more and he had to let some of it out. 'I'd better see how soon I can book a flight back to London. No reason not to head back tomorrow if it's possible.'

Anahera's shocked intake of breath was overtaken by the wail of the baby she was holding, which was probably why Sam didn't notice, but Luke heard it, and it cut through him like a knife.

He'd lost control of his anger but he hadn't intended directing it towards Anahera.

He could see exactly how she was interpreting his words in the way her eyes darkened and the frozen expression on her face. He was telling her that she wasn't a reason to want to be here. That he didn't want any more to do with her.

For a heartbeat Luke stayed where he was. He even opened his mouth to say something that would mollify his dismissal of his time here, but nothing came out. The baby was sobbing now, and Luke could see the grand-mother, Marama, coming towards them. She would probably smile at Luke and add to the number of people thanking him for the care he'd taken of Tane.

He couldn't take any more of it. Any of it. What was the point of trying to talk to Anahera anyway? The kind of conversation he'd had in mind was a minefield of mak-ing yourself vulnerable and then having to deal with pain, and he'd had more than enough of that today.

It was far easier to turn on his heel and follow Sam, who was already moving towards the office where the grim paperwork would need to be completed, so that was exactly what Luke did.

CHAPTER SIX

So that was it?

Luke was simply going to turn his back on Wildfire Island—and *her*—and ride off into the sunset without a backward glance?

Talk about hitting someone when they were already down.

Tears flowed freely as Anahera worked with Kura and Marama to prepare Tane's body to be returned to his home and the churchyard where he would be buried within a few days.

She removed the tracheal tube, the IV lines and ECG electrodes as carefully as if her patient could still feel every touch. She brought scented water and warm, fluffy towels so that Tane's wife and mother could bathe him. She listened to the traditional, soft songs of grief and her heart broke a little more with every verse.

The undertaker had been summoned, and Tane would have to be in his care for a while before his final voyage back to his own island. Anahera joined the solemn procession of family and friends to accompany his body to the boat. Sam walked by her side, but Luke was nowhere to be seen.

'He's taken it hard,' Sam said quietly. 'I suspect he's

got used to saving people even when they get to a critical stage. From what I hear, that's what he did for that sheikh—Harry—who's poured a fortune into developing the new vaccine. It's a personal failure for him.'

'It's personal for all of us. These are *our* people.'

'They are.'

His glance reminded Anahera that Sam had no island blood in his veins. He had been born and raised in Britain—like Luke—but he never talked about his old life except to say he was happy to have left it behind. This young doctor had virtually washed up on the shores of these islands and then had never left, but even if it hadn't been so long ago, he would be one of her people. There was something about him that meant he had been one of them from the moment he'd arrived.

'Is he really going to leave tomorrow?'

'I've asked him not to. He thinks we can sort all the details of setting up the clinical trial for the new vaccine by internet connection but...' Sam shook his head. 'I get the feeling he needs to be here longer for his own sake as much as mine.'

Anahera's heart skipped a beat. Had Luke said something? About *her*? About his 'unfinished business'?

They stood a little apart as Tane's immediate family said their temporary farewells until they could have their loved one with them again. A heart-rending wail from Kura split the air as the undertaker's boat pushed off from the jetty.

'We have to do all we can to make sure this doesn't happen again,' Sam said, his voice raw. 'And that's the way forward for us all. A way to deal with the grief and any sense of failure. I don't want Luke to go off and carry this on his own shoulders. He saved Harry and he was there when the whole concept of developing the vaccine started. Actually being here himself to set up and start the trial would give him something a whole lot more positive to take away from here.'

It should have been a relief to hear that Sam had no knowledge of a personal past history and that he thought any benefit to Luke staying longer had a professional basis. It should have been a relief that she might not have to make that decision of whether or not to talk to Luke and what to tell him when she did, because the moment his plane took off, her life would go back to exactly what it had been.

Anahera was nodding but yet another piece of her heart was breaking. This wasn't right. Of course Sam had intuitively picked up that there was something Luke badly needed to heal his life that he would only find here. He just didn't know that it had a whole lot more to do with her than this tragic case he had inadvertently taken responsibility for.

But what on earth could she do about it?

'You okay?' Sam pulled her into the kind of hug only a brother or a very good friend could provide. 'It's been a rough couple of days.'

'I think I need a walk, that's all. A bit of quiet time to sort my head out. I might go and watch the sunset.'

'The tide's out. You could walk around to Sunset Beach from here and get the best view of all.'

'Sounds like a good idea.'

Or not. Sunset Beach had been the place she and Luke had shared their first ever kiss. Where they'd made love for the first time.

'Can I do anything? Want me to pick Hana up and look after her for a while?' Sam's smile was crooked. 'I love time with kids. I reckon that's all I need to sort *my* head out.'

'Mum will have already gone to do that. She had almost finished packing up the extra food to send back with Tane's family when I talked to her before we left the hospital.' Anahera returned his smile. 'But go and visit. Take Bugsy with you.'

Bugsy was a gorgeous golden retriever who belonged to Maddie—one of the FIFO doctors—and Sam looked after her on Maddie's regular weeks back on the mainland. 'Mum would love to see you, and Hana adores Bugsy. And her uncle Sam. Like every other kid on these islands.'

Her smile faded. In the years that Sam had been here she'd never seen any sign of him wanting to find a relationship. Would he ever have children of his own to spend time with?

Would Luke go on to find someone else and have a child he could knowingly call his own?

What if he didn't and she was depriving him of the kind of joy she had been blessed to have ever since Hana had been born?

'I might do that.' But Sam was frowning. 'Bugsy needs a walk. But are you sure you don't want some company? You look…'

'I'm fine.' Anahera's interruption was swift. If he said anything else, she might burst into tears and confess everything. 'Or I will be. Tell Mum that for me, will you? And not to worry if I'm not home for a bit.'

Sunset Beach was the only place Anahera could go to watch the sunset given how close it was as the last of Tane's family piled onto the ferry that would take them home. To one side of the harbour was the rocky promontory with the church on top, and the only way round was the road that led to the village. The beaches on that side would have groups of children shouting and splashing in the calm water sheltered by the reef and she really didn't want company right now. Far better to pick her way past the rock pools exposed by the low tide to get to the beach with the shadow of the cliffs beside her that would catch fire as the sun said its goodbye for the day.

She took her sandals off as soon as she was past the rock pools to feel the sand beneath her feet and paused again, a moment later, to pull the fastening off the end of her long plait and unravel her hair so that it could flow down her back and get ruffled by the delicious sea breeze.

This was exactly what she needed. To be alone and immerse herself in the elements. The sound of the gentle waves breaking and the leaves of palm trees rustling overhead, the smell of salt mixed with the sweetness of unseen flowers and the caress of the sun's warmth made perfect by the cool breeze.

Anahera could centre herself here. She could let herself become one with the beauty surrounding her and realise what a microscopic piece of the universe she—and her problems—represented. Maybe some of those worries would simply ebb away with the pull of each wave and they would be diluted by the vastness of this ocean that cradled her home.

She watched the waves and then looked past where they were breaking to where the water changed from turquoise to a deep blue. It was only then that she saw the swimmer. Someone who was swimming hard and fast, as though they were trying to wash away whatever demons were chasing them.

It could have been anyone, but Anahera knew instantly that it was Luke. Of course it was. The exclusive bures built for the new conference and research facility were just around the rock fall at the other end of Sunset Beach. Had some part of her agreed with Sam's suggestion of a destination because she'd known there was a chance of her path crossing Luke's?

It didn't matter. She was here now and this had been meant to happen.

She had to shade her eyes from the sun as it dipped lower and it made it increasingly hard to see the movement in the water, but she stayed exactly where she was and simply waited. The cliffs behind her were turning a spectacular blood red as the dark shape finally emerged from the shallows, and even though the light behind him made it impossible to read Luke's expression, Anahera could tell the moment he saw her by the way he stopped—as though he'd walked into a brick wall.

And then he started walking again.

Towards her.

Anahera's heart picked up speed. She tried to remember what it was she had wanted to tell him when they got a chance to talk but it was scrambling in her head. Something about her parents. About not repeating history…

But here they were, alone on Sunset Beach, and that was repeating a history that was making Anahera's legs feel like jelly and making rational thought increasingly impossible.

She had no idea how she was even going to greet Luke, let alone say anything of any significance.

She didn't need to say anything. Luke came close and his smile said it all. He knew exactly why she had come here. Why she had needed to. His single word summed it up.

'Better?'

She nodded. 'You?'

He mirrored her nod. 'I'm sorry.'

'What for?' Anahera held his gaze. She couldn't let it fall because he was standing so close to her and he was virtually naked, droplets of sea water probably clinging to every inch of that smooth, olive skin. The shiver she had to repress had nothing to do with the sea breeze.

'The way I left. What I said. Sam was right. I can't walk away yet. I've got to get this trial set up. It occurred to me while I was swimming that we're going to have to comb every record of encephalitis cases on the island so we've got statistics to use as a measure for how effective the vaccine is. It's a massive job, and I'll have to show Sam how to carry it on when I've gone. The data entry and so forth...' Luke pushed his wet hair back from his face. 'And then there's the tea-leaves. I still need samples but that made me think, too. If it's got any use against the mosquitoes and the bushes grow on French Island, why did Tane get bitten?'

Knowing that Luke wasn't going to vanish from her life immediately was like taking a huge gulp of a very heady cocktail. There was relief there. And something a whole lot stronger. Like joy?

Anahera had to press her lips together to suppress a smile. Had to focus to remember what it was that Luke had been saying.

'Maybe Tane didn't like the tea.'

'That's something we'll have to find out. That's going to be a whole study in itself. Brrr...' Luke rubbed his arms. 'That swim was cooler than I thought it would be.'

'The sun's almost gone.' Anahera let her gaze drop now. To the soft sand that had encrusted his feet and had been kicked up to stick as far as his knees. Up to swimming shorts that were dripping, past an impressively flat abdomen and then…yes, the water was still clinging, especially to the sprinkle of dark hair on his chest between nipples standing out like tiny pebbles in the chill. Hastily, she returned her gaze to his face.

'Where's your towel?'

'Back at my bure. I kind of forgot.'

'You probably need a shower.'

'What I really need…' Luke wiped a hand across his face but didn't drop the eye contact '…is to talk to you.'

Here it was. The opportunity that had been impossible to find since that time in the hospital garden. They could talk. Part on good terms, even?

Anahera's mouth felt suddenly dry. It was hard to swallow. 'I'll…I'll come with you, then. I don't have to be home for a while.'

There was a moment's silence, long enough to make it clear that Luke was registering the significance of her offer. Long enough for the wash of a wave to be heard, along with a mournful cry of some unseen sea bird.

He didn't say anything but he didn't have to. His nod and that slow smile told her that he welcomed the idea. Maybe that it was more than he had hoped for.

The silence continued as they walked together. Along to the other end of Sunset Beach, as the last of the colour drained from the cliffs towering alongside, leaving the pattern of their footprints in the sand. The tide was still out far enough to make it easy to get around the rock fall at the end of the beach, and within moments they could glimpse the first of the bures that had been built to accommodate the visitors to the conference and research facility.

The smell of the shrubs planted to screen the bures from each other made Anahera draw in an appreciative breath.

Luke smiled. 'It's lovely, isn't it? I'd forgotten the scent of ginger flowers.'

'I haven't seen these bures before. This area has been fenced off for ages. The first time I've been here for years was when Sam and I came down to that doctor we thought was having a heart attack at your conference.'

'Charles.' Luke nodded. 'I had an email from him yesterday. They brought his coronary angiogram forward as soon as he got home. He ended up with three stents to fix his arteries and he reckons he's good for another forty years or so.'

'That's good to hear. He was lucky.'

This was an easy way to break the silence. To talk about people other than themselves.

'He said he wants to come back. I must ask Harry if they're going to rent out these bures to people who might just want a break. They could make a fortune if they did.'

'Turn it into some kind of resort?' Anahera frowned. 'I don't think the Lockharts would allow that to happen on Wildfire Island. But then, I didn't think they'd lease even part of it like this. I'm sure it was Ian's idea, not Max's.'

'Ian's his brother, isn't he? I seem to remember hearing some opinions about his character that were not very flattering.'

'Nobody likes him. He was the black sheep of the family and was apparently no support at all when Max's wife died and he was struggling to care for the twins. I think he did his best to bleed the family fortune dry even when Max needed so much money to get care for Christopher.'

'Caroline's twin, yes? The one with cerebral palsy.'

'Yes. Max has been living in Australia with him for years. Ian was given the job of running the mine a few years back but Mum says that he was just using the money for himself, probably gambled it away, and then he just took off. The mine's been closed recently because it isn't safe. Ian hasn't been seen for weeks and nobody knows where he is. Caroline came back just last month and she was horrified by how run-down everything's become but she's determined to save the mine and the jobs for everyone.' Anahera turned to follow Luke up a pathway from the beach that led to one of the bures. 'Maybe it's not such a crazy idea, starting a resort.'

Stepping inside the bure, her eyes widened.

'This looks like a resort already. Like something you only see in a magazine.' Her gaze followed the round walls with the louvred windows, up to the coved ceiling and then down to where the softly draped mosquito nets framed a huge bed made up with crisp-looking white linen. Whoever had serviced the room had sprinkled frangipani blossoms over the cover, which made it look even more inviting.

Romantic, even…

Luke had no idea she was finding it hard to take in a new breath.

'Have a look at the bathroom while I find my clothes. It's astonishing…'

It was. Anahera looked at the bowl on the vanity bench, where a pretty pattern of colourful petals had been left as decoration beside a pile of fluffy white towels. At the design of the fish in the mosaic of the shower floor. At the stone walls and the rainhead fitting. And then she imagined Luke standing in here, naked, under the fall of water, and she had to close her eyes and step back. To lean against the wall for a moment, even.

'Ana? Are you okay?'

She opened her eyes to find Luke standing close. Too close. She could see the tiny flecks of gold and brown that made his eyes hazel more than green. He had some dry clothes in one hand but he was still wearing only his damp swimming shorts, and looking at his face couldn't remove that bare chest in her peripheral vision. It had been manageable out in the open space of the beach, with the sea stretching for ever on one side, but nothing could mitigate the effect of him standing so close, in a confined space, with all that skin within touching distance. She could feel the heat of it. Could smell the salt of the sea and something else that opened an avalanche of memories.

The smell of… Luke…

Anahera opened her mouth to say she was fine. Tensed every muscle in her body that she would need to move. To slip past Luke and into the safety of a larger room.

But nothing happened. No words emerged. No muscle twitched.

And Luke was just as still.

The soft thud of a handful of clothing being discarded barely registered, and the touch of Luke's hand on her face was so intense that she had to close her eyes again. She still hadn't closed her mouth after that abortive attempt to say anything, and it was too late by the time she felt the touch of Luke's lips.

It was too late to talk. To move. To *think*…

'Oh… *Ana*…' The word was almost a prayer. Luke's

hands had trailed down her body, over her breasts and then slipped up under the top of her uniform to touch her skin by the time his lips were lifted enough for him to speak. 'Do you want this as much as I do? I can stop…'

The sound that came from Anahera's lips was no more than a whimper of need. She had wanted this for ever. She just hadn't known how much.

It was a tiny sound but it had the effect of unleashing something huge. Luke had the hem of her green tunic in his hands now and he was lifting it. Anahera raised her arms to make it easier to shed the item of clothing that represented a barrier between his skin and hers. It had to go, along with everything else she was wearing. So that Luke could touch her anywhere. Everywhere.

Especially *there*…

Her legs were losing the ability to hold her upright but it didn't matter. Not when there was a pair of strong arms to support her. To scoop her up and carry her and then lay her down amongst the fragrant lemon-and-white blossoms of the frangipani. Blossoms that released even more scent as they were crushed by her body lying on them. Then Luke stepped back, turned and retrieved his wallet from the dressing table. She watched him fumble through it, searching for a condom. He turned to face her, a question in his eyes: *Are we going to do this?*

Nothing needed to be said. They had never needed to ask what was needed or preferred because they had been in tune with each other from that very first time of such gentle, passionate lovemaking. This was nothing like that first time. The sex was hard and fast. Almost desperate—as if they'd both been wanting this for ever. As if they were grabbing something illicit because they knew they might never have another opportunity?

And then they lay facing each other, their faces only inches apart, as they both tried to catch their breath and wait until their hearts stopped racing.

It was Luke who broke the silence.

'I wish I could turn back time,' he said softly. 'I wish I had the chance to change things.'

Anahera's smile was wistful. 'What's that saying? If wishes were horses, then beggars would ride...'

'I've gone over and over it, you know. Wondering why I *didn't* tell you—or anyone else—about Jane. I think it was because I was...escaping, you know?'

Luke had the most beautiful face Anahera had ever seen on a man. She loved the intensity of his eyes. The way he could control his face when he was in a professional setting but he could let it go sometimes, like now, when every emotion could be seen in the subtle dance of muscle movement. It was how she knew how open he was being. How honest.

'Those years with Jane in the coma. Being married but having no wife... It was the loneliest place you could imagine. And I was trapped in it. As trapped as Jane was in her own body. It never occurred to me that I'd want to be with anyone else, though, because when I was in London I knew she was lying in a bed in the same city and it would have felt like cheating.' He closed his eyes for a moment. 'It *would* have been cheating.'

Had Jane known how much she had been loved? How many men were capable of such loyalty and devotion?

'Coming here—to Wildfire Island—was a crazy idea that my boss came up with because he said if I didn't take a break, he'd either have to fire me or I'd kill myself by overworking.'

A smile tugged one corner of his mouth. 'And coming

here was like being set free from that trap. London was a world away. I couldn't visit Jane. There was nothing here to even remind me. It was a fantasy break and I had been given permission to forget—just for a few weeks. I guess telling anyone would have broken that fantasy.'

Anahera's head dipped in a slow nod. She could understand that.

'I hadn't expected to meet you, though. To…to fall in love…'

The words seemed to explode in her head. Luke *had* loved her. He still did, if the expression in his eyes were anything to go by. And then he touched her face again, and she had to close her eyes. Tightly, but that wasn't enough to prevent a tear escaping.

'I know I hurt you.' Luke's voice was raw now. 'And if I could change anything by turning back time, that would be the one thing I would change. But by the time I did try to put things right it was too late, wasn't it? And I'd been in a bad space when I called you anyway. It was just after the funeral. I didn't expect to be forgiven and I was right so I let it go and never tried again. And you'd already moved on to a new life. You'd found Hana's father…'

Another tear escaped. This was it—the moment of truth. But how could she destroy the love she'd seen in Luke's eyes and inflict more pain on someone who'd already been through too much? Or wipe out the blissful reminder of what it was like to be made love to by someone who thought about her that way?

'Would it have made a difference, Ana? If you'd known about Jane right from the start? Would you have let me close if you'd known I still had a wife?' His sigh was heavy. 'There's another saying—that timing is everything. If only I'd waited a few months before taking that break…'

In the silence that followed his words Anahera made her decision. Maybe it would have been a different one if he hadn't given her such an opportunity but there it was—a perfect lead in to what she'd seen as a framework to cling to.

'It was a fantasy, Luke.' Her voice sounded almost rusty and she had to clear her throat gently. 'For me as much as you, I think. History trying to repeat itself, I think.'

'You've said that before. About raising Hana by yourself.' Luke was frowning. 'I'm not sure I understand what you mean now, though.'

'I mean that I knew it couldn't have worked. I only have to remember my mother crying over photographs of my father to know that.'

She felt the touch of Luke's hand as he stroked her hair. 'I remember you saying that he'd died when you were very young. That was a tragedy.' Luke's smile was crooked. 'But I'm not planning on dying any time, soon, Ana.'

'That's not what I meant. The real tragedy was that they loved each other so much but couldn't find a way to be together all the time because they came from such different worlds. And he died in France. Mum couldn't afford for us to go to his funeral even, and his family wouldn't pay. They thought he'd been crazy, marrying a girl from a Pacific island who didn't want to live in Paris.' Anahera could see that Luke was processing what she was saying. Was he relating the story to himself? Wondering if she had no desire to live in London?

'She tried,' Anahera added. 'She took me to Paris

when I was a baby and we lived there for a few months. She said that, despite being so in love with my father, it was the loneliest time and that she couldn't live without the sun. And he couldn't live full time in a place that was a holiday destination for him. It had just been a fantasy...'

Luke's face had stilled. Whatever emotion he was feeling was hidden. 'So you're saying you wouldn't consider trying something like that? Living in a different place? Did you hate being in Brisbane that much?'

Given different circumstances, Anahera would have loved Brisbane, with the vibrancy of a big city and new things to entertain and challenge her. But she couldn't tell Luke that because it would undermine the integrity of her framework.

'I needed to come home,' she whispered. 'I needed my family.'

Luke nodded. 'I think I understand,' he said slowly.

His hand was on her shoulder now. He traced the length of her arm until he found her fingers and he raised her hand to place a kiss on her palm.

'You were in love with me, too, weren't you, Ana? Or did I imagine that?'

'You didn't imagine it.' Her voice cracked but she carried on. 'I loved you more than I thought it was possible to love anyone. I...' She had to bite her lip so that she didn't tell him she still felt exactly the same way.

'And I felt exactly the same way about you,' Luke murmured. 'We never really got round to telling each other that properly, did we?'

'No.'

'And it's too late now.'

Anahera's heart was breaking. But this wasn't just

about her, was it? She had to remember that and hold on to it.

'It was always too late, Luke. We just didn't know it.'

In response, Luke drew her into his arms and held her close. She could feel his heart beating against her own. An echo of his voice rumbling in his chest.

'If this *is* just a fantasy…would there be any reason for us not to enjoy it for a bit longer? Just a few days more?'

He was kissing her hair now. Stroking her back. Their lovemaking had been so wild and fierce as they'd slaked their pent-up need for each other. What would it be like to do it again—the way they used to make love, with that slow tenderness that took its own sweet time to build to such a passionate release?

'How soon do you need to be home?'

With a sigh, Anahera let go of rational thought and lifted her face as she pulled Luke's head close enough for her to touch his lips with her own.

'Not for a while,' she murmured. 'Long enough…'

CHAPTER SEVEN

SOMETHING WEIRD HAD happened today.

Perhaps it was some kind of emotional alchemy from a mix of grief, desire and that bone-deep contentment that only came in the wake of complete physical fulfilment.

If someone had asked, Anahera would have said with absolute conviction that it wasn't possible to love Hana more than she already did.

And yet here she was, looking down at her sleeping daughter, filled with love that had a new depth, and it was overwhelming enough to make her heart ache and for slow tears to trace the outline of her nose.

Was it because she'd been part of the grief of Tane's family as they'd faced the loss of someone so deeply loved?

It couldn't be that simple. It wasn't the first time she'd lost a patient, and while every death saddened her it was a part of the job she had chosen to do and one that was as much a part of her as being a mother. Even the really tragic cases like Tane and little Hami—the child they'd lost to the same, awful disease of encephalitis a couple of years ago—could be processed in a way that made her a better nurse. A better person even, because they served to remind her how precious life was and how important it was to show the people in her life how much they were loved.

This new level of love for Hana felt like she had tapped into a mysterious vault where there was a vast new wealth of love to be found—and shared.

Could it be because she felt loved herself in a way that nobody but Luke could have made her feel?

The soft mosquito netting slipped through her fingers as Anahera stepped back from the bed after a final kiss and murmurs of love, but her train of thought was not interrupted.

Was love like some kind of emotional currency and the more you could put into the bank, the more you had to draw on?

The smile of greeting from Vailea as she went onto the veranda almost started her tears again. How could anyone get so much understanding and sympathy into one smile?

'You've had such a day, love. Come and sit. Eat. I've made the paella you love.'

Anahera glanced at her favourite chair that she couldn't wait to sink into and at the plate of fragrant rice and seafood—one of Vailea's specialties—that was waiting on the little round table beside the chair. She took a step farther away first, though, so that she could press her cheek to her mother's hair for a long moment.

'Thanks, Mum. Love you.'

'And I love you. Now sit. Eat.'

Anahera sat. And ate. And smiled.

She had all the love she needed in her life, didn't she? From Hana and her mother. From her friends like Sam and Hettie and Keanu and Caroline. From the island community that was more like a huge, extended family that willingly shared the joy of celebrations and was there as a solid rock of support when things weren't so good.

But the love that Luke could give her was different, her mind whispered.

Important...

Her mother sat there quietly, keeping her company as she ate her meal. Every so often she would glance at Anahera, who smiled back but said nothing. She needed this comfort. The delicious food, the company of someone so dear and the peacefulness of home that wrapped around her like a cosmic hug.

It was Vailea who broke the silence.

'I was worried about you,' she said. 'I knew you'd gone walking because you were so upset about Tane and I thought you still would be when you came home but...' Her glance was quizzical. 'There's something different about you.'

The last mouthful of her food was a little difficult to swallow. Just how much could her mother see?

'I'm just the same, Mum. I am still upset about Tane— of course I am—but I feel better than I did. The sunset was beautiful. I...guess I found some peace on the beach...'

'Mmm...' It was obvious that Vailea knew she was being fobbed off. She wouldn't push for more of an explanation and maybe that was partly why Anahera felt she deserved more.

'I met Luke,' she added. 'And we talked. He was even more upset than I was, I think. He took losing Tane as a personal failure. He told Sam there was nothing more he could do here and that he was going to go back to London tomorrow.'

'But what about all that research? Didn't he want to go and collect tea-leaves and things?'

'I think he's changed his mind and he's going to stay for a bit longer. He was angry with himself, I think. Like it was his fault Tane died.'

'That's ridiculous. I've never seen a doctor work so hard to save someone. Or care so much. He's an extraordinary young man.' She sighed. 'You know, when he was here the first time I had hopes that something might happen between the two of you. He's just the sort of man I could see you with. I hear he's good with children, too. Marama has been helping me in the kitchen and she was telling me all about the football game over on French Island.' She shook her head. 'It was such a shock to find out he was married.'

'His wife died just after he went back. It's a really sad story. She'd had a dreadful accident and was in a coma for years. The only time she opened her eyes and spoke was when he was here. That's why he rushed back like that.'

'Ohhh…'

Anahera could almost hear the wheels turning in her mother's brain.

'Even if I was looking for a partner—which I'm not—I wouldn't choose someone who lives half a world away. I know how that works.' Her smile was poignant. 'I saw you crying too often when I was little.'

Vailea's eyes widened. 'But that was because Stefan *died*. I lost the father of my baby and the man I loved with all my heart…'

An echo of Luke's voice was as clear as if he was whispering in her ear.

I'm not planning on dying any time, soon, Ana.

'But you couldn't live together. He came from Paris

and you said it was cold and horrible and you couldn't live without the sun.'

'I didn't want to live without Stefan either.' Her mother's voice was quiet. Sad. 'We would have found a way to make it work. Paris in the summer is probably wonderful, and who wouldn't have wanted to escape a European winter by living in a tropical paradise? We were working it out. We *would* have worked it out but he…he died.'

'Oh, Mum…' Anahera reached over the little table to hold and squeeze her mother's hand. She could hear the tears in Vailea's voice, and the old grief was contagious. It didn't matter how much love she or Hana or anyone else could give, did it? There was still that gap that could never be filled.

And maybe she needed the comfort of touch herself. The conviction in her mother's voice had shocked her because they had knocked the bolts from the framework of the rationale she'd been using as the justification to keep the truth from Luke and maintain the foundations of the future unchanged. Her mother truly believed it would have been possible to live in different worlds and to be with the man she loved so much. To have a whole family.

The bolts were gone. It would take no more than a puff of breath to topple the emotional structure completely, and then where would she be?

Nursing even more guilt than ever before, that was where.

'He wasn't going to let you grow up without a daddy. He adored you. And me…' Vailea sniffed and sighed again. 'There's never been anyone else for me. I doubt there ever will be.'

'I'm…sorry…'

Inadequate words but the sorrow Anahera was feeling was genuine. For her mother, but for herself, too. She couldn't remember her father so she couldn't miss *him* but she had always been aware of that gap in her life so she had always missed having him in her life. Having a father like the other kids had.

It was in that moment that she knew what she had to do.

It was wrong to keep the truth from Luke. She had to tell him. She had to tell Hana, too. She wasn't just depriving Luke of a daughter. She was depriving Hana of a father. If her daughter ever found out the truth, she would never forgive her mother.

Anahera would never forgive herself.

She would also have to tell her mother—something she should have done right from the start.

Maybe that would be the easiest way to start. Anahera took a very deep breath as she tried to collect the words she needed.

'Mum?'

'Yes, love?'

'There's something I need to tell you.'

'What's that?' Vailea was distracted, fishing in the pocket of her apron. 'I'm sure I've got a hanky in here somewhere...'

Her sniff revealed that she was still crying. How could Anahera make things worse by dropping the bombshell hovering on her lips right now?

And, if she told her mother, it was only a step away from telling Luke and that was...

It was terrifying.

Even if she started by telling him that there was a chance they could work things out and be together, she would have to destroy whatever hope that engendered by telling him the truth about Hana and then she would be back to square one. He would hate her for lying to him and he might demand a share of Hana's life but exclude her from the time he had with his daughter and everything she had feared the most would come to pass.

She had dug a huge hole for herself and there was no way out. She couldn't even see the frayed ends of a rope.

Vailea had found her handkerchief and she blew her nose. Then she patted Anahera's hand and smiled, signalling that she had pulled herself together and things were going to be fine again.

'Look at me…sitting here crying when I have so much I can be thankful for. When other people have so much more to try and bear. Poor Tane. And that poor little baby, who's going to grow up without a daddy. Like you did…' She shook her head. 'What was it that you wanted to tell me, love?'

Her words felt like a judgement and as if she was the guilty party. Confessing had suddenly become so much harder. So much scarier.

Anahera swallowed hard. 'Just…that I love you.'

She didn't dare meet her mother's eyes because she knew that too much would be seen. In the heartbeat of silence following her words, she knew that avoiding that contact hadn't been enough.

Vailea might not know what was wrong but she certainly knew that that there was something she wasn't being told.

'I love you, too, Anahera.'

Her heart sank. Her full name was only ever used when things were serious.

'And you know that my ears are here for whenever you want to talk about anything.'

'I know,' Anahera whispered. 'I…I can't, Mum. Not yet. There's…um…someone else I probably need to talk to first.'

This silence was broken by the creak of the old wicker chair as Vailea got to her feet. By the clink of cutlery against china as she picked up Anahera's plate.

'It's hard to do the right thing sometimes,' Vailea said quietly. 'But, in the end, sometimes the right thing is the only thing you *can* do.'

Anahera nodded.

She knew that.

She just had to find the courage she needed to do it.

Of all his five senses, Luke decided that the one he would least like to lose might be that of smell.

It hit him even before he opened his eyes as the first fingers of light poked their way through the slats of the shutters the next morning.

That had been the thing that had hit him like a brick the moment he'd set foot on this island again, hadn't it? That gentle, tropical breeze with the sweet waft of flowers like frangipani and jasmine.

For him, it would also remind him of the scent of Anahera's hair. Of her skin.

He kept his eyes shut as he took a deep breath, his nose still half buried in the soft pillow.

Her scent was still on his sheets, but even if it hadn't been, it was so deeply embedded in his memory that it would be an instant connection for the rest of his life. Interesting how closely it was related to the sense of taste because that was what filled his mind now as he surfaced to complete consciousness.

The taste of Ana…

Good grief…and how close were they both to the sense of touch? The memories were so recent and real it felt like he could roll over and start making love to her again this very second, and the desire to do exactly that was so powerful he threw back the covers with a groan and pushed his body to get his feet on the floor and start moving.

Towards the shower. Preferably a cold one.

Or maybe a swim would be more effective. Grabbing a towel and a dry pair of swimming shorts, Luke headed out into the soft light of dawn and jogged along the track to the beach. He dropped the towel without pausing and kept running until the water was deep enough to slow his momentum and then he dived and started kicking. By the time he surfaced and could use his arms, he was swimming as hard and fast as he had been yesterday, in an attempt to wash tension from his body and calm the kaleidoscope of thoughts and emotions in his head.

When he started to tire, he rolled onto his back and floated on gentle undulations of the deep water and watched the sun climb over the ragged mountaintops.

He never saw the sun rise in London. Rarely noticed a sunset either. And he never, ever went swimming because he could only do that in a pool and the smell of chlorine was one he associated with grief because that had been the scent of Jane's skin when he'd arrived at the emergency department that dreadful day.

This was, indeed, a very different world.

A fantasy?

But it felt real. He could feel the water around his body and he could see the clear blue of the lightening sky that heralded another perfect day. If he turned his head he could see the curve of that gorgeous beach with the twisted shapes of the old fig trees near the bottom of the cliffs, and if he let his mind wander just the tiniest bit he could see Anahera standing on the sand, waiting for him.

The image was real enough to start him swimming towards the shore, but as he stood up and shook the sea water from his eyes he could see that he was alone on Sunset Beach.

Of course the image had been a fantasy. Anahera would be at home with her family, caring for her daughter and getting ready for work. Getting on with a life that was so far removed from his own life that her words came back to haunt him.

'The real tragedy was that they loved each other so much but couldn't find a way to be together all the time because they came from such different worlds...

'I needed to come home... I needed my family...'

She'd been right. It was a fantasy because it was too much to believe that real life could deliver this kind of paradise.

It wasn't the setting. Luke draped his towel over his shoulders and took in a last glance of the dramatic beauty around him before making his way slowly back to the bure and the luxury of the shower. Everyone could visit this kind of tropical paradise that travel agents loved to advertise with huge posters in their windows to lure in Londoners in the grey depths of winter.

That it was paradise for him had nothing to do with being on a remote island.

It had everything to do with being with Ana.

And she belonged here. She needed to be here. How could he even think of taking her away from the sun? To a place where the scent of flowers might fade from her hair and her skin and that light in her eyes that was like a personal sun might begin to dim?

Would it make it all the harder to go home if they made the most of the few days they could have together now?

As if he had a choice...

A wry smile curled Luke's lips as he flicked the shower on and reached for the soap that had yet another scented reminder of Ana to release.

It didn't really matter if it made things harder. They were going to be unbearable for a while anyway.

'So that's it.' Sam spread the pages he had just collected from the printer on the staffroom table in front of where Luke was sitting. 'The whole plan for the rollout of the clinical trial. We've covered every island and hopefully we'll get a good cross-section of the population to sign up.' He grinned at Luke. 'Not a bad day's work, is it? Could I interest you in a beer?'

'Sounds good.' The glance Luke sent in Anahera's direction was hopefully casual. 'You going to have one, Ana?'

'Why not?' Anahera opened the fridge and took out some cans. 'It's been the longest day. Too quiet...'

They only had a couple of inpatients and there'd been no dramas. Nothing to push the awareness of that empty bed in the intensive care room to the background. Nothing to break the sad silence that seemed to echo in the corridors and wards. It would be nice to sit here for a few minutes and celebrate something as positive as the start of a trial that could prevent future tragedies from fatal cases of encephalitis.

'We still need to map out the epidemiological study

that you want me to do.' Sam popped the tab on his can and took a gulp of the cold beer. 'And what about the tea-leaves stuff? Do you want to leave that to me, too? Or there's always Keanu... Hey...' Sam grinned at Anahera. 'I forgot to tell you that Keanu's coming back next week.'

'Is he? Is Caroline coming with him?'

'Are you kidding? As if they'd let each other out of their sights right now...'

She couldn't help catching Luke's glance as she smiled. She knew how that felt—not wanting to let some-one out of your sight. And then her smile faded as she hurriedly looked away. It hadn't just been the empty bed she'd been so conscious of all day. Knowing that Luke was in the hospital, working with Sam, had been in her mind just as much. The day had been so long because she'd been counting the minutes until they might be able to have some time alone together.

Time that she would have to use to tell him the truth.

Anahera stared at the can of beer she was holding so tightly the chill from the metal was seeping into her hand. It was time that would spell the end of life as she knew it but her mother had hit the nail on the head. Sometimes you simply didn't have a choice and the only thing to do was the right thing.

It took a moment to tune into what Sam was saying to Luke.

'So it was Keanu's father who started the first research into the tea but it all stopped when he died.'

'What happened to him?'

'Got killed in a rock fall, apparently. Keanu was just a toddler but he's grown up knowing how special his dad was. There's a big picture of him in his graduation gown in the entrance to Atangi School. He was their brightest star back then, and the Lockhart family funded him to go to the mainland to get his degree.' Sam nodded with satisfaction. 'I reckon Keanu would see the project as a way of honouring his dad's memory. He'd love to be involved.'

'I'd still like to see where the bushes grow and take some photos. I'd like to take some leaves back to London, too, and get the experts to analyse them to see what makes them different.'

'I could help you collect them. I know where the bushes grow.' Anahera's brain was buzzing. French Island was the place they'd really started talking to each other. It would be the ideal place to have an even more significant conversation, wouldn't it—except that would mean having to wait. 'We couldn't do it tomorrow because it's Tane's funeral but the day after that, we could visit the island.' She was speaking fast because this felt like a plan coming together. The first step in putting things right. 'We'd have to take a boat, though. We couldn't justify a helicopter when there isn't a clinic happening.'

'Make a day of it,' Sam suggested. 'Take a picnic. Take Hana with you. Hey…take Bugsy with you. He loves a boat ride.'

Luke found himself smiling as he listened to the conversation. It sounded like a great idea. How amazing would it be to be out with Anahera and her gorgeous little girl, with a dog bounding along beside them?

Like the perfect picture of a family outing…

Another image for the fantasy gallery he'd be able to treasure for the rest of his life?

Anahera didn't seem so keen on the idea, though. Weirdly, she was looking…nervous?

Sam was still on a roll. 'Speaking of Hana, don't forget she's due for her vaccination.'

'What?' Anahera's eyes widened. 'You want to start the encephalitis trial with *Hana*?'

'I'm talking about her four-year vaccination. The one for diphtheria, tetanus, whooping cough and polio. And the MMR, if she didn't have it at eighteen months.'

The colour had suddenly drained from Anahera's face, and Luke stared at her in astonishment. Was it that big a deal for her to take her daughter to an appointment that involved a painful injection? She was a nurse, for heaven's sake—she knew how important vaccinations were.

Sam was taking another pull of his beer and didn't seem to notice her odd reaction. 'Did she have the MMR at eighteen months? You were still in Brisbane then, weren't you?'

'I'll find the records for you. She's not due for ages yet.'

'Two weeks isn't ages. I noticed the reminder on my calendar this morning.'

Luke was still staring at Anahera and barely listening to Sam. It wasn't just her face that was pale. Her hand was squeezing that can so hard her fingers looked white. Any harder and…yes…the can crumpled and a whoosh of foamy liquid spilled over her hand and onto the table.

'Oops…' Sam scooped paper out of harm's way.

Anahera leapt up to grab a tea towel.

Luke was aware of an odd buzzing in his head like static as his brain finally caught up with what Sam had said. He didn't stop to think before saying something. He wasn't actually aware he was saying it aloud.

'Hana's only three and a half.'

'No…' Sam was tapping the sheaf of paper in his hand on the table top to straighten the edges. 'She turns four in a couple of weeks. Vailea's already talking about the cake she's going to make, isn't she, Ana?'

For the longest moment the only sound in the room was the last edge of the papers being tapped.

The moment was more than long enough for Luke's brain to focus on a few simple calculations.

Calculations that lead to a blindingly clear result.

Anahera had lied to him.

Hana was six months older than he'd been led to believe. Anahera hadn't hooked up with someone as soon as she had moved to Brisbane. She'd already been pregnant when she'd left Wildfire Island.

Hana had to be *his* daughter…

CHAPTER EIGHT

'ANA? ARE YOU OKAY?'

It was the concern in Sam's voice that made Anahera realise that she was frozen to the spot, the tea towel dangling from her hands while the foamy puddle on the table spread out and started dripping from the edge. She looked up slowly but her gaze didn't connect to Sam's. It was drawn, inexorably, to Luke.

The shock on his face was only to be expected but the darkness behind it was far more disturbing. Anger? No, it was worse than that. It looked more like…devastation.

In her peripheral vision she could see Sam's head turning to look at Luke, too, and even someone who had only a fraction of his intelligence and compassion would have realised that something major was happening between Anahera and Luke.

'I…ah…I'd better go and file these papers so I don't lose them.' Sam took a step towards the door but then hesitated, and this time Anahera looked at her friend directly because she knew what he was thinking. She was in trouble and he would do whatever she wanted him to do to help.

The almost imperceptible shake of her head told him

that she didn't need him to stay. That this was something she had to deal with by herself.

She was still staring at the door after he left, too afraid to look back at Luke, so his quiet words made her jump.

'I'm right, aren't I? Hana is my daughter.'

'Yes.' Her response was no more than a whisper.

'Were you going to tell me?' His voice was cold now. So cold that Anahera felt a shiver trickle down her spine.

'*Yes...*' She gulped in some air. 'Today. But...but then...then I thought that if we were going to go to French Island together that would be a better time but...' The words were tumbling out with desperate haste. 'But you liked Sam's idea of a picnic and taking Hana and that wouldn't have been...' Her voice cracked, and Anahera knew that she wasn't going to be able to hold her tears at bay.

The urge to throw herself into Luke's arms so that he could hold her while she sobbed out the overwhelming mix of guilt and apology and...yes...*relief* was so strong she could feel her body leaning into the movement.

'I don't believe you.'

The words—and the tone—were a brick wall that Anahera slammed against. Her balance had tipped enough for her to need to catch the back of a chair and the support was comforting enough to make her slip into the seat.

'You lied to me, Ana.'

There was a note of outrage in his voice. Disappointment that was so personal it was a direct body blow. She'd been right to fear that he would hate her for what she'd done.

'*No...*' It wasn't that she was trying to contradict him—more like she was trying to ward off what she knew had to be coming next—but her response drew a huff of disbelief from Luke.

'*No?*' A chair scraped as Luke pulled it out and dropped himself into it. The tension in his body seemed to be transferred through the tabletop like the faint aftershock of an earthquake. 'Oh…right. You told me the truth, didn't you? That Hana was born in Brisbane. That her father was a doctor. That—what was it you said exactly? That her father wasn't in the picture because there'd never been any chance of a relationship with him?'

'I didn't think there was. I thought you were married. Living in London. I didn't *know*…'

'And whose fault was that, Ana?'

'Mine.' She had to hide her tears so she put her elbows on the table and covered her face with her hands. '*Mine*…'

'And the only relationship you thought to consider was one you might have yourself? Did it not even occur to you that I might have had the right to have a relationship with my own child? My *daughter*?'

The sound that escaped Luke now was—horrifyingly—close to a sob. And then he was completely silent, as though the enormity of what he'd just found out was only now sinking in.

The silence went on. And on. But all Anahera could do was wait. To wallow in the revelation of how selfish she'd been.

How wrong…

He had a daughter.

Something was swimming through the shock of the discovery and the disbelief that he hadn't been told. A feeling Luke couldn't identify clearly because he'd never experienced it before.

Maybe it was a very personal kind of amazement. He had a daughter. A small person who carried his genes. Who was a part of himself. A child who was about to reach the milestone of being alive for four years and he knew nothing about her, except that she was beautiful.

And she loved butterflies.

And he could have gone back to London and carried on with the rest of his life and never known that she even existed.

'How could you do that?' The words burst out and he wasn't surprised that they made Anahera flinch.

The pang of disappointment in himself that he'd scared her might well come back later to haunt him, but in this moment he didn't care.

'When you knew the truth, you still didn't tell me. How could you have been with me last night...?' The memory of how it had felt to hold her in his arms—to make love to her—was trying to swamp him. Like a drowning man, he had to kick hard to reach the surface.

'It was all a lie, wasn't it? You can't tell someone you loved them more than you thought it was possible to love anyone but...but know that you're doing something like *this* to them...' He stared at Anahera's bent head, willing her to look up and meet his gaze.

'I thought I knew you,' he said sadly. 'But I don't, do I? And you know what?' The scraping of his chair on the floor was as harsh as his tone as he stood up. 'I don't think I want to any more.'

The need for distance was imperative—before he said something he knew he would regret. Something cruel that would make her feel a fraction of the pain he was feeling right now.

But he hesitated for a heartbeat.

'Why, Ana?' He closed his eyes on a sigh. 'Just tell me why. The real reason, not that cop-out about history repeating itself. Why didn't you tell me when you had the chance? When we were sitting on that cliff and I asked... I *asked* about Hana's father? When I said...' His breath came out in an incredulous huff as he opened his eyes again. 'When I said he must have been over the moon to have a daughter like Hana. You could have just said that he didn't know he had a daughter and I would have put two and two together.'

Luke ran stiff fingers through his hair and ended up holding his head as if there was too much inside and it might explode.

'Why?'

Finally, Anahera raised her face and looked directly at him. Her eyes were so dark they looked like bottomless pools. And they were so full of fear Luke felt the hairs on the back of his neck stand up.

Her voice was so strangled it sounded nothing like her. 'I thought you might take her away from me.'

Unbelievably, there was a new pain to be experienced. One that held the threat of a chasm he really, really didn't want to see into.

'I loved you, Ana.' It was even painful to try and swallow. 'How could you believe that I would have done something to hurt you?'

Loved.

Past tense.

It was no more than she had expected, but she hadn't expected it to hurt *this* much.

Anahera watched Luke walk out the door of the staffroom and knew that she hadn't ever really known what loneliness felt like until now.

Luke's parting words had been a mutter about needing space. Or time to think. She'd barely heard them because the implications of that choice of tense had been crowding into her head with the singsong kind of 'I told you so' taunt. And her heart had been dealing with the sensation of the distance between them increasing as he'd moved towards the door. Of a bond being pulled beyond capacity and snapping with a vicious whip-like crack that was leaving blood to well in its wake.

The worst had happened.

Or had it? Maybe there was worse to come. Maybe Luke wouldn't have tried to take her daughter away from her when he'd loved her but now he didn't know who she was and he didn't even *want* to know so there was no chance he would ever love her again, which meant that there was no barrier to him doing something that might hurt her. When he'd had time to think, would he decide that it might be a good idea to take Hana away from someone who treated the people she loved the way she had treated him?

Oh…God…

Telling the truth was supposed to lessen guilt, wasn't it? So why was it worse? The need to protect her family and her life by keeping the truth hidden had outweighed the guilt until now, but now that side of the scales had been replaced by fear and it seemed in perfect balance with the guilt on the other side.

Whatever was going to happen, she had brought it on herself.

But that didn't mean she couldn't still fight to protect her mother and Hana and herself, did it?

Her hands were steepled on either side of her nose. Moving them apart, she scraped away the tears beneath her eyes as she took in a deep breath that sounded like a final sniff. Sitting here, crying, wasn't going to help anyone.

Luke wouldn't be sitting around anywhere. He was probably swimming by now. Powering through the ocean as he cleared his head and decided what he was going to do next.

Or had he gone to find his daughter?

The thought was appalling. What if Luke told Hana who he was before Anahera had had time to prepare her for something that would be confusing and probably frightening?

It was enough to propel her from her chair and through the door. It was only luck that stopped her barrelling straight into her mother.

Vailea rarely left her domain of the hospital kitchens to come into the staffroom and, by the look on her face, she hadn't come to check the supplies of cold drinks in the staff fridge.

'So Sam was right…' Vailea shook her head. 'Oh, love…'

'Sam doesn't know…' Anahera stepped back. She could see the fear in her mother's eyes. She *knew*… Did everybody know now? 'What did he say?'

'Just that you seemed to be upset about something. That Luke was, too. And it had been something he'd said about Hana that had caused it. About how old she was…' Her breath came out in a sigh. 'It wasn't hard for him to guess, love, and…and I've always had my suspicions.'

'You never said.'

'I thought he was married. I thought…last night that

you'd decided to tell the truth and it seemed like the right thing to do was to tell him first.'

'I didn't get the chance. And now he doesn't believe that I was ever going to.'

'Well, I can tell him *that* isn't true.'

Anahera shook her head. 'It wouldn't make any difference. Not now. I should have told him before…before…' Tears threatened again. Before she'd made things worse by deliberately *not* telling him? Before she'd given in to the temptation of making love with him again?

'He's not even here now. I don't know where he is and I'm scared he might have gone off to find Hana…' The need to get to Hana first came back with renewed strength, and Anahera started to move but Vailea caught her arm.

'Hana's safe. Luke went storming off towards his bure and Sam's gone after him.'

'Why?'

'To talk to him. To try and help.'

'Talking won't be enough. I need to get legal advice. Maybe Caroline or Keanu could help me find someone while they're still on the mainland. I'll ring and talk to them tonight. I'll fix this, Mum. I won't let him take Hana away from us.'

'Oh, darling…why would he want to do that?'

'Because…' The calm tone of reason in her mother's voice was taking the wind out of the sails Anahera had hoisted in readiness for the new fight she might have to protect her family. Her voice dropped to a whisper. 'Because she's his daughter…'

'And I suspect that the only thing he'll want to do right now is to meet her properly. And he has every right to do that, hasn't he?'

'Yes…'

'That's why I told Sam to bring him round to our house later. For dinner.'

'*Mum*…' Anahera was horrified. Home was her safe place, only secondary to these islands. Having the truth in the open was making her feel vulnerable enough. Having Luke in her home with her daughter—*their* daughter—was a terrifying prospect. Were they going to tell Hana who Luke really was? How? And when?

'It's a start,' Vailea said quietly. 'Remember what I said to you last night? About the only thing to do being the right thing?'

Sometimes her mother could make her feel like a child again. A child who still had a lot to learn. Anahera nodded.

'Well, this is one of those right things. Now, why don't you go and pick up Hana and go home? See if you can find some pretty flowers on the way and she could help you make a bowl for the table. I want to go down to the boats and get some nice fresh fish.'

'He won't come. He doesn't want to see me at the moment.' Her voice dropped. 'He…he hates me, Mum. Because I lied to him.'

'He doesn't hate you.' Vailea touched her daughter's cheek gently, and the expression in her eyes made Anahera want to cry.

'If he hated you, how could you both have made something as perfect as our little Hana?'

'That was then. It's different now.'

'True love never dies. He's angry right now and he has every right to be like that. He's probably confused, too. It changes you, being a parent. You had nine months to get used to the idea. Imagine if someone just handed you a baby and told you that you were a mother now. How would you feel?'

'Terrified,' Anahera admitted. 'I wouldn't have the first idea what to do.'

'Exactly. And how much harder would it be if the baby was big enough to have her own opinions and tell you what they were?'

Being terrified was not something she would ever have thought Luke would have to contend with but her mother's words were making sense. Whatever emotions Luke was experiencing had to be strong enough to need an outlet, and anger was usually the fastest route to ease the initial pressure, wasn't it?

It had been for her.

That apparent betrayal in finding out that Luke was married had made her angry enough to slam the door on his attempt to see her again and put things right. She had convinced herself that the last thing she ever wanted was to see him again.

Luke couldn't slam that kind of door because Hana would be left on the other side and however difficult it might be for him to face the woman who'd betrayed *him*, Anahera knew instinctively that Luke would never contemplate turning his back on his own daughter.

Neutral ground would have to be found. If nothing else, maybe they could end up with a kind of friendship and that would be better than nothing, wouldn't it?

Vailea looked over her shoulder as she turned to leave. 'Let's make Luke welcome in our home, love. He's part of our family. And we have something to thank him for, don't we?'

Anahera was still trying to answer the question she had just posed for herself. 'Do we?'

'Think about it.' With a smile, her mother was gone.

But Anahera's thoughts were still on her question about whether friendship would be better than nothing and she'd found her answer by the time she headed out into the heat of the late afternoon to collect Hana from the Lockhart mansion.

No. It definitely wouldn't.

Friendship with Luke would be a minefield of memories that would taunt her with 'what might have been' and it would reinforce the level of where a bar had been set and she would never meet anyone else who could possibly match that level.

But what could she do?

If she fostered a less-than-amicable relationship with her child's father, she would be bringing nuances of hostility into the life of a little girl who had never known— or shown—anything other than love.

The smile on Hana's face when she saw her mother was more than enough to convince Anahera that she couldn't do something that would affect her daughter's happiness. Especially something that would prick the happy bubble she lived in right now, where everybody loved each other and nothing could threaten that ultimate security. The tight hug she received from those tiny arms was enough to remind her how incredibly lucky she was to have this small person in her life.

And that was when the penny dropped.

This unimaginable joy that loving and being loved by Hana bestowed was what Luke deserved thanks for.

Without him, Hana would not have existed.

CHAPTER NINE

LUKE HAD FACED life-changing moments before.

Like the moment his pager had sounded as he had been preparing for an early-morning ward round to relay the message that his wife was being rushed to the emergency department of his own hospital, under CPR.

He'd known that his life was never going to be the same and he would never forget the way he'd felt as he'd run through those corridors, dodging people and beds and trollies—barely seeing what had been around him as he'd run headlong into an unknown and frightening future. That feeling of fighting against a force that had the potential to suffocate him. A force that could make it impossible to breathe and make his whole world grow dark. A force that he had no ability to control.

Even if he hadn't been able to remember it so well, it would have come flooding back right now, as he walked towards the village beside Sam and Bugsy. How, exactly, had Sam persuaded him to come here?

'You need a bridge,' he'd said, *'to get past the gap that's just appeared in the ground in front of you. It's much, much harder to build a bridge like that by yourself. When you've got other people around you, they can help*

*find what you need to build it with. Besides, it's about
time you met your daughter properly, isn't it?'*

Maybe the beer had helped, when Sam had taken him
to the conference centre's bar. And maybe it was the reminder that this was the exact spot he'd first seen Anahera again had been why he'd had another one.

Whatever. He was here now, silently walking up the
garden path that led to the village house where the Kopu
family lived.

His daughter was inside that house.

Or maybe not. A tiny figure was crouched beside a
bushy, flower-laden shrub and she hadn't noticed the new
arrivals until Bugsy sat beside her, his feathered tail waving vigorously enough to tickle a small brown bare leg.

'No, Bugsy! You can't eat it.' Hana's head turned and
there was a worried frown above those huge, dark eyes
that Luke remembered from the one time he'd seen her.
'Make him go 'way, Uncle Sam.'

'What's up, chicken?'

Stepping away from Luke, Sam crouched down beside
Hana with an ease that gave Luke a pang of something
that felt like jealousy. Sam already had a relationship with
Hana—clearly one they were both very comfortable with.

'Oh, I see… It's a caterpillar.'

Hana nodded her head. 'A patercillar. And Bugsy
wants to eat it and if he does, it won't turn into a flutterby.'

It brought a smile to Luke's lips, the adorable way
Hana jumbled her words, but the smile wobbled and he
realised—with horror—that he was on the verge of tears.

'Bugsy won't eat it,' Sam was saying reassuringly. 'He
knows that caterpillars don't taste nice. And he thinks

he's a person, not a bird or a gecko. He wants some of that yummy food that your nana is cooking for us.'

Hana heaved a relieved sigh and scrambled up to throw her arms around the dog's neck.

'I love you, Bugsy.'

The prickle of tears was more insistent. Luke cleared his throat to regain control, and the sound made Sam glance up.

'Hey, Hana. This is Luke. He's a friend of mine and Mummy's.'

Her cheek was pressed against Bugsy's golden coat but two eyes swivelled to look directly up at him. He could sense the shyness. The space, hanging in time, that would eventually lead to a decision about whether or not he would be granted entry into her special world.

That space felt like an impassable distance.

'Luke comes from London,' Sam continued. 'That's a country a long, long way away over the sea. Do you reckon they've got butterflies in London?'

'No-o-o…' Hana giggled and peeped up at Luke again.

He smiled. 'We do,' he told her. 'In a place called the London Zoo there's a special house that got built to look like a big caterpillar and inside there are hundreds and hundreds of butterflies.'

Had Sam provided the perfect foundation for a bridge to span that daunting space? It certainly felt increasingly easy to talk to this little girl.

'Big ones and tiny ones,' he continued. 'All different colours, like black and white and orange and red and yellow.'

Hana's eyes widened. Sam was grinning.

'How would you know that, Luke? Don't tell me you're a butterfly fanatic, too.'

'I do love butterflies,' Luke admitted. 'Always have. I've got a big book about them that I got given for my birthday when I was about Hana's age.'

'Are there blue ones?' It was the first time Hana had spoken directly to Luke. 'Blue ones are the bestest.'

'There are loads of blue ones.' Luke's smile widened. 'They *are* the bestest.'

Sam snorted. 'Let's go inside,' he said. 'Before your skills in the English language deteriorate any further.'

Standing up, Sam extended a hand as if it was an automatic thing to do, and Hana scrambled to her feet and put her hand in his. And then she looked up at Luke and it felt like a completely natural thing to do to extend *his* hand on her other side.

And, dear Lord…the feeling when those tiny fingers curled around his was…indescribable.

Huge…

He couldn't find even a single word of greeting as he reached the steps to the veranda, and Anahera appeared at the door of the house. Not that she was looking at his face. Her gaze was fixed at a lower point. At where his hand was holding Hana's.

Maybe they could all feel the shock wave emanating from Anahera because they all stopped moving at exactly the same time. Even Bugsy, who was happily trailing in their wake.

For a heartbeat they were all frozen. Sam wasn't going to find it easy to suggest any building materials for the bridge that was needed here because they would need to be quite substantial.

The help came from a very unexpected direction.

'Mumma…' Hana's face split into a wide grin. 'Bugsy

tried to eat my patercillar and Uncle Luke said he loves flutterbies and he said he lives in a patercillar house.'

'You need to wash your hands, darling.' The words were a little difficult to get out from a suddenly dry mouth. 'It's time for dinner.'

How could Luke have done that? Won her daughter's trust so easily? Had he used the knowledge he'd had of Hana's passion for butterflies to his own advantage?

But...*Uncle* Luke? He certainly hadn't taken any unilateral decision to let Hana know who he really was.

A small percentage of the tension in every cell of her body drained away. Enough to relax her lips to allow a subtle curl to the corners of her mouth.

'A caterpillar house? Really?'

Luke looked embarrassed. 'I was telling her about London Zoo. They have a butterfly house that's shaped like a caterpillar.'

Hana had got as far as the front door. She tugged on her mother's skirt. 'Can we go, Mumma? To the flutterby house?'

Anahera's smile vanished. So the conflict of parents living in worlds apart was beginning already. She couldn't help the tight tone to her voice.

'We'll see. Now scoot—I'm going to check in a minute to see if all the dirt gets washed off those hands.'

Hana's disappearance left a silence that could have been awkward except that Sam started moving up the steps. 'Come on, Bugsy. You stay on the veranda. I'll go and get you a bowl of water.'

The distraction increased as Vailea came to the door, wiping her hands on her apron.

'I can do that. Why don't you all sit out here on the

veranda? It's much cooler. I'll bring you boys some beer. One for you, too, Ana?'

'I'll get that.' The excuse to escape for a minute or two and try to get used to what was happening was irresistible. She opened bottles of beer and put them on a tray, along with some glasses. Her mother was filling an old enamel bowl with water at the sink.

'You're doing well,' Vailea said quietly. 'And it'll get easier. I'll feed Hana first and then she can go to bed. I don't imagine Sam and Bugsy will stay late and I'll get out of your way later so you and Luke can talk.'

The prospect was terrifying. Anahera had to make an effort to keep her hands steady so that the rattle of glass wouldn't betray her nervousness as she returned to the veranda.

At least she didn't have to try and start a conversation. Hana had beaten her back to the veranda and she was standing beside the low table, her hands clasped together and her face shining with pride as Luke exclaimed over the bowl with its petal mosaic framed by the turquoise glaze.

'You *made* this? Wow...'

'Mumma helped.' Hana was bouncing from one foot to the other. 'We picked the flowers on the way home. I picked all the yellow ones. And the pink ones.'

'It's an art form you'll find on most Pacific islands.' Vailea was smiling at Bugsy's enthusiastic appreciation of his drink. 'We love our flowers.'

'They're pretty,' Hana told Luke with the solemn tone of imparting great wisdom. 'Like flutterbys.'

'They are indeed.'

Luke was smiling at Hana and Anahera found herself staring intently at his face. She knew that expression. Her heart did a funny double flip thing. This was it, wasn't it? The moment he had fallen in love with his daughter.

Sam and Vailea were smiling, too. As if they thought everything was going according to some plan she wasn't privy to. Nerves kicked in again and she had to break the moment before something even more momentous happened—like someone telling Hana who Luke really was.

'We got most of the flowers from around the lagoon. I couldn't believe how bad the mosquitoes were for that time of day. I've never seen so many.'

'I know.' Vailea clicked her tongue as she sat down and started to pour a drink for herself. 'It's appalling. Nobody's been able to get hold of Ian Lockhart. We're hoping that Caroline can sort out the aerial spraying when she gets back next week.'

'Maybe I'll just sort it out myself,' Sam said quietly. 'We can't afford to wait any longer. People are getting bitten far more than in previous years and it's Russian roulette whether they are infected mosquitoes or not.'

Hana was listening to the adults talking. Was it Anahera's imagination or had she edged closer to where Luke was sitting? She took a deep breath. If she had, it was probably because Bugsy had settled at Sam's feet, on Luke's other side.

'*I* got bitten,' Hana said proudly.

'*What?*' Any need to observe the signals of a developing relationship between Luke and Hana evaporated. '*When*? Why didn't you tell me?'

The happy glow faded from Hana's face. She clearly thought she was in some kind of trouble and she didn't know why. And Luke was frowning. Did he think she was a bad mother because she hadn't noticed?

'Wasn't it itchy?' Luke tilted his head to catch Hana's

gaze. 'Did you have to scratch? Like this?' He demon-
strated scratching by crossing his arms and tickling his
armpits. Hana laughed and the sound cut through the
sudden tension in the group.

It had had even more of an effect on Luke. The way he
was looking at Hana now brought a lump to Anahera's
throat. She knew how that felt—the unbelievable joy of
hearing Hana laugh for the first time. It was something
she would never forget. Like the feeling when she'd seen
that first smile and witnessed those first, wobbly baby
steps.

Luke had missed out on so much and she wanted to
make up for it somehow. To share all those things. Would
he want to see the baby photos and videos or was it too
soon? It might be like rubbing salt into a very raw wound
at this point.

'Bessie fixed it,' Hana said. 'She put *magic* stuff on
it and it stopped scratching. See?'

Twisting her little body, she pointed to the back of
her knee. A small red dot was barely visible. No wonder
Anahera hadn't spotted it at bathtime.

She raised her gaze to find Luke watching her and for
a long moment they held the eye contact. The telepathic
conversation was the kind that only parents would have
when they were sharing the same worry about their child.

And it felt…*good*. As if something huge that had been
missing from her life was suddenly there.

Someone to share the worry. Coming home to live
with her mother had given her that kind of relief but this
was different. Her mother was more like an extension
of herself. Luke was Hana's father—the missing piece
of the puzzle.

'It must have been days ago,' she said aloud. 'It's almost gone.'

I'll be watching her, her gaze added. *Like a hawk. Don't worry...*

'I wonder what the "magic" stuff was,' Sam said. 'Maybe it's an ointment made from the same bushes they make that M'Langi tea from?'

'I'll ask Bessie,' Vailea said. She held out her hand to Hana. 'Come on, darling. I'm going to give you some dinner and then it's time for your bath.'

Luke was still watching even when they had disappeared into the house. He was struggling a bit with how overwhelming this was.

Anyone would have found Hana an adorable child. Listening to her talk, seeing the wonder of life shining from her eyes, hearing her *laugh*... To know that this was his daughter made it so much more powerful. The connection was already there—he could feel it in every cell of his body. The love was there, too, ready to be bestowed, and the need to offer protection was so strong he'd felt a moment of sheer panic when she'd told them about that mosquito bite.

How ridiculous was that? The odds of it having been from an infected mosquito were very low and she was obviously perfectly healthy days after the event. It could have been more than a week ago, in fact, and she could be well past the time when symptoms of encephalitis could appear.

'An ointment is a bit different from tea,' Anahera was saying to Sam. 'Maybe they use a different part of the bush. Like the bark. Don't they use the leaves for the tea?'

'It wouldn't be the bark.' Luke tried to refocus his attention on the conversation. 'I've been doing a bit of reading about the medicinal uses of hibiscus. The tea's usually made from an infusion of the flowers from crimson or magenta-coloured flowers. Leaves can be used, too, but the bark's only useful for making rope or caulking ships.'

'Have you found any scientific evidence of effects?' Sam leaned forward, clearly interested in the subject. Anahera had turned her head to glance at the door to the house. Would she prefer to be inside with her family?

'There's been quite a lot of studies done,' he told Sam. 'There's some evidence that it acts as a mild diuretic and it can lower blood pressure in people with type two diabetes.'

'That could be useful. Type two diabetes is getting to be an increasing problem in all the islands.'

'It can also act as a gentle laxative, apparently. And an anti-inflammatory. It's supposed to be good for stomach irritation. Some researchers think it may contain chemicals that work like antibiotics.'

'Not so farfetched to think it could work like an antiviral, then?'

'Hmm. I read something about it potentially being able to kill worms so maybe going down the track of an insect repellent is valid.'

It was so much easier having Sam here. For a short time Luke had been so immersed in this discussion he'd been totally distracted from where he was—and why...

But then Hana appeared again and this time she was wearing a pair of pink pyjamas that had a butterfly print on them. Her hair was a mass of damp ringlets and her face was full of the joy of life again.

'Come over here, chicken,' Sam said. 'I want my goodnight kiss.'

Hana happily scrambled over Bugsy and held her arms up for a cuddle. Sam tickled her until she shrieked with laughter and then kissed the top of her head with a loud smack.

'Sweet dreams,' he said.

Hana wriggled out of his arms. Anahera stood up. 'Bedtime, sweetheart,' she said. There was a tiny silence as everybody noticed the little girl wasn't moving. Anahera cleared her throat. 'Don't forget to say goodnight to Luke.'

There was shyness back in those big brown eyes. She'd just been released from a loving farewell from her uncle Sam but this was new ground and she wasn't sure how to say goodnight to this new person in her life. How had Sam made it seem so natural? Oh, yeah… Luke smiled and held out his arms.

He wasn't really expecting Hana to accept the offered hug. Not this easily anyway, but she didn't hesitate. She knew what to do now and those little arms went round his neck and squeezed hard. For just a precious few seconds Luke could feel the whole shape of that little body. He could feel her heart beating and the puff of her breath on his neck.

The feeling of loss when she wriggled free was equally unexpected and Luke found himself blinking hard as he watched Anahera scoop Hana into her arms. She clung like a little monkey, her arms and legs wrapped around her mother, and he could see the way the little body instantly relaxed, her head burrowing into the dip below Anahera's shoulder and her eyes closing. By the look of it, she would probably be asleep by the time she was put into her bed. There was no mistaking the bond between these two as Anahera's head tilted to press against

Hana's drying curls. Nobody else existed for either of them in that moment, and Luke felt the exclusion so clearly it was a physical ache. Was it even possible to become a part of that human unit?

Again, he found himself staring at the empty frame of the front door when Anahera had carried Hana inside.

'That went well,' Sam murmured. 'Don't you think?'

Luke didn't respond with anything more than a grunt and he picked up his beer to avoid having to try and articulate what he was thinking.

He wouldn't have known where to start anyway. Instead, he let his gaze drift. To the bowl of petals on the table and then over the railings of the veranda to the village surrounding this small house. The sun was setting but there was a group of children playing football farther down on the dusty road. The faint sound of their laughter could be easily heard.

Could he imagine his daughter living in London? Where would you go to find brightly coloured petals there? Where were there any roads that would be a safe playground?

He couldn't imagine it. Anahera was right—merging their lives would never have worked.

And he'd been right, too. She had never *really* loved him. Okay, he could accept why she'd kept Hana's existence a secret at first but to keep it up when she knew the truth… That was unacceptable. Unthinkable. How could anyone do that to someone they cared about?

Discovering just how much he had missed out on was making it all the worse.

His appetite had fled and he was hard put to do more than taste the delicious meal that Vailea had prepared.

'Must be something in the air,' she said. 'Hana wasn't hungry either.'

'Well, I've made up for them both.' Sam sighed. 'We might need to take the long way home, Bugsy.'

'I'll come with you,' Luke said. 'I'd like to talk about the M'Langi tea study with you some more.'

There was a sudden, awkward silence. And then Vailea reached for his half-empty plate and it sounded like she was deliberately trying to keep her tone casual. 'I thought you and Ana might like a chance to talk,' she said. 'I've got some coffee brewing.'

Anahera was pushing a bit of fish around her plate. Maybe her appetite hadn't been any better than his own. She looked up, and he was reminded of the moment they'd met, when he'd been horrified to see what had looked like fear in her eyes. How had it come to this—that she could be afraid of him and what he might do to her life?

He couldn't go there now. It would be so hard and he was already emotionally exhausted.

'We'll have plenty of time to talk,' he said. 'Thank you, Vailea. This has been…been…' He couldn't find any words. What had happened here this evening for him was simply too huge.

'It was a pleasure.' Vailea touched his arm before picking up the plate, excusing him from having to say anything more. 'You're welcome here any time, Luke. You're part of our family now.'

Sam must have sensed that this was the best note to end this introduction on. He clicked his fingers to summon Bugsy and hugged both Vailea and Anahera. Maybe Luke was expected to follow suit but it was all suddenly too much. He could only mutter his thanks and duck his head in farewell before following Sam.

'It was a good start,' Sam said. 'You all need a bit of time now to get used to things. You'll work it out.'

'I hope so.'

'You're a lucky man, you know that?'

Luke's breath came out in a huff. 'It's a mess, mate. How come that's lucky?'

'You have the most beautiful daughter on earth. I'd give my right arm for a gift like that.'

They walked in silence for a while, and Luke found the colliding thoughts and feelings in his head beginning to slow down and find a pattern.

A gift.

Yes. Despite the fact that he had lost his trust in Anahera and knew they could never have a future together, their child was a gift that would change his life for ever in a very good way.

He should find happiness in that and he did. Of course he did. It was just unfair that opposing emotions seemed to be two-sided coins. Love and hate. Happiness and sadness. That particular coin seemed to be spinning on its side for him right now. Which side would end up showing? The unimaginable happiness of having Hana in his life?

Or the sadness in losing Ana?

CHAPTER TEN

'I DON'T WANT IT.'

'But mango's your favourite. Would you rather have an egg? With soldiers?'

'No.' Hana rubbed at her eyes with tight little fists, and Anahera cast a worried glance at Vailea, who was almost ready to leave for work. She kissed the cloud of curls in need of brushing and moved towards her mother as she lowered her voice.

'She barely ate anything last night either. And look at her—she looks like she needs to go back to sleep.'

'It's early.' Vailea's smile was reassuring. 'You could both go back to bed for a bit, love. It's your day off, after all.' She picked up her bag. 'If you're worried, bring her up to see Sam later.'

Anahera nodded. She felt Hana's forehead. She put her hand on her own forehead and then felt Hana's again. Was it warmer?

'What are you doing, Mumma?'

'Just checking. Do you feel sick, sweetheart? Have you got a sore throat or a sore head?'

'No.'

'Are you still tired?' Anahera was tired herself, which was hardly surprising after another night of sleep eluding her. Her mother's suggestion was starting to seem rather attractive. 'Shall we go and have a cuddle in Mummy's bed for a bit and have a story?'

Hana smiled and nodded and slid off her chair. 'I'll get my book. The *big* book…'

The worry ebbed. The big book was an illustrated version of old fairy tales that Hana loved. The day would soon get too hot to laze in bed but she could enjoy some time reading aloud with her daughter cuddled deliciously under her arm, tiny fingers ready to help turn the pages and point out the most fascinating things in the pictures.

Time out. If she was reading aloud, her mind couldn't wander and fret about Hana's lack of appetite.

Or when they were going to see Luke again.

And what the future might hold…

For a while it was lovely. Hana dozed off, and Anahera soon followed her example. She probably didn't sleep for more than an hour but it was the uncomfortable warmth that woke her. Hana's skin felt hot and sticky, and a wave of panic washed through her.

'Hana? Wake up, darling.' Her grip must have been firmer than she realised because Hana woke up with a start and immediately burst into tears. Anahera pulled her into a cuddle. 'Oh, I'm sorry…I didn't mean to give you a fright.'

'Go away, Mumma.' Hana was trying to wriggle free as her sobs quickly subsided. 'You're too hot…'

She was hot?

Of course she was. The sun was well up and streaming into her bedroom and they'd been lying under the covers together. She didn't normally panic like that. What was wrong with her?

'Let's have a shower. We'll pretend we're under the waterfall up by the lagoon.'

That was lovely, too. Hana was smiling under the cool rain of the shower and she even ate a piece of mango afterwards. It was Anahera whose appetite had vanished now.

'Shall we go to the beach and have a swim? Or up to the lagoon?'

Hana shook her head.

'Where would you like to go, then? Or shall we stay at home today?'

'I want to go to the patercillar house.' Big, brown eyes held a pleading edge. 'With Luke.'

Anahera's heart sank.

'But that's in London, sweetheart. It's a long, long way away.'

'I want to go.' There were tears rapidly filling her eyes now and it wouldn't be long before they were rolling down her face. It was so unlike Hana that Anahera was alarmed.

Children could pick up on things that had been left unspoken. Was she unsettled by Luke's appearance in her life without knowing why?

Or was it something more serious? As a medical professional, Anahera knew that a mother's instinct was not something to be ignored.

'Tell you what. Let's go and visit Uncle Sam. He might let us take Bugsy for a walk around the lagoon.'

It was a particularly hot day. The humidity was high and the walk was long and slow. Bone-dry dust coated their feet and geckos basked on the rocks, oblivious to their steps. Even the bright yellow trumpets of the allemande vine looked wilted and maybe it wasn't surprising that Hana was definitely not her usual, chatty self. Anahera didn't want to upset her by trying to force conversation so, for the most part, it was a silent companionship. She frequently found her mind wandering, and every time it logged into the circuitous worry about Luke and the future that was rapidly becoming a well-worn track.

She normally loved her days off and time to spend with her daughter like this but happiness was elusive today. She tried to remember what it felt like to be really happy in the hope that she could turn her mood around in case that was something else that Hana was picking up on.

When had she been the happiest in her life?

That was easy. When Hana had been born and she'd held the miracle that was her new baby in her arms for the first time.

Or maybe it wasn't so easy. Impossible not to also think of the time she had believed she was the happiest it was possible to ever be—when she'd been head over heels in love with Luke Wilson. In that happy bubble that she'd been so careful to protect so that nobody would know and do anything to dim the rainbow shine it had had.

Such different kinds of happiness. Mother love was deep and warm and for ever, but the *in* love one was shinier and amazing. Both had a piercing sweetness, but the mother love was more solid and dependable. Nothing could change that.

Luke had had his first taste of that parent-child bond last night. Was he even more aware of everything he'd missed out on now?

The guilt was still there but it had changed shape. Now it was about what she had stolen from Luke instead of what she was keeping hidden. Things that she could never give back—like the miracle of Hana's birth and the milestones of her babyhood.

Did he hate her even more?

It hit her like a mental slap that she was doing it again. Making this about herself.

Being selfish.

She couldn't change what she had done, however wrong it had been, but she could try and do the right thing and that was to make up for it in some way, no matter how hard it might be.

She could welcome Luke back into her life as Hana's father and she could share the parenting. Hana would get a daddy who loved her and—if she was lucky—maybe he would eventually forgive her and she would end up with the best friend she could hope for.

It seemed like a big step in moving forward and for a moment Anahera could feel enormous relief. But then her treacherous mind came up with another angle of how it might impact on her. What if Luke got married again and presented Hana with a substitute mother?

Was the thought so shocking it transferred itself through her hand to Hana and made the little girl stumble?

Whatever the cause, Hana was in tears yet again and she had grazed her knee.

'I don't want to walk any more, Mumma. My legs are sleepy.'

'I'll carry you. It's not far now. We'll visit Uncle Sam and then go and see Nana in the kitchen for lunch, okay?'

''Kay…' Still sniffling, Hana let herself be lifted and wrapped her arms around her mother's neck as she settled onto her hip.

Anahera kept walking up the hill but it was even slower going now. When had Hana become so heavy?

The sniffles stopped after a short time and she could feel Hana's body going floppy as the little girl fell asleep, which seemed to make her even heavier. By the time she reached the hospital it was becoming quite a struggle to keep carrying her. Entering the walkway, Anahera headed towards the staffroom, hoping that Sam might be in there for lunch by now, but the only person present was Luke, who had papers spread over the table and was working on a laptop.

'Hi…'

'Hello…' Luke got to his feet. 'I thought this was your day off.'

'It is. I've brought Hana up to see Sam. She's…a bit off colour, I think.'

'In what way?' Luke was close enough to touch Hana within a couple of swift steps. He smoothed back her hair and dipped his head so he could see her face. 'Hey, Hana…what's up?'

Hana moved her head as if the touch was irritating but didn't open her eyes or make any response. Luke's gaze flicked up to meet Anahera's.

'She's barely touched any food and she's…just not herself. She keeps crying and she almost *never* cries…'

Luke had his hand on her forehead now. 'She feels a bit warm.'

'It's pretty hot outside. It was a long walk up the hill.'

'Is she usually this sleepy at this time of day?'

Anahera shook her head. 'She gave up on naps by the time she was eighteen months old.' Oh, help. She could see the shadow that flicked over Luke's face. Sadness that he hadn't known this fact about his own daughter?

She had to look away. Had to try and change her grip on Hana, too, because her arms were really aching now with the effort of holding her.

'Let me take her,' Luke said. He matched his words with action and gently scooped her out of Anahera's arms. 'It's probably nothing more than a cold or something coming on but let's go and check her out.'

'Do you know where Sam is?'

'Doing an outpatient clinic.'

'We need to head that way, too. We could use one of the treatment rooms in the emergency department.'

Luke flicked a glance over the mop of curls nestled into his shoulder. 'Would you rather Sam had a look at Hana?'

This was the first chance she'd had to show Luke that she wasn't going to keep him shut out of his daughter's life any more but she didn't get the chance to say anything because Luke answered his own question.

'He probably should. I'm not actually working here and you aren't supposed to treat your own children, are you?'

'But you're the expert,' Anahera said quietly. 'If it is... You know...' She couldn't voice her worst fear that this was, indeed, another terrifying case of the dreaded encephalitis.

'Right now, I feel more like a father than a doctor.' Luke was staring straight ahead now and he spotted the figure in the green uniform first. 'Hey, Hettie? Could you grab Sam when he has a moment, please? We'll be in the treatment room with Hana. She's not feeling so great.'

'Oh, no!' Hettie was looking worried as they walked closer. 'We're almost done with the clinic. We'll be there in a tick.'

Hana woke up as Luke put her on the bed in the treatment room.

'Hullo, sleepyhead,' he said softly.

Hana just stared up at him. She didn't smile but she didn't burst into tears either. For a long moment they just seemed to stare at each other, and Anahera was sure she'd been right. Whether she was picking up on nonverbal signals or if it was some unexplained genetic connection, Hana knew there was something very important about this new man in her life.

The moment was broken when Sam, closely followed by Hettie, came into the room.

'What's happening?' His glance at Anahera was reassuring and his tone was cheerful as he directed his words at Hana. 'You haven't gone and caught a naughty bug, have you, chicken?'

Hana's head rolled from side to side. 'I'm not naughty.'

'Not you. It's the bug that's naughty if it's making you feel sick.'

'I'm not sick.'

'Good.' Sam's smile was enough to make everyone in the room relax a little. 'You won't mind if I have a look at you to make sure, though, will you? Hettie? Let's get some vital signs.'

'I can do that.' Anahera was already stretching out her arm to get the tympanic thermometer to check Hana's temperature but Hettie stepped in front of her.

'My job.' She smiled. 'You're the mummy here, remember?'

She was. It was her job to reassure Hana and explain what was happening so she didn't get frightened by any of the tests that Sam might want to include in his examination, and she knew it would be a thorough one because

Sam loved Hana and he knew that Anahera wouldn't have brought her in unless she was genuinely worried.

But it seemed that she wasn't needed to keep Hana either distracted or co-operative because Luke was already doing her job.

'Let's get your T-shirt off. That way Uncle Sam can see if you've got any spots—like a butterfly.' He was helping her to pull it over her head. 'Do you like the butterflies with spots the best? I do.'

'I like the yellow ones.'

'What about blue ones? Do you get those really tiny blue ones here like this?' Luke held his thumb and forefinger a centimetre or two apart.

'Temperature's well up,' Hettie reported quietly. 'So's her heart rate.' She wrote on the form, and Anahera had to swallow hard as she watched the clipboard being hung on the end of Hana's bed. Had her daughter just become an official patient?

'I'm going to feel your neck,' Sam said as he checked her lymph nodes after peering down her throat. 'You tell me if it's sore.'

Anahera edged closer to the bed to read the figures Hettie had written on the chart. She should have been able to pick up that Hana had a fever. Or had her temperature spiked during the walk when she'd been so hot herself it had been hard to tell?

'Tummy-tickling time,' Sam announced. 'And then we're going to play with the stethoscope.'

It was certainly a very thorough examination. Anahera could see Luke nodding at some unspoken question that came from Sam and then he started on a neurological assessment, checking strength and sensation and pupil reaction, and all Anahera could do was stand there and wait for the verdict and try—unsuccessfully—not to be reminded of Sam doing all these tests on little Hami when he'd come in with the fever that had been the first sign of his fatal encephalitis.

This small treatment room seemed crowded with people who had all the knowledge in the world that could be needed but it was still possible that they might all be helpless in the face of a disease they couldn't control.

Anahera had never been more scared in her life.

There had been times in his career when Luke had wished there was more he could do for his patients. Times when he felt frustrated—angry, even—like he had when he'd been powerless to save Tane. He'd had patients he'd grown very close to, like Harry, and many that he'd cared about deeply enough to experience memorable joy in their recovery or sadness for their outcomes.

But he'd never, ever felt like this.

Scared…

Hana looked so little and fragile, sitting on a bed that was too large for her, in nothing more than a pair of knickers that had—surprise, surprise—a butterfly print.

He could see her ribs clearly outlined beneath that perfect olive skin and the wave of protective tenderness that washed through him was almost unbearable.

He could also see the flushed cheeks of a rising fever and the concern in Sam's gaze as he looked up, still moving the disc of his stethoscope gently over that small chest and back.

'Something's certainly going on,' he said quietly. 'The question is—what?' He took his earpieces out. 'It could just be a cold. Her throat is slightly inflamed and her ears are a bit red. Chest's clear, though, and there's no sign of any rash. Let's get a dose of paracetamol on board and I'll get some bloods off but…'

His raised eyebrow invited Luke's input and he had to say it. 'Given the history of the mosquito bite, a lumbar puncture would tell us what we really want to know.'

Anahera's intake of breath was audible, at least to him. It wasn't a pleasant procedure for parents to watch. He could feel his own gut tightening at the thought of a needle being stuck between those tiny vertebrae he could see protruding from Hana's back as she sat with her little shoulders hunched.

'I can stay with her,' Hettie offered. 'And we'll put a good dollop of anaesthetic cream on now. By the time that's taken effect, it'll be painless.'

She would still have to be held very still and it would be frightening.

'I'm not going anywhere,' Anahera murmured. 'If anyone's going to hold her, it's going to be me.' She took the dose of paracetamol syrup from Hettie's hand.

'Of course it is,' Luke said. He caught Anahera's gaze as she stepped closer to give the medication to Hana and he held it, trying to offer what reassurance he could. Trying to let her know that he was in her corner. That Hana had both her parents here to worry about her. As her gaze clung to his for a heartbeat, and then another, he was aware of a new strength coming from somewhere. Something strong and good. He could do this and he could help. He was helping already because some of that fear was ebbing from Ana's eyes.

'In that case, I'm probably superfluous.' Hettie smiled. 'I might go and get on with some work in the ward, unless…' The glance in Luke's direction was curious but everybody knew he was the encephalitis expert. Of course he'd want to be involved in this case.

'I know my way around a manometer,' he told her. 'I can assist Sam.'

Hettie paused on her way out of the treatment room. 'Want me to get a bed ready?'

'I think so.' Sam nodded. 'We'll want to keep an eye on her for a while yet.'

Hana was intrigued rather than frightened by the application of the topical anaesthetic cream both to her back and the crook of her elbow beneath sticky patches, and her eyelids were drooping noticeably as Anahera gave her a cuddle and then tucked her up with a light sheet as a cover. She was asleep—yet again—almost instantly.

'We'll give it an hour to make sure it's done its thing,' Sam said. 'I might grab a bite of lunch and I'll let Vailea know you're here. Can I bring you a sandwich or something, Ana?'

She shook her head. 'I'm really not hungry.'

'Neither am I,' Luke said. 'We'll just stay here and look after Hana.'

Sam's gaze travelled from him to Hana and then to her mother and back to him. His slow nod suggested that this arrangement was exactly as it should be.

'Come and get me if anything changes. Won't be long.'

Luke arranged chairs on each side of the bed, and they sat with their sleeping child between them.

'I can't believe this is happening,' Anahera whispered.

'Try not to worry. We don't know if it's anything to worry *about* yet.'

'When it's your baby, you worry about everything.'

'Yeah…' Luke's voice cracked. 'I'm discovering that.'

There was a long silence and then Anahera spoke in

no more than a whisper. 'I'm sorry, Luke. I'm sorry for everything but most of all that I didn't tell you about Hana. That you've missed so much...'

'I could have gone my whole life not knowing what I *was* missing,' he told her. 'Without knowing what this could feel like. It's... It feels like...a new beginning.'

'I don't blame you for hating me...'

'I don't hate you, Ana.'

It was true. He might not trust her any more and he might be angry that she could have gone as far as to make love with him and still not told him the truth. He might be feeling betrayed and hurt as well, but hate didn't come into it. That coin would never land on that side because he had truly loved her once.

Anahera's head was bent now. Was she trying to hide the fact that she was crying? She reached out to smooth an errant curl that was stuck to Hana's flushed little cheek and as she put it back where it belonged, her hand stayed there, gently cupping her daughter's head.

Luke could feel the strength of that love. A bond that nothing could ever break. He could feel the fear, too.

'It'll be okay,' he murmured. 'I know it will.'

Anahera didn't look up. 'You don't know that.' Her voice was raw. 'We had a little boy come in once, not long after I came back home. His name was Hami and he was the same age as Hana. His mum brought him in because he had a fever and she couldn't wake him up properly and...and...'

'He had encephalitis?'

Anahera nodded. She didn't have to tell him how the case had turned out. He could see the fat tears rolling down her face. He could imagine what it must have been like to have a patient who reminded you of your own child. How devastating it would be to lose the fight. He'd only discovered he was a father yesterday but he knew already that his interaction with paediatric patients would never be the same. He might have thought he understood how precious they were to their parents and how hard it was, but you never really knew, did you, until you walked in their shoes? How amazing that he'd only needed to take a few steps to feel like he'd stepped onto a new planet.

A planet that put a whole new perspective on everything, and there was a downside that was all too obvious now because it gave you new things to be afraid of.

Anahera was afraid. She'd been afraid of *him* when he'd turned up so unexpectedly in her life and he'd felt like a complete jerk because he'd assumed that fear had sprung from how badly he'd hurt her by not telling her the truth about Jane.

But she'd been afraid of losing Hana, hadn't she? Just the way she was now.

He recognised that fear because he could feel it himself. This feeling of needing to protect a vulnerable child might be very new but it was astonishingly powerful. He would do whatever it took to make sure Hana was safe.

Anahera thought she had been protecting Hana by not telling him the truth. Protecting herself, too. Trying to hang on to the safe place she'd thought she'd found for her family.

And hadn't he done exactly the same thing to her?

He hadn't told her about Jane because it would have destroyed the safe place that Wildfire Island had been for him. It would have destroyed the miracle of finding love, which had been the last thing he'd expected.

It hadn't *felt* like lying, though…

He'd been protecting himself. Just the way that Anahera had been.

Luke was staring at Anahera, even though he could only see the top of her head. That shiny, soft black hair that rippled down her back because she wasn't working today and hadn't braided it. His fingers tingled as they reminded him what it felt like to have the weight of that hair slipping through them. She had taken her hand from Hana's head and traced it over the little, bare shoulder and down the arm until she could take her daughter's hand gently in her own. Bowing her head even farther, she lifted Hana's hand to touch it with her lips.

The gesture was so tender it made Luke's heart ache but his head was still grappling with new thoughts that seemed increasingly important. Maybe Anahera had convinced herself she wasn't really lying to him. She had, after all, told him part of the truth.

But she'd made love with him and still hadn't told him.

He'd done the same thing, though, hadn't he? He'd made love with her without telling her anything about Jane. Hana had been conceived on one of those stolen nights. How many opportunities had he had to tell her the truth? Opportunities that had only became impossible to grasp because he'd known that if he had, Anahera would never have allowed that kind of intimacy. He'd wanted—*needed*—it too much to risk that.

But that had been then and this was now.

The destruction of his trust in Anahera ever since he'd learned the truth made the idea of being that close to her seem abhorrent. You couldn't make love with someone you couldn't trust.

His head was spinning. Anahera must have felt like that when she'd lost her trust in *him*. Even if they'd been in the same place, she wouldn't have wanted to talk to him, let alone be close enough to touch.

What had changed?

She must have forgiven him, that was what it was.

And she must have wanted to be with him as much as he had wanted to be with her.

She'd told him that she'd loved him more than she thought it was possible to love anyone.

Had.

Past tense. She'd also said that it was too late.

It was always too late, Luke. We just didn't know it...

'It's *not* too late.'

'What?' Anahera's head came up with a jerk.

Oh, God...had he said that aloud? This wasn't the time or the place to talk about anything in the past or even what could still be between them now. This time was about Hana. Nothing else mattered.

Her face was white. 'Did you say it was *too late*?'

'No...the opposite. I said it's *not* too late.'

'I don't understand...'

Luke was spared having to try and explain by Sam's return. He had Vailea with him, and Hana woke up and then it was time to take a blood sample and get the procedure of the lumbar puncture over with.

The topical anaesthetic on her elbow had made getting that sample relatively painless but it was still frightening for Hana, and when the sticky patch was peeled from her back she knew there was more to come and her co-operation ceased.

'I need you to lie on your side, darling. And curl up.' Anahera was trying to bend Hana's knees and get her bent so that the spaces between her vertebrae were as wide as possible.

'*No-o-o*... I want to go *home*.' Hana pushed at her mother with her arms and kicked her legs, and her sobs were becoming heartbreaking.

Sam was pulling on a pair of sterile gloves and looked at Vailea with a head tilt to ask for her help but the older woman was looking almost as upset as Hana. She had a hand pressed to her mouth and it was shaking visibly.

Luke touched her arm. 'You go,' he said quietly. 'It's not as bad as it looks. And it'll be over soon. I'll come and find you.'

And then he stepped closer to the bed and crouched so that his head was on the same level as Hana's.

'Hana?' He had to raise his voice to cut through her wails and be heard. And he tried to sound as if he had something very exciting to tell her.

It didn't work. So Luke clicked his fingers in front of her face. Then he did it again, above his head.

'What's this, Hana?'

He clicked them again, close to Hana, to one side of her head and then the other. Up high and down low beneath the level of the bed.

'Do you know what it is?'

Hana had stopped crying. She stared at Luke as she rolled her head slowly from one side to the other to say 'no'.

'It's a butterfly,' Luke told her. 'With hiccups.'

The small, miserable face crumpled again, but this time it was with a smile. A sound emerged that could be a giggle.

But laughter could turn to tears very easily.

Luke knew he had only a very small window of time to do something a bit more heroic.

* * *

It was the worst thing in the world for a mother to have to restrain her child to allow someone to do something frightening and potentially painful. Anahera couldn't blame her mother for being unable to help or even watch.

This was killing her.

And then Luke stepped in and caught Hana's attention. In the surprising silence that fell, he began talking in a quiet, gentle voice that was utterly compelling.

'You know how butterflies are caterpillars first and then they change?'

Hana didn't say anything or nod but she was clearly listening. The gasping breaths that had fuelled the terrified crying were subsiding into rapid breathing with just the occasional hiccup.

'Did you know they make themselves a little house called a chrysalis so they can hide inside and not come out until they're a real butterfly?'

'A…a patercillar house?'

Luke nodded. 'And you know what? They have to curl up inside that house. Just the way Mummy wants you to curl up now. Could you do that, sweetheart? Could you curl up like a caterpillar?'

It was the first time Anahera had heard him use an endearment for someone other than herself. The first time she had heard that level of caring. Weirdly, it was making *her* feel loved so surely Hana could feel it, too?

She could. The little girl gave an enormous sniff. ''Kay…'

'That's my girl. Caterpillars have lots and lots of legs. How many have you got?'

'Two…'

'That's right.' Luke's smile was genuinely impressed. 'And they curl them up just like that…'

It was easy now to slip her arms into place and rest them on Hana's legs so that she could prevent any movement.

'There's going to be a little bit of rain on top of your chrysalis now,' Luke said. 'Can you feel the cold water dripping on your back?'

Sam had a lopsided smile on his face as he swabbed Hana's back with antiseptic. He was clearly as blown away as Anahera was with how effective the distraction was that Luke was providing.

'There might be a little twig that pushes on you, too. It doesn't hurt, does it? You can just feel it pushing.'

Sam had injected local anaesthetic into deeper tissues through the numbed top layer of skin. Then he slipped the needle into where it needed to be without so much as a whimper or twitch from Hana. Spinal fluid was always so slow to drip into the test tubes but Anahera couldn't believe how fast it was all over.

'You can come out of your chrysalis now, sweetheart.'

'Will I have wings?'

'You sure will. Very soon.'

Anahera widened her eyes. Luke was new to being a parent but surely he knew he shouldn't make promises he couldn't keep?

Not that it mattered. The procedure was over and Hana was happy and it was all thanks to Luke.

She had never loved him more than she did right then. Releasing the gentle hold she'd had on her daughter, she looked up to meet his gaze, and his eyes were as gentle as his tone had been with Hana. The smile that curled his lips was slow and *so* beautiful. The kind of smile she'd never thought she'd receive from him again.

Was it so impossible to believe that he could forgive her?

That, somehow, in the midst of this apparent crisis, he'd done so already?

'I'll go and start testing this.' Sam was collecting up the test tubes. 'She might have a bit of a headache for a while but hopefully the paracetamol she's got on board will deal with that. We'll top up the dose soon.'

The anti-inflammatory did seem to prevent the headache that was a common side effect from having some spinal fluid removed. It seemed to be helping with the fever, too. Hana's cheeks were looking less flushed. She fell asleep again, but this time it seemed less alarming—the sleep of a small child who was worn out by unusual events.

Or was that wishful thinking?

Like Hana growing wings?

'She'll want them,' she warned Luke. 'Those wings you promised her.'

'I wouldn't promise anything I couldn't deliver.'

Anahera's heart skipped a beat at the serious note in his voice. He was giving her a message that had nothing to do with a promise made to a child.

But then he smiled. 'I was playing around online last night, wondering what I could get for Hana for her birthday. I found a pink sparkly fairy outfit that comes with a set of wings. I admit I'm no expert in such things, but it looked to me like fairy wings are pretty much the same as butterfly wings. It should be on the next supply plane that comes out.'

'Oh…' Why on earth had she never thought of that? 'She'll *love* that…'

If she was well enough. A lot could happen in the few days before the next plane was due from the mainland.

It was an opportune moment for Sam to come into the room. He had Vailea with him and her smile made Anahera catch and hold her breath. Did she already know something? Something good?

'First results look great,' he said. 'Completely normal. I really don't think we're looking at anything more than your average kiddy bug. We'll still keep her in overnight for everybody's peace of mind but I wouldn't be at all surprised if she bounces back to her normal gorgeous self by tomorrow morning.'

Anahera burst into tears and threw herself into Luke's arms.

Or maybe he had pulled her into them.

It didn't matter. They both needed this fierce hug that was a release from the worst fear in the world.

They needed each other.

CHAPTER ELEVEN

'HERE. THIS IS the place.'

It was the wooden bench in the hospital's tropical garden where Luke had kissed her as the sun had risen after that long night when Tane had been admitted.

Vailea had been happy to sit with her granddaughter. She'd practically shooed Anahera and Luke out the door of the room when they'd finally stopped hugging each other.

'Go.' She'd smiled. 'Find a quiet place. You two need to talk.'

And Luke had chosen this place. The spot where he'd been able to drag her back in time and make her realise that she'd never stopped loving him.

She never would.

And it felt… It felt like Luke didn't want her to. He had taken her hand as they'd left Hana's room and he still hadn't let it go by the time they sat down on the bench. If anything, he was holding it even more tightly. Looking at her as if there was something of the utmost importance that he wanted to say but was struggling to find the words.

'I'm sorry,' he finally managed. 'You're a better person than I am, Ana.'

'*What?*' Anahera blinked.

'I judged you. I couldn't get my head around how you could have slept with me when you hadn't told me the truth, and then I realised I'd done the same thing to you when I didn't tell you about Jane.'

'But that was a long time ago. And it was me who judged *you*. And I was wrong. I knew that as soon as you told me.'

'And you forgave me, didn't you? Otherwise you wouldn't have… You couldn't have been so…'

He had to be referring to that intense connection between them when they'd made love. Had it only been the night before last? The memory was still fresh enough to bring a flush of colour to Anahera's cheeks and a very noticeable warmth to far more private parts of her body.

She managed a smile. 'Of course not. There's nothing to forgive anyway, because I understand. It was my fault. I should have listened when I had the chance. I—'

Luke's finger on her lips stopped her words.

'And I understand now, too. What it feels like to be a parent. There's nothing for me to forgive either.'

'But you've missed so much…'

'Then let's make sure I don't miss any more. I still love you, Ana. I will never stop loving you. I know you think there's no way to make it work but…but we have to *try*, don't we?'

Anahera nodded as tears filled her eyes. She already knew that she'd been wrong to base assumptions on the tragedy that had been her mother's love story but there would be another time to tell him about that. She had something more important to say.

'I love you, too, Luke. And we'll find a way to make it work. You're right. We have to. For Hana's sake.'

Luke's smile was crooked. 'For my sake, too. I can't imagine my life without you. I want to marry you, Ana. I want to have more children with you. I don't know how we'll do it but I want… Dammit, I want it *all*.'

This time it seemed quite okay to be a bit selfish.

'I want it, too,' Anahera whispered. 'Every bit of it.'

In some ways this kiss was very like the first one they had shared in this very spot. It was inevitable. A reminder of every past touch—every loving gesture.

It was still the feeling of coming home.

But at the same time, it was so much more than the last kiss had been because this time it held a solemn promise of what the future would hold.

And yet Luke was frowning as he finally let Anahera take a proper breath.

'I'll have to go back to London very soon. I'll have to sort out how I'm going to change my job.' He smiled again. 'You know, my senior registrar has been eyeing up my job for years. If I gave him the chance to job-share, I think he'd be over the moon.'

'So you could spend time here on the island as well? That would be perfect.'

But he shook his head. 'Not when I'll have to leave you behind. And Hana, when I'm only starting to get to know her.'

'We could come with you. I'm not going to let you completely sacrifice the life you already have. And certainly not your job. You're doing things that are too important—for people like our islanders, amongst others.

You and that friend of yours—Harry? You're going to change a lot of people's lives if this vaccine works.'

'But it's winter in London at the moment. It's cold and grey and…you'd hate it. Hana would hate it.'

'Not if she could go to the patercillar house.'

Luke's smile made the corners of his eyes crinkle in a way Anahera had never seen before and she fell a little bit more in love with him—the way she had when she'd been there to share the way he had calmed and distracted Hana so that what could have been a horrible procedure had become almost a game. And the way he had cared for her mother, making it okay for her to leave when she'd been finding things unbearable.

As if it was an extension of her thoughts, Vailea appeared on the garden path, looking a little tentative as she approached in case she was interrupting something important.

'Hana's awake,' she told them. 'And she really wants an ice cream. I can get one from the kitchen, but I thought you might like to be the ones to give it to her.'

She had to be feeling a lot better if she was asking for ice cream. A smile curled Anahera's lips and then kept growing.

'We can give her something even better to go with that ice cream,' she told her mother. 'We can give her a daddy.'

Luke's sharp intake of breath was an echo of the expression on Vailea's face.

'It's not…too soon to tell her?'

'No.' Anahera caught Luke's hand and stood up, bringing him to his feet as well. 'It's not too soon.'

She was still smiling like the happiest woman in the

world as she looked up at the man she loved. 'And you were right. It's not too late either.'

Luke bent his head to kiss her again. 'Let's do it,' he whispered into her hair. 'Let's make a family.'

And that was exactly what they did.

* * * * *

MILLS & BOON®

MEDICAL ROMANCE™

THE ULTIMATE IN ROMANTIC MEDICAL DRAMA

A sneak peek at next month's titles...

In stores from 25th February 2016:

- **The Socialite's Secret** – Carol Marinelli *and*
  London's Most Eligible Doctor – Annie O'Neil

- **Saving Maddie's Baby** – Marion Lennox *and*
  A Sheikh to Capture Her Heart – Meredith Webber

- **Breaking All Their Rules** – Sue MacKay
- **One Life-Changing Night** – Louisa Heaton

Available at WHSmith, Tesco, Asda, Eason, Amazon and Apple

Just can't wait?
Buy our books online a month before they hit the shops!
visit www.millsandboon.co.uk

These books are also available in eBook format!

0116_MB518

MILLS & BOON®

Why shop at millsandboon.co.uk?

Each year, thousands of romance readers find their
perfect read at millsandboon.co.uk. That's because
we're passionate about bringing you the very best
romantic fiction. Here are some of the advantages
of shopping at www.millsandboon.co.uk:

* **Get new books first**—you'll be able to buy your
  favourite books one month before they hit
  the shops

* **Get exclusive discounts**—you'll also be able to buy
  our specially created monthly collections, with up
  to 50% off the RRP

* **Find your favourite authors**—latest news,
  interviews and new releases for all your favourite
  authors and series on our website, plus ideas for
  what to try next

* **Join in**—once you've bought your favourite books,
  don't forget to register with us to rate, review and
  join in the discussions

Visit **www.millsandboon.co.uk**
for all this and more today!

MILLS_WEB

MILLS & BOON®

Why not subscribe?
Never miss a title and save money too!

Here's what's available to you if you join the exclusive **Mills & Boon®** Book Club today:

+ *Titles up to a month ahead of the shops*
+ *Amazing discounts*
+ *Free P&P*
+ *Earn Bonus Book points that can be redeemed against other titles and gifts*
+ *Choose from monthly or pre-paid plans*

Still want more?
Well, if you join today, we'll even give you
50% OFF your first parcel!

So visit **www.millsandboon.co.uk/subs**
to be a part of this exclusive Book Club!